MEET ME IN ZANZIBAR

A NOVEL

GRAY DOYLE

Meet Me In Zanzibar

First published in 2025

Copyright © 2025 Gray Doyle

All rights reserved. No part of this publication may be reproduced, stored in a retrieval system, or transmitted in any form or by any means—electronic, mechanical, photocopying, recording, or otherwise—without the prior written permission of the copyright holder, except for brief quotations in reviews or articles.

ISBN (Paperback): 978-1-0693727-0-3

ISBN (E-book): 978-1-0693727-1-0

Published by Gray Doyle

"Never doubt that a small group of thoughtful, committed citizens can change the world... Indeed, it is the only thing that ever has." — Margaret Mead

This book is dedicated to my son, Cameron, who never gave up on me. His unwavering support and belief in me carried me through my darkest hours. And for Jo. If it were not for her love, dedication and support, this book would not have been published.

In loving memory of Dr. Gil Asoy, Divine Word Hospital, Tacloban City, The Philippines.

Author's Note:

To all the volunteer aid workers across the world — those who go where angels fear to tread, putting their lives on hold to bring hope to those who have lost everything, including hope itself. To those serving in conflict zones, internally displaced persons camps, refugee camps, and natural disaster areas. To those who have made the ultimate sacrifice in the effort to make a stranger's life a little better, and to the friends and families they left behind.

You — the EMTs, paramedics, doctors, nurses, dentists, teachers, pilots, truck drivers, and countless others who step forward, often with nothing more than a big heart and a passion to help — are the heroes no one sees. You are a true gift to humanity.

Preface

There are places in this world that exist only in the margins of most people's awareness — remote landscapes marked by war, resilience, and humanity's unyielding spirit. This novel takes you to those places.

Meet Me in Zanzibar is, at its core, a story of redemption, sacrifice, and the profound impact of human connection. Inspired by my own experiences as a volunteer aid worker, this book blends reality with fiction, offering a glimpse into the lives of those who risk everything to bring hope to the forgotten corners of the world.

Through the journey of Dalton 'Mac' McBride, a former airline pilot seeking atonement in the chaos of a conflict zone, you will navigate the perils of war, the fragility of love, and the devastating cost of loss. Mac's story is not just one of survival, but of transformation.

As Mac navigates the dangers of war-torn Africa, Andrew, a paramedic and Emily, a dedicated volunteer teacher, embark on a mission to bring hope and healing to the storm-ravaged Philippines. Their stories, though separated by geography, are bound by a common thread — love, sacrifice, and the relentless pursuit of light in the darkest places.

This is neither a history lesson, nor a political statement — it is a tribute to the courage of those who stand in the face of suffering and

Preface

choose to help, to heal, and to love, despite the odds. Some of the places in this book may seem unfamiliar, their struggles distant, but they are real, as are the people who inspire them.

I invite you to step into a world where redemption is hard-won, love is fleeting yet powerful, and even the smallest act of kindness can change a life.

Gray Doyle

Chapter 1

"We have to leave now. It's not safe!" Father O'Donnell called, spotting Emily and rushing to her side.

He grasped her hand and propelled her towards the battered Peugeot 404, his words allowing no hesitation, only immediate action. Maintaining a firm grip, he pulled her along as they stumbled through the school courtyard. Emily's heart pounded in her chest, the morning sun already scorching the dusty ground beneath their feet. The suffocating panic in the air was tangible.

"Thank God you're okay." He pushed her into the passenger seat, jogged around the car, and slid in behind the wheel of the idling vehicle. "Do you have your passport?"

"It's at home... in my room." Emily managed to say, her voice ragged.

In the tight confines of the parking lot, he executed a K-turn and raced down the driveway, neither stopping nor pausing at the exit. He careened onto the main road, spewing rocks as he slid, skidded, and then straightened out while shifting gears. Emily sat, stunned, staring blankly out of the smeared and bug-encrusted windshield.

Father O'Donnell's voice broke through the silence, faster now but controlled. "I've been trying your number and Ms. Mossekka's for the past two hours. I feared the worst when I couldn't reach either of you. I finally got through to her moments before I arrived, and she told me she was on her way to evacuate the school." His tone shifted, the panic in his voice subsiding just enough to let relief seep in. "There have been rebel attacks up north, and it's spreading fast."

Tearing into the driveway of the homestead, they saw the doors flung open and the staff — babies secured on their backs with blankets — fleeing across the open fields. Smoke billowed in the distance, all but blotting out the morning sun. Emily's heart sank. She knew they had attacked the neighbouring village. Many of her students came from there. She would often walk with them, either on the way to or from school. Her eyes filled with tears, but she swallowed them down, forcing herself to focus. She had to keep it together — now wasn't the time.

Scrambling from the car, she dashed up the three steps onto the polished concrete veranda. She slipped on the smooth surface, nearly sending her to the ground, but she caught herself on the door jamb. Without pausing, she sprinted down the hallway and burst into her room. She flung open the free-standing antique wardrobe. Pulling aside two planks, she revealed a hidden compartment. Inside was a small safe containing her money, credit cards, passport, a small first aid kit, and a fully charged backup GSM cell phone. She grabbed the safe, a pair of running shoes, and scooped up a jacket as she exited the room.

The acrid stench of smoke filled her nostrils, and the sound of distant gunfire echoed as she crossed the veranda. She was back in the car in under three minutes. The world felt like it was collapsing around her, a slow, suffocating spiral she couldn't escape from. She had barely slammed the door shut when Father O'Donnell stomped on the accelerator, the car jolting forward as they tore down the driveway. They careened onto the N4, heading east, willing the almost forty-year-old car to carry them to safety.

"I spoke with Travis and Andrew a few hours ago, and they'd witnessed a similar scene. They packed up camp and are heading our way. I hope to meet up with them by ten at the market, if this old clunker can hold on till then." he said, referencing the car. "I've also been in contact with an aviation company in Goma trying to coordinate a rendezvous at a remote airfield in Beni for the final portion. But for now, we're on our own." His face contorted with worry.

Emily sat stiffly in the passenger seat, her fingers digging into the worn fabric beneath her. The road ahead was clogged with families — women balancing bundles on their heads, men pushing bicycles loaded with salvaged belongings, children clutching their parents' hands or scrambling to keep up. The air was thick with dust and despair.

Father O'Donnell clenched the wheel, his knuckles white, swerving to avoid a toppled cart. "Lord, have mercy!" he muttered under his breath, then glanced at Emily. "Are you holding up, lass?"

She hesitated, blinking away the sting of tears. "No. Not really."

The priest's gaze softened. "It's a lot to take in. Even for me. And I've seen a fair share of madness in my time."

She looked out the window again, her voice quieter now. "Maybe I should've stayed in England. My parents wanted me to. My mum, anyway. My dad said I should follow my heart." She swallowed hard, her voice thick. "I thought this was my calling."

Father O'Donnell kept his eyes on the road, but his tone softened. "You've a good heart, Emily. Don't let fear make you second-guess that."

The road opened up briefly, and he accelerated, the engine groaning in protest. The temperature gauge was well over the normal operating range. "Aye, we'll meet Travis and Andrew soon enough." he said, as if reassuring himself.

"And this flight company in Goma, do you know them?" Emily asked.

"Clarke Aviation, aye. They've brought doctors, medicines, and supplies to the mission. If fortune is on our side, they'll send Mac." A faint smile flickered across his face. "He's as Irish as they come. A good man, though a troubled one. Solid, reliable. If he comes, we'll be in good hands."

Emily nodded, drawing her jacket tighter around her. She wanted to ask more, but the words wouldn't come. Instead, she watched the fleeing masses and her mind returned to the school, her students, and teachers. She admired many of her colleagues, led by a firebrand of a headmistress who, despite not being paid in almost a year, showed up daily to lead her staff. Like her, none of them had been paid either. Most walked or rode bicycles to school, some a distance of more than ten kilometres each way, yet they were always punctual and impeccably dressed. The students, likewise, were punctual, their uniforms always clean and pressed. Ms. Mossekka firmly believed that the children were the future and that education was the only way the country could move forward. Her staff and students felt the same. No one took a day off, pay or no pay. Together, they believed they could change the trajectory of their war-ravaged country. Emily wondered how many of their lives would be reduced to memories before this was over.

Outside, the horizon blurred with smoke and peril, but the battered car pressed on, carrying them toward a fragile hope. Knowing what was behind them, what was beside them, and what lay ahead, their escape remained uncertain.

Chapter 2

He woke with a scream. Sweat slick on his skin, his breath sawing in and out of his chest. Twisted damp sheets clung to him, the pillows scattered across the floor. Mac sat bolt upright, his heart hammering against his ribs.

"Fuck!" He swung his legs off the bed and sat hunched, head in his hands, forcing air in and out of his lungs. When the trembling finally subsided, he pushed himself upright with a groan, and shuffled to the bathroom.

He steadied himself on the basin, turned on the faucet and splashed cold water over his face. He ran his fingers through his hair and caught sight of the stranger in the mirror. "Feck me!" he muttered. The man staring back looked a decade older, his salt-and-pepper hair a far cry from Mac's once-jet-black shock. The accident, four years since, had hollowed him out. His eyes, once the colour of stonewashed denim and full of light, were now sunken and dull. Worry lines carved deep into his chiselled features.

A former senior pilot at Shamrock Air, with over 18,000 hours in the captain's seat, Mac's reputation now lay in tatters after a controversial finding by the National Transportation Safety Board. An accident that haunts him daily.

Of the 227 souls on board; only 73 had survived. Mac had done everything by the book, drawing on every ounce of his twenty-eight years of flying experience. He'd flown the crippled aircraft to the bitter end, guiding it all the way to impact.

The crash came on the heels of two major incidents the year prior, piling public and governmental pressure on the NTSB to explain how a seemingly flawless aircraft fell into the Irish Sea. Missing components, misplaced documentation, and Mac's messy personal life, made him an easy target. The media didn't hesitate to convict him.

Three years later, the official report was inconclusive, but its strong hints at 'pilot error' had left a permanent stain. Mac and many others in the industry knew he'd been at the helm of a doomed plane long before it left the ground.

Of course, everyone knew Captain Dalton McBride; his face had been in every newspaper — the front page for months — and on every news channel for just as long. Having grown weary of the death threats, the constant sideways glances, and the hushed voices that seemed to stalk him wherever he went, Ireland, his beloved home, was not his anymore. Finally, one dreary November day, he locked his home for the last time and drove to the airport, abandoning his old car in the long-term parking lot at terminal two. Mac had no destination in mind; he simply purchased a ticket on the next outbound flight, boarded it, and watched the lights of Dublin until he could no longer see them, somewhere over the Atlantic.

As far back as he could remember, Mac knew he would be a pilot. It's all he dreamed about, all he ever talked about. Mac, as a child, had spent endless days watching the planes take off and land at Dublin Airport. There, in the green space adjacent to the airport, alone with his imagination, he could fly away... fly to those sun-kissed beaches and swaying palm trees he had seen on the brochures in the travel shops on Grafton Street. He could flit off to those exotic far-off destinations seen in his National Geographic magazines he received every month. As a pilot, he could escape the bleak weather that blankets Dublin in the winter and visit those cities, some he had not yet learned to pronounce.

Now at forty-six years old, the years of training, the long nights studying, and countless hours of little-to-no financial reward, building flight hours to reach his goal as an airline captain, had come down to this. His airline career shattered, his life in ruins. His body and mind just strong enough to pass the required flight medical to keep him in the air... but not in the airlines. Not that the medical stood in his way — the cloud of doubt that was cast after the investigation all but guaranteed he would never captain an airliner again.

At one time, Mac appeared to have it all. A lovely home on the Ward River in Swords, a prestigious career, and married with two lovely kids. Catriona, his daughter, now twenty-two and attending the University of Toronto in Canada, and Connor, his son, seventeen, who was finishing up his last year at Ballantine Boarding School in Dublin.

Mac's marriage, however, was on shaky ground. It was a disaster from the outset and he had long since forgotten what had attracted him to Fiona. She was a ruthless solicitor who brought her bilious arguments into the home, and her couple of 'harmless' drinks to 'take the edge off' would often exacerbate the situation. Not that she was a raging alcoholic... she did, however, drink with determination.

After Mac's plane fell apart, he too fell apart. If it affected Fiona at all, it only affected her positively. She seemingly took great pleasure in his pain. Divorce proceedings were well into the sixth month, and the latest jabs and barbs became intolerable. Mac gave up the fight for the house, he signed whatever documents needed to be signed, packed a small bag, and rented a shabby bedsit above an equally shabby corner shop on Talbot Street in the heart of Dublin. Mac shut out the world and was simply going through the motions of life, until it stopped.

Chapter 3

Just shy of seven, Andrew was jolted awake by frantic yelling outside the tent. Before he could register the words, the sharp tang of burning wood reached him.

"Travis." He shook his friend urgently. "Wake up!" The sound of hurried footsteps and a young voice crying, "They're coming! The rebels are coming!" got them both moving.

They stumbled out into the early morning, blinking against the blinding sunlight, squinting at plumes of black smoke clawing at the sky. Andrew's chest tightened as he felt the thick, suffocating tension in the air. His mind raced, still foggy from sleep, but the dread was unmistakable. Somewhere behind them, Travis's phone buzzed angrily from inside the tent. Travis ducked back in, rummaging underneath the sleeping bag, but it stopped ringing before he could grab it. Andrew's phone immediately picked up the baton, shrill and insistent.

"Andrew, this is Father O'Donnell. Are you boys okay?"

Andrew rubbed his temple, trying to focus through the fog of sleep. "We're fine, Father, but what in the Sam Hill is going on?" They quickly updated each other on the rebel attacks of the morning. Andrew's throat tightened as he swallowed, the words sinking in.

"I'm on my way to the school to check on Emily — I haven't been able to reach her. I fear this is going to be big, and we don't want to get caught in the middle of the mess!" Father O'Donnell continued, his voice laced with urgency. "From what you lads are telling me and what I'm seeing, our routes out of harm's way are diminishing rapidly. Where are you now exactly?"

"We're about twenty kilometres east of Komanda at the Sisulu Mission Clinic, roughly two kilometres north of the main Bunia-Mambasa Road," Andrew replied, still struggling to absorb the reality of the situation.

"Might I suggest a plan?" Father O'Donnell's voice was already forming solutions, despite the danger pressing in. "I'm worried my old car might not make the journey. We may need your help to get out of this predicament." He paused, catching his breath.

"Sure, tell me what you need." Andrew said, trying to hold onto some semblance of calm.

"From where you are, to the crossroads at Mambasa, is about the same distance as from Emily's school. I suggest we meet at the market just south of the junction. You know the one, on the west side of the road about five kilometres from the turn-off?"

"Yeah, I know the market." Andrew answered, the location already familiar in his mind.

"Good. Let's try to rendezvous there. How long before you can get underway?" Father O'Donnell asked.

Without hesitation, Andrew's voice was sharp. "Ten minutes. We can be at the market in about an hour and forty-five if we push it, but let's say two hours to be safe. And you guys?"

Father O'Donnell exhaled deeply. "God willing, we'll be there in just over three hours. The roads further east... they're... well, let's just say they're problematic."

"Okay. Let's say we meet there around ten a.m.?" Andrew's voice was firm, despite the tension tightening his chest. "Keep us posted."

"That should work. Then we can ride along with you to Beni and onward to Goma, getting in around nightfall." Father O'Donnell's plan came to a close with a note of hope. "Let's keep the line of communication open and check in every thirty minutes or so, to be on the safe side."

Andrew agreed, cutting the call quickly.

Travis had the hood of the Land Rover up, adding oil to the motor and checking the rest of the fluids and belts. Travis had only heard one side of the conversation, but it was enough to know things were escalating rapidly.

Andrew snatched up belongings in the tent — tossing clothes, flashlights, and their passports into a pile — before grabbing Travis's trauma bag. "Let's roll!" Andrew barked, slamming the Land Rover's rear door shut, as Travis dropped the hood.

Both still dressed in their scrubs, they opted not to change or pack the tent. It was a fight-or-flight moment, and they chose the latter. They jumped into the Land Rover, Travis at the helm and Andrew riding shotgun. Travis woke the sleeping diesel engine, and it came up clattering, then purring, and finally roaring, as it warmed up.

As Travis slammed the gear stick into place, Andrew drawled, "We've got an hour in our favour, but Father O'Donnell is riding in that French tin-can of his, and I reckon that's fixin' to be a problem."

The smoke on the horizon thickened, and the Land Rover's engine growled as they made their way down the two kilometer poorly maintained eroded dirt track from the mission to the main road.

Chapter 4

Travis Johnson and Andrew Koch hailed from a sleepy town twenty miles north of San Antonio, Texas. Bulverde, often referred to as the 'front porch' of the Texas Hill Country, had a charm as expansive as the sky itself. Growing up there was every Texan boy's dream; summers filled with cedar-scented air, riding dirt bikes through mesquite scrub, shooting cans with their first .22s, floating down the Guadalupe River on tractor inner tubes, and endless trails and caves that seemed to stretch far beyond what any two boys could ever explore.

Their families had been long-time neighbours, settling in the area since the days of German pioneers. Andrew liked to playfully brag that his great-uncle Carl had been the town's original mail-keeper, back when letters still arrived by horseback.

Childhood revolved around the simple, yet profound pillars of life in Bulverde; school, football, church, and family missions. The Johnsons and Kochs travelled together on dozens of church-sponsored trips, spreading faith and lending hands across Central America. By the time they graduated high school, Travis and Andrew had rebuilt storm-wrecked houses in Honduras, handed out care packages in Guatemala, and helped dig wells in Haiti after the devastating 2010 earthquake.

But it was Africa that truly captured their hearts. In 2011, a mosquito net distribution program in Malawi brought them halfway across the world. For two months, they travelled dirt roads, through sun-scorched villages, handing out nets and learning to move to the rhythm of the continent. Africa wasn't just a place to them — it was an adventure, a calling.

That same summer, Travis married his childhood sweetheart, Andrea, with Andrew standing proudly by his side as best man. A year later, the two were planning their final mission before Travis would become a father. Andrea gave her blessing on one condition; he'd be back in time for the baby's arrival.

They landed in Uganda with one mission; to distribute one thousand mosquito nets to families across Western Uganda and Eastern Congo. But plans had a way of changing in Africa.

Chapter 5

Mac made a cup of tea, slipped his cigarettes into the pocket of his robe, and stepped out onto his private balcony at the expat complex. The world below was steeped in crepuscular hues. He stared absently at the airport, where the sun crept over the horizon, chasing the moon into retreat. Dawn spilled magnificent hues of gold, tangerine, and fuchsia across the sky, softening the jagged edges of Goma, a war-scarred city on the edge of the Democratic Republic of the Congo. A country that was arguably the most beautiful in Africa.

Below the surface, the country's splendour hid scars; the March 23 Movement — M23 rebels — fought for control, blood diamonds funded warlords, and children toiled in illegal Coltan mines, unearthing the tantalum that made the world's technology hum.

His phone alerted him to an incoming text. BRIEFING ROOM URGENT 08;45. "Shite." he muttered, the word hanging heavy in the air. He hadn't expected a summons this early. Urgent. In Goma, that word meant something much more than simply 'important.' He tossed his phone on the table and rubbed the back of his neck.

He downed the last dregs of his Earl Grey tea, stubbed out his Camel cigarette and stepped back inside the room. He closed the French doors, dropped his robe on the tiled floor, and padded into the bathroom.

Mac showered quickly, dressed, threaded his epaulettes, slipped on his shoes and pocketed his phone. He flipped off the lights, and made his way downstairs to the kitchen. There, a large dining table sat, made from reclaimed teak railroad ties, and eight chairs, six of them already taken with his two-man security detail, two paramedics, a flight nurse, and another pilot, all chatting amicably and digging into a hearty breakfast.

"Top of the morning, Mac." they jovially teased in unison.

Mac groaned, rolled his eyes, and replied, "And the rest of the day to you, too!" He knew they were teasing him; his eye roll and groan were just for effect, his cadence conveying a playful warmth that made the jest feel like a shared secret.

"Oh, come on Mac. Maybe that greeting will make a comeback." one of the nurses said.

"Good God, I hope not!" Mac replied, pulling up a chair.

Platters of bacon, sausages, fried tomatoes, toast, croissants, marmalade, and homemade preserves were already on the table when William, the cook, stepped from behind the kitchen counter.

"Jambo, Captain. How do you want your eggs?"

"Jambo, William." Mac responded, in the typical Swahili greeting. "Three over easy, thanks. And how is your family today?"

Mac had a natural affinity for William. He was a hard-working local man who always seemed to go the extra distance for what William affectionately called his 'guests' and ran his kitchen as if it were a five-star restaurant. William was smart and dedicated to his work. Oftentimes, you would find him looking up recipes for the multinational crew that rotated in and out of the compound. He was married to Aminata, who worked in the local café, Bon Pain, a favourite hangout for the NGOs and expats. Aminata also helped at the compound and ran a small but profitable business doing laundry for the community. Their two children, Bamboula, a seven-year-old mischievous little boy, and Prisca, his older sister, were being schooled at the expensive Athenee Royal Private School. Much of what William and Aminata earned went towards their education. They wanted the best for their children and, unlike many of their peers, Bamboula and Prisca spoke French, English, and German fluently and were often at the compound after school, practising their language skills with the expats.

Mac turned to Peter and Ryan, his security detail. "Lads, we are to be in the briefing room in an hour, so we best get on with our breakfast."

Chapter 6

Peter McCabe stood six feet, six inches. He was a fitness fanatic and former SAS trainer and was Mac's head security — and running partner three days a week. Peter had mustered out of the SAS with honours after eleven years of service, with three tours of duty behind him. One earning him the Victoria Cross and one the Conspicuous Gallantry Cross, before returning to England as a trainer for the SAS Special Projects Team, specialising in hijacking and counter-terrorism at Credenhill, on the outskirts of Hereford.

Peter had retired to a quaint marina in Northumberland in the North East of England, where he had purchased and moored his 1989 Bruce Roberts Bermudan cutter, a 45ft sleek blue water sailboat. He spent his days lovingly restoring her to her former glory and spent his evenings researching and charting his course to circumnavigate the globe. His weekends were spent out on the North Sea, honing his skills in the open water. Peter adored his boat with its gleaming teak decks, a beam of almost thirteen feet, and seven feet of headroom — a definite advantage for someone of Peter's stature. After a twelve-hour daily regime of working on the boat and two hours at the chart table, he would retire to the double aft cabin suite, where sleep came easily as the waves gently lapped the hull of 'The Wanderer'.

Some eight months and twenty-odd ports later, Peter and The Wanderer sailed into Cape Town's Royal Cape Yacht Club. Once docked securely, Peter signed in at the club and followed the directions to immigration and customs across the street. An hour later he was back aboard The Wanderer armed with a cold Amstel lager and a six-month visitor's visa.

At five the following morning, Peter was on the deck enjoying a coffee and watching the sunrise lighting Table Mountain as the waves gently rocked the boat. He had an eight o'clock meeting with the yard manager to book an appointment to have his boat hauled out for some dry dock maintenance. Of utmost importance was repacking the stuffing box and replacing a worn cutlass bearing. And of lesser importance, a thorough pressure cleaning of the hull and a cursory check of the bow thruster. By ten he was in the gantry adjusting the last of the straps on the travel lift and by eleven, she was resting on the stands in dry dock.

Peter was caressing the dripping hull, while intently looking for any other damage that might need attention, when his concentration was broken by a stocky, fit, sun-weathered man. Peter assumed he was somewhere in his mid-forties, dressed casually in khaki Bermuda shorts, an untucked white cotton short-sleeved shirt, blue Hang Ten sandals, and a five-o'clock shadow.

"She's a real beaut! You the skipper?" Ryan van Oldenburg asked in his thick South African accent. Not waiting for a response, he continued, "England, hey?" noting the registration. "You better watch out! You're not playing the Aussies this weekend; the Bokkies are going to donner you on Saturday."

Peter assumed that Ryan was referring to the fact that the South African Springboks, affectionately known as the 'Bokkies', were going to thrash the visiting England team at Newlands Rugby Ground in Cape Town on Saturday for the upcoming Rugby World Cup. Peter enjoyed rugby, and England was on a hot streak, beating Australia forty-nine to seventeen two weeks earlier and strongly favoured to beat the struggling Springboks.

"Not the way you play!" Peter jovially retorted and put out his hand introducing himself. "Peter McCabe." he smiled. Ryan shook hands and introduced himself.

"You have a boat here?" Peter asked.

"Ya." Ryan replied, pointing at a gleaming thirty-five-foot catamaran bobbing in the water. "She needs a bit of rigging work and I have a new jib on order. Have you had breakfast yet?" he continued.

They threaded their way into the old quarter and found a table on the sidewalk outside a small diner off the main tourist route, somewhere south of John Street, nestled between a bustling florist and an antiquarian bookstore.

By the end of the day, they were like old friends, having found common ground in their military background, sailing, and everything sports-related. The next two weeks were spent taking in the sights of Cape Town, climbing Table Mountain, driving the peninsular route, and visiting Robben Island, where Nelson Mandela was imprisoned for eighteen of his twenty-seven years of incarceration.

After a day of sailing on Ryan's catamaran, he and Peter were enjoying a couple of cold beers while moored in the harbour. Ryan, feeling at ease in Peter's company, felt comfortable sharing some of his background.

"You know, I grew up during the apartheid era and it shames me that I loathed the black majority, especially the ANC. I could not understand the world's views of South Africa and the love they had for that terrorist, Mandela. I'd been fed the lies and propaganda, and I eagerly drank the Kool-Aid. I desperately wanted to be a part of protecting South Africa from the blacks.

As soon as I was old enough, I joined the South African Police Services, a week after my eighteenth birthday. I was driven by hate, fuelled by the jaded news. By the time I was twenty-five, I had specialised in every known weapon available in South Africa and had read every counterintelligence and counter-terrorism book in print."

Peter sipped his beer as jet skis and motorboats churned up the water in and out of the harbour. Peter was a listener. And he listened, as the boat gently rocked. "Sure you want to continue?"

"Ja, man. I'm not proud of it, but it's who I was then. I was a confused young man... but hell-bent on learning. I studied the German

GSG9; the British SAS; the Israeli Yamam; and then applied to join the SAPS Special Task Force — kinda like your SAS — bad asses, but the most disciplined. We trained as hostage negotiators, paratroopers, and counter-terrorism experts.

In 1993, a Royal Swazi Fokker F28 was hijacked with twenty-one passengers and three crew members and was sitting at the then-known Jan Smuts Airport, now Oliver Tambo Airport, just outside of Joburg. I led a twenty-two-member hostage rescue team and was told to retake the plane at all costs. It was harrowing, man. We killed the hijacker and rescued the passengers, albeit one with a shoulder wound… oh, and the pilot was shot in the leg."

"Holy shit! Mate… you have my utmost respect." Peter raised his bottle and dipped his head. "Another beer?" Peter asked, digging around in the cooler and pulling out two Amstels.

"Cheers." Ryan said, taking a long swig. "A year later, Nelson Mandela was sworn in as the first black president of South Africa and, man, tensions were high. One day, there was a knock on my office door. Nelson Mandela wanted to see me! I was thinking 'Fuck… why?' Then before I could even stand, he was in the doorway, telling me not to get up. He walked in slowly, calm but purposeful, with that same warmth you see in all his photos. He apologised for intruding… Nelson… bloody… Mandela — I mean, come on… it was surreal!" Ryan gazed off, lost in the memory.

"No fucking way! *The* Nelson Mandela? Man, I would have shit my pants."

"Ja, I nearly did! The man was just there, right in front of me, smiling."

"Fuck, you met Nelson Mandela! Lucky bastard! What did he want, man?"

"He wanted to thank us personally for our part in rescuing the hostages. He said he was proud of us. You know, Peter, no-one — not even our own Police Commissioner — came by to thank us. A year passed, and this man, who I considered a terrorist, went out of his way to stop by and commend us and shake our hands. That moment was life-changing for me. It was not 'my' South Africa, it was 'our' South Africa. A few weeks later I was invited to Mr. Mandela's home.

"What?!"

"Wait, it gets better. He offered me a position on his personal security detail. I served under him until he retired in 1999."

"No bloody way! You? You were Nelson *fucking* Mandelas bodyguard? Oh man, that's gotta look good on a CV. Fuck me, I'm drinking beers with Madiba's bodyguard." Peter laughed aloud, leaned over and clinked bottles with Ryan. "You, my friend, are a legend!"

"Why, thank you, sir!" Ryan laughed. "I still work in close security and VIP protection, freelance mostly, for Gryphon Enterprises. In fact, I leave next week for Kinshasa to work with some NGOs, providing protection for the cargo and ambulance pilots. You know, we could always use some help if you're interested. The pay is great and the detail is easy."

Peter sipped his beer, mulling over the idea in silence. He missed military life — the structure, the camaraderie, the discipline. "Text me their number. I'll give them a call."

Peter contacted Gryphon Enterprises, shared his credentials, and after an extensive background check, some weapon requalifications, and advanced training, Peter was hired and sent to Goma on his inaugural mission. A couple of months later, after his second in command was stricken with malaria and sent home, Ryan was reassigned and transferred from Kinshasa as a replacement.

Chapter 7

Mac was finishing his breakfast. Peter and Ryan excused themselves to get ready for the drive to Goma Airport, and so began their daily routine. They collected and checked their weapons. They both carried Heckler and Koch HK MP5 H3 submachine guns, the model with a folding stock, specifically designed for close combat work. They carried three extra clips with thirty rounds of spare ammunition in each and one in the machine gun, bringing the total to one hundred and twenty rounds. They also carried Glock 17C sidearms with a seventeen-round clip and three spare magazines. On completing their checks, they donned their bulletproof vests and went outside to talk to the night security guards based around the perimeter of the complex. Earlier that morning, they had made back up discs from the security cameras, labelled them, and stored copies in a fire-resistant safe in the safe room.

Their vehicle was a modified armoured conversion Toyota Landcruiser series 76, complete with run-flat tyres, forty-millimetre bullet-resistant glass, and weighing in at six thousand six hundred pounds. Ryan inspected its undercarriage with a mirror and walked around her twice checking for any signs of tampering. He stood at a distance, before clicking unlock on the remote. Deemed safe, he approached the vehicle and popped the hood. After carrying out a fluid and belt check, he drove her out and parked near the front door, engine running and air conditioner on.

Peter had finished supervising the changing of the local guards and collected their log sheets from the previous night. He trotted up the driveway and stood by the rear passenger door, awaiting Mac's arrival.

Mac drank the last of his coffee, checked his watch, picked up his flight bag, and walked out into the bright African sunlight. Of all the things he disliked about this job, this for him was by far the worst part... he simply loathed being driven around by a protection detail. The guys were great, and he enjoyed their company immensely; although he had told himself, this was not Afghanistan or Iraq, it was Goma. He had given it a three out of ten on the danger scale, there were no kidnappings or violent clashes, and this was the general consensus of many of the expats living and working there.

Mac slipped into the rear of the cruiser and Peter slid in beside him. Ryan took his place behind the wheel, locked the door, put the vehicle into first gear, and drove slowly towards the gates of the large complex. Pressing the remote control, the heavy metal gates slid smoothly on their tracks and the tyre spikes retracted below ground. The local guards stood to attention as they passed by and Ryan scanned the exit before accelerating and shifting gears.

Although the airport was less than a kilometre away, as the crow flies, they had to take a heavily congested, pot-holed, and lava-damaged anfractuous route in stop-and-go traffic. Peter and Ryan were on high alert, their eyes scanning constantly. Both agreed with Mac as to the safety of Goma. But they were highly skilled and trained soldiers, and safety was their priority. If there was to be an ambush, attempted kidnapping, or hijacking, it would happen somewhere in this four-kilometre, thirty-plus-minute route.

Ryan flashed his security clearance badge at the bored guard, who lifted the boom, admitting them into the secured area of the airport, and they drove towards the general aviation section. The checking of the security badge was almost comical; the runway was often dotted with pedestrians taking shortcuts from the markets to the neighbouring Bunia settlement, and kids were constantly wandering about in the prohibited area.

In 2002, Mount Nyiragongo erupted a mere fourteen kilometres away, spewing molten lava which ran like a river through the main streets of Goma and across a thousand metres of the airport's only runway, reducing it from three kilometres to two. This had resulted in a number of aircraft landing long and careening into a four-metre-high lava field, before the approach plates were updated. Many of the accidents rendered the aircraft unsalvageable. These, combined with relics of abandoned war-damaged planes, had turned the end of runway 36 into a rather large playground for the neighbourhood children.

Ryan pulled the cruiser to a stop at the side entrance to hangar 12, home to Clarke Aviation Services, and unlocked the doors of the vehicle. He and Peter slid out simultaneously, scanning every direction, more out of habit than necessity. Peter held the door for Mac, who clambered out, shielding his eyes from the harsh glare of the metal buildings.

"Thanks, lads. I can find it from here." Mac smiled, and walked into the cavernous hangar.

Ryan got back into the driver's seat, drove out onto the apron, and backed the large Toyota into his assigned canvas-covered parking spot on the north side of the hangar. He slung his MP5 over his shoulder, closed and locked the doors, and ambled into the hangar, meeting Peter at the entrance.

"Another long, hot, muggy, tedious day." he mumbled at Peter, as they walked towards the smell of freshly brewed coffee drifting from the cooler, air-conditioned waiting area.

"Morning fellas. Don't get too comfortable. You will be escorting Mac on his flight today to Beni." Pierre, the flight op's manager, said, as he came out of the briefing room, a stack of folders under his arm, a coffee in his free hand and a croissant balanced atop the mug.

Ryan poured the coffee as Peter pulled out his Thuraya Satellite phone, punched in the South African office number and asked to be connected with Simone. Simone was a woman who could find anything, on anyone, at any time. If it happened anywhere on the globe, she knew about it. And if she didn't, she would in a few hours. There was a pause, a few clicks, a low-pitched buzz, and then Simone answered.

"Hi Simone. Pete here. I need some intel on Beni. Can you send me the latest ASAP, and fax it to Clarke Aviation in Goma? Thanks."

"Hi Pete. And good morning to you too!" she retorted.

He could imagine her smiling on the other end of the phone. Sufficiently chastised by his lack of manners, he replied. "Sorry for being so blunt! We are on the move this morning and wanted a heads-up. Good morning, Simone." He said politely, before reiterating the urgency.

"I'm on it! Give me twenty." she replied, as she disconnected the call.

Chapter 8

The briefing room was cramped. Peter and Ryan stood in the corner while assignments were handed out to freight and passenger pilots, and scheduling was organised for the air ambulance and medical crews. Mac alternated between all three divisions, and today he was on passenger detail. They listened intently as Mac received his assignment.

"Dalton." Pierre was one of the few who called Mac by his given name. Mac looked up, as Pierre continued in his thick Belgian accent. "We have a situation brewing up North with the M23 rebels. Last night they hit a village just south of Bunia and left a trail of devastation, as they do. This is the third village in the past week, and it appears they are now moving south towards Beni. Although we are not privy to all the details, we can assume the usual horrors — rape, kidnap and the indiscriminate slaughter of those who are of no use to them.

We were contacted late yesterday afternoon by the Catholic Archdiocese in Kinshasa. They are worried about one of their priests, Father Keith O'Donnell, who is conducting fieldwork in the area. They need him brought safely back to Goma and then onward to Kinshasa. We reached him at six this morning. He was already on the move after hearing heavy fighting and seeing the flames of razed villages in and around Isiro. That makes two hits today that we are aware of at this time."

Pierre tapped a map, pointing to two locations. "The good Father is meeting up with a young British teacher in Nia Nia. He was roughly an hour from the school when we last spoke." Checking his watch, he estimated, "He should be about ten minutes from the school now. He intends to pick up the teacher and try to rendezvous with two American medics before heading south to Goma. I asked him to collect the girl, try for the boys, and keep heading to Beni, avoiding the Komanda road. He will keep us posted so we can send you guys in to meet them."

"Dalton, take your guys with you as a precaution, and take the 208B Nine Quebec Alpha, Kilo November." Pierre instructed, referring to the Cessna Grand Caravan 208B with registration 9Q-AKN. "It's a routine flight to Beni where Father O'Donnell should be waiting. Collect him, and any others, and bring them back. We'll arrange a flight to Kinshasa tomorrow."

Mac hesitated for a moment before asking, "Isn't there a MONUSCO base on the outskirts of Beni?" He referred to the United Nations' peacekeeping mission, *Mission de l'Organisation des Nations Unies pour la Stabilisation en République Démocratique du Congo.*

Pierre nodded. "There is, but it's 30 kilometres northeast. The Father and the NGOs are somewhere around here." Pierre pointed again at a large map on the wall, circling an area close to Nia Nia and Mambasa. "The two Americans are hopefully heading east from Komanda towards the southern bypass from Mambasa to Beni." he continued, tapping the map thoughtfully. "But if they're delayed, they might run into trouble. The rebels are raising hell southbound, and the army's trigger-happy. This is their best shot — a better than 75% chance of slipping between both groups undetected."

Fax in hand, Peter interrupted the conversation with new intel. "The area north of Beni was a green zone 24 hours ago. It's been upgraded to orange and may become a red zone in 36 hours, as the rebels move south. The Blue Berets are on alert, but they're not authorised to engage yet. That might change soon. I agree with Pierre — this route is safest for now, but we need to move quickly."

Mac checked the time on the large clock above the whiteboard. "If that's all, we best saddle up, lads. Looks like you guys will be keeping me company. See you later, Pierre." He smiled, as he headed for the restroom.

"Bon chance!" Pierre replied, before returning to the day's briefings.

Peter handed Ryan the intel. "We've got some stuff to go over." he said, pouring coffee and grabbing a croissant. Peter spread out a detailed topographical map on a large table, and they began discussing escape routes in case things went wrong.

"In the words of Jack Reacher, 'Hope for the best, plan for the worst'." Ryan joked.

Peter shook his head in mock disbelief. "Tell me you don't read that shit! And I'm going into a conflict zone with you?!"

Mac returned, wiping his hands on his chinos. "Will they ever get towels in here? I'm tired of looking like I peed my pants!" Grinning, he asked, "So, what's the craic, gentlemen?"

"We're reviewing the intel and mapping out options. Seems okay, but we're planning for the worst." Ryan replied.

"Brief me on the way. I'll get the bird ready." Mac said, and headed out onto the apron.

Ryan and Peter studied the map intently, and Ryan called the office in Johannesburg for more information. Simone was ahead of him. She'd spoken to the communications officer already and had asked Captain Singh at the UN base, MONUSCO, for an eye-on-the-ground update.

"All the rumours had been confirmed. The rebels were moving south and were expected in Beni somewhere between twenty-four and thirty-six hours," she said, "unless the FDNA (Congolese National Army), who were currently approaching from the west, could head them off. Actual numbers on both sides were vague, with estimates of the FDNA ranging from 300 to 600 strong, and the rebels anywhere between 150 and 200."

Ryan thanked her, and she wished him well as the line disconnected.

"There's both good and not-so-good news." Peter said. "The not-so-good first. Rebels are approaching from the north, and the FDNA from the west. There are some pockets of rebel sympathisers in and around Beni. The good news is that the intel is solid and fresh. Communications are not great, so the sympathisers may not be as informed as we are about the incoming rebel group, but I want to prepare in the event that they might be."

The pair spent a further fifteen minutes etching out a plan. Beni airport was small, with a single two-thousand-metre east-west gravel runway. Two small buildings and a large corrugated hanger were all to the south of the field, and a dense forest to the north. There was roughly a two-hundred-metre open space between the buildings and the runway, and then the same from the tree line. There was an aircraft turn-around one hundred and fifty metres from the west end of the runway.

Pierre came out of the briefing room, and Peter turned to him, asking, "Do you have that dossier for me?"

Pierre flipped through a stack of manila folders and handed one to Peter. Peter opened and scanned the couple of pages inside, entered the names and numbers into his phone, and assigned speed dials to each.

"Thanks, Pierre." he said, as Ryan folded the map, and the pair walked out to find Mac.

"Just to be on the safe side, I'm gonna grab that concealed vest for Mac." Peter said, as he jogged off to the Land Cruiser to get it.

Mac had completed his walk-around, fuelled the plane, filed an open flight plan, and was just finishing his cockpit checklist when Ryan reached the aircraft.

"Peter is just fetching you a little gift. I'm sure you'll love it!" Ryan joked.

A few minutes later, Peter arrived with the vest, and Mac groaned.

"You really think that's necessary?"

"Lest I remind you of your quote about the six P's — 'Proper Preparation Prevents Piss Poor Performance'. Now, be a good lad and put it on." Peter smiled, and winked at his friend.

"Aye, catch yourself on." Mac responded, removing his shirt, slipping into the vest, and buttoning his shirt back on.

"We're not completely sure of the situation, but according to our latest intel, this country is a tinderbox. We're not exactly expecting any issues, but we're certainly not taking any chances. There's a small group — or a few small groups — of M23 supporters milling about, waiting for something to happen. Let's not give them a reason to practise on us!" Ryan stressed.

"What Ryan means is, let's get in and out as if our arses were on fire." Peter added.

Sitting in the club configuration of the aircraft, with a chart spread on the table, the trio went through the plan twice to ensure nothing was amiss. Due to the winds coming from the Rwenzori mountain range, it would be best to land from the west. This had its pros and cons. Landing from the west would make it easier to make the turnaround and pickup, and keep the doors towards the buildings. The downside was that they would have to taxi uphill before passing the buildings again. If they encountered resistance and the rebels mounted an offensive, the group could be in trouble if they weren't quick enough.

Mac studied the chart again and added, "I need a quarter of the runway for landing — around five hundred metres — and a third, or six hundred, for takeoff. I can execute a sideslip landing and shave off a bit more, but we're landing on gravel, so let's go with the maximum. In short, I can stay on the west side of the runway, away from the buildings if that helps. The only drawback is, we'll be on the steepest part of the slope for takeoff, but we'll still have about eight hundred to play with. I can work with either, so lads, whatever makes your mission safest and easiest."

He leaned back in his chair.

"Okay, gents, we have a plan. Let's hope that the good Father and the flock he's shepherding can coordinate and be on time." Peter said. "I'll give them a call now so we can get a fix on the timing. How long is the flight?"

Mac, who had flown into Beni on several occasions, didn't need to calculate. Turning in his seat, he said, "One hour and ten minutes."

Peter punched speed dial one, and Father O'Donnell's number began ringing. It rang six times, then went to voicemail. He hit speed dial two, Emily's. As the ringtone buzzed in his ear, a young woman's voice answered on the fourth ring.

"Hello, this is Emily." she said, a just hint of an Oxfordshire accent still detectable.

Peter introduced himself and asked if she was okay, where she was, and with whom. Emily detailed what had transpired, bringing Peter up to speed with the situation in Isoro, Nia Nia, and Komando, and that she was with Father O'Donnell and would, with any luck, be meeting the two American paramedics at Mambasa.

Peter relayed the plan in detail; the timing and where to watch for the arrival and descent of the plane, making certain Emily knew to be on the west side of the runway, away from the buildings. He gave her directions to a small maintenance track they had gleaned from scrutinising the satellite images of the airport.

"It is imperative that you are neither early nor late. We need to be on the ground for as short a time as possible. I need you to be pulling up to the runway as we land. I cannot stress this enough!" he remarked firmly.

"Got it!" she replied. "I'll call you when we meet up with Andrew and Travis with an update. If all goes to plan, we will be in a white Land Rover 110 Discovery." She read back Peter's satellite phone number before breaking the call.

Peter turned gravely towards Mac and Ryan and said, "It's worse than we expected. There have been multiple hits. Not just Bunia — Isiro was hit, another just outside Nia Nia, and other unconfirmed reports. And, from what Emily just told me, it seems the two American paramedics were roused out of bed around sunrise, with a skirmish just north of them." He continued, indicating an area on the map near Komanda.

"This is not one group." Ryan interjected, "It looks like a coordinated strike, moving from north to south."

"And what does that do to our timing?" Mac enquired.

"They will be at the airport at one-thirty, if all goes well." Peter confirmed. "Emily appears, by all counts, to be a competent person. She'll be keeping us posted."

Chapter 9

Emily Esposito, a petite twenty-five-year-old woman, hailed from Towcester, a small English town with a population of around ten thousand. Standing no more than five foot three and weighing in at ninety-eight pounds, Emily's stature was small, but her determination was immense. She had inherited her striking beauty from her Irish mother, including her hard-to-miss, captivating green eyes, and a mop of curly, strawberry blonde hair, which cascaded midway down her back. Her father was Italian. She credited him for her stubbornness and hand-gesturing communication skills, some certainly inappropriate for those under eighteen.

She had grown up travelling and was comfortable most anywhere on the planet. Emily was fluent in Italian, English, French, and functional in Spanish. Her parents wanted the best education available, so she was enrolled at Quinton House, a private school in Upton, from the tender age of five until her graduation at eighteen. She then went on to study linguistics at the University of Central Lancashire (UCLAN) and soon discovered the difficulties of finding employment in the UK. Being 'quadrilingual', as she often quipped, together with her love of travel, she decided to combine the two. And there was no better way to accomplish that than globetrotting and teaching.

This passion had taken her to Vietnam, Thailand, Cambodia, India, and then Zimbabwe, where she met Rene, the son of the French Ambassador to the Congo, based in Kinshasa. Emily and Rene's romance was not unlike a forest fire. It was all-consuming. It burned fast, hot, and furiously, finally burning itself out somewhere on the banks of the Victoria Nile in Uganda. There were no ill feelings. They both knew their time together had run its course. One morning Rene picked up his already-packed backpack, kissed her on the cheek, stepped out the door, crossed the dusty road, and hailed a matatu that would take him to the bus and onward to Entebbe airport, and finally, the flight home to Paris.

The following week, Emily collected her mail at the post office in Jinja. The letter she'd been hoping would arrive, had. She ran excitedly back to her shabby one-room shack, packed her belongings, and made her way to the DRC embassy in Kampala to obtain the visa that had been pre-arranged by the school for her teaching assignment. Two days later she was boarding the commuter flight from Entebbe to Goma, and within the week was ensconced in her new quarters at a rural school on the outskirts of Nia Nia.

Chapter 10

Travis turned west out of the clinic, his eyes focused on the battered road ahead. He manoeuvred the Land Rover with practised ease, pushing it to its limit over the pot-holes and eroded patches. Andrew stared out the window, his gaze fixed on the dark smoke that clawed its way upward. It was different from the fires back home — this wasn't an accident or a natural disaster. This was deliberate. Malicious. Set by people whose hearts and souls were filled with hate. They had guns. They had machetes. And they would use both without a second thought.

Andrew's mind raced. There was no discretion in this violence. Men, women, children, the elderly. All unarmed. All would suffer. None would be spared. Some would be taken as 'spoils of war' — a fate far worse than death, in Andrew's view. There was no prosthetic for a tortured soul.

The anger and pain gnawed away at him. It was almost tangible. Travis seemed to sense the storm inside his friend. Eyes firmly fixed on the road, he reached over, handing Andrew a bottle of water from between the seats, and laid a hand on his shoulder. The simple gesture was enough to crack Andrew's composure, and he felt the swell of tears threatening to spill over.

"They were good people. Simple folk." Andrew murmured, his voice rough. "They didn't hurt no-one. They had next to nothin' — not a pot to piss in, nor a window to throw it outta — but they were always grateful for any kindness." Andrew smiled, though it was weary, almost hollow. The faces of those people flashed in his mind — happy, unburdened by wealth but rich in spirit — and for a moment, the pain eased.

The silence settled back between them, thick and heavy. They were alone with their private thoughts, each lost in a grief too deep to share. Plumes of smoke from other razed villages sullied the skies to the north of them. The Land Rover bobbed and weaved on and off the road, away from the nightmare, westbound to safety.

Chapter 11

In his usual unruffled manner, Mac continued in the tone of a person about to embark on a scenic pleasure flight.

"So, if you want to be home in time for dinner, may I suggest one of you fine gentlemen take care of the loading? You'll need to know how to operate the starboard passenger door." he said, slipping between the seats and making his way aft.

Bending over with Peter and Ryan on either side, he explained, "Exit the aeroplane through this door here. Pull the upper door section's inside handle from its locked position, rotate the handle clockwise to the open position, and push the door outward. When the door is partially open, the automatic door lift will raise the upper door section to the fully open position. Next, rotate the door handle of the lower section over here, up and backward, to the open position, and push the door outward. The telescoping gas spring will lower the door to its fully open position, and the integral steps will deploy. Closing it is pretty much the same."

Mac demonstrated as he spoke. "Just make sure you give the upper door a good yank so these paws latch firmly. And then do the bottom door." he cautioned.

Both Peter and Ryan took turns carrying out the procedure until they had mastered it.

With the tutorial complete, Mac went forward, slipped into his seat, and strapped into his five-point harness.

"Ready, lads? All strapped in? I know you know this shite, but there are two exits back there and two up front here. The fire extinguishers are behind the rear seats, before the cargo compartment, and one up here." he said, checking his watch and starting up the powerful six hundred and seventy-five horsepower Pratt and Whitney PT6A turbine engine.

Mac contacted the tower and taxied to the edge of the apron, glancing left and right. He checked for pedestrians — something he was quite certain he would never get accustomed to — and proceeded onto the runway. Sitting in position, he checked and rechecked his watch. At twelve twenty, he released the brakes, and the Caravan lumbered down the runway.

At ninety knots, he rotated, pointing the nose skyward, and soon they were climbing at a rate of one thousand feet per minute, just over one hundred and ten knots.

Reaching their relatively low cruise altitude of 8000 ft, Mac levelled off and punched the speed up to 170 knots. He checked his lap chart, did a few calculations, and then relaxed for the remainder of the flight.

This time of year, the skies were calm, the air smooth, and the ceiling unlimited. Three months from now, this would be a whole different flight, Mac thought. The rainy season brought with it a very different sky here in the Congo.

Peter unsnapped his belt and hunched over, as he made his way up to the cockpit, gesturing at the right seat.

"May I?" he said.

Mac just nodded and handed him a spare headset, showing Peter where to plug it in. Peter adjusted his mike and said, "You okay, Mac?"

"Aye, sure, you know yourself. It's an interesting day, my friend. A strange world we live in over here." he answered, turning to look at Peter.

Peter glanced back, watching Ryan as he rested... feet up on one seat, ankles crossed, arms folded, and eyes closed. Peter thought back to his days in service, when they were trained to sleep whenever they got the opportunity.

The flight was remarkably smooth, and the deep hum of the Cessna Caravan's powerful engine had a soothing effect. Even in the face of uncertainty, Mac exuded an air of calm confidence. His experienced eyes continuously flicked between the array of instruments and the vast horizon beyond the cockpit's windows. His hands rested lightly on the controls, a gentle touch that belied the intricate dance he performed with the aircraft. It was a genuine pleasure to observe a master craftsman skillfully navigate through the complexities of the machine. If Mac was worried about the mission, it certainly didn't show.

Chapter 12

Father O'Donnell continued to wrestle with the old Peugeot, dodging and avoiding as many potholes as he could, still hitting at least two out of every five with a loud bang. The perpetual slowing down, shifting gears, accelerating, and almost stopping to navigate the dismal road, was causing the old car's cooling system to protest.

The temperature needle kept edging its way north of the normal operating range, creeping higher and higher before the thermostat kicked in and it dropped marginally. However, it constantly hovered above the mark, which was not at all comforting to Father O'Donnell.

Emily called Andrew to check in on their progress and could sense his sadness. His usual rambunctious deep Texan drawl was now subdued, and he seemed to be struggling with his emotions.

"We've been on the road for forty-five minutes and are making decent time. How are you guys making out?" Andrew asked.

"Father O'Donnell is worried about the car overheating. People fleeing, potholes and the road conditions are horrendous. We're constantly having to slow to a crawl. He says there's a stretch up ahead where it's a bit better, and hopefully he can cruise and bring the temperature down." Emily replied.

She took a deep breath and added, "There are fires everywhere.

People are heading in all directions, running scared. I'm terrified, Andrew!"

Father O'Donnell was attempting to coax every last breath out of the sick and dying car, but no amount of begging, pleading, or praying could help the old girl. She was now running on three of her four cylinders, and the temperature gauge was rapidly marching into the red zone. Finally, thirty or so kilometres west of Mambasa, the needle's march to the red zone was successful. There was an almighty bang, followed by loud hissing, as steam billowed from beneath the hood. A loud metallic rattle followed, and the engine coughed its last breath. Father O'Donnell took the car out of gear and slowly coasted to the side of the road.

Emily was back on the phone to Andrew as the Peugeot reached its final resting place. The phone only rang once. Andrew answered, and she relayed their predicament. He had previously informed her that they were safely at the market and that the Land Rover was already fuelled for the remaining leg of the journey. Andrew looked at his watch. It was nine-thirty.

"We'll be there in twenty minutes." he reassured her. She heard the Land Rover fire up before ending the call.

Ten minutes later, on the outskirts of Mambasa, Andrew and Travis encountered a police roadblock.

"Son of a bitch!" Travis cursed.

They slowed down for the shabbily dressed officer, who was ambling nonchalantly towards them, signalling for Travis to stop. He sauntered around the vehicle in no apparent hurry. Travis had his driver's licence and passport in his hand, ready for the officer. He wound down the window, and they exchanged greetings in passable French. Travis explained they were medics, on their way to pick up a priest and his 'niece' and take them to the clinic in Mambasa. He pointed at their scrubs and trauma bag to emphasise the point.

The policeman was clearly disinterested and was not going to hurry on any account. He signalled that Travis should pull off the road for an inspection. Travis obliged, opened his door, and got out. He followed the officer to the rear of the vehicle, and as much as he loathed bribes and prided himself on never having paid one, he slipped his hand into his pocket and pulled out twenty-five US dollars.

"We desperately need to get to the Father. He is not well!" Travis said, folding the bills and handing them to the officer. "Will this speed up our journey there and back?"

The policeman grinned and replied in perfect English, "Now why didn't you say he was sick in the beginning? You could have just proceeded." Travis smiled through gritted teeth, thanked the officer, jumped into the driver's seat, and sped off.

Andrew spotted the pair first, sitting under the shade of a mature Iroka tree, next to the dead — still-smoking Peugeot, its hood standing open. Travis slowed, drove off the road, executed a U-turn, and pulled up alongside them.

"Emily, you're in the front!" Andrew hurriedly called out as he bounded out of the vehicle. "Father, you're in the back with me." Travis pulled away as they explained the roadblock and the ruse.

Andrew pulled a space blanket out of the bag and covered Father O'Donnell. He fitted the blood pressure cuff, looped the stethoscope around his neck, and splashed water on Father O'Donnell's face. He drenched the front of the Father's shirt to make it appear he was sweating.

"Good. You look like you have a fever, possibly malaria." He smiled as they bumped along. Travis flashed his lights as he approached the roadblock and accelerated, wound his window down, waved, and yelled, "Merci beaucoup, Monsieur." as he sped past the corrupt officer.

As they turned onto the Mambasa-Beni road, Andrew checked his watch. It was ten-fifteen, and their one-hour window had been whittled down to fifteen minutes. He let Travis know and asked Emily to update Peter. Barring further hiccups, they would be in Beni around one-fifteen and Beni airport ten minutes later, putting them on the bottom of the maintenance road at one-thirty at best.

"See if you can buy us ten minutes." Andrew said to Emily, as she punched Peter's digits into the phone.

Chapter 13

The buzz and vibration of Peter's satellite phone startled him. He whipped off his headset and answered quickly. "Emily, what's happening? Is everyone okay?"

"Hi Peter. We're fine." she said, relief evident in her voice. "Just a little car problem, but we're with Andrew and Travis now. We just got onto the Mambasa-Beni road. Travis says we will be cutting it fine, but could be at Beni airport at one-thirty at best, but probably one forty."

Peter looked at his watch and asked Emily to stand by while he conferred with Mac. He slipped his headset on and pressed the push-to-talk button. "What's our ETA?"

Mac checked the map, his watch, and the airspeed indicator. "Thirteen twenty hours." he replied.

"Any chance of slowing it down a bit? They encountered a few issues and will be pushing it to make thirteen thirty. Can we buy them ten minutes without us being exposed?" he asked.

"Aye, sure. I can slow her down a bit and deviate from the route, which will get us in at thirteen forty-five, if that helps."

"Thanks, mate." Peter replied, as he slipped his headset off and got back on the phone with Emily. "Okay. We're deviating and slowing down, so plan to be in at one forty-five. Remember, this has to be a quick exit. Please relay that on to whoever is driving! We'll see you soon and get you out of there. Hang tight!" Peter concluded, reassuringly.

Chapter 14

Emily turned to Travis, patting his arm affectionately. "Thank you. You're a good man. And you." she added, turning in her seat to look at Andrew. "You really came through for us today. Not that I ever doubted you, but I don't come across many people like you two. Your families must be proud, both for what you do at home and here as volunteers. You leave an indelible mark wherever you go, and I'm honoured to know you."

Emily felt a little embarrassed as the words spilled out, uncensored. She flushed slightly and looked down. She'd only met these guys a handful of times.

Andrew chuckled softly. "Well, shucks, ma'am. You sure know how to make a guy feel good."

Travis, still focused on the road, glanced over with a small smile. "Lordy, girl. It's what we do and what we know. Just part and parcel of being a community." He shrugged, his voice steady, no bravado. Just the truth. "Here, you and Father O'Donnell are our community, and we aim to take care of you." His slow, deep drawl made his words feel like a sermon from a southern baptist church.

Emily smiled at his sincerity, warmth radiating from his every word.

It was hard not to believe him. She leaned back in the seat, closed her eyes, and propped her feet up on the dashboard.

Father O'Donnell was dozing in the back. Andrew twisted in his seat, contorting himself into an uncomfortable position halfway between the two front seats. He rested his head against the corner of Emily's headrest, the discomfort of the position forgotten, as he turned to Travis.

The quiet hum of the road and the rumble of the engine filled the space as the two men spoke softly, their words a mixture of reflection on the harrowing day, how stability was so ephemeral in Africa...not unlike sand always slipping through one's fingers.. Andrew teased Travis about his upcoming fatherhood. "...and if he grows up to be anything like you, man... I feel sorry for Andrea," he said, a grin tugging at his lips. "That kid'll be running circles 'round y'all before he can walk. Before ya know it, I'll be getting calls to come simmer you down a spell and get the little fella out of a tree, or some other crazy shit."

"Well then, hell, we'd better pray we're having a little girl... so she can play dollies with her uncle Andrew!" Travis bantered back.

The repartee went back and forth, their laughter a respite in the otherwise heavy silence of the car. Emily opened her eyes, unable to keep a smile off her face at the easy camaraderie between them.

"Sorry." they said, almost in unison.

"No, don't apologise." she murmured, shifting slightly in her seat. "I wasn't asleep. I was just... enjoying the show."

Chapter 15

"We are three minutes out." Mac squawked into the headset.

Peter stared out of the cockpit window. "Three minutes?" Peter said, quizzically. "I don't even see the runway."

Mac smiled at his friend. "Trust me, I've got this. I am going to keep her high, deploy the flaps, and drop in. Aye, it's a bit unconventional, but under the circumstances, so is this whole bloody day!" he grinned, as he finished the sentence.

Peter glanced back and signalled to Ryan that they were descending. At the same moment, as if on cue, they both started scanning the terrain below, looking for anomalies.

Mac was still high when the runway came into sight. Peter glanced over at him, wondering what he was thinking. Mac winked, and said, "We're going in." Mac transitioned the aircraft from cruise to approach by quickly pushing the propeller control all the way forward and pulling the power back to stop. He selected full flaps and the big aeroplane went from soaring eagle to gracious downhill skier in seconds, yet the airspeed never exceeded 80 knots.

Peter and Mac spotted the upward-swirling dust generated by a white Land Rover bouncing along the rutted road. Ryan too noticed it. "Perfect timing. Let's bring them home." he yelled up to the cockpit.

Mac raised the nose gently, shaving off more speed, and touched down as smoothly as one could on a bumpy gravel runway. He applied the brakes, stopping about a hundred feet east of the Land Rover. He executed a perfect turn-around and taxied up to the idling vehicle, as if choreographed.

Peter quickly scanned the one hundred and eighty degrees available to him through the cockpit windows and quipped, "Keep the meter running, my good man." bringing a modicum of levity to the situation. He unsnapped his harness, shuffled out of it, and was halfway down the aisle, scanning left and right out of the windows.

Ryan had the door open, the steps were falling into place. Peter was only two steps behind. Both had their MP5s slung over their shoulders.

Peter tapped Ryans right shoulder, covering him. Ryan jumped to the ground and crouched low, his weapon ready, safety off. He swept the muzzle from left to right. Peter jumped out, ducked and scurried below the tail of the Caravan. He, too, scanned the area, port side, just aft of the cargo door.

Nothing stirred. The only sounds were the large idling PT6 aircraft engine, and the TD5 diesel engine knocking below the hood of the dusty, battered Land Rover. Peter signalled the driver to kill the engine as he approached the vehicle.

Travis killed the throbbing TD5's engine and stepped out. The rest of the occupants followed. Ryan was now at the tail of the aircraft, continuously monitoring the situation, covering the open door, and Peter's back. Peter lowered his MP5 slightly as Travis started crossing the fifteen or so paces that separated the two men. Travis smiled, his arm outstretched, ready to shake hands and introduce himself, his youthful face aglow with a mixture of pride and relief that he had completed what he had set out to do, against all odds.

Peter began ushering the group to the awaiting aircraft, as the first shots rang out from deep within the copse of trees. Travis stopped mid-step, his arm still extended, his smile still broad, yet now staring through lifeless eyes. His knees buckled and he crumpled to the ground, a bright red patch spreading over the front of his scrubs. His injuries were catastrophic. Within seconds his heart would stop beating, and he would be dead moments later.

Ryan was the first to return fire into the trees, deploying short, quick bursts in the general direction of the muzzle flashes. Peter yelled, "Down! Everyone down!" as he dived to the ground, rolled twice, and came up returning fire.

Andrew screamed, "No. No. Nooo!" Defying the danger, he was up and sprinting towards Travis. Shots thudded into trees all around him, but Andrew kept running. He skidded into the dirt at Travis's side, turned him over and felt for a pulse. He ripped open his shirt, trying in vain to plug the gaping holes in his chest. Andrew sat cross-legged in the dirt, refusing to believe Travis was dead. He cradled his head in his lap and rocked back and forth. Andrew sobbed loudly, seemingly oblivious to the ongoing gun battle.

Peter flanked Ryan and they advanced cautiously and methodically, firing short bursts. Ryan scored the first kill as one of the rebels exposed himself in an attempt to throw a grenade in their direction. Ryan saw the movement and fired a short four-round burst into the man's chest. The rebel fell back and dropped the grenade where he fell. A few seconds later, the fragmentation grenade exploded, screams followed. Frantic activity erupted in the dense grove, and both Peter and Ryan stood up and ran forward, firing at the distracted rebels. They each found a tree where they could take modicum of cover and started scoring further hits within the shocked and now — retreating rebel force.

Emily and Father O'Donnell had belly-crawled to where Andrew was sitting with Travis. Emily, tears streaming down her face, wrapped her arms around Andrew's torso but said nothing. Father O'Donnell said, "We need to bring him with us. Here, let me help you."

Andrew said nothing. Still clutching his head in his arms, he ran his hand over Travis's wide-open, unseeing eyes, gently drawing his eyelids down.

"Let's get him to the plane so you can take him home." Emily said, soothingly, while gently rubbing Andrew's back.

Peter and Ryan began scoring a hit with every burst, until the only sound was Andrew's wailing and the aircraft idling patiently.

"You good?" Peter asked Ryan.

"Yeah. You?" Ryan responded.

They scanned the area again, standing still and listening for any other sound.

"Body count?" Ryan asked Peter.

"No time. Let's hope there are no survivors, we need to get in the air ASAP before more arrive." Peter said. He started retreating, walking backwards as Ryan gave him cover. They reached the small group just as Andrew was lifting Travis's body. Both men knew not to say anything; their job was to cover the group and keep them moving as fast as possible to the plane.

Out of the cockpit window Mac had witnessed the whole scene. One of the boys walked confidently towards Peter, his big smile and friendly, confident face, forever etched in Mac's mind — and no doubt in Peter's. He had heard the first shots and watched as his body twitched twice, lost momentum, and then stood still. Mac looked on helplessly as this young man's life spurted and seeped out onto his pale blue shirt, turning it crimson as he slumped to the ground. Mac scanned the area to see where the shots were coming from, and before the full effect of what was happening had time to register, Mac had unsnapped his harness and was moving aft to help with the body retrieval. The ferocious gun battle lasted only a few minutes, and he saw Peter and Ryan reach the group through the port side windows.

Still half-turned and scanning the rear, Ryan ushered the small group towards the plane. No more than two hundred feet from where Ryan was standing, a Toyota pick-up truck blasted through the trees in a cloud of dust. Within seconds, he knew they were not the military. Instinctively, his training kicked in. He dropped onto his left knee, rested his right elbow onto his right knee, pressed the rifle butt firmly into his shoulder, and fired his first five-round burst into the windshield of the fast-approaching truck.

At least one of the well-placed rounds found its mark. The windshield shattered and turned red with the blood of the driver. The vehicle careened out of control and slammed headlong into a tree, coming to a hard and abrupt halt, slamming the remaining four insurgents into the back of the truck's cab and propelling two over the roof onto the hood, and finally landing on the ground.

Ryan fired another short burst into the bed of the truck as the two targets bounced off the cab. He caught one squarely in the chest, at least three rounds finding centre mass, confirming he was out of the game permanently. He staggered into the last standing rebel, and they both toppled out of the truck on Ryan's blindside. Ryan had lost count on the second magazine, so quickly ejected it and snapped in a fresh one.

Peter fell back to cover the rear of the terrified group, swiftly urging them on, all the while keeping an eye on Ryan's progress. He saw Andrew reach the door and Mac helping him with Travis. He saw Emily disappear up the stairs, with Father O'Donnell close on her heels.

Peter crouched low and skirted around, ensuring a clear line of sight to the rear of the truck. One of the insurgents came up firing a nonstop burst from his AK47, a full thirty rounds, spraying indiscriminately in Ryan's general direction, pinning him down. Peter had witnessed this type of behaviour before from ill-trained and panicked soldiers.

Peter knew the rebel had seconds until his weapon ran dry. He needed to get a bead on the attacker before the rebel ducked out of sight to change magazines. Peter's patience and predictions paid off when the rebel's rifle clicked dry. The rebel looked at the rifle, confusion washing over his face, before realising he was out of ammunition. That three-second hesitation was the last time he would ever hesitate. Peter had him in his sights and snapped off two rounds. He probably didn't need the second; nonetheless, he put both in the centre of his head. The insurgent fell as his rifle clattered into the truck bed.

"How many, Ryan?" Peter yelled.

"Two more, I think." came his friend's response. "Twelve o'clock and a hundred yards from your position and injured," he responded.

Peter and Ryan continued with hand signals and advanced cautiously. Peter spotted the rebel. He was kneeling behind the tree where the truck had come to rest. He was well protected by both the tree and the crumpled front end of the truck. The rebel had a clear view of Ryan's approach. "Ryan, eleven o'clock, behind the tree!" Peter yelled a warning. Ryan dropped to the ground, rolled left, and came up firing. Peter fired at the same time, and the rebel fell onto the hood of the Toyota with a significant amount of his head missing. The remaining adversary began firing haphazardly and without any discipline. Neither Ryan nor Peter could see him. Peter hit the deck and found a little cover behind a stump, but Ryan was in the open, completely exposed. Ryan saw a flash reflecting in the trees and then movement to his left nearer the back of the truck, yet still hidden. "Coming your way! Twenty yards behind the truck bed." Ryan whispered.

A few seconds later, Peter detected movement within the treeline. He had just changed his magazine and was lying stock-still behind the three-foot stump, his rifle hard into his shoulder, as he watched the rebel moving between the trees. He followed his trajectory, took a bead on the next gap, exhaling gently as the rebel walked into his sights. He squeezed the trigger. The MP5 coughed once, and the round found its mark. The rebel collapsed, dying as he hit the ground.

Ryan and Peter waited a further minute and a half before moving stealthily. Then Ryan called the all-clear. Peter joined him, and they checked the four bodies — definitely bad guys, definitely dead. Peter peered into the cab. There were two bodies inside, blood obscuring the faces. One body was slumped over the steering wheel, and the passenger was half on the seat, half in the footwell.

"Clear!" Ryan yelled, and they both raced towards the idling plane.

Ryan reached the steps first and was ducking into the cabin, Peter right behind him. They dropped their MP5s onto two unoccupied seats and turned to take care of the door. Mac was already strapped in, the engine spooling up, when Ryan called, "Door secure. Clear. Let's roll."

Travis's body was lying behind the last row of seats, covered with a couple of cabin comfort blankets — only his feet visible. Andrew sat next to his friend, with his hand on Travis's chest. Father O'Donnell and Emily were seated in the last row, their faces ashen and tear-stained. Shock was setting in. Peter, at a loss for words, simply squeezed Andrew's shoulder as he walked past towards the cockpit. Ryan strapped himself in opposite Emily and Father O'Donnell as the plane started lumbering up the runway.

Chapter 16

The rebel leader stirred and felt his head, the knot huge from where he had hit it on the dashboard, and blood from the open gash blurred his vision. He wiped his eyes and sat upright in the seat, surveying the carnage. His driver was dead, and it all started coming back to him; he had heard the initial conflict and raced in for support. Two white soldiers escorting some civilians had opened fire on his truck.

He kicked at the crumpled passenger door repeatedly until it opened a fraction but did not have the strength to open it any further — the damage was too extensive. He pulled the seat forward, reached behind, and retrieved the jack. He placed it between the door and the pillar, prying the door open as far as the jack would allow, just enough for him to wriggle out.

He fell headlong onto the ground and slid his legs out. He slithered a few more feet until he was clear of the vehicle before rolling onto his back and breathing deeply. He began assessing himself. He hurt like hell, but was relatively unscathed. He'd suffered some bumps and bruises, yet his arms and legs seemingly worked well and it appeared he had no broken bones.

Getting onto his knees, his head swam for a moment. He wobbled and focused on the door of the truck, his vision blurred, coming back into focus as the dizziness passed. He stood up and walked on unstable legs towards the battered Toyota. Reaching in, he retrieved his AK47, webbing belt, and a canteen of water. He took a few swigs, washed his face with the cool liquid, and poured the remainder over his head to help awaken his senses.

The commander felt his rage brewing. He could have had, what, four or five hostages and an aeroplane? Those fuckers would have paid handsomely for the return of their people, and their plane! That money would have benefited his cause no end. He could've funded a small army and taken over one of the mines controlled by some rag-tag outfit... that's how those idiots raised money to arm themselves sufficiently; you get some hostage money, raid a few villages, kidnap the kids to work for you — young boys to work the mines, and girls as 'gifts' for the officers. It was so easy when you had weapons and money.

His dream, now dissipating. The would-be hostages were gone, his men were dead, and he was back to square one. Back to building another team but without the resources. He cursed aloud and booted the destroyed vehicle in anger.

Just then he heard the throb of a large engine whining. He turned to see dust swirling on the runway. He could not believe he'd been given a second opportunity! The commander, still a little shaky and in pain, judged the distance he would need to cover to intercept and shoot at the plane before it took off. With fortune on his side, he could have one, maybe two survivors... and with any luck, one would be the little white girl. He could certainly have some fun with her before he handed her back to whomever paid the ransom. 'White people would buy her back, broken or not... they are so sentimental.' he thought.

He shook off the pain and began running at a forty-five-degree angle towards the runway. His lungs were burning, his vision swimming, but he was determined to intercept that plane and finish what he started. The stakes were too great to ignore. He was ahead of it by at least a hundred and fifty feet when he burst out of the trees and onto the centre of the dirt strip. He raised his rifle and began firing.

Mac stared fixedly out of the windshield as the Caravan lumbered uphill, struggling to gain speed. The quiet in the cabin was suffocating, broken only by the sound of the engine growing louder, and the tyres crunching on the loose gravel. Peter, hunched over, entered the cockpit and collapsed into the right seat, slipping into his harness and putting his headset on. Mac's hand was on the throttle, his eyes flitting between the runway and the airspeed indicator, which was indicating sixty-five knots.

Mac glanced over at Peter and said, "You okay?" Peter just nodded and tapped Mac's shoulder in response.

The air in the cockpit was thick with the heavy scent of gunpowder clinging to Peter's clothes, as if the very atmosphere had been soaked in the violence that had just unfolded. It had been a hellish ordeal and he felt so very bad for Andrew at the loss of Travis. Peter was wondering what was next for everyone in this godforsaken country, as he caught sight of someone at the edge of the runway moving quickly.

"Fuck!" he yelled, "Rebel with a gun! We need to be airborne, now!"

Mac's eyes darted to the airspeed indicator. It was now hovering just above seventy five knots. He needed ninety at this altitude and temperature to get aloft. Taxiing uphill was costing him precious seconds, but Mac decided to attempt a lift-off anyway. An aircraft barreling down the runway had a set course, but if it was airborne or somewhat airborne, the large plane would be a harder target. He pulled firmly on the yoke as the first bullets struck just below the cockpit.

Peter yelled into the cabin, "We're under fire!"

The engine screamed, and the plane lifted off. It swayed right and left over the runway. It lost lift and touched down on the nose wheel and starboard wheel, before lurching into the sky once more, beginning its ascent.

"Come on. Come on! Climb, you son of a bitch. Climb!" Mac growled through gritted teeth, as the second burst of gunfire stitched holes along the fuselage.

Mac screamed out in pain, and the plane's nose lowered dramatically and banked to the right. There were more screams from the main cabin area. Peter looked over at Mac, who was holding his lower left leg. Blood was seeping through his fingers, his chinos sodden. At second glance, he noticed blood pooling under Mac's upper right thigh.

The engine was still at full throttle. Peter had some flying experience; he placed his feet on the rudders while pulling up gently on the yoke, simultaneously gaining altitude and straightening out the plane.

"Mac!" he screamed. "Get back in the game, my friend. We need you. Can you hang in there and get us straight and level?"

Mac was perilously close to losing consciousness, but he set the propeller and throttles, checked the airspeed, and retracted the flaps. He talked Peter through a few life-saving rudimentary steps, programmed the autopilot, and passed out. Peter checked that the plane was climbing and double-checked that the autopilot was set. He unsnapped the harness and lurched back through the cabin.

"Everyone okay?" he called out.

"All good." Ryan answered, already up and out of the seat.

"Andrew." Peter yelled, "I need your help up front! Mac is badly hit. There's a trauma bag over there?" He said, pointing at the cargo hold.

Both Peter and Ryan were experienced field medics, but Andrew was a trained paramedic, freeing up Peter and Ryan to assess the damage and figure out how to get the plane safely on the ground.

Andrew, still dazed, nodded, stood up, and walked towards the cockpit, wiping the tears from his face on his shirt. Ryan hoisted the trauma bag from behind the cargo net and followed Andrew. Peter slipped into the right seat and surveyed the instruments to ensure the plane was still flying on autopilot.

Ryan unsnapped Mac's harness and Andrew helped him manoeuvre Mac from his seat, dragging him into the cabin — no easy feat in the cramped quarters. They laid Mac, supine, between the cabin seats. Andrew was fully focused now, his training kicking in, and he took control of the scene.

He set the trauma bag down, unzipped it and familiarised himself with the contents. He looped the stethoscope around his neck, wrapped the BP cuff around Mac's upper arm, and placed the pulse oximeter on his middle finger. Andrew was efficient, organised, and highly adept in his duties. He completed the initial ABCD trauma assessment rapidly (airway, breathing, circulation, disability) and took Mac's blood pressure and oxygen levels, scribbling his initial findings down on the vital statistics notepad.

"Shears." Andrew called out to Ryan.

Ryan handed Andrew the shears, and he proceeded to cut open Mac's blood-stained chinos. Ryan anticipated Andrew's needs, setting out the contents of the kit. He set aside the gauze, pressure bandages, a tourniquet, and a bag of Chitosan haemostatic dressing. Although Mac's breathing was shallow, his airway was open, and he was breathing on his own. Mac was tachycardic due to the blood loss.

Ryan set up the oxygen tank, laying it flat and wedging it under the seat legs to prevent it from rolling around. Andrew placed the non-rebreather mask on Mac and made certain the oximeter was visible. Andrew noted that Mac had an entry wound mid-calf, and an exit wound higher up. The projectile had re-entered just above the knee, in the rear of his thigh, and the round was now lodged there. Andrew could see no spurting blood, but there was a large quantity of pooling darker venous blood.

Andrew and Ryan rolled Mac onto his side and discovered a further upper thigh wound. This did not look good. The second bullet had become deformed after penetrating the thin skin of the fuselage, then the seat, through the cushion, before finally entering Mac's upper thigh and travelling upward through his body, possibly carrying with it shards of metal, cloth, and foam, thus tearing muscle and tissue, before becoming lodged somewhere in his lower abdomen. This could quite possibly cause internal haemorrhaging, and Andrew would need to monitor him closely. Andrew had to stem the blood loss quickly or Mac could bleed out.

"Do you know how to use the tourniquet?" Andrew asked Ryan.

Ryan nodded, unwrapped the tourniquet, and secured it as high as he could on Mac's thigh. Mac writhed in pain, momentarily opening his eyes and screaming as Ryan tightened the tourniquet until Andrew could no longer detect the distal pulse. Ryan grabbed a marking pen and wrote the time on Mac's forehead. Meanwhile, Andrew busied himself cleaning and disinfecting the wounds. He applied the haemostatic dressings to further stave off the bleeding and applied a pressure bandage as tight as he could.

He was aware the trauma bag contained a bag of lactate Ringer's solution and instructed Ryan to hand it to him. Andrew struggled to find a vein but finally succeeded and promptly set it up. They had successfully stemmed the external blood loss, but they suspected he was still bleeding internally.

Andrew could do nothing more except keep some fluids flowing and monitor Mac's progress. His systolic blood pressure was certainly not stable, and Andrew considered using the epinephrine, however he would continue monitoring and use it as a last resort.

"Emily, can we get some blankets and pillows up here?" Andrew called out.

Emily rushed around, gathering all that she could find. They stuffed pillows around Mac to prevent any unnecessary movement and covered him with several blankets to keep him warm. Ryan grasped Andrew's shoulder firmly and said, "Well done. Great job! Have you got him from here? I need to be in the cockpit."

Andrew looked up, his face tense but determined. "Thanks. And yes, I've got him."

Andrew noted that Mac was beginning to respond to voice commands. Originally, his eyes opened only when Andrew pinched him. This was a good sign. His verbal responses had gone from no response to confusion. Again, a good sign, and his motor skills were improving. As the aircraft continued its turbulent flight, Andrew knew they were a long way from safety, but for now, Mac was stable, and that in itself was a small victory.

Ryan slipped into Mac's vacated, bloodstained captain's seat, secured his harness, and interrupted Peter, who was familiarising himself with the instruments, controls, and reading the QRH (Quick Reference Handbook). "Got any flying time?" Ryan enquired.

"Only air cadets - gliders, a Blanik L-13 — when I was fourteen. And you?" Peter responded.

"I took a few lessons when I was seventeen. Got about twelve hours, soloed, and then ran out of money — probably twenty hours in total. But that was a long time ago, and nothing like this." Ryan replied, gesturing to the array of complicated instruments in front of him.

Handing over the QRH to Ryan, Peter said, "The autopilot is set, so we're okay for a while. Mac needs a trauma centre, now! Goma is useless for that, and Kinshasa is out of range, if I'm calculating the fuel correctly. I need to get Pierre on the phone and I want to keep the conversation private. He'll know best, but I think we need to head to Kampala."

Peter pulled out his satellite phone and called Pierre's private cell phone.

Chapter 17

Pierre had just returned from lunch. He dropped into his comfortable, well-worn, leather high-back chair and was bringing himself up to speed with the morning's outbound missions. Some were already back, and some were not due in for a few more hours. He should be hearing from Mac soon if the timing went to plan, he mused.

A slew of messages had flooded in whilst he was out, and he busied himself arranging them in order of importance. He picked up the landline and was dialling South Africa regarding a King Air 350 propeller that was being serviced. There had been one delay after another, and he really needed it by the weekend. His cell phone lit up and began to hum, vibrate, and dance across his glass-top desk. He was about to ignore it, as the line to Johannesburg had just started to ring. Then he noticed it was Peter McCabe's satellite phone and instinctively knew something was not right.

He immediately cut the call to South Africa and snatched up the buzzing cell phone. Pierre sat stunned, listening. His elbow on the desk, head bowed and cradled in his left hand. His eyes closed, cellphone pressed hard against his right ear, trying to hear over the drone of the aircraft's engine, at times drowning out Peter's voice. He dared not allow himself to imagine what they were all going through. 'Mac. Merde! Not Mac.' he thought.

When Peter finished explaining their predicament, silence ensued — five seconds that seemed like an eternity - before Pierre was able to respond. "Okay, Peter. I wish I could tell you everything will be okay, but there's no sugar-coating the situation — it's gonna be a rough ride. We'll be with you every step of the way."

Pierre sighed, exhaling a long breath and pinching the bridge of his nose while squeezing his eyes shut. He continued, "First things first. Let me get another Caravan pilot in here to talk you through the process. Meanwhile, keep reading the checklist and make notes on the most important settings — approach, landing speed, flap settings. You guys have a little flight experience, and both of you are sailors, so you have a better than average chance of getting this bird on the ground. Hang in there; I am going to get that pilot for you now.. I'll call you in ten minutes."

He finished and hung up the phone. As the connection fell silent, Peter felt as though their lifeline had been severed. Ryan said nothing. They both felt very alone up there. The lives of four souls, not including their own, were hanging in the balance of a combined total of thirty hours flight time, some twenty-odd years in the past.

Pierre rolled his chair back and leaped up. He walked briskly out of his office, phone in hand, already calling the fuel depot. He reached his secretary's desk, and while waiting for the fuellers to answer, he told her, "Andy just touched down. Tell him, drop everything, including his post-flight report, and get him in here as fast as possible. We have a life or death situation with Mac."

He finished just as the fuel desk answered the phone. "I need the fuel records for 9Q-AKN in the briefing room as fast as you can... preferably twenty minutes ago!" He disconnected the phone and listened as his secretary relayed his message over the radio to Andy. Pierre hurried into the briefing room and was happy to find it empty. He picked up a chart of the area, spreading it out on the large table, and was studying it intently when Andy entered the room.

Chapter 18

Ryan took charge of flying the plane, while Peter handled the radios, navigation, and checklist. Peter was on the satellite phone relaying the day's events with Hendrick Viljoen, head of security at Gryphon in South Africa. Hendrick would liaise directly with Pierre, and Pierre would be the go-between, saving a lot of back and forth communications. Hendrick wished them luck and hung up the phone.

Ryan had located the seat adjuster and got himself comfortable, his feet rested on the rudders and his hands lightly on the yoke. The aircraft's avionics package was daunting at first, compared to the spartan analogue equipment Ryan remembered from way back when. According to the manual Peter was holding, it was now an all-in-one Garmin G1000 avionics flight suite. On closer inspection, Ryan noted that pretty much everything he needed was on one display screen. Of course, there were two sets of instruments, one for each pilot, which made their situation a little more hopeful. Peter could monitor, figure out which knobs and buttons did what, and relay the info to Ryan. Meanwhile, Ryan was feeling out the controls. He had kept the autopilot connected, he neither knew how to deactivate it, nor wanted to. He just wanted to familiarise himself with as much as he could before actually taking the controls. He knew his flying would not be pretty. However, this plane felt much like an oversized Cessna 172, and he could possibly manage, with a little help and a lot of luck, to get her on the ground.

To Peter and Ryan, it felt like they had been in the air for hours, but a quick check on the time told them they had only been airborne for just under fifteen minutes. Peter's phone rang. He flipped off his headset and answered.

"Peter, Andy Tomlinson here. How are you guys managing?"

"Not great." came Peter's candid response. "Ryan has more experience, so he has the left seat. Mac is hurt pretty bad, and one of the volunteers was KIA. Mac needs a trauma centre."

"Understood." Andy replied. "We're working on getting you to Entebbe. It's a two-hour flight from where we think you are. Pierre is on the phone getting permission, but you may be detained and questioned when you arrive. We'll deal with that issue if and when the time comes. Let's just get Ryan comfortable and get the plane on the ground."

Peter checked the sat phone battery — three hours of constant talk time. It would have to be enough. He tapped Ryan's shoulder and handed him the phone.

"Hey, Ryan." Andy greeted him. "How's it going?"

"Okay." Ryan responded. "Glad you could join us. Wish it were you in my seat... it would make my life a whole lot easier."

"Ryan, I'm right here with you, mate. We're gonna get you guys down. First off, locate and squawk 7700 into the transponder. That will ensure you are an official mercy flight and have declared an emergency. Everything is in front of you on the large display. Take your time. Next I need you to read out your heading, airspeed, altitude, and fuel. I am going to be right here checking what numbers I have for your fuel situation and doing some calculations."

Andy switched the phone to speaker mode and asked Pierre to get his charger and plug the phone in as he poured over the map. Andy scribbled calculations taken from Ryan's readings, information from the fuel slips, and time/distance and fuel burn, concluding they would have ample fuel to reach Kampala.

"Okay, Ryan. Good news!" Andy said reassuringly. "You have enough fuel to get to Kampala, plus an hour's reserve. Your altitude is good, and when you are ready, I need you to turn off the autopilot and keep the speed at a hundred and sixty-five knots. Set the prop at one thousand six hundred rpm and make a gradual left turn, heading one one eight. This will set you on a course to Entebbe. They'll give you headings and runway designation, etcetera, once you are over the Rwenzori mountains and into Ugandan airspace. As of now, you are officially a mercy flight and will be afforded all rights that come with that designation."

Ryan clenched and unclenched his fists, spreading out his fingers and wiping his clammy hands on his trousers. Peter located the autopilot, his fingers hovering at the switch. He turned to Ryan and said, "You've got this! Ready?"

Ryan gripped the yoke, his knuckles white, then released it. 'Gently' he reminded himself. Memory or instinct? He didn't know which. His breath quickened, and the cockpit felt smaller, suffocating. He returned his hands lightly on the yoke, placed his feet on the rudders, and nodded with a modicum of trepidation.

"Okay. Let's do it."

Peter disengaged the autopilot, and Ryan instantly felt the resistance. He began his unsteady turn, passing one one eight before returning to the correct heading and holding her true. Although the air-conditioning was on, his brow was moist and sweat ran from his temples. His palms were still sweaty, but for now, he dared not remove them. His masseter muscles visibly tensed as he tried to ignore his rising anxiety and the pounding in his chest. Desperately trying not to allow the panic to overwhelm him, he thought, 'Concentrate... breathe... focus... relax'.

"Okay. We're heading on one one eight and props and airspeed are good." Ryan informed him.

"Nicely done!" came Andy's elated response. "You okay?"

"Been better!" Ryan nervously replied.

"Well, I'm going to make things a little easier for you now. Do you see the flight management system?" Andy asked.

A brief pause ensued, and Peter pointed to the FMS.

"Yes," Ryan answered, "but I'm gonna hand-fly her in!"

Mac was still lying in the aisle, covered in blankets, completely ashen. His vitals were proving difficult to stabilise. He was certainly hypovolemic and in dire need of a hospital.

Peter turned in his seat and hollered, "Everyone okay back there?"

Andrew was as spent as he had ever been, yet he diligently checked Mac's vitals and logged his findings and times. He had done what he could, with what he had, where he was. Andrew called back, "Mac is stabilising, but the blood loss and added fluids mean he is hovering around the hypothermia mark, and I'm struggling to keep him warm. Can you turn off the air conditioner?"

Peter promptly scanned the controls, located the switch, and shut down the A/C.

Emily had made an improvised hook through the overhead air vent and hung up the lactate Ringer's solution. She sat down next to Andrew on the cabin floor, her knees pulled up tightly against her chest. She desperately wanted to hold him, comfort him, and cry with him and for him. He had lost so much today, yet he had found a reserve of strength to care so diligently for Mac. She resisted the urge to embrace him, instead just placing a hand on his knee.

Father O'Donnell sat sombre-faced, completely drained and defeated, in an aft club seat just ahead of Travis's lifeless body. He watched in awe at the valiant efforts unfolding before him, his mind replaying the events of the day in a futile attempt to make sense of a senseless situation. For the very first time in his life, the age old adages 'God knows best', 'The Lord works in mysterious ways' and 'All things happen for a reason', gave him pause. He so desperately wanted - no, not wanted, needed - answers! Today's senselessness brought a whole new meaning to 'senselessness'... and Father O'Donnell was a man on intimate terms with senselessness. He had worked on the fringes of hell throughout some of the most ruthless and bloody countries in Africa. He'd buried so many bodies — so many lives stolen — by the violence of Africa's darkest corners. He'd come to believe that 'God knew best' in the chaos, that everything had a reason. But today, in the face of Mac's blood-soaked body, Travis's untimely violent death and the hollow gaze of a dying world, even Father O'Donnell had to question the validity of that faith.

Chapter 19

After a gruelling fourteen-hour night shift in the ER at the International Hospital in Kampala, Uganda, Ingrid Svenson felt as though her head had only just hit the pillow when she was abruptly awoken by the shrill ring of her cellphone. Her hand searched blindly in the darkness, fumbling for the annoying, vibrating instrument of interruption on her nightstand. Hitting the answer button and clearing her throat, she mumbled, "Please tell me I'm dreaming. If not, this had better be good!"

Originally from Gothenburg, Sweden, Ingrid, forty-two, was a statuesque, handsomely attractive, no-nonsense woman. She worked tirelessly as a dedicated ER doctor and trauma surgeon at the world-renowned Sahlgrenska University Hospital until her own parents were wheeled in one night after a drunk driver ran a red light. Her father was pronounced DOA and she had frantically paced the hallways outside the OR as a team of surgeons attempted to save her mother. At one-forty-five a.m., she heard the crushing words she had so often used herself; "I'm so sorry. We did everything we could."

Six months after burying her parents, Ingrid had boarded a flight to Africa. Her grief had no place in Sweden; there, it was too close, too raw. But here, in Uganda, she could lose herself in the demands of the hospital, in the urgent needs of others. It was easier to ignore when you kept moving. It was easier to heal the ache of your own heart when you were saving others.

She threw herself into work at the emergency room at IHK, a hundred-bed, state-of-the-art private hospital. After two years and a handful of senior doctors leaving, she accepted the esteemed position of Head of Department.

Ingrid was compassionate, kind, and well-liked. She was respected by her fellow doctors and loved by the nurses. She cared passionately for her adoptive country, and her days off were spent travelling to one or another refugee camp, or internally displaced people's camp, to volunteer her services.

Untangling herself from the sheets and duvet, she swung her bare feet out of bed, placing them on the thick pile carpet. Stifling a yawn, she listened intently, her Blackberry cradled in the crook of her neck. She switched on the bedside lamp, shielding her eyes from the harsh glow, and blinked rapidly, willing the bedside clock to come into focus. Finally able to read the green numerals, she asked if it was two-thirty a.m. or p.m.

"Two-thirty in the afternoon, Doc." came the reply.

Ingrid groaned into the phone. She'd had barely four and a half hours of sleep. The duty nurse began to relay the message. "We have an inbound mercy flight. The pilot has been shot and details are sketchy. We know he is being attended on board by a paramedic, but no further details."

Pausing and taking a deep breath, she continued, "It may get worse. There are six other passengers on board and no qualified pilot. If they make it to Entebbe, the landing could be catastrophic. The weather is worsening and becoming unpredictable. We have scrambled the medical chopper from Kajjansi Airstrip and have three ambulances on the way. Entebbe has the fire and rescue services at the ready. We are in the process of clearing the parking lot, and the helicopter ground crew are on their way to assist with the landing."

Ingrid felt her pulse quicken as the gravity of the situation hit her. A mercy flight, a shot pilot, a non-pilot trying to land in a storm? This was no routine day at the ER. The clock was ticking. "ETA?" Ingrid enquired, suddenly fully awake and alert.

"Sixteen hundred hours." came the response.

"Okay. Assemble my team, prep the OR and cancel all elective surgery. Prep the ER for a multi-casualty incident and have the burn team staff on standby. No-one goes home until we've assessed the situation." Tossing the phone onto the rumpled bed, she blew out a long breath, stretched, and padded into the bathroom, stripping off her nightgown and tossing it into the wicker laundry hamper as she went. Standing naked on the cold bathroom tiles, she shivered as the cool air blasted her from the overzealous air conditioner. Ingrid reached into the shower and turned it on, catching a glimpse of herself in the mirror and sighing at how tired she looked. She stepped into the cubicle, welcoming the piping-hot water. She tilted her head back, combing her fingers through her thick hair, and allowing the water to assault her tired body.

Twenty minutes later, Ingrid was in fresh scrubs and a white lab coat, her well-worn leather handbag slung over her shoulder, a cup of green tea to go, and car keys in hand. She hurried into her attached enclosed garage, unlocked and swung the car door open. She clambered into her road-weary Nissan Patrol, a far cry from the sleek Mercedes coupe she had once sported in Gothenburg, but the big, rugged Nissan served its purpose, traversing the unrelenting terrain of Africa.

Pressing the remote for the automatic garage door and fastening her seatbelt, she fired up the engine and stared through the filthy windshield over the mud-spattered hood, promising herself, once again, she would have it washed if she ever found the time. She depressed the clutch, slipped the Nissan into reverse, and backed out of the garage until the bull bar cleared the opening. She pressed the button and watched as the door closed fully before backing onto her quiet residential street.

Dark, ominous clouds blanketed the sky, and the winds gusted ferociously, forcing the mature jacaranda trees to sway and bow. The suspended overhead traffic lights swung violently on their cables, and most anything not tethered down became a projectile. Tin garbage cans blew across the street, emptying household refuse onto the pristine gardens. Carelessly discarded plastic bottles, soda cans, and bags pelted her car as she navigated her way to the hospital. This storm was going to be intense, and she could not help thinking about the stricken aircraft with a non-pilot at its controls having to deal with a storm of this magnitude. She had been a passenger on countless occasions all over the region while conducting her volunteer work and had encountered her share of inclement weather. Even with skilled bush pilots in control, it was a terrifying ordeal.

Thunder boomed and crashed most violently. Lightning, not unlike a hundred small missiles, streaked from the dark roiling clouds, so bright and ferocious as to cause Ingrid temporary blindness. She grasped tight the steering wheel and turned on her headlights just as the rain began in earnest, drumming hard against the sheet metal. Fat drops exploded on her windshield — the cacophony loud enough to drown out the radio — as the windshield wipers beat mercilessly in a valiant, futile effort to ward off the deluge. Within minutes, the road had become a shallow river as the drainage system fought in vain to cope with the heavenly onslaught.

Living in the leafy upmarket area of Muyenga, also known as Tank Hill, had its advantages. It was close to many of the embassies, had good restaurants, and breathtaking views — not that that mattered today — you could not see twenty feet in front of you. The downside to this idyllic neighbourhood was the lack of entrance and exit roads onto the main thoroughfares. Ingrid had to navigate the labyrinth of small streets from Diplomate Road to Tank Hill Road, and finally onto Bambossa Road, which was now choked with stalled cars and fender benders. To make matters worse, the traffic lights were not working. Ingrid inched forward as the rain continued its barrage. Blaring horns, combined with the storm's racket, made for a nerve-wracking forty-minute drive — a journey that would normally take no more than fifteen minutes.

She turned left into the staff parking lot, relieved to see the welcome sight of the grey, three-story hospital structure. A sodden security guard checked her identification. Once satisfied, he raised the boom and directed her to park on the west side of the car park, leaving the centre clear for the inbound helicopter.

Ingrid parked, turned off the engine, and wrestled to get her umbrella out from behind her seat. The opportunity to drink her tea had evaded her, both hands having been glued to the steering wheel.

Cold now, she decided to leave it in the cupholder. She whipped her bag over her shoulder, opened the door just wide enough to poke the umbrella out, and pressed the spring release. The rain pounded the bright yellow umbrella as she ducked under it and locked the car.

Making a beeline for the entrance, the rain stopped as abruptly as it had started. Steam rose from the black asphalt. The air, in contrast, was cool and fresh. The sweet, pungent aroma of ozone hung in the air. Ingrid squinted in the bright afternoon light and instinctively reached up to retrieve her sunglasses, which were normally perched on her head. Cursing softly, she could see them sitting on the kitchen counter. 'A fat lot of good they will do me there!' she thought, as she strode with purpose. By the time she reached the pathway intersecting the manicured gardens, a kaleidoscope of vibrant-coloured butterflies had ventured out from hiding and were sitting atop broad-leafed plants, sunning themselves and drying out their wings.

She closed her umbrella as she skipped up the steps. The automatic doors opened, and she felt the welcome blast of cool air. Throngs of people milled about, talking excitedly about the storm as they shook off wet umbrellas and shod their rain jackets. She threaded her way through the small crowd, her focus returning to the incoming stricken aircraft.

Chapter 20

Ryan's hands were steadier now, his breath more measured, as he controlled the descent, but the weight of responsibility still pressed heavily on him. They had just cleared the Rwenzori mountains and entered Ugandan airspace, midway between Fort Portal and Kasese, eleven thousand feet above Rwimi. Andy was still connected to Peter via the satellite phone.

"I have contacted Entebbe airport and another Caravan pilot, who is climbing the stairs into the control tower as we speak. He will take over in a few minutes and guide you guys down. For now, tell Ryan to maintain his heading of 105 and contact Entebbe Centre Control on 128.5. Jot this down. It's important!" Andy continued, "Entebbe coordinates are N02.45/E3226.43, elevation 3784.0." He had Peter read it back, before wishing them well and disconnecting the call.

Peter dialled in the frequency on Nav 1, looked over at Ryan, took a deep breath, and said, "Ready?"

Ryan nodded. Peter keyed the mike and contacted Entebbe Airport.

"Entebbe control. Cessna Caravan Niner Quebec Alpha Kilo November. We are declaring an emergency."

The air traffic controller responded quickly. "Entebbe control.

Alpha Kilo November — state your emergency, intentions, fuel quantity, and souls on board."

Peter relayed the pertinent information, the situation, how many souls were on board, and where they wanted to go. Peter asked, "Is the Caravan pilot in the tower with you?"

"Stand by, Alpha Kilo November." the controller responded, immediately starting to hand off all other aircraft to different frequencies handled by other controllers, to avoid transmissions getting garbled. He scanned his screens. It was relatively quiet. He barked out orders to divert whatever traffic could be diverted and hold any aircraft still sitting at the gates.

"Alpha Kilo November, Entebbe." the radio squawked. "We just cleared the channel. Your pilot has arrived and is on the radio." the controller calmly said.

"Peter. Ryan. Mike Sellers here. You're doing great! Now, let's get you on the ground. You are about fifty minutes out. I see you are at eleven thousand and heading one zero five at one seven zero knots. Firstly, let's get your altimeter set, then we are going to start you on a slow descent to eight thousand, okay?" He continued, "You'll need to reduce speed, so pull back on the throttle gently and maintain one five zero. Once stabilised, you can start your descent. Five hundred feet per minute, try not to exceed it."

Ryan repeated the commands, followed the instructions and began his adjustments.

"Alpha Kilo November, you are looking good. You are approaching eight thousand feet. Add a bit of throttle as you reach eight thousand and level off. Don't fret if you go through eight thousand — you have all the airspace you need. Right now, we're showing some weather to the east."

"Oh, of course you are. Fucking great!" Ryan mumbled, just loud enough for Mike to hear. Peter looked at his friend and smiled nervously.

Ignoring the comment, Mike continued, "I am going to have you make a slow turn to the south to avoid it. You're still looking good at eight thousand. You're doing a great job. Alpha Kilo November, confirm you are hand flying."

"Entebbe, Alpha Kilo November. That's affirmative." Ryan responded. With the air-conditioning off and his body armour still on, his shirt clung, drenched, to his body. The overwhelming stress compounded the altogether uncomfortable situation.

"Alpha Kilo November, copy that. Okay, begin your turn to the south. You will want to follow a heading of one eight zero. Hold and maintain eight thousand. Your speed is looking good."

Ryan completed his turn. He looked out of the port side window and could see the storm. Dark clouds, pregnant with rain, filled his field of vision. Sheet lightning brightened the horizon and his pulse quickened. He turned back and barked into the cabin, "Buckle up! And secure Mac as best as possible. It's gonna get bumpy!"

Emily and Father O'Donnell strapped themselves in, but Andrew refused to leave his post. Mac was his patient and there was no arguing with him.

Although they were flying on the edge of the storm, the winds were still fierce. Ryan fought the controls and adjusted the trim. The aircraft rocked violently, and it appeared by all counts that the turbulence had a personal vendetta against Ryan and this fragile group. The heavy trauma bag, the rifles, and anything that was not stowed was tossed about. Andrew crouched over, shielding Mac as best he could.

Fifteen minutes later, after being talked down to two thousand feet and having gone through a series of flap settings in stages, the aircraft was almost configured for landing. They passed over the western edge of Entebbe Airport and were soon over Lake Victoria. Under the calm guidance of Mike, Ryan followed a series of turns and lined up for runway three-five. The winds were calm again, at zero two zero and four knots. A Precision Air Bombardier Dash Eight was exiting the runway, and Ryan was cleared to land.

"Alpha Kilo November, you are looking good. Reduce speed to one hundred and twenty knots and set flaps to thirty."

Ryan maintained his equanimity and responded, "One-twenty, and thirty on the flaps. Alpha Kilo November." He stole a glance at Peter. "Here we go. It's been a slice!" he said, as he lined up with the runway.

"Alpha Kilo November. Remember, landing speed is around seventy-five to eighty-five KIAS, slight nose up, and when you touch down, bring the power back to idle, allow the nosewheel to drop and apply the brakes. Remember to fly it all the way to the ground... all the way, until the main gear touches down. Good luck, Ryan." Mike said, signing off. He slipped his headset off, stood slowly, shook hands with the controller, and went to the window to watch the landing as Ryan crossed the outer perimeter of the airport

Everyone in the tower was standing, and every available pair of binoculars was trained on the stricken plane as it cleared the threshold. The silence was deafening.

A medivac helicopter, two fire trucks, and three ambulances sat on the apron — every piece of equipment had their engines running, bar the chopper, whose flight crew and paramedics were standing at the ready.

Ryan was over the runway, twenty feet above ground level, floating past three hundred feet, then four hundred. Finally, at five hundred and fifty feet beyond the threshold, he felt the main gear make contact with the asphalt. He quickly reduced the power to idle, and the nose wheel bumped down gently. The stricken bird was on the ground, slowing under his gentle braking, finally coming to a full stop with two thousand feet of runway to spare.

Mike and the Air Traffic Controllers let out a collective sigh of relief before the cheering began. Mike was handed a portable radio tuned into the aircraft's frequency and talked Ryan through the shutdown procedure, including setting the parking brake. He congratulated Ryan as the ambulances and fire engines raced towards the aircraft.

Peter and Ryan shook hands as Peter quipped, "And now the fun begins!" referring to the weapons and the rest of the mess they had on board. Peter unsnapped his harness and went into the cabin. He collected all the weapons, cleared the breeches and emptied the magazines, placing them in full view on the table. He collected the handgun that was still in Ryan's shoulder holster, unloaded it, and placed it with the others. He asked Andrew how Mac was doing, checked everyone was okay, then opened both doors just as the first ambulance arrived.

The helicopter's rotors began spinning and the whine of the turbines carried across the still airfield. Peter watched it lift off and hover across the runways, gently settling just ahead of the Cessna. Andrew finished up his report on Mac's condition; his findings, what he'd done, and the times he had done them. He reset the tourniquet, updated the time on Mac's forehead, and met the paramedics at the door as he called out for the litter. One paramedic went to retrieve it and Andrew discussed his findings with the other. He handed over the notes and informed them that Travis was deceased, and Mac was the only other injured. He watched as Mac was loaded onto the litter, wheeled across and into the helicopter, before being spirited away to the hospital.

Travis was loaded onto a gurney and moved to the ambulance, with the obligatory white sheet covering him completely. Andrew walked alongside his friend, his hand on Travis's chest, as the tears flowed once more. "Can I please have a moment alone?" he asked, and the paramedics respectfully moved away. Andrew pulled the sheet down, exposing Travis's colourless face. He bent down and kissed his friend's forehead, vowing to take care of Andrea and their unborn child. He replaced the sheet and nodded to the paramedics, his voice choking with emotion, as he turned to them and said, "Please take care of him. He was one of us, and a good man." He walked over and stood numbly next to Emily and Father O'Donnell.

Mike arrived in an airport security vehicle, and after greetings and thanks were exchanged, climbed aboard the Cessna. He fired it up, taxied her off the runway, and onto the apron, where he tied her down. He was met by two uniformed police officers who commandeered the keys and sealed the doors with bright yellow police decals. They strung a ribbon of crime scene police tape around the perimeter of the bullet-riddled Caravan before taking up station in their Toyota Land Cruiser. The engine idled, affording them a modicum of comfort, having the power to run both the air conditioning and the red, blue, and white light bar. Peter, Ryan, Andrew, Emily, and Father O'Donnell were rounded up, squashed into the security vehicle and whisked off to the airport police station to give statements. The airport reopened.

Chapter 21

Cruising at forty-one thousand feet above sea level at nine hundred kilometres per hour, somewhere just south of Lake Kariba and about five minutes before they entered Zambian airspace, Patrick Kinsella, CEO of Gryphon Security, was sitting in the luxurious cabin of the company Gulfstream G550 when he received notification that Ryan and Peter had landed safely. They were, however, being detained by airport police and awaiting the arrival of the Criminal Investigation Branch. He learned that Mac was at the hospital, being prepped for surgery.

Patrick was travelling with Hugh McDonald, an international attorney, and Rick Jones, his fixer. They had been airborne for just over an hour and fifteen minutes and still had another two and a half to go before they landed at Entebbe. Rick had a briefcase containing two hundred thousand US dollars, which he could use at his discretion, should Hugh not be able to secure everyone's release. Patrick would do whatever it took to prevent any of his guys from spending a single night in a wretched African prison. He had played this game before.

As the jet streaked north into the fading light, the three sat around the conference table, finalising the plan. Simone had compiled a dossier of all the players who might need to be coaxed into sweeping the arms issue under the rug. The trio poured over the intel.

The dossier was comprehensive. It contained names, ranks, phone numbers, details of their family members, where they lived, their daily routines... and if and when they had ever accepted a bribe. Evidently, they all had! Bribery and corruption were deeply rooted in these guys. And Gryphon Security had the facts! Right down to the last detail; day, date, time, amount, and for what purpose... often backed up with photographic, audio, or video evidence.

The flight attendant refilled the coffee carafe, setting it centre table, together with cold bottles of Perrier water. She asked if they wanted anything to eat. They all declined, politely. She retreated up to the cockpit, asking the pilots if they needed anything. They also declined, and she took her seat, keeping a watchful eye, in case they needed any refills.

Chapter 22

Peter, Ryan, and the rest of the group were hustled out of the security vehicle and ushered through the backdoor of the airport police detachment. No-one spoke. They walked single file down a narrow corridor. An overweight, slovenly police officer led the way, while a young, bright officer brought up the rear, stopping at a steel door with a centre tray slot. Ryan knew this long day was going to turn into an even longer night. The unkempt officer fumbled a large bunch of keys from his belt, tried a few, before finally unlocking the door, pulling it wide on its rusty hinges. The screech echoed through the hallway. His arm outstretched, fleshy palm up, he gestured to Ryan, "Please!" breaking into a broad, condescending grin — all teeth — bright in contrast with his ebony skin.

Ryan knew the drill. He placed his hands high against the cell door frame, spread his legs, and was duly searched. His wallet, keys, watch, and other personal effects were taken and placed in an evidence bag. He was relieved of his bulletproof vest, belt, and boot laces before being shoved, unceremoniously, into the dingy six-by-eight-foot cubicle. The steel door slammed with a resounding thud. The lock was turned.

Ryan listened to the sound of receding footfalls and another door opening. Muffled voices filled the corridor. He could not make out what was being said but surmised that Peter was going through the very same scenario. He heard the cell next to him close and the group shuffle off.

Ryan took in his surroundings. There was no window and the only light came from a dim, single caged bulb, high in the ceiling. The painted cinder block walls could only be described as 'institutional green'. They were filthy. The toilet was merely a dented, rusty, steel bucket. Standing on the opposite side of the room was a plastic bucket, half-filled with water. Ryan was cognizant that this would be his ration — quite possibly his entire allocation — for both drinking and ablutions.

There was a single metal cot bolted to the unfinished concrete floor, topped with a thin, crusty, stained mattress. The entire cell reeked of untold misery; sweat, dirt, hopelessness, and fear. Names and dates were crudely scratched into the walls, telling a partial history of some of the unfortunate souls who had passed through this little slice of hell. There were etchings on the cinder block just above the bed, where a man might lie. A series of four vertical lines and one diagonal line through each set, most assuredly depicting the time in days where one of these poor souls had languished. All told, there were seven completed and two vertical, totaling thirty-seven days. Absurdly, Ryan couldn't help wondering why the hapless sod had not scored them in sevens... but that was a fleeting thought.

Ryan went to the wall that separated the two cells and used the tap code, or sometimes referred to as the knock code, to send Peter a message. He waited, then repeated it, perfecting his method.

Ryan had become intrigued with this form of communication after reading about it being used by American POWs in Vietnam. He studied and sometimes taught this to others in his line of work and hoped Peter knew it too. After half a dozen attempts, he got a response. He smiled at this little victory, and he and Peter began the tedious archaic method of messaging, oftentimes having to repeat themselves, both rusty.

Emily and the other two were ushered into separate interrogation rooms, all identical and spartanly furnished, with a long metal table in the centre and two uncomfortable-looking plastic chairs. They were each offered a bottle of water and told to wait. Emily sat down in the chair, her back to the wall, facing the door, and began revisiting what was undoubtedly the worst day of her life.

The day's images ran like a timelapse. The narrative bounced haphazardly through her mind, reminiscent of a pinball — Father O'Donnell's panic, the burning villages, people fleeing, their mad dash to safety, Travis and Andrew's rescue, the plane arriving at Mavivi, the relief... and then the gunshots, and Travis's death. So unnecessary, and so tragic. And then there was the pilot. She hadn't even had a chance to be properly introduced, and tried to recall his name — Mark, Mick... Mack?

She placed her head in her hands and her elbows on the table, as she felt the warm tears run down her cheeks. 'Am I entitled to a phone call? If so, who would I call?' She pondered that question for a long time. She was terrified — as terrified as she had ever been — and she wept openly. She wept out of fear. She wept for the kids at her school. She wept for their families. She wept for the senselessness of it all. But mostly, she wept for Andrew and his tragic loss.

Andrew shuffled into his interrogation room, oblivious to his surroundings. Numb and spent from this godforsaken day, he placed his back to the wall and slumped down on his haunches. He stared down at his pale blue scrubs, stained with the blood of both Travis, a friend he could not imagine his world without, and the pilot. He prayed Mac would be alright... however, he did not hold out much hope. He had lost a great deal of blood, and it would take some sort of miracle for him to survive the helicopter flight to wherever they were taking him.

Traumatised and alone, Andrew struggled to hold onto his overwhelming and daunting thoughts long enough to make sense of them. How was he going to break the news to Andrea? When could he tell her? Would he be allowed to make a call? If he was granted only one call, then to whom? Travis's wife? Travis's parents? His own parents? Where was Travis? How would he get him home? Would the embassy help? Is there even an embassy in Kampala? If there was, he certainly would not want them to break the news — that was on him.

Incoherent and unfinished thoughts bombarded him. Andrew's breathing became shallow and rapid. His mouth was dry. He was moving headlong into non-medical shock. He began taking long, deep breaths in an attempt to control his breathing and rapidly elevating heart rate. He closed his eyes, trying to erase the last moments of Travis's life and allowed his mind to play like an old movie; he and Travis in Texas, horse riding, camping, long sunny afternoons swimming in the creek, sitting on the patio at Max's Roadhouse listening to bluegrass over a few beers... anything but those large hazel eyes staring blankly as he lay in Andrew's lap at the side of a dirt runway in the middle of Africa.

Father O'Donnell had been praying fervently for the past hour. A man of the cloth. A devotee of forty years in the ministry. A man who thought he had seen and heard everything he could ever see and hear. A man whose faith was non-negotiable. Yet today, doubt was not only setting up camp... it was building a house. He prayed for guidance. He prayed for his doubts. He prayed that his faith would not waiver. He could not allow it. His small entourage, a mini flock if you will, needed him... needed his faith and his strength.

He discovered he was almost chanting, as opposed to reciting, Isaiah 41;10. "So do not fear, for I am with you; do not be dismayed, for I am your God. I will strengthen you and help you; I will uphold you with my righteous right hand." He scoured the deepest recesses of his mind, seeking further assurances, and in his time of need, he found the comfort he was searching for in Deuteronomy 31;8. "The LORD himself goes before you and will be with you; he will never leave you nor forsake you. Do not be afraid; do not be discouraged."

He had finished praying for himself. He had found his strength, and with renewed vigour, he bowed his head and prayed out loud. He prayed for all the injustices of the day. He prayed for the two courageous security personnel, their names escaped him currently, if ever he knew them. Surely, if it were not for them, and of course, his God, they certainly would have perished, or worse still, been taken hostage. He prayed for the pilot he never got to meet. He prayed for Travis's soul and for Andrew, who would need all of his faith and strength to get through the coming days. But most of all, he prayed for Emily — he knew all about young women incarcerated in countries where law and order was merely a suggestion.

Chapter 23

The powerful twin-engine Eurocopter EC135 raced across the sprawling city at just over two hundred and fifty kilometres per hour. The flight doctor and flight medic worked feverishly to keep Mac alive. His pulse was weak, his breathing shallow, his heart rate rapid, his systolic pressure was below seventy, and he was tachycardic. His body was cool and clammy, and he had not regained consciousness. He was in stage four hypovolemic shock. By all indications, he had lost about forty percent of his blood volume. His heart was doing its job, desperately pumping whatever blood and oxygen he had left to his vital organs, while his body was shutting down the flow to less important areas. If he were to survive, they would need to have him in surgery within the hour.

The steam was still rising from the hot asphalt as the helicopter touched down in the parking lot of the hospital, a mere fifteen minutes after leaving the airport. A trip that would have taken more than an hour by road; a trip he would not have survived.

A flurry of activity ensued as the pilot shut down the chopper, applied the rotor braking, and gave the all-clear for the medical team to disembark. The flight doctor finished her trauma notes as the medic unfastened the litter. The ground crew raced in a crouch, placed the safety cones around the bird, and jogged aft, unlatching and opening the large clamshell doors. They received the thumbs-up affirmative signal from the medic and rolled the litter out onto the tarmac, the wheels of the gurney dropping down and locking with a clattering of metal. The medic slid open the side door. He and the doctor jumped out and caught up to the ground crew, who were wheeling Mac across the parking lot through the rising steam.

Seeing the chopper touch down, two orderlies and an emergency room doctor hurried out of the hospital to meet the incoming patient. The flight doctor jogged with the ER doctor alongside the gurney, relaying her findings and the pre-hospital treatment. She handed him her written report, along with Andrew's report, before turning back towards the waiting helicopter. She raised her right hand, pointed her finger skyward, and rotated her wrist clockwise — the international signal to light the engines in preparation for takeoff.

The ground crew latched the clamshell doors, cleared the safety cones, and flashed a thumbs-up. The pilot nodded as the medical team jumped aboard, sliding the door shut with a decisive *clunk*. Within seconds, the rotors surged, and the chopper lifted off — back to base in under ten minutes.

Ingrid's pager alerted her that the inbound helicopter with the critically injured pilot was on the ground, she headed down to the ER immediately to assess the situation herself. The trauma team had just enough time to assemble. Every second mattered when dealing with gunshot wounds.

As the stretcher was rushed into the trauma bay, Ingrid joined the team, already moving with practised urgency. The flight doctor's rapid handoff summarized the pilot's condition; severe blood loss, a thready pulse, probable intra-abdominal injury, possible intrathoracic injury.

"Let's transfer him." she instructed. The team swiftly moved the patient onto the ER trolley, its radiolucent frame designed for immediate imaging. "Secure the C-spine. Airway?" she asked, her voice calm but firm.

"ET tube already placed. Airway patent." the anaesthetist confirmed.

"FAST scan, portable X-ray, and full blood workup." Ingrid

ordered. The ultrasound technician began the scan while another team member drew blood, expertly inserting a second large-bore cannula on the opposite limb from the medivac-inserted cannula.

The monitor displayed images that confirmed her fears; internal bleeding in the abdomen and signs of vascular damage. "Probable hemoperitoneum." she muttered, already formulating a surgical plan.

"BP is holding with fluids, but barely." the anaesthetist added. "He's tachycardic."

"We're not wasting time here." Ingrid said. She turned to the theatre manager, who had been coordinating from the doorway. "Is Trauma One ready?"

"Yes, cleared and prepped."

"Good. He's going up." she announced.

As the patient was wheeled out, Ingrid's mind raced through the next steps. The pilot's injuries required immediate surgical intervention to control the bleeding and repair the damage. She kept pace beside the trolley, her focus unwavering despite the controlled chaos around her. The radiologist had confirmed there was no time for a CT scan — they would have to rely on the FAST findings and clinical judgment.

In the operating room, the team awaited her arrival. The anaesthetist updated her as they transferred the patient to the surgical table. "We're maintaining oxygenation and circulation, but he's on the edge. Be ready for massive transfusion protocol."

Ingrid scrubbed in, her thoughts methodical and precise. The OR staff worked in synchrony, each member knowing their role in this high-stakes battle.

Chapter 24

Three well-dressed detectives from the Criminal Investigative Branch arrived just after five-thirty in the evening. They showed their credentials to an alert and 'by-the-book' airport security police officer. After a bit of posturing and a few heated words, they reluctantly surrendered their sidearms, as per airport regulations. They signed the register, their weapons were locked in the airport armoury, and they were escorted to the interview rooms.

Adroa Odongo, the self-declared lead detective cut an imposing figure. Tall and heavyset, his once-athletic frame now bearing the marks of years of overindulgence. His skin was the colour of polished ebony. Too many late nights, too many cigarettes, and a near-perpetual scowl etched lines deep into his face. His demeanour — prickly and often malicious — left little room for doubt about the state of his character. While his two partners held the same rank, Odongo's reputation as a bully and saboteur was well known. He was a man who didn't tolerate dissent and wasn't afraid to settle scores in the most underhanded ways. He was the pack's Alpha, and in his eyes, that meant everyone else was expendable.

"Okay!" he barked at his two partners, then paused to check his file. "We will interview Ms. Esposito, Father O'Donnell, and Mr. Koch separately, one-on-one. Then we meet in an hour to compare notes. After, we will interview the two security men, or more than likely, 'mercenaries', in their cells. We may have to school them on how things are done in Uganda." he said with a sneer.

Emily's interview did not begin well. She agreed to give her statement of the day's events but insisted that the interview be both written and verbally recorded, to make it more difficult to tamper with or alter in any way. Odongo claimed they had only one recording device and it was being used in one of the other interview rooms. He was overbearing and intimidating, but Emily, though afraid, stood her ground. Folding her arms across her chest, she said politely, "That's okay, I'll wait."

Usually, Odongo had a knack for sniffing out the runt of the litter for interrogation purposes, but he had clearly underestimated the fiery nature of this small, demure young woman.

He slapped his large palm on the table with such force that Emily's water bottle bounced, toppled, and rolled onto the floor. She flinched and pushed her chair back with a start. He smiled at his small victory. Frustrated, he bellowed, "You are in a lot of trouble, young lady! You imported illegal weapons into our country. You and your friends violated our airspace without permission. You had a dead man on your plane — one of you probably shot him. Your pilot was shot. So, you'd better start telling me what happened! You could go to prison for a very long time, and let me tell you, prison is not a nice place for a young pretty white girl."

Leaning in, elbow on the table, palm upwards, clenched in a fist, he threatened quietly, "I hold your future in my hand." Then, unclenching his fist and gesturing with an open palm, he continued, "or secure your release."

Despite the fear clawing at her insides, Emily forced herself to remain composed. She turned her gaze away from Odongo, as though weary of the charade, her breathing steadying with each controlled inhale. After a long moment, she met his gaze again, her voice calm but resolute. "Well in that case, I want a lawyer and a phone call to the British Embassy before I say another word."

Infuriated, Odongo picked up his briefcase, tossed in his notepad and pen, and snapped it shut. He exited the room, slamming the door behind him, only to return five minutes later carrying an archaic-looking recorder and microphone. He set up the equipment and placed it in the centre of the table. Wordlessly, he removed his jacket, draped it over his chairback, and retrieved the notepad and pen. "Happy now?" he asked sarcastically.

"Will be, when I see it working." she said, nodding at the recorder.

After it was tested and Emily was satisfied, he rewound the test section and pressed record. He stated the date, time, Emily's full name, his name, and their location. He was very professional and thorough, but Emily's intuition told her he was not to be trusted, and she was glad she had insisted on the recording.

As painful as it was, she was determined to recall every last detail, regardless of its significance. She started with the burning of the villages, followed by Father O'Donnell's arrival, their escape, the car breaking down, the calls to Andrew and Travis, and their subsequent rescue on Komanda Road. She recalled the phone calls from Clarke Aviation in Goma and their arrangement to meet at Beni airport in Benin. She relayed the details of the attack, her voice faltering as she recalled Travis's final moments. She wanted to give Odongo the facts, but this man did not deserve her pain. Keeping her emotions in check was a battle she would ultimately lose. She concluded her statement with the details of Mac being shot, and Peter and Ryan flying the plane to Kampala.

By the time she had relived the entire horrific day, tears were streaming down her face and her eyes were rimmed red. "Please could I have another bottle of water and five minutes to compose myself?" she said through choppy breaths, anticipating that Odongo's questioning was sure to take up much of the evening.

He stopped the recorder and slid the notes over the table, saying, "Read this. If this is what happened and you agree, sign it, with the date and time... which, by the way, is 19;43."

Emily was still scrutinising the written statement when Odongo returned with a bottle of water, a box of tissues, and her personal effects that had been confiscated earlier. Once satisfied, Emily signed the document and handed it to Odongo.

"Ms. Esposito, I have no questions at this time and you are free to go. As this is an ongoing investigation, I am going to have to hold your passport. I will make a copy of it and sign it. You can use that for identification purposes if required for hotel bookings, etc. I will release you on your own recognizance. You are not to leave the country, and you need to inform me once you have made accommodation arrangements. I will require your contact details and you must come to the police department when summoned. No excuses! I don't want to have to come and find you, Ms. Esposito. If I do, I will arrest you and you will go to jail. Understood?"

Emily did not doubt him. She shuddered at the thought and nodded in acknowledgment. He left and returned ten minutes later, handing her a signed photocopy of her passport and escorted her to the main concourse.

Father O'Donnell's interview was much the same as Emily's, and he was being released, sans his passport, of course. Like Emily, he was told not to leave the country.

Andrew, on the other hand, was having a difficult time. He had left his passport in the Land Rover during the attack and only possessed his driver's licence, his paramedic's identification, and a couple of credit cards. After ten minutes of being verbally abused and threatened by Detective Odongo, Andrew decided it was a fruitless endeavour to argue. In the heat of the moment, Andrew's mind drifted back to his father's quirky advice, 'Arguing with an idiot is like playing chess with a pigeon… no matter how good you are, the bird is going to shit on the board and strut around like it won anyway'. He could almost hear his father's deep, comforting, slow southern cadence, and it brought with it a boost of confidence.

Andrew stated confidently, "Sir, I think this interview is over. I want to call the US embassy's after-hours emergency service and have them send over a lawyer." The detective scowled, snatched up his things, and stormed out. Andrew hoped that after the call, a representative from the embassy would arrive with a lawyer in tow and this whole miserable day would soon end.

Chapter 25

The Gryphon Gulfstream touched down at Entebbe at 19;45 hours, twenty minutes ahead of schedule, thanks to a moderate tailwind. The pilot taxied the aircraft onto the apron and onward to the designated parking area, where the two powerful Rolls-Royce BR700 engines whined to a stop.

The pilots had requested customs and immigration personnel to clear the passengers onboard. moments later, a white Toyota Hiace minivan arrived, 'EBB Customs and Immigration' emblazoned on its doors. The national flag in black, yellow, and red with the grey crowned crane encircled in white sat proudly below the lettering.

The captain announced that immigration was on the scene as two men alighted the vehicle, looked up at the cockpit, and nodded a greeting to the captain. The captain saluted them in a form of returned greeting. The flight attendant opened the door, deployed the stairs, and welcomed the two aboard. Both men were impeccably dressed in their slate blue slacks, crisp white shirts bearing the Ugandan flag on their sleeves, green epaulettes identifying them as immigration and customs officers, and green berets, which they removed respectfully when entering the aircraft.

Patrick Kinsella greeted them warmly, impressed with their

professionalism and courteous act of removing their headgear, and gestured for them to take a seat opposite him at the conference table. He slid the passenger manifest and passports to the immigration officer, who checked the names and passports against the passengers and crew. Once satisfied, he asked how long they intended to stay and their purpose of travel.

"Business, and no more than forty-eight hours." Patrick responded with a smile.

The customs officer had stayed an extra hour to clear this late arrival. He was hungry, tired, and fed up, so instead of the usual due diligence, he simply muttered, "Anything to declare?"

Again, Patrick responded for everyone, "No. Just our laptops and personal effects." He omitted the fact there was two hundred thousand US dollars in cash — technically, it was not going to enter Uganda, and if pressed, it was fuel funds, in the event they ended up in an airport whose credit card machine wasn't working — 'This is Africa and these things happen' would be his excuse. Their passports were stamped, and they were welcomed into Uganda.

Patrick and Hugh put on their jackets and ties, disembarked, strolled into the main terminal, and followed the signs to the airport police office. Rick and the flight crew remained on the aircraft. Rick stayed with the money, and the crew readied the plane for a quick turnaround. The pilots called for the fuel truck and ordered fifteen hundred gallons of Jet A1, while the flight attendant cleaned and checked the stock. If she needed any further supplies, she would take a quick trip to duty-free.

Chapter 26

The three detectives met in the hall, briefly discussing and comparing Emily and Father O'Donnell's notes. They were very similar and had no obvious discrepancies.

"Tomorrow, we will have them come to the CID headquarters to be questioned, and then see if their stories hold up." Odongo announced. "Mr. Koch will remain in custody, as he has no passport. We will come back to him later. Tell him he will have to wait until the morning for his phone call. Process him and move him to the holding cell. Fucking Americans and their demands! He is in my country now." he growled. "Okay. Now let's see what the soldiers have to say for themselves."

After a quick discussion, primarily consisting of Odongo talking and the others agreeing, it was decided that all three would interview Peter first.

Peter heard the footfalls echoing down the hallway and could tell there were at least two, possibly three, men coming either to his cell or Ryan's. He stood up, placed his back against the wall furthest from the door, let his arms hang loosely at his sides, legs akimbo, and his eyes fixed on the door. He heard the keys jangle, then enter the lock. The metallic snap. The scraping of metal on concrete, as the door creaked open. All three detectives squeezed into the cramped space and fanned out into an arrow formation, one in each corner on either side of the door, and the lead investigator standing two steps in front of Peter.

Peter's eyes darted quickly around the room, he was calculating the distance, the size of the men, and chances of a victory if it became an abusive situation. He was confident he would prevail, but then what? Well, then, he presumed, he would be in a great deal of shit! But he would deal with that if it came to it. One thing was abundantly clear... he would not allow himself to be beaten by this bunch.

"I am Detective Chief Inspector Odongo and you, I believe, are Mr. Peter McCabe." Odongo said, looking up and holding eye contact with Peter, not bothering to introduce his fellow detectives.

"I am," Peter replied, holding Odongo's stare, "and I want a lawyer and a representative from the British embassy present if this is a formal interview."

Odongo didn't blink and showed no intention of backing down. He simply replied, "This is Uganda, Mr. McCabe, not America or Britain. We are a sovereign nation and you have broken... let's see..." he said, counting each violation, imaginary or not, theatrically on his fingers, "...at least five of our laws, and I am sure I can come up with many more. I can hold you for as long as I want on terrorism charges, maybe even place you in one of our less pleasant prisons, which will make this place..." pausing for effect, and sweeping his arm dramatically, "...seem like your Buckingham Palace."

Peter never flinched or blinked, and just repeated, "Law-yer." He broke the word into two syllables, as if teaching a toddler. He watched as Odongo's fist clenched, smarting at the insult.

"I would think twice before attempting to use that fist. I can assure you it will not end well for you." Peter said, in a calm tone, just above a whisper.

Chapter 27

"Miss Esposito?" came the inquiring voice at the door. Startled, Emily looked up to find a small, rotund female police officer, wearing a warm smile, something she had not seen all night.

"Yes." Emily responded as she stood up.

"Don't forget your belongings. Follow me, please." The officer led Emily down the narrow hallway, with its flickering and humming fluorescent lights.

"If you need a hotel, I suggest the Serena in downtown Kampala. It's safe and close to all the embassies. Use only the yellow official airport taxis. It'll take about an hour and a half and will cost around fifteen US dollars."

Wordlessly, she flashed her badge at the immigration man and escorted her into the terminal. "This is where I leave you. Good luck, Miss Esposito." she said with a smile before she turned and headed back the way they came.

Emily stood in the near-empty terminal and gazed around. She needed to sit for a minute and collect her thoughts. She spotted a brightly lit café that was still open but had no clientele. Clutching her meagre possessions tight against her chest, she started hesitantly over to the café. Out of the corner of her eye, she noticed two well-dressed

Caucasian men in dark suits. One carrying a briefcase, both walking with purpose, being led by one of the policemen she had seen earlier. The officer nodded in recognition as the group passed not ten feet from her.

The older, tall, athletic man with silver hair seemed to pause for a second, then continued walking. Emily too continued walking.

"Miss Esposito?" She froze, not sure what to do. She did not turn to face the summons but started walking again, pretending she had not heard her name being called out in this shabby airport.

"Wait up, Emily Esposito!" She did not 'wait up'. Quite the contrary, she hastened her step.

"Emily, I am Peter and Ryan's employer. Please stop. I just want to know that you are okay." His accent was definitely South African, and his plea sounded genuine. She stopped mid-stride and turned to face him. He was approaching her with a concerned, almost parental, caring look across his handsome features. The airport police officer had stopped in his tracks and was waiting patiently as Hugh joined in the pursuit and was only a few paces behind Patrick.

"Hi Emily. My name is Patrick Kinsella and this is Hugh McDonald, our company's international attorney." he said, reaching out his hand to shake hers. "We flew in from Johannesburg on our private jet as soon as we heard about what had happened. I heard you lost a friend today. My deepest condolences. Are you okay?" His deep, honey-coloured eyes hinted at compassion, tenderness, honesty, and integrity. His voice, calm, warm, and caring, invited Emily to respond.

Emily started babbling and the tears flowed again. "I don't know where they are. They separated us when we got here. I haven't seen Andrew or Father O'Donnell. I don't know what happened to Peter, or your other man."

"Ryan." Patrick informed her, handing her a clean handkerchief.

She continued, "Travis is dead and I don't know where they took him. I think your pilot is dead too. I am so sorry." Mac was not their pilot. He did not correct her; he just let her continue.

Her words came out fast and choppy, stammering and falling over each other, at times incoherent, punctuated by gasps of breath. She was hyperventilating and struggling to get a grip. She tasted the tears as they passed her lips and clung to her chin, uncertain whether to take the plunge onto her already damp and blood-stained shirt, much like a cliff-diver standing on the precipice, calculating his odds of survival. She dragged her wrist and the back of her hand across her mouth and chin, dispersing her tears and muffling some of her words.

"It's okay. Calm down. Try to relax. You have nothing to be sorry about. It's not your fault. It will all be okay. We are on our way to see Peter and Ryan. What is your friend's last name?" he said soothingly.

"Er... mmm... Koch. Andrew Koch." she stammered, wiping the tears from her eyes.

Patrick said, "Go get a coffee and a bite to eat. We are going to see what we can do. Don't leave the café. We will be back, I promise. Do you need any money?"

"No thanks," she replied, "I have some Ugandan shillings. Please make sure Andrew is okay. He is in a complete state!"

"Of course I will." Patrick said, as he stepped in and embraced Emily in a fatherly hug, kissing the top of her head before stepping back and retracing his steps.

Emily smiled a weary smile as she trudged over to the Crane Cafeteria. It was brightly lit and sported an impressive mahogany bar, in juxtaposition to the few cheap Formica tables. There were hot and cold stainless steel food cabinets, a steam table offering a selection of curries, stews, rice, and some kind of vegetarian option all neatly on display in polished chafing dishes. Unidentifiable music was coming from a small transistor radio, perched on a cluttered shelf behind the counter. She had not eaten since morning and was ravenous but did not think she could hold anything down. She ordered a latte, paid for it, and found a table where she could sit and keep an eye on the concourse.

Emily cupped both hands around the hot mug, staring down into the frothy drink and blew absentmindedly into the latte. She was suddenly drained and oh, so very tired. She longed for a hot bath and a warm bed where she could climb under the covers and block out this entire day. She looked above the rim of the cup as she drew it to her lips and saw Father O'Donnell shuffling slowly beyond a bank of chairs. He had seemingly aged ten years since she last saw him a few hours earlier. His gait was uncertain and he appeared bewildered. He looked not unlike a lost grandfather with early onset dementia. His hair was dishevelled, his clothes rumpled, his shoulders slumped and his head bowed.

She pushed her chair back with a screech. The leg caught an uneven join in the tile and toppled over with a loud clatter, bringing the sleepy staff awake as she rushed forward to intercept Father O'Donnell. He looked up with a start and then smiled a tired smile, "Oh, Emily! Are you okay? I have been worried about you, so I have!"

"And I you." Emily responded. "Come and sit. Let me get you a cup of tea. Are you hungry?" she continued, so relieved to see him again.

"No, thank you. Just a pot of tea, my dear girl."

Emily righted her chair, apologised for the disturbance, ensured Father O'Donnell was seated and comfortable, and ordered his tea.

Chapter 28

Dr. Ingrid Svenson's role was that of a general surgeon, while Dr. Francis Nabirye, one of the best vascular surgeons in sub-Saharan Africa, was called in as the attending vascular surgeon. International Hospital Kampala had fought hard to keep him in the country and working in their hospital.

Together, they reviewed Mac's scans and blood work, ensuring that emergency blood products and the rapid infuser were set up to counter his substantial haemorrhage. The anaesthetist, who had monitored Mac's initial resuscitation in the ER, confirmed adequate vascular access through large-bore IV lines, with close monitoring of his core temperature and central venous pressures. They maintained urine output checks and adjusted vasopressors to support his blood pressure.

In the OR, Dr. Nabirye carefully released the tourniquet around Mac's upper thigh and exposed the wounds. He began by performing anastomoses on the severed femoral vessels, restoring critical blood flow to the leg. Moving to the lower leg, he bypassed the injured popliteal artery with precision, ensuring stable blood supply despite the damage. With the vascular repairs completed, Ingrid moved to perform a splenectomy to control the internal bleeding in the abdomen. Both projectiles were safely extracted without further tissue damage.

After surgery, Mac was transferred to the ICU, where he remained intubated to support his recovery. The medical team closely monitored his vital signs and clotting factors as his anaesthesia gradually wore off. Wrapped in a warm-air blanket to stabilise his body temperature, Mac's blood pressure and venous pressures showed signs of improvement. A steady infusion of morphine and Propofol kept him comfortable and sedated as his condition stabilised.

Although the surgery was successful, Mac's condition was fragile. He would remain in the ICU, closely monitored by his medical team for any signs of complications. His journey to recovery would be long and arduous, but he had overcome the immediate crisis.

Chapter 29

Detective Odongo was weighing his options. He really wanted to smash Peter's bright white teeth, destroy his handsome face, teach the 'mzungu' a lesson, and some much-needed manners. But he wasn't sure if he could. If he was honest with himself, the mzungu was bigger, certainly fitter, and reminded him of a leopard - stealthy, confident, and likely already having scoped out the lay of the land with a plan of attack.

Odongo, on the other hand, was the typical textbook bully. He sat behind a desk, only cracking the heads of scared, petty thugs or criminals already in handcuffs. His dilemma ceased to be a problem when there was a knock on the metal door.

"We are in the middle of an interview!" Odongo barked. He tried not to break eye contact with his detainee, but the more he stared at Peter, the more uneasy he felt. He sensed his adversary was highly-skilled, very intelligent and potentially dangerous. Odongo was seldom intimidated, but this man rattled him.

Determined not to lose face in front of Namatovu and Bako, Odongo maintained his charade by pointing his index finger at Peter's chest. However, his false bravado faltered, and he stopped just shy of making contact. He desperately wanted to jab Peter with his finger, but he erred on the side of caution. He knew it could be a dire mistake and might result in him wearing a finger splint for the next few weeks.

"Mr. McCabe's lawyer is here." came the voice from behind the steel door, followed by the sound of keys entering the lock. Odongo gritted his teeth and hissed, "McCabe, don't think this is over. I'll be seeing you."

"Thank you, Detective Odongo. I look forward to that." Peter calmly and pleasantly responded. Odongo turned on his heels, spittle glistening on his lips, and stormed out, pushing past Patrick and Hugh, with Namatovu and Bako close on his heels.

Hugh called out to the retreating detectives. "Detectives, a minute please." Namatovu and Bako stopped, but Odongo continued walking defiantly. "Who is the lead detective and what are the charges?"

Odongo pulled up short, spun around abruptly, and barked out loud, "I am Chief Inspector Odongo. Your men are charged with multiple crimes against our sovereign nation. Just for starters — violating our airspace; terrorism; impeding an investigation; hijacking; illegal entry into the country without proper identification; suspected murder; and attempted murder. Of course, this will change to murder if the pilot dies. I am sure I will have more." Even Bako and Namatovu rolled their eyes at the absurdity, which Hugh did not miss.

Peter and Patrick were talking quietly, leaning against the cell wall, not wanting to sit on the filthy cot. The airport cop stood guard at the door.

"What a fucking shit-show." Peter said, his mind replaying the incident over and over. "I haven't had time to piece it together. The mother-fuckers knew we were there. They were ready! Mac did everything possible to ensure we wouldn't be spotted. He stayed out far, stayed high. They couldn't have followed the Land Rover because they were already in place. It was a fucking ambush! The only thing that makes sense is that we were a target of opportunity. There isn't enough traffic going into Mavavi for them to have been there just waiting. They must have been expecting someone else... and we stumbled blindly into the ambush."

Peter drew another breath and was about to continue when Patrick interrupted. "Listen, Peter. You and Ryan did your jobs. It was a miraculous performance under the conditions, and no-one could have asked more of you. I'm not gonna blow smoke up your arse, but that's why we hired you. You two are exemplary soldiers. You did what you were hired to do, and more. Let it go for now, and let's work on getting you out of here."

Patrick Kinsella was a no-nonsense, straight-shooter and a man who did not linger in the past. In short, he was a 'reasons or results' kind of guy, and reasons did not count in Patrick's book. Peter had to admit, this was why he took the job in the first place.

Chapter 30

"Detective Odongo. Is there a free room where we can talk?" Hugh asked politely.

Odongo feigned indignation, as if he had nothing better to do than deal with a terrorist's lawyer. He looked at his watch, sighed impatiently, and said, "I can give you ten minutes. You two, wait here." He addressed Namatovu and Bako as if they were mere ancillary staff, not his equals. Bako, clearly irritated by Odongo's posturing, retorted that they would be in the Crane Cafe when he was ready to leave. Anger flashed in Odongo's eyes, but he quickly controlled himself. He simply nodded and told Hugh to follow him.

Once seated in the interrogation room, Hugh took his time. He removed his jacket, hung it on the back of the chair, and brushed an imaginary piece of lint off his shoulder. He carefully placed his handcrafted Lugro ostrich-skin briefcase on the table, unsnapped it, and withdrew a yellow legal pad, a recorder, a microphone, and his Waterman pen from its custom teak box. He dusted off the chair with his handkerchief before sitting down. He noted the time and marked it on the legal pad along with the date. He asked Odongo for his full name, rank, and identification, extending the same courtesy in return.

Dispensing with the formalities, Hugh informed Odongo that the interview would be recorded. He started the recorder and began. "I am representing Peter McCabe, Ryan Van Oldenburg, Andrew Koch, Emily Esposito, Father Keith O'Donnell, and Dalton McBride. My local counsel, who is not present at this time, is Edwin Mbabazi." He paused for effect. Edwin was a well-known Ugandan criminal attorney with a reputation for taking on corrupt officials. His fearless approach had made him an enemy of the state, resulting in numerous threats and attempted assassinations.

Odongo was visibly shaken. He crossed his arms and struggled to maintain his composure. "Detective Odongo, please refresh my memory. You mentioned a slew of charges against my clients. Could you please repeat them? And have my clients been officially charged at this time?" Hugh asked, purposely not requesting the charge sheets, which had not been drawn up yet.

Odongo seized the opportunity to rattle off charges, real or imagined, employing the shotgun effect to see what would stick. "At this time, it's an ongoing investigation. We haven't had time to process the aeroplane, which is being treated as a crime scene. But for now... illegal entry into Uganda without proper identification; illegal importation of military-grade weapons; suspected murder of one man who was DOA and attempted murder of the pilot; terrorism; flying an aircraft without a licence; entering Ugandan airspace under false pretences; and resisting arrest." he said smugly.

"I assume you've interviewed the witnesses and have their written statements. We would like copies of those along with the charge sheets, which I presume you have. Could you please send them over to Mr. Mbabazi's office in the morning?" Hugh inquired.

Unruffled, Odongo responded, "We'll process the plane tomorrow, complete our report, and get all the pertinent information to Mbabazi's office when we are done with the investigation. It may take a week or more. There's a lot to process." Odongo glanced at his watch, as if this was an inconvenience. "If we're done here, I have transportation to arrange for the prisoners, reports to file, and a forensics team to notify for the aircraft inspection." he said with a sneer.

Hugh smiled back, putting his pen away and methodically repacking his briefcase. As Odongo stood up and walked confidently towards the door, Hugh said, "Good night, Detective. Thank you for your time. I know you're a busy man, and I really appreciate it."

Odongo paused, half-turned with a self-satisfied smile, and replied, "My pleasure, Counsellor. Don't mention it."

"Oh, I almost forgot," Hugh remarked, the recorder still running, "one more question, Detective, on a different matter. How is your case going against Ms. Acin? It's such a shame you were charged with assaulting and raping that young woman. I heard her two witnesses — oh, what were their names...?" Hugh continued nonchalantly, pulling out a dossier and flipping through it, "Ah yes, Ms. Masika and her boyfriend Mr. Namutebi — had disappeared! Thought to have gone into hiding or fled the country, according to reports. There are those who believe they were paid off and threatened. Such a ludicrous allegation! Well, it would be, if it weren't for this." Hugh said, patting a large manila envelope.

Odongo's face visibly slackened, his eyes darted about the room as if seeking an escape. It was fleeting but Hugh did not miss it. "Do you want to see it? It's not your finest work, Detective. Moreover, you're not so photogenic. Apparently, the luxury apartment you keep for your sordid trysts, unbeknownst to your wife, is sponsored by the shakedowns of local businesses. A protection racket you've run for..." pausing for effect, "the past four years. You are quite the busy boy, Detective! I hope you'll show a little more professionalism in dealing with this case at hand."

"For you, my friend. Watch and read at your leisure." he said with a smile. He switched off the recorder, placed it in his briefcase, and snapped it shut. He shrugged into his jacket and pointed to the door. "After you, sir."

Chapter 31

Emily gasped when she saw Detectives Bako and Namatovu walking into the Crane Cafe. Father O'Donnell placed a comforting hand over hers and whispered for her not to worry, but she could do nothing but worry. It had been the worst and longest day of her life. She silently chastised herself for not leaving the airport immediately.

Namatovu and Bako both smiled and greeted them pleasantly. Bako said, "How is the coffee? You know it's grown here in Uganda. It's some of the best coffee in Africa. Don't believe the stories that Kenyan coffee is the best — it's just the most marketed." he added warmly.

Namatovu chimed in, suggesting Emily and Father O'Donnell should get something to eat. "Raj here," he gesticulated at the small man behind the counter, "makes the best butter chicken in all of Kampala! It's not on the menu, but if you ask him nicely, he'll make it fresh for you. You both could use some nourishment after the day you've had."

Emily relaxed as the two detectives wished them a good evening and went to banter with Raj, who was delighted to see them. Bako looked back at her and Father O'Donnell. "We're ordering some butter chicken and naan bread. You don't want to miss out on it." he smiled warmly.

Emily surrendered to her hunger and said, "Sure, we'd love a couple of orders, if it's not too much trouble. Thanks."

"It will be my pleasure." Raj said, disappearing into the kitchen.

The two detectives took their seats a few tables away from Emily and Father O'Donnell and sipped on fresh tropical fruit drinks.

It wasn't long before Emily's olfactory senses were treated to the enticing aromas of fresh exotic spices wafting from the kitchen. Garam masala, ginger, cumin, and turmeric hung in the air. The sound of chicken sizzling in ghee was only interrupted by Raj's singing as he toiled over his signature dish and she was momentarily transported to a happier time from the not-too-distant past. One gorgeous autumn day, after a trip to Robben Island off the coast of Cape Town, she had arrived back famished. On the hunt for a quick bite to eat before visiting the old castle, she stumbled upon the Eastern Food Bazaar on Longmarket and Plein Street. The food there had been incredibly fresh. The smells coming from Raj's kitchen now were reminiscent of that happy day, and she welcomed the distraction, however fleeting.

Her sense of smell teased mercilessly, her mouth salivating and her stomach beginning to grumble audibly, she bashfully apologised to Father O'Donnell and quipped, "I didn't realise I was that hungry."

A young jovial waiter appeared with a beaming smile, precariously balancing an overburdened tray consisting of cutlery; crockery; a wire basket brimming with warm naan bread; two finger bowls with hot water and lemon; two dinner plates; a pitcher of iced water with cucumber slices; and a couple of glass tumblers. He cleared away the coffee and teacups, and draped a starched white tablecloth over the bare Formica, transforming the casual airport café into a pleasant restaurant.

He laid out the utensils. "Prepare yourselves for something super!" He proclaimed, omitting the 'er' from 'super' and replacing them with the least four 'a's.

"I shall return." he said, as he scampered into the kitchen.

His mannerisms were jolly, and it brightened their evening. As promised, he came back with a steaming platter of butter chicken and an oversized bowl of garlic rice. The aroma wafted ahead of the dishes, teasing and tantalising, as if announcing something spectacular was on its way.

He placed the bowls in the centre of the table, and with a flourish, stepped back, swept his hand over the food, and declared, "Dinner is served." With a theatrical bow, he slipped silently out of view.

"Flamboyant little bugger." Father O'Donnell whispered conspiratorially. Despite the ordeal they had just endured — or possibly as a consequence of the day and nervous tension — they both began giggling, which, with time, became unbearably difficult to curtail, let alone belay. Emily, aware of the two detectives sitting in close proximity and how inappropriate giggling may seem, finally excused herself and retreated to the restroom in an attempt to compose herself.

Chapter 32

It was almost midnight when Ingrid turned into her driveway. She pressed the remote and waited patiently for the garage door to whirr to a stop before driving in. After closing the overhead door behind her, she shut down the clattering diesel engine and silenced Van Morrison, who was pleading for 'one more moondance under a cover of October skies' on the radio, keeping her company during the drive home. Thankfully, the roads were nearly empty, and she arrived home in just under ten minutes. She was exhausted.

Entering the darkened house, Ingrid killed the chirping alarm, resetting it for 'stay' to deactivate the indoor motion sensors. She kicked off her shoes at the door and padded on stockinged feet, turning on lights as she went. Dropping her bag on the armchair, she made her way through the living room and into the kitchen.

She set the forgotten cold green tea from the car this morning on the counter and swapped it for the leftover half bottle of Barolo Vigne Dei Fantina, a gift from a visiting Italian neurosurgeon. She decided it would pair well with a little Cesaria Evora, a wonderful Cape Verdean singer she had recently discovered, a few years after the barefoot singer had passed.

Taking a glass from the dishwasher — something she should have emptied three days ago — Ingrid retired to the living room. She slipped the CD into the stereo, plopped down on the couch, poured herself a glass of wine, and tucked her legs under her. With her eyes closed, she let the singer's melodic, melancholy voice wash over her, as she savoured the exquisite wine.

Chapter 33

Hugh closed the door quietly behind him and noticed Detective Odongo stomping heavy-footed up the corridor approaching the main terminal. Hugh smiled to himself and began walking casually in the opposite direction towards the cells where Peter and Ryan were being detained. He knew the young paramedic was not in a holding cell, and he wanted to see him to assure him all was being done to get him released as soon as possible. He went in search of one of the airport police officers and almost collided with a young policewoman exiting an interview suite.

"Excuse me." he said politely, as he stepped aside to allow her room to pass in the narrow hallway.

She smiled back at him and asked if she could help.

"Sure. That would save me a great deal of time, which is in short supply. Too many doors and not enough hours. I'm representing the crew that came in on the flight from the DRC, and I need to see Andrew Koch. He is in here somewhere."

"Oh, sure. No problem. He is in interview room six. I just brought him a sandwich and a bottle of water. Here, let me take you there." she said, as she turned to lead the way.

He followed her down the corridor, passing a series of identical doors. She stopped at the final door, unlocked it, and said, "In here."

Hugh smiled, thanked her for her help, and bid her goodnight.

Hugh stepped into the room and did not immediately see Andrew, who was sitting on the floor in the corner, his knees pulled up to his chest, his head bowed and a bottle of water clutched in his hands between his knees. The unappetizing sandwich sat, still wrapped, on the table. Andrew made no attempt to move or look up. He appeared to be a man beaten by life, utterly broken and dejected.

"Hey, Andrew. I am so sorry to hear about your friend." Hugh offered his condolences.

Andrew was tired of everyone being sorry. He was tired of Africa. Tired of this place. Tired of the corruption and injustices. He yearned for Texas, the open spaces, the comforts of home, surrounded by people he could trust, but most of all, he yearned for his friend. He just wanted to be on a flight home with Travis — the Travis he knew twenty-four hours ago — alive and joking.

Andrew finally looked up at the distinguished-looking gentleman and asked, "Are you from the embassy?"

"No, I'm Hugh McDonald. Peter and Ryan work for us, and I am the lawyer representing you and everyone else who was on the flight today. Rest assured, you will all be released tonight."

Hugh held his hand out to Andrew to help him up. "Come, take a seat." he said gently.

Hugh realised Andrew was about his son's age, and he could not imagine his boy going through what this young man endured today. All he wanted to do was take him in his arms, hold him, and tell him everything would be okay, but he knew that would be a lie. Nothing in this young man's life would ever again be okay.

Andrew accepted Hugh's hand and stood up on cramped legs. He stretched and walked slowly to the chair, taking a sip of the lukewarm water as he sat down and stared at Hugh through bloodshot eyes.

"What time is it?" Andrew asked.

"Almost midnight, and I can say with absolute certainty, you and everyone else will be released within the hour, with no pending charges. Plan A is in play, and in the highly unlikely event that goes to shit, plan

B always works, believe me. This is not my first rodeo." Attempting to bring a modicum of levity, Hugh finished by saying, "As you Americans like to say, that's why they pay me the big bucks."

Andrew smiled at the familiar phrase, spoken with an Afrikaans accent.

"Now, get that water into you, and I'll be back soon. Do you need anything else?"

"No. But I don't have a passport."

"Got that covered. Not a problem. We'll get you into a hotel tonight and to the embassy in the morning. It will take a bit of finagling, but like I said, rodeos and big bucks. Hang in there, it's almost over."

Andrew managed a weak smile and asked, "By the way, Mr. McDonald. How's the pilot?"

"Alive because of you. I heard you did an amazing job. Last I heard, he was in surgery. We'll get an update when we are out of here."

As he stepped into the corridor, Hugh saw Detective Odongo pacing the halls.

"Detective." he greeted him cheerfully, as if they were old friends. "What are you still doing here? I thought you'd be home by now. It's been a long day for you. I was just telling Mr. Koch he was being officially charged and that he would be transferred to the prison sometime tonight, pending a hearing, along with Mr. McCabe and Mr. Van Oldenburg. Has something come up?"

The two men were now walking towards each other, stopping a few paces apart. Odongo looked at Hugh with a mixture of loathing and defeat in his eyes. Hugh stood erect, tall and poised, briefcase in hand, an impassive look on his face, and waited.

Odongo foraged for the words he had probably rehearsed over the past forty or so minutes. "We have decided to drop all charges against everyone aboard the flight. Whatever happened, happened in the DRC."

Hugh understood that, for Odongo, it was all about not losing face, and he was fine with that. He anticipated what was to follow. Odongo's words tumbled out in a rehearsed cadence, the official spin he'd practised over the last hour. He was trying to rewrite the narrative, but the cracks in his delivery were unmistakable. "The flight was a mercy flight, and we did everything in our power to facilitate its safe landing in Kampala. We arranged the transfer of the critically injured pilot. The rest of the people on board were never detained, only accommodated and questioned respectfully as to the events of the day. We have discussed the passport issues with immigration and arranged a temporary stay in our country for those that are without their passports. I will arrange a press conference tomorrow, and I want you or Mr. Kinsella to be there. I expect you to thank our department, immigration, and air traffic controllers for our outstanding work and hospitality."

Odongo paused as he searched for the best way to bring up the delicate matter of his abuse of power and corruption. He held no cards, and he had to tread carefully.

"I hope we have both gotten what we wanted, and this will be the end of our arrangement."

Hugh placed his briefcase on the ground, stretched out his hand to shake Odongo's, which he took and shook reluctantly. Hugh said, "Sure. We are done, as soon as you release my men. Good night, sir."

The afternoon airport police had finished their shift, leaving only a few crew members on duty. An officer escorted Hugh to Ryans cell. Two hardback chairs had been brought into the room, and both Patrick and Ryan were deep in conversation when the door was unlocked, and they were released.

Hugh brought them up to speed while the three men stood in the hallway. "I will take care of the paperwork at immigration. Could you ask the crew to arrange two minivans and hotel accommodation for two nights for everyone?" Hugh called over his shoulder, as he followed the officer to Peter's cell.

With Peter freed, he left the three men in the hallway and hurried to secure Andrew's release.

Hugh opened Andrew's door, poked his head in, and said, "Come on, young man. Let's get a coffee into you, a hot shower, and a comfortable bed. We'll deal with everything else in the morning."

Chapter 34

Emily and Father O'Donnell had long since finished their dinner and were nursing their second pot of tea. Fatigue and apprehension were beginning to set in. The restaurant was now deserted. Bako and Namatovu had left after receiving a call some fifteen minutes earlier. Raj bid them goodnight, as did the funny little waiter, but not before giving Emily his email address and asking her to write to him.

Father O'Donnell, struggling to keep his eyes open, agreed when Emily suggested they take a walk in the empty concourse.

"It will do us both good to stretch our legs."

She informed the barman, who was bored and scrolling through his phone, that they would be back in ten minutes.

As they turned right out of the restaurant, they heard voices and footsteps echoing through the terminal. Emily glanced over her shoulder, and her heart hitched at the sight of the bedraggled group approaching. She let out an involuntary screech and spun Father O'Donnell around so quickly, he barely maintained his footing.

Peter and Ryan, were carrying their flak jackets, flanked by Patrick and a portly man in a rumpled suit toting a metal briefcase handcuffed to his wrist. Andrew followed behind in his stained scrubs, with the lawyer's arm draped over his shoulder. Bringing up the rear was an impeccably dressed, handsome flight crew.

Waves of relief flooded over her. She bolted towards the group, tears of joy streaming down her peaches-and-cream complexion. She almost knocked Peter off his feet as she hugged him, jumping up and down with excitement. She hugged and kissed everyone in turn, her joy infectious. Father O'Donnell soon joined the melee, as the flight crew stood on the periphery smiling at the reunion.

Once Emily had calmed down and composed herself, Patrick informed them of the arrangements. Rooms had been booked at the Serena hotel, and platters of finger food, tea, coffee, and cold drinks would be available upon their arrival.

Outside, two minivans waited curbside. Patrick suggested they go immediately. Tomorrow, they would meet at ten in a pre-booked conference room to go over the coming day's events.

Patrick woke early. The group was safely ensconced in the hotel, and Patrick assumed they were still asleep. He, however, had been up since five-thirty and was burning up his phone. He had roused Simone out of bed, updated her, and asked her to get the American ambassador's private cellphone number in Uganda. He had spoken to Pierre, who was relieved to hear that everyone was released and would be couriering Ryan's and Peter's passports to the Serena hotel by FedEx overnight. He had located Travis, called the hospital, and checked on Mac, who was still heavily sedated in the intensive care unit. He had badgered the staff at the hotel to find an independent boutique with a wide selection of clothing. The entire group was in desperate need of fresh clothes, especially Andrew. He stumbled upon some good luck when the concierge hinted that 'he might know a man, who knows a man'. Patrick tipped the concierge twenty US dollars for the name and number.

At seven-thirty, which Patrick perceived to be a respectable hour, he called the owner of 'La Boutique' and spoke to a still-sleepy Leo. He relayed his predicament.

"I need a range of clothing for a variety of people. Different styles, different sizes. They will need complete outfits, from head to toe. In short, could you possibly bring a wide selection of your stock and set up shop at the Serena hotel? I know it's an inconvenience, but I'll make it worth your while."

Leo, although mildly confused, was curious. Business was slow mid-month, and it would consider it an outing.

"No problem. I trust this will be a cash sale. I don't take cards." he said in a friendly, business-like manner.

"Cash it is!" Patrick replied.

As Patrick waited for Simone to call him back, he ordered another Bodum of coffee, his third today so far, and he was certain it would not be his last. He called his wife — just missing out on speaking to the kids — they were already bundled into the car for the school run. He updated her and told her the mission was a success, and he would be home sometime the following day.

Simone called back and furnished him with the ambassador's number. He called without delay and brought the ambassador up to speed regarding Andrew and Travis. He invited him to come to the Serena for the meeting. The ambassador agreed, thanked Patrick for his help, and confirmed he would see him at ten. Patrick plugged his nearly-depleted phone in to charge, slumped into a high-back chair, stared out of the window, and sipped his coffee.

Leo arrived shortly after nine. A lanky, sun-weathered man with skin the texture of aged leather and of undeterminable age; he could be forty, or he could be fifty-five — it was hard to tell. He had closely shorn hair and a neat beard. He was dressed in distressed Levi 501s; boat shoes — no socks; a black V-neck henley shirt; a tan casual jacket with the sleeves pushed up to his elbows; and a straw-coloured aerated Panama hat. He looked as if he had stepped out of a *Miami Vice* set from the eighties.

He commandeered a handful of the hotel staff and luggage carts — the ones with the chrome poles designed for hanging suits — and brought everything up in the freight elevator. Accompanying him was his tailor, the perfunctory measuring tape draped around his neck, wheeling in a sewing machine on a dolly, ready to alter or hem anything to suit. He greeted Patrick warmly, and Patrick thanked him for accommodating his needs so readily.

Patrick was suitably impressed as Leo went about setting up *La*

Boutique in the conference room, as the tailor unpacked and readied his sewing machine. Patrick explained briefly what had happened. It would be a sombre morning in the juxtaposition of the bright clothing and elaborate breakfast buffet being set at the far end of the room.

Andrew entered, dressed in a white hotel terry robe, barefoot, his eyes bleary from lack of sleep. "I'm sorry. I couldn't bring myself to put my scrubs on again." He said to Patrick.

"Don't worry. We've taken care of everything. Leo will sort you out. Did you get any sleep?"

"A little. I still haven't called home." Andrew said, still wearing the tormented look on his face. "I just don't know how I'm gonna do it. I'm dreading it. It's a call that will devastate not only our two families, but our community."

"Andrew, we're here for you and will do anything to help. Grab some clothes, take a shower; the American ambassador will be here at ten. We'll go over everything and put a plan into action. Now, go and let Leo sort out your wardrobe. Select a few outfits — it will be a couple of days before you get home. Don't worry about the cost, it's on us."

Chapter 35

Ingrid had fallen asleep on the couch when nature rudely awoke her at a ridiculous hour. The music had stopped, the wine was mostly gone, and the house was still. It was dark outside as she stumbled to the bathroom, dropped her scrubs and panties on the floor, relieved herself, and brushed her teeth. She padded into the bedroom, collapsed onto the unmade bed, drew up the duvet, and fell into a deep, much-needed sleep.

She woke again at ten, stretched, yawned, and decided she needed a run to blow the cobwebs from her mind. She dug out her running gear, peeled it on, and limbered up before going in search of her phone. She finally found it between the cushions on the couch.

She selected her running playlist, put in her earbuds, disarmed and rearmed the alarm, and stepped out into the bright African morning. She set her timer and began her run as Katy Perry was belting out 'Roar'. It had taken Ingrid a few frustrating months of trial and error to find a good five-kilometre run, as her neighbourhood had a number of cul-de-sacs and dead-end streets. One would have thought the city planning department was inebriated when they designed it. It was not the case. There simply was no planning whatsoever.

After the Obote regime fell in 1986, the government coffers were ransacked by high-ranking politicians and government officials who built elaborate homes haphazardly on Tank Hill, with no planning permission. No thought to roads, sewer, or drainage systems. The results, twenty-five years later, were not unlike navigating a maze.

Ingrid was holding a steady pace as she passed in front of the Hotel International, some four thousand feet above sea level. A tired old hotel with unobstructed, breathtaking views over the neighbourhood. Burnt orange terracotta-tiled roofs, lush green lawns, a combination of flowering fruit trees, lilac-blooming Jacaranda trees, and flaming Flamboyant trees led down the slopes to the shores of Lake Victoria and the Rwenzori mountains in the distance.

Ingrid never tired of the scenery. The lake, one day azure and as still as a monastery, the next dark and ominous. She wove her way along the broad streets, past the International University, before picking up her pace for the final kilometre home. As if on cue, Pharrell Williams' upbeat song 'Happy' blasted through her earbuds and she smiled at the line, 'Sunshine, she's here. You can take a break'. "Not likely!" she called back to the song. Drenched in sweat, she stopped her timer, rested her palms on her knees, and panted heavily. She glanced at the stopwatch and punched the sky. Thirty-four minutes and fourteen seconds! She was ecstatic.

Ingrid was not working today; however, she felt the need to see how her patient was getting on. It had been a gruelling three hours of surgery, and he was still in serious condition. She showered, made a fresh fruit salad, and mixed in a yoghurt for breakfast. Dressed in her kimono and with her hair wrapped in a towel, she sat at the kitchen counter, one long elegant leg draped over the other, watching NBS TV, the Ugandan news channel. There was no mention of the ill-fated flight. She switched to CNN, then Al Jazeera. Nothing there either. Something about it was odd, and she suspected the incident had either not yet leaked to the media or the police had censored the story, a common practice in this part of the world.

She dressed in a conservative, cornflower-blue, knee-length, button-front floral cotton dress adorned with sunflowers that accentuated her flame-blue eyes. Her summer-wheat, shoulder-length hair - still damp - hung free today. She wore no make-up. She rarely used it. She selected a pair of brown, distressed leather, flat, slip-on shoes and headed out to the hospital.

Chapter 36

Shortly before ten, the group began filing into the conference room. Chafing dishes filled with hot breakfast items; a cereal station; assorted breads; muffins; cinnamon buns; and croissants stood along one wall. A fresh juice, coffee, and tea bar made up the L of the breakfast table. Patrick greeted everyone warmly but refrained from asking if they slept well. He already knew the answer.

"Please, everyone, help yourself and take a seat. We have a lot to go over this morning." Patrick said as he closed the door behind the assembled group.

Emily did a double-take when she saw Andrew walk in a few minutes later. He was now dressed in smart blue jeans, a pale blue linen shirt, black socks, and no shoes. He was clean-shaven and his hair was neatly combed.

"You look great. Hey, nice shoes!" she said, regretting the comment as soon as it left her mouth - of course he would not want to put on his blood-soiled sneakers. "I'm sorry, that was insensitive. I didn't mean anything by it." She stumbled over her words, her face flushing, scrambling for something else to say in an attempt to rectify her blunder. She drew a blank. Andrew smiled reassuringly and hugged her.

Everyone was seated and tucking hungrily into a hearty breakfast when the door opened and the American ambassador stepped in, apologising for his tardy arrival. Patrick greeted him, pointed towards the buffet, and beckoned him to help himself. Patrick had not yet eaten, but was anxious to lay out the plan for the coming days. He walked to the head of the table just as the ambassador sat with his plate and coffee.

Patrick cleared his throat and began. "I know you all had a very trying day yesterday, and I wish the outcome was different. I am disturbed and heartsore at the events that unfolded, however, I'm grateful it was not worse. You all lived through that horrific event, and I am not going to dwell on it. I just want to find the best solution under the current circumstances. I have taken the liberty to arrange as much as possible and get you all where you are supposed to be. Feel free to come and see me afterwards if there is anything further I can do or change.

Firstly, Mac is in the ICU following surgery. He is heavily sedated but is expected to make a full recovery." There was a collective sigh of relief as he pressed on. "Father O'Donnell, I have made contact with your church in Kinshasa and arranged for your flight tomorrow at noon. Your ticket will be waiting for you at the Ugandan Airlines desk, and your party will meet you on arrival." Patrick paused and sipped his coffee before addressing Andrew.

"Andrew, we are making travel arrangements for yourself and Travis's remains. At this time, the best we can do is have you fly with us to Johannesburg. Travis will be flown on a commercial flight. We will meet the remains in Joburg, where you will both board a British Airways flight, connecting with American Airlines to Dallas, and on to San Antonio."

Tears streamed down Andrew's face at the mention of Travis's remains. He apologised, pushed his plate away, and excused himself, standing up and leaving the room. Emily followed. Patrick waited until the door closed before continuing.

"Peter. Ryan. Your passports will be here tomorrow. Pierre just sent us the FedEx confirmation, and you guys will come back with us to Johannesburg. The officials are going through the shit you guys left at Mavavi, and it's a bit too hot for you to return for a while."

He turned to the ambassador and said, "How soon can you arrange a passport for Andrew and clearance to have Travis's body moved?"

"Tomorrow morning. I just need to get some identification from Andrew, and passport photos, which we can arrange. I will have the coroner here send me fingerprints for Travis's identification. You said he was a paramedic or firefighter, so his prints will be in the database."

"Okay, that's good. Thank you." Patrick continued as he turned to the flight crew. "You guys, get the plane ready for a noon departure tomorrow. Pick up some casual clothes from our man Leo over there." He pointed to Leo, who was standing perplexed next to a rack of clothing. "Get your uniforms dry cleaned. I'm sure Leo can arrange that. I will get you the passenger manifest tonight. I'm not yet sure if Emily is coming or not." He finished by thanking everyone and then getting himself some breakfast and another coffee.

Emily jogged along the hallway and caught up to Andrew, as he fumbled to get his key card to work in the door. She gently took the card from him, flipped it around, and inserted it. A green light illuminated, and she pushed open the door to his room. He shuffled in. She followed, then quietly closed the door behind them — not before placing the 'DO NOT DISTURB' sign on the outside handle.

He sat on the edge of the bed, and she went into the bathroom. She poured him a glass of water, brought in the box of tissues, and gently sat next to him. He declined the water but took the tissues, mumbling his thanks.

"I can't go home with Travis like that. How am I gonna tell..." he broke off, then continued, "Hell, I just can't tell Andrea. I promised her we'd be safe. She asked me to take care of him. I didn't. And now he's dead." he wailed. His shoulders shook uncontrollably. He was wracked with guilt.

Emily wanted to tell him it wasn't his fault; a cliché so overused in situations like this, and so totally useless. She, instead, placed a hand on his knee and allowed him to talk without interruption.

Emily had witnessed the unbreakable bond and friendship the boys had shared through their many visits to her at the school. She had been privy to their joshing and banter in the Land Rover just before the horrific incident. Andrew had lost someone he loved and admired, and she knew nothing could ever replace Travis. She, of course, had friends, but nothing came close to what these guys had.

"I haven't told his parents nor mine. I've picked up that phone so many times... but I can't do it. I feel like a dang coward. They deserve to know. They need to know. But I cannot bring myself to call."

Emily interjected, "Andrew, sweetheart," surprised at herself by the use of the endearment, "we can do this. We were there." She paused, choosing her words carefully, deliberately avoiding the word *survived*. "We endured this together. Andrew, let me be there for you — all the way to Texas. I want to do this!"

He sobbed louder at her genuine compassion. She pulled his head onto her shoulder, buried her face in his sandy hair, and kissed his head, as her tears, too, began to flow. His face in the crook of her neck, his tears spilling and soddening her blouse, and hers dampening his hair. Nothing more was said. Nothing could be said. They just clung to each other, rocked and sobbed.

They finally broke the embrace, and Emily, again, surprised herself by kissing him gently on the cheek. She said, "Let's go and see the ambassador, and ask Patrick to help with the travel arrangements. It's too early to call the States. We can make the calls when we come back."

They took turns washing their faces in his bathroom and strode back down the hallway to the conference room. Most had left. Just the ambassador and Patrick remained, talking in hushed tones. The wait staff were silently and efficiently clearing the buffet, and Leo was helping the flight attendant with her garment selection when they entered the room.

The sound of the sewing machine clattered as the tailor hemmed a pair of trousers. The ambassador stood and introduced himself to Andrew, putting his arm around Andrew's shoulder and drawing him aside. Emily went to talk to Patrick. She brought him up to speed on her and Andrew's plans.

"I'm going to travel with Andrew to the States. He could really use the support. I have a credit card. I just need to know which flights to book."

Patrick told her in no uncertain terms that he would cover all expenses, and it was not up for negotiation. "You will need some travelling clothes, so quickly go and grab a few outfits from Leo. He needs to leave shortly."

She smiled a tired smile and she didn't have it in her to argue. She just hugged Patrick.

Emily selected a few dresses, a pair of jeans, a blouse, and suitable attire for Travis's funeral. She only hesitated when it came to choosing her undergarments, and Leo walked away respectfully as she rifled through the selection of intimates. She went into the conference room bathroom and tried on the items. She was pleasantly surprised that everything fitted, except the jeans, which needed hemming. Trousers of any kind were always too long for a woman of her stature.

She emerged from the bathroom, clutching her jeans. "Is there time to hem these?" she enquired hopefully, indicating the amount by using her index finger and thumb. "About this much."

"Ten centimetres." he replied, jotting it down and taking the jeans over to his tailor.

Leo, cognisant of her bashfulness regarding the lingerie, handed Emily a large paper bag with sturdy handles and a pair of scissors, and asked her to cut the tags off. She smiled at his old-fashioned gentlemanly manners.

"You guys need some shoes? This is what I have in the shop." he said, handing her a brochure. "I can bring whatever you want later today."

"Did Andrew get some clothes other than the ones he is wearing now?" she asked.

"No." Leo responded.

She walked over to Andrew and excused the interruption. "Hey, Leo is leaving in a few minutes. Can I grab you a few outfits, and if so, what shoe size are you? Don't worry, I have good taste." She assured Andrew, who had composed himself and appeared to be doing better.

"Sure, that'd be great. Size ten on the shoes please, thirty-two thirty-three on the jeans, fifteen on the shirts, and large on the t-shirts." he said in response.

Returning to the table, she selected a pair of trainers for herself and a pair of sensible flats for the funeral dress. For Andrew, she picked out a pair of ostrich skin cowboy boots — a bit extravagant, but Andrew always wore boots, and she suspected they were left behind in the abandoned Land Rover — a pair of nondescript black trainers, a few plain t-shirts, a handful of casual shirts, some jeans, socks, and underwear. Leo bagged Andrew's garments. He promised the shoes and her altered jeans would be delivered to the hotel reception shortly after lunch.

Patrick ambled over to Leo as Emily was just finishing up. She thanked him profusely and said, shyly, "These are not all mine! The other bag is for Andrew."

He smiled and said, "Young lady, you can have whatever you want. Thanks for being there for Andrew. Keep an eye on him for me, and if you need anything, just ask. You will call if you need anything, right?"

She hugged him and said she would.

"Okay, then. We'll see you later. Oh, before I forget, you both missed the end of the meeting, so just to bring you up to speed, we are going to check on Mac today and update you all. All accommodation and meals are on the company. Just charge whatever you want to your rooms. We will meet together as a group tomorrow at seven in this room for breakfast to confirm flights, etcetera. We've arranged to drop Father O'Donnell at the airport for his flight to Kinshasa. Like I said, call if you need anything."

Emily thanked him again and took her leave.

Patrick shook Leo's hand and conveyed his gratitude. "I'd better grab a few things while you're still here."

He made his selection and Leo added it to the total. "So, including the dry cleaning, your total is two thousand eight hundred and eighty-seven dollars and eighty-five cents. Just call it two thousand eight hundred."

Patrick said nothing. He walked over to the metal briefcase, took out three thousand dollars, handed it to Leo, and said, "Let's call it three. Thanks again!"

He shook the shopkeeper's hand and requested that he put a rush on the dry cleaning.

"Already have. The uniforms will be here by midnight. The crew can collect them in the morning from the front desk."

"Thanks, Leo. Your efficiency is quite something for someone who lives in Africa." Patrick quipped.

"You can take the German out of Germany, but you can't take Germany out of the German!" replied Leo with a wry smile.

Chapter 37

Ingrid took the elevator to the third floor. She greeted the staff warmly and located the nurse in charge of the ICU.

"Doctor Svenson, what a lovely surprise! What are you doing here? I thought you were off for the next forty-eight hours."

"Good morning, Nurse Otim. How are you? I was just checking in on Mr. McBride. How's he doing?"

"He's doing okay. No changes from last night. His vitals remain stable. He's still heavily sedated, per your instructions. We changed his dressings and catheter bag about an hour ago. There was a call from a man in South Africa. I don't recall his name." She rifled through a stack of messages. "Ah, yes, here we are — Mr. Patrick Kinsella. He's in the country and wanted to stop by. He's not family, but was quite insistent. He left his number and asked that the attending doctor call him so he can explain his connection. We also received a call from a Mr. Pierre Arquette. Apparently, Mr. McBride works for him as a pilot; they are based in Goma. I told him Mr. McBride is stable, but in the ICU. I did not tell him anything else. He, too, wants a doctor to call him."

"Thanks, Nurse. I'll just pop in and check on him. Please have those numbers for me. I might as well make the calls while I'm here, so I can enjoy the rest of my time off." Ingrid replied with a warm smile as she opened the door to Mac's private room.

Ingrid picked up the chart and studied it for a while. She checked the medication dosage, the arterial line, and read the cardiac monitor, and was satisfied with his vitals. She checked the infusion pump and set the chart back at the foot of the bed. The nurse poked her head through the door and handed Ingrid the phone numbers.

She thanked the nurse and said, "If there are any changes whatsoever, put me down as the primary call." She did not know why she said that; there were many capable doctors on call, and she was off duty.

Ingrid strode down the hall, fished her keys from her pocket, opened her office door, and made the first call to Pierre. After putting his mind at ease, Pierre went on to tell her a little about Mac, probably more than he should have. Being a chatty fellow, he couldn't help but boast and praise one of his best pilots. She soon learnt he was well-loved and respected, originally from Ireland. Twenty minutes later, she managed to end the call, and phoned Patrick. After a brief conversation, she added him as an approved visitor.

She quickly stopped back in to see Mac before she went about her chores for the day. He was a handsome man, even in this state, but life had certainly not been kind to him. He had obvious stress lines around his eyes, and his hair was flecked with silver. She had to admit, he had piqued her curiosity. This former airline captain was now flying dangerous missions in Africa... and the Congo of all places.

Chapter 38

Andrew and Emily walked down the carpeted corridor. She shared her recent conversation with Patrick, and Andrew, in turn, brought her up to speed on his talk with the ambassador. "They're fixin' a replacement passport, and I gotta get photos done at the embassy this afternoon. They're arranging the transportation and paperwork, so that Travis can be on the same flight as me."

Emily interrupted. "You mean the same flight as us."

Andrew was taken aback by her comment. "You really meant that? I just thought…"

She cut him off with a gentle smile. "Hey, no overthinking. You guys meant the world to me. I want to be there for you and say my goodbyes to Travis. Besides…" her tone turned playful as she nudged his shoulder lightly, "Patrick bought me a dress, so I have to show it off somewhere, right?" She let her hand slide down his sinewy arm before taking his hand in hers.

She pulled him up short in the corridor. "Look at me." she said. "I really want to be there, but if you don't want me to come, I'll completely understand."

Andrew shook his head, overwhelmed. "I want you to come, but…" She interrupted him again. "Shhhh, that's all I wanted to hear. Now that's settled, you have a couple of calls to make. Again, I want to be there, but if you want to…"

This time, it was Andrew who interrupted. "Please, I want you to be there. I don't think I can do it by myself." They resumed walking towards his room.

Once inside, they left the 'DO NOT DISTURB' sign on the door again. Andrew tossed the bags of clothes on the bed. Emily told him she'd arranged some shoes for him and that the reception would call when they arrived. "Give me half an hour to shower and change, then we can make the calls." she said, rubbing his arm gently.

"You can shower here if you're comfortable with that." he replied, not really wanting to be alone, the full weight of the task ahead bearing down on him.

"Sure. No worries. I'll be quick." she answered. She picked up her bag and stepped into the bathroom, closing the door behind her. She turned on the shower, waiting for it to get hot, and noticed Andrew's soiled scrubs and sneakers in the trash can. She tossed her dirty clothes in with his, tied the bag liner, and set it by the door for room service to collect. Selecting a new dress and clean undergarments, she hung them over the towel rail and stepped into the shower.

Ten minutes later, dressed, her hair still wet and wrapped in a towel, she re-emerged. Andrew was perched on the edge of the bed, his elbow on his knee, head resting in his hand, nervously tapping the back of his cellphone with his index finger. Emily dropped the soiled clothes into the hallway and joined him on the bed. "Ready?" she asked.

"No. Not really." His eyes were already moist. Emily climbed onto the bed behind him, perched on her knees, and wrapped her arms around his chest, resting her chin on his shoulder. "Whatever happens, I'm here." she whispered. She felt him nod, as his finger tapped more urgently on the phone, before he turned it around. Inhaling deeply, he dialled. Emily gave him one final squeeze, kissed his neck, and slid off the bed to sit beside him. The long-distance ringtone pierced the quiet — a long shrill ring followed by a silent pause.

"It's six in the morning in Texas. Is it not too early?" Emily whispered.

"No." Andrew responded. "We're up by five at home."

The phone seemed to ring endlessly. Andrew wondered which of Travis's parents would pick up, and quietly prayed it would be his dad.

"Hello." A female voice with a heavy Texan accent finally answered. "Hello-o." she repeated in a chirpy sing-song tone. Emily felt Andrew's body tense, ready to deliver the sentence that would shatter the woman on the other end.

Static filled the line, and she likely assumed it was Travis. The connection to Africa was often poor. Then she said it, and Andrew broke. "Travis? Darlin', I can't hear you, Sweetheart. You have to speak up."

Andrew's voice cracked. "Mrs. Johnson," he spluttered, "i-i-it's Andrew." he stammered, squeezing his eyes shut in a futile effort to hold back the tears. "I'm so, so sorry. I have some terrible news." he choked. "We were ambushed yesterday a-a-and..." His struggle to find the right words failed him, words of comfort eluded him, and before he knew it, he had blurted out, "Travis is dead."

A blood-curdling scream echoed through the line. Andrew knew that scream would haunt him forever. He heard a loud thump, glass shattering, and the phone crashing to the floor. He didn't need to be told where she was; he could picture the hallway, adjacent to the kitchen, lined with family photos. He had stood there countless times. He knew that the shattering of glass was the vase that always stood on a small table, freshly filled with flowers Mrs. Johnson had picked from her garden. A moment later, a deep baritone voice came through the phone, trembling with a mix of confusion and alarm. "Who is this? What the hell is going on?" Mr. Johnson's tone carried the fear of a man who already sensed the worst.

Andrew's breath caught. "Mr. Johnson, it's Andrew Koch." He paused, struggling to keep his voice steady. "I'm so sorry... Travis was killed yesterday."

Silence stretched over the line — a heavy, suffocating silence. Andrew could hear faint, ragged breathing, then the sound of the other phone being picked up. Mrs. Johnson was now on the line from the living room. He imagined her slumped on the brown leather couch... crushed.

Andrew somehow managed to tell them what had happened and

that he would be home, likely by Saturday, with Travis's remains. He would update them once plans were confirmed. When he mentioned calling Andrea, Mr. Johnson insisted they would drive over and tell her in person. She would need support, and Andrew agreed.

The call culminated with a long silence punctuated by sobs, before Mr. Johnson said, "We'll meet you at the airport. Send us the details." He said goodbye and disconnected.

Andrew dropped the phone onto the plush carpet and collapsed onto the bed in a foetal position, pulling Emily down with him. He sobbed. Sobbed for his loss. Sobbed with relief at having told the Johnsons. And he sobbed at the guilt that the relief brought with it.

Finally, Andrew picked up the phone again to call his parents, going through the whole painful story once more. By the time he'd finished, he was utterly drained. Untangling himself from Emily, he walked unsteadily to the bathroom, where he shut the door, sat in the shower tray, and let the water pour over him until it ran cold.

When he returned, Emily hadn't moved. "I have to meet the ambassador," he said, quietly, "but please be here when I get back." She nodded. He kissed her on the top of her head and mumbled, "Thank you." She heard the door click shut, then bolted from the bed, remembering his shoes. "Don't forget, your shoes are at reception." she called, catching him in the hallway. He waved an acknowledgement, but did not turn around.

Chapter 39

Detective Odongo had called Patrick and requested that they meet on the front steps of the hospital where Mac was recovering. He had arranged for a press conference to be held at five in the afternoon. Patrick agreed and decided to use this time to visit Mac. Although they had never met, Peter and Ryan held him in high esteem, and he wanted to leave a personal note for Mac to read when he recovered.

Patrick had kept one of the two minivans on retainer for the duration of their stay. Currently, it was shuttling Andrew to the embassy, which was conveniently located less than ten minutes away on Ggaba Road, for his 3 o'clock appointment. Everything had been pre-arranged by the Ambassador and Andrew was scheduled to return in less than an hour.

At three forty-five, the van deposited Andrew at the front doors of the hotel. The driver called Patrick, alerting him that he was free.

"Okay, perfect. I'll be down in five minutes."

Patrick quickly called Hugh as he was heading to the lobby and informed him he was on the way to the press conference. He stopped at the reception desk to check if any packages had arrived. Nothing had. He met Andrew coming out of the hotel convenience store, having just purchased a few toiletries.

"Everything sorted, Andrew?" Patrick asked, in passing.

"Hey, Patrick. Yes, thanks. My passport will be here tonight around seven. Thanks for everything." Andrew replied.

Patrick smiled and waved over his shoulder as he hurried out towards the waiting minivan. He snapped his fingers as he remembered something and called out to Andrew, who was making his way to the reception desk to pick up Emily's jeans and his other pair of shoes.

"Andrew, a second please. Could you get yours and Emily's details over to me tonight, so I can book tickets? I'll need your DOBs and your names as they appear on your passports." He did not mention Travis, he had asked the ambassador to arrange the release of the body, and to stand by for travel updates.

"Sure thing. And again, thanks." Andrew replied.

Patrick clambered into the minivan and told the driver to head over to the International Hospital.

"Are you alright, sir?" the driver asked, obviously alarmed at the request.

"Yes, thanks. I'm just visiting a friend."

"Ah, that is okay then. The traffic is not good. If you were sick, I would suggest an ambulance. It would be faster." the driver explained, showing his concern.

As promised, the traffic was indeed a mess. By the time they had navigated their way through three traffic circles, endured an inordinate amount of hand gestures, a cacophony of blaring horns, and witnessed a fender-bender that had deteriorated into a full-blown fistfight, they arrived at the fourth traffic circle. Their exit onto Makwana Road was blocked by yet another accident. They circled the roundabout three times, before being able to squeeze by and continue their journey. Once they had made the left turn onto Eighth Street, the traffic began to flow with a sense of normalcy.

"You do this every day? You are a patient and brave man." Patrick said jovially to his nonplussed driver.

"Every day, sir!" the driver replied cordially, making eye contact with Patrick in the mirror and smiling.

They arrived, miraculously unscathed, at the hospital's main gate at four fifteen. The driver spoke to the security guard in Swahili, and the boom lifted. He drove in and stopped in front of the admissions door. He quickly exited the driver's seat and had the sliding door to the rear open before Patrick could put his hand on the handle. Patrick handed him ten US dollars, asked him to park, get himself something to eat and drink, and wait for his call. The driver thanked Patrick and agreed to stand by.

Patrick entered the hospital, located the reception, stated his business, and was directed to the elevators. He checked his phone while waiting. A mechanical ding sounded, the metal doors slid open and a throng of people exited. Patrick held the doors for a minute, until the stale odour followed the group, as if to say, *'Hey, you forgot something'.*

He was the sole occupant. He pressed '3', hoping he would ascend as the only passenger. The elevators in hot muggy climates had a tendency to carry an odour of sweat and unbathed bodies, which hung in the air and settled on your clothing. He made a mental note to take the stairs on his return.

Patrick stepped onto the third floor and followed the signs to the intensive care unit, along the brightly lit, spotlessly clean, white-tiled hallway. He passed two nurses in pale blue scrubs, talking in hushed tones. Surgical masks adorned their faces, covering their mouths and noses. He could not see their smiles as they passed him, yet their eyes conveyed the greeting. He smiled back.

He reached the nurses' station, which was being manned by a large woman, her skin the colour of dark chocolate. Handel's *Water Music* was playing softly in the background. The scent of pine cleaner, mixed with the sweet, unmistakable antiseptic hospital smell, permeated the air. She looked up from her paperwork, a pair of tortoiseshell half-frame glasses perched on her wide nose.

She greeted him warmly and asked if she could help. He introduced himself, inquiring about Mac's condition. He said he had spoken to Doctor Svenson and was wondering if he could leave an envelope for Mac.

In a sweet voice, she said, "Ah, Mr. Kinsella You are on the list. You can leave it in his bedside drawer. Room 4, the second door on the right." She pointed in the general direction of Mac's room. "He won't know you are there, but you can visit him for fifteen minutes."

He stepped into the room and closed the door quietly behind him. This was not how he wanted to meet Mac. He had been told by both Peter and Ryan that Mac was the most undemanding and friendly client they had the privilege of protecting.

He glanced around the sterile room. The blinds were drawn, and a beam of sunlight shone through a gap, settling on a pitcher of water and causing light refraction. There was a silvery hourglass shadow on the wooden table and a small rainbow reflected on the stark wall. The only other light was coming from a low-wattage bulb on the nightstand.

The silence in the room was punctuated by the persistent beeping of his monitor and the rhythmic up-and-down whoosh and hiss of the ventilator that kept breathing for Mac. He looked pale and drawn. Dr. Svenson had told him Mac would be on a ventilator for the next few days, and although it looked frightening, it was just precautionary.

Patrick opened the bedside table drawer and saw Mac's watch, passport, and wallet. He slid the envelope underneath the personal effects, then quietly closed the drawer and slipped silently out of the room. He thanked the nurse and asked for directions to the stairwell.

Back on the ground floor, he found the cafeteria, ordered a latte, and chose a quiet corner table, still processing the events of the past twenty four hours.. He checked his watch; he still had twenty minutes before the press conference. He pulled out his cellphone and called Doctor Svenson.

Ingrid answered on the third ring. "Hello, Mr. Kinsella. How are you?"

She must have put his number in her contacts, and he appreciated the gesture.

"Please, call me Patrick," he said.

In turn, she said, "And I am Ingrid. How can I help?"

"I have just come from visiting Mac, and I'd like you to do me a favour. He has his watch, passport, and wallet in his bedside drawer. Could you please put them away for safekeeping? I am not concerned with your staff, but the police may come and interview him. It is they I do not trust!"

"No problem, Patrick. I will take care of that as soon as we hang up. Is there anything else?"

"No, Ingrid, that's it. Except, thanks for everything. We will be leaving tomorrow, but please keep me informed of his recovery, or any changes. I'm going to locate his family and let them know what happened. I know he is divorced, but has two grown children who will need to know." They exchanged goodbyes and promised to keep in touch.

Patrick finished his latte, tossed the paper cup into the trash receptacle, and walked outside. He donned his sunglasses to ward off the harsh sunlight, which was low in the western sky. He adjusted his tie and saw Detective Odongo arranging the reporters. The two largest local TV networks were present — Ugandan Broadcasting Corporation (UBC) and the state-operated Uganda Television — alongside Al Jazeera, CNN, and BBC Africa Service.

Patrick shook his head and muttered to himself, "Fucking Odongo." The man was clearly grandstanding, and was about to spin a tale so far from the truth, as to make himself and his department the heroes. Patrick looked around and noticed that the other two officers, who were professional and cordial, were absent. This solidified his instinct; Odongo was looking to take all credit.

Odongo saw Patrick and smiled broadly, whilst jogging up the few steps to meet him.

"Mr. Kinsella." he bellowed, his arm outstretched. "How are you? How is Mr. McBride?" He grasped Patrick's hand, shook it vigorously, and leaned in, still grinning. "I kept my end of the bargain. You keep yours, and everyone goes away happy. So play nicely, okay?"

Patrick kept his composure, and responded, "A deal is a deal." returning Odongo's smile.

"Showtime. Lights, camera, action." Odongo whispered, only loud enough for Patrick to hear. Patrick groaned inaudibly, and whispered to himself, *"Ladies and gentlemen... The Fucking Odongo Show!"* as Odongo approached the lectern.

Wires led from a plethora of microphones perched precariously on the lectern, each bearing the names of the organisations recording the hastily assembled conference. Word had not yet leaked about the incidents of yesterday, and the media were more than a little curious. Odongo was going to reveal the news to the world and revel in this, his moment of glory. An international newsworthy event that he, Odongo, would release. He was giddy with that knowledge.

"Good afternoon, ladies and gentlemen of the press. My name is Detective Adroa Odongo, Chief Inspector of the Criminal Investigation Department of the National Police Force of Uganda. Welcome all, and thank you for coming. Today is a day for celebrating the combined efforts of our department, the Ugandan Civil Aviation Authority, and our hospitals... this one in particular." he said, sweeping his hand back towards the entrance of the hospital, conveniently omitting that it was actually privately owned. "Yesterday, the Civil Aviation Authority was alerted to an aircraft in distress entering Ugandan airspace. This plane was carrying seven foreign nationals; two Irish, two American, two British, and one South African. The flight had originated in our neighbouring country, the DRC. It was originally a domestic flight sent to collect an Irish Catholic priest, two American medics, and a British school teacher — all volunteers, all in Africa — assisting where they can in impoverished areas, all innocent people just wanting to help. Their plane and crew were ambushed. Sadly, one of the young American medics was killed, and the pilot gravely injured. He, thanks to the joint efforts of my department and the CAA, is recovering right here in our hospital, being cared for by the very best Ugandan doctors and nursing staff. Once we learned the pilot had been shot and the flight was in peril, the CAA immediately diverted all air traffic. One of our highly qualified air traffic controllers assisted one of the survivors to fly the plane by giving him lessons over the radio."

Patrick could hardly believe the outlandish claims. He bowed his head, rolling his eyes in frustration, careful not to be caught on camera. He would give Odongo credit where credit was due; he was articulate and convincing as hell, albeit bullshit, Patrick thought.

His speech was reminiscent of their former insane dictator, Idi Amin, when, in 1976, an Air France Airbus was hijacked en route to Paris from Tel Aviv while on a layover in Athens. Two members of the *Popular Front for Liberation of Palestine — External Operations*, and two supporters from the German cell, had taken control of the flight and diverted it to Entebbe. Idi Amin knew of the hijacking from the onset, and he not only supported the hijackers, but welcomed them to

Uganda. The passengers had been held in two groups; Israelis, and one hundred and forty-eight non-Israelites. The latter were released two days later, and Idi Amin claimed the credit in a speech, much like the one playing out before Patrick's eyes. Seemingly, Odongo had ripped a page out of Idi Amin's playbook.

Odongo continued, "A fast-acting air traffic controller contacted our national air rescue services, who quickly dispatched a helicopter to the airport to await the stricken incoming plane and transport the critically injured pilot to the hospital. It landed right there." he said, pointing at the parking lot. "We made sure we had the best trauma team on standby. The pilot was rushed in and immediately taken into surgery.

I personally went to the airport to make sure the rest of the passengers were safe. I arranged food and drinks for them, and I was ready to bring in a team of grief counsellors, but they declined our offer.

We have arranged transportation for those survivors who are able to travel, and they will be going home soon to be with their loved ones.

We, on behalf of Uganda, wish them a steady recovery and a safe flight home, and hope they come back and visit us, and remember fondly our efforts and hospitality.

Yesterday, Uganda, known as the Pearl of Africa for its natural beauty, extended that claim to the beauty of its people. I, Chief Inspector Odongo, and all those who assisted in making this a success, did so on behalf of all Ugandans, because we, the Ugandan people, are peace-loving and compassionate.

At this time, I would like to introduce my new friend, Mr. Patrick Kinsella, whose two-man security detail thwarted the attack on the plane and allowed our paths to cross."

Patrick stepped up to the lectern, thanked Odongo for his kind words, and shook his hand. *My three minutes of bullshit start now*, he thought.

"I would like to extend my gratitude to Detective Odongo, the CAA, and the hospital staff for their professionalism and quick actions that saved my men, the crew, and passengers aboard the doomed plane. If it were not for them, many more lives would be lost.

In particular, I would like to thank Detective Odongo, who could have delayed the truth from being revealed — sadly common practice in some less-scrupulous countries of our beautiful continent. Detective Odongo saw, clearly, this was a mercy flight. People's lives were at risk, and the pilot's protective detail was just that; two trained men protecting precious cargo and no threat to the beautiful country of Uganda and her people. So, thank you, Detective Odongo."

Patrick shook Odongo's hand. Odongo embraced Patrick for the cameras and whispered, "We are now even."

Patrick said nothing; he just smiled and thought, *not by a long shot, arsehole.*

Questions were being yelled out, and Odongo wisely thought to quit while he was ahead. "Sorry, ladies and gentlemen. We do not have time for questions, but feel free to contact my office for further comments." With that, he turned to leave.

Patrick was already cutting through the hospital, making his way to the emergency room entrance and on the phone to the driver, telling him where he was and to pick him up outside the ER.

Patrick was frantically dialling the group as his driver arrived. He hopped into the van and instructed him to go back to the hotel. He reached Hugh and gave him a quick rundown, warning him not to take any calls from unknown numbers. Then Peter and Ryan received the same caution. Finally, he managed to get hold of Emily and informed her of the situation, asking her to pass the information on to Father O'Donnell. Emily mentioned that 'breaking news' snippets were already airing and promises of more were to follow.

He was making his last call as they pulled up to the hotel. The phone was ringing, and he signalled the driver to wait, as he got out of the van to speak to Ingrid.

"Hi, Ingrid. Listen carefully, please. We just had a bullshit press conference outside your hospital. I did and said things necessary in order to protect the group. We are out of here tomorrow, but you and Mac are still here. I don't think anything will come of it, but I suspect you will be called by news organisations looking for comments. Please refrain from commenting or divulging Mac's name. Turn on your TV, any channel, and you'll see what I'm talking about."

Ingrid was calm and unruffled by his speech. "I live here, Patrick. I've seen and heard the way things are twisted and I'm used to it, but I will be a little more vigilant until things die down. Rest assured, my patients come first. Mac is in safe hands."

They wished each other a good night as they hung up. Patrick walked back to the van and the waiting driver.

"Sorry about that." Patrick said. "I need you and your friend tomorrow at nine to take the group back to the airport. If you watch the news tonight, do not tell anybody that you know us, or where we are staying. There's an extra hundred dollars for your discretion. Please tell your friend the same."

"I have never seen you before, so how do I know where you are staying?" The driver winked, waving as he drove off.

Patrick smiled at the comment as he walked into the hotel and went to the front desk. He asked to speak to the duty manager, who was just walking by, when he heard Patrick's request.

"Good evening, sir. I am the manager."

"Good evening. My name is Patrick Kinsella. My group and I are staying here. I am sure to be all over the TV tonight, and I believe the reporters are going to want further information that I am not prepared to divulge at this time. I don't want it leaked that we are here. It's a sensitive matter to the group, who have already been through too much. As far as you and your staff are concerned, we are not here. You do not know us and have never seen us. Does that work for you?"

"No problem, Mr. Kinsella. I'll spread the word."

Patrick thanked him, went to the lobby bar, and ordered a single malt scotch just as *'The Odongo Show'* was airing. "Fuck sake!" he mumbled.

By now the speech had been edited, spliced, cleaned up, and was airing worldwide. The talking heads were having a field day, and the police department's switchboard was overloaded. News anchors from as far afield as Canada, Ireland, the United Kingdom, and the United States were seeking comments or sound bites, and Odongo was happy to give them what they wanted. The multinational group aboard the plane had grabbed the attention of the international community.

Chapter 40

In Andrew's absence, Emily had housekeeping make up his room. She had called her parents to assure them she was okay and that she would be coming home in a few weeks after attending Travis's funeral. She grabbed her clothes and went to her room and took a quick shower. Feeling refreshed, she trotted down the hallway, knocked on Father O'Donnell's door and invited him for a cup of tea downstairs, poolside.

Peter was in Ryan's room where Ryan was swearing at the television and threatening to toss it out of the window.

Peter quipped, "A lie will make it halfway around the world before the truth has had a chance to put its shoes on."

Ryan laughed at the saying he had not heard before, and retorted, "Odongo's lies made it all the way around the world before the truth could get out of bed!" They both laughed, clinked their bottles in a salute, and took another swig of their beers.

The Gulfstream captain had filed his flight plan and was going over the latest weather updates with his crew. He contacted the catering company to arrange the meal service, and the local FBO to organise a cleaning crew to pump out the toilet and give the interior of the plane a basic vacuum and wipe down. He had called the airport authority, paid the parking fee over the phone with the company credit card, and arranged to collect the receipt in the morning.

Patrick joined Hugh and Rick in the lobby bar for a drink and were discussing *'The Odongo Show'*, as it had been aptly named.

"This motherfucker is going to get sole credit, and all he wanted to do was lock everyone up. I heard he was ready to take on Peter in his cell, but thought better of it." Hugh said.

"Well, at least he didn't get any of the money, thanks to Simone's brilliant detective work. I swear, that woman can find anything, on anyone, at any time. She is one fucking scary woman." Rick said, raising his eyebrows and crunching on a block of ice he had fished out of his now-finished scotch. "I wouldn't want to cross her. I don't know what we are paying her, but she just saved us a couple of hundred grand. Flowers might be in order. Another round?"

"No thanks." Patrick and Hugh replied, in unison.

"Patrick, you are looking a bit perplexed. You have that look in your eye that scares me. What are you up to? I know it can't be good." Hugh said, quizzically.

Chewing on his thumbnail, his elbow on the table, and looking at his empty glass, Patrick replied, "I am going to send a copy of Odongo's files to the press. Anonymously, of course. Then a copy to Edwin Mbabazi, that local lawyer. And another to the internal affairs department. I hear the guy at the top is trustworthy and is hell-bent on quashing police corruption. Mac is my problem. He is still in the hospital and would automatically become a target in retaliation. There may also be a bit of fallout on Doc Svenson. She does not appear to take any shit from anyone, so it's my guess she will protect Mac's well-being and get caught up in Odongo's revenge. I may have to wait, time it right, but it's gotta be done. Well, gentlemen, I have to call my wife and kids, I missed the boys this morning. I also need to get Simone to check on the tickets." He said, getting up and pushing his chair back in place. "Rick, will you square up the bill? Get an early night, guys. See you at breakfast."

Chapter 41

Emily and Andrew had just finished a more-than-satisfactory dinner. They were savouring the last of the crème brûlée and washing it down with the half bottle of surprisingly good South African Cabernet Shiraz. Room service then brought in a carafe of coffee and cleared their dinner service away. Andrew signed the tab, tipped the waiter, and thanked him.

They had long since turned off the television and were listening to some quiet classical music on Emily's phone when Andrew asked, "Would you stay the night? As friends, of course. I just don't want to be alone."

Emily pondered the question for a little while and smiled. "Okay, but I need one of your t-shirts. I don't have any pyjamas." adding, "I'll go to my room and collect my toothbrush and clothes."

"I'll go get my things, scroll through the TV and find us some mindless entertainment. I think they've some pay-per-view movie channels. You know I'll be grading you on your choice." she teased.

An hour later, they were lying on the king-size bed, under the duvet, and propped up on the oversized pillows. Emily was dressed in one of Andrew's t-shirts, which ended just above her knees and hung off of her shoulders. Andrew was in his boxers and a t-shirt. Both were playfully arguing about the movies in his selection. A sense of normalcy hung in the air, providing a brief respite from the reality they were living.

"So, we are down to *The Life of Pi*, which gets my vote, *The Impossible*, which comes in a close second, and two chick-flicks. *Bridget Jones's Diary*, isn't that a comedic love story about a ditzy Brit? That might give me an insight into British culture," he laughed as she pounded him with a pillow, "or *Love Actually*, a Hugh Grant love story, which is getting a thumbs down. No self-respecting Texan male would ever admit to wanting to watch that."

"If it were up to you, we'd be watching *Rocky*, or worse, *Fast and Furious - Part 87*. Don't those movies ever die?" she groaned, playfully.

"No, of course not. That's why there are sequels," he replied.

Emily rolled her eyes. "Just choose a bloody movie, will you?"

"*Life of Pi* it is!" he said, as he made the selection and turned off the bedside light.

Emily stretched out his arm and snuggled in. His warm, musky scent washed over her, and she felt secure in his arms. The anxiety of the past twenty-four hours started to melt away and she began to relax. Andrew looked down at her strawberry blonde mop of hair cascading over his arm and onto his chest. He wondered how he would have fared if she, too, had been lost in the catastrophic events of the previous day. He blocked out all the troubling images and savoured the moment with this beautiful, brave, and compassionate woman.

He awoke, slowly, at six. The television was off. Emily was spooned around his back, her arm across his chest, one leg draped over his thigh. He could feel her breathing deeply — the gentle rise and fall of her chest pressing against his back. The last recollection of the night was something about a boy on a lifeboat attempting to outwit a tiger. He closed his eyes again until the first chirp of the alarm brought him fully awake. He reluctantly untangled himself, and slid to the edge of the bed.

"Staaaaay, I was having a nice dream." she mumbled.

He smiled, kissed her on the cheek, and got out of bed.

"Nooooooo!" she pleaded, reaching out, the fabric of his t-shirt slipping through her fingers. "Okay, Mr. Koch, have it your way. Let the record reflect, I offered and you declined." She teased, as she clambered out of bed. "Good morning, mister. I'll order coffee, you jump in the shower first."

"I have a better idea. How about I go to the bathroom, you order coffee, and *we* take a shower?" he said, his tone a mixture of teasing and flirting.

"Nice try, cowboy. Remember, I offered, you refused. Your loss," she replied sassily, as she called room service.

Whilst Emily was in the shower, Andrew pulled on yesterday's jeans, a fresh button-down shirt, and his new boots. He packed his clothes in the bag and called out through the bathroom door, "I'm just going downstairs to pick up my passport." He lingered in the lobby, giving Emily a chance to get dressed before he returned. He knocked softly on the door before inserting his key card.

Emily was standing at the window, bathing in the warmth of the soft morning sun, finishing the last of the coffee. She was dressed in a yellow, form-fitting sundress that stopped just above her knees and accentuated her hourglass figure. Her hair, illuminated by the sunlight, flowed down her back in loose curls.

Chapter 42

Rick was at the table, his plate full to overflowing, and Patrick, as usual, had his phone glued to his ear, pacing up and down the conference room. Peter, Ryan and Hugh were chatting. All three were drinking coffee, and Ryan was chewing on a cinnamon bun. Emily hardly recognised Peter and Ryan without their fatigues, combat boots, and flak jackets. They were dressed in casual slacks, polo shirts, and blazers. They exchanged the perfunctory morning greetings from across the room.

Emily and Andrew walked over. Emily paused a few steps shy of Ryan and sheepishly said, "I have not seen much of you guys since Tuesday, and just wanted to thank you both for what you did." She stretched up, standing on tiptoes, awkwardly embracing and kissing each in turn.

She turned and saw Father O'Donnell alone, eating his breakfast. She signalled that she was coming over to join him, as Andrew conveyed his thanks to the two security men and shook their hands warmly, before joining Emily at the breakfast buffet. He took her bag so she could plate her food and placed them on the end of the conference table.

Father O'Donnell stood and hugged them both, as they pulled up seats on either side of him. Emily told Father O'Donnell she was going with Andrew to Texas, and he thought it was a fantastic idea. They chatted amicably, as they ate.

At 8;45, Patrick announced, "Okay, everyone. It's time to head to the airport. Meet in the lobby in 15 minutes. The vans are waiting."

At nine o'clock, they all piled into the minivans, except for the flight crew, who had departed earlier in a taxi and were already at the Gulfstream. The group arrived at the airport just before ten and clambered out at the main terminal. Patrick instructed the driver to circle the airport and wait to take them to the private jet section. He would call when they were ready.

Patrick called a number he'd been given and arranged to meet the chief immigration officer, who stamped their passports without question. The group then escorted Father O'Donnell to the Ugandan Airways desk, where he checked in for his flight to Kinshasa. He hugged and kissed Emily, promising to keep in touch, shook hands with the men, and thanked them all in turn, especially Ryan and Peter. Turning to Andrew, he gave him a heartfelt hug, telling him to be strong and look after Emily.

Patrick called the driver as they walked towards the exit. Once back in the van, he gave him directions to the secure airside entrance. The two vans moved off in convoy. After clearing security, they followed the access road towards the apron, where the jet stood gleaming in the mid-morning sun. The door was open, and the flight crew stood post at the bottom of the steps.

They exited the van for the last time and made their way to the waiting jet. The auxiliary power unit was running, keeping the aircraft cabin cool. Patrick lingered and chatted with the drivers. He handed over the fee they had agreed upon, plus an extra two hundred dollars each. The drivers protested, but Patrick insisted, "Take a few days off and take your families away. We took a lot of your time, and we are grateful."

Patrick then pulled his driver aside. "I know I can trust you. Here are three packages, all postage paid. I'll call you in a few weeks, when I want you to drop them at FedEx, using the overnight drop box. Do not park in front of the building because of the cameras, and wear a baseball cap — I don't want you to get into any trouble. These are sensitive documents, and some high-ranking official is going down. Are you okay with that?"

The driver responded eagerly, "If you tell me it's that snake Odongo, I'll give you your money back. It will be an honour to bring that bastard down." He took the plastic bag containing the packages, and said, "Consider it done. I look forward to your call, Mr. Kinsella, 'the man who was never here'."

Chapter 43

The Clarke Aviation Cessna Caravan sat forlornly against the fence where they had last seen it, cordoned off by yellow police line tape. The group collectively stared at it as they passed, each lost in their own memories of that fateful flight.

The flight crew greeted them respectfully, as they climbed aboard the luxurious jet. The pilots took their seats, and the flight attendant assisted in stowing the clothing bags while everyone took their seats. Ryan and Peter settled into the oversized camel-coloured leather chairs, one either side of the aisle. Hugh, Patrick, and Rick sat in the club seating configuration around the conference table, while Andrew and Emily took their places on one of the two leather couches, their backs against the windows.

The flight attendant demonstrated the location of their entertainment screens, covered the safety briefing, pointed out the exits, and showed them where the life jackets were located. She handed out headsets and informed them that she would return with drinks once they were airborne.

Andrew and Emily admired the jet's plush leather seating, cherry wood trim, and well-equipped galley. They watched as the pilots adjusted knobs, threw switches, and communicated on the radio. The flight attendant retracted the stairs, closed, locked, and armed the cabin door. She then went up to the cockpit, leaned in to speak with the pilots, and took her seat, buckling in. She smiled discreetly at Andrew and Emily and gave them a small thumbs-up. Emily smiled back, returning the gesture. Andrew, lost in thought, was clearly wrestling with painful memories. Emily held his hand, knowing he would talk when he was ready.

The plane began moving slowly, taxiing off the apron and holding short at the edge of the runway for a few minutes, while a blue KLM jet hurtled past and took off. After a brief radio exchange, the sleek jet turned into position and waited. Emily watched as the pilot advanced what she assumed was the throttle, and the plane thundered down the runway. Trees flashed past the windows, the terminal building quickly vanished, and they lifted into the bright, clear sky.

Soon, they were soaring over Lake Victoria, climbing faster than she had ever experienced on a commercial flight. She gazed out of the window as they ascended and banked. The blue of the lake gradually gave way to the rich, red earth of the African landscape, dotted here and there with patches of green. The vast forests below were rapidly diminishing. A stark reminder of the environmental changes occurring across the region.

The plane levelled off at forty-five thousand feet, and the flight attendant came through the cabin taking drink orders. Emily opted for an orange juice and a bottle of water; Andrew just wanted water. The rest also ordered non-alcoholic drinks. Ryan and Peter were each engrossed in movies, Rick had his eyes closed, apparently napping, while Hugh was going through some paperwork. Patrick, in customary form, was on the phone.

Andrew was lost in his private thoughts, as Emily watched the landscape change below them, at just under one thousand kilometres an hour. The red patchwork quilt of Tanzania, gave way to the large bodies of water of Malawi, and then the vast emptiness of Mozambique. Half-dozing, she caught glimpses of the turquoise blue of the Indian Ocean through the port side windows.

The flight attendant was saying something. "Sorry," Emily smiled, "I was far away with my thoughts. I missed what you asked."

"No problem," she said warmly. "We have chicken Caesar salad or an antipasto."

"Antipasto, please." she responded.

"Anything to drink with that?"

"Mmm, no thanks. I'm fine for now."

Andrew had stretched out, his boots neatly standing next to the couch, his head on a pillow, a blanket covering him, and wearing an eye mask.

"How long has he been like that?" Emily enquired, alarmed at the apparent loss of time.

"An hour or so." the flight attendant responded politely.

"How long have we been travelling?" Still alarmed, Emily looked at her watch.

"Just over three hours. We will be on the ground in an hour and fifteen. Let me get you your lunch." she said, patting Emily gently on the arm.

Andrew sat up, removed his eye mask, and smiled, a pained and tired smile. She knew he had not been sleeping; he just wanted to be alone with his thoughts. His face was tear-streaked and his eyes were red-rimmed. He excused himself and went to the bathroom.

Hugh, who was facing Emily, mouthed silently, "Is he okay?"

She smiled, nodded, and signalled palm down, a left and right movement indicating the 'so-so' gesture. Andrew returned, sat down, and fastened his seat belt. The flight attendant came by and asked if he'd like anything to eat or drink.

"Just another bottle of water for me, thanks. Sorry, I'm not hungry." he said.

Emily asked for an Americano, and Andrew said, "Actually, make that two, please."

The plane began its descent, and the flight attendant busied herself with clearing the cabin and securing everything in the plush galley. Emily looked on, fascinated, as items were stowed. She watched in amazement as the espresso machine disappeared at the press of a button; the countertop opened up, and the machine descended into the cabinetry below. She turned to Andrew and said, "I want one of those!"

Andrew, still preoccupied, simply smiled and nodded.

Chapter 44

Emily resumed looking out of the window, as the landscape changed rapidly and became closer as they descended. The harsh brown of the Mozambican terrain, with muddy brown rivers dissecting the earth, gave way to small villages and brown narrow roads meandering in every direction.

By landscape alone, she could tell they were now over South Africa. Wide black roads replaced the narrow brown ones, and there was far more greenery. Big concrete structures were more prevalent, and there was a lot more traffic. She could see Pretoria and Johannesburg through the cockpit window — a horizon of skyscrapers, tall, even at this distance and altitude. Clouds of pollution rose upwards from large chimneys, and the haze of an industrial city blanketed parts of the skyline. She, of course, could not tell where one city started and the other ended. There seemed to be no end to the buildings.

The captain announced they were fifteen minutes from landing and instructed everyone to please fasten their seat belts. As the landing gear whirred down, clunked and locked into place, Emily felt Andrew's hand brush hers. She opened her hand and felt his fingers interlace with hers. They closed their hands together. She turned to look at him and smiled. He smiled back. No words were needed; their eyes met, and their body language conveyed an unspoken understanding and appreciation for each other.

The plane touched down lightly at Lanseria Airport and taxied onto the apron. There were a dozen or so small jets and turboprop aircraft, most of which were parked and quiet. A few were moving slowly towards the runway, as the pilot shut down the plane.

A few minutes later, Patrick asked for everybody's passports and bundled them together, along with the passenger manifest. The flight attendant opened the door and a rush of warm air filled the cool cabin. She deployed the stairs, and an immigration official boarded the plane.

"Good afternoon. Welcome to South Africa." he said, with an inviting smile. "Welcome home, Mr. Kinsella. I hope you had a pleasant journey."

"Good afternoon, Tembe." Patrick greeted him cordially, as the two men shook hands. Tembe took the vacant seat next to Rick and greeted him and Hugh. They obviously knew each other, as the atmosphere was warm and the conversation light.

Tembe took the manifest and passports and said, "I see we have some guests. Welcome to South Africa, Mr. Koch, Ms. Esposito, and Mr. McCabe. How long will you be staying?"

Patrick answered to avoid any confusion. "Ms. Esposito and Mr. Koch are only here for one night. They are staying at the Intercontinental Johannesburg, as my guests. Mr. McCabe will be here for a few months. He will be staying on his boat in Cape Town."

Tembe asked Peter if he wanted him to extend his visitor's visa, and Peter said that would be great. The passports were stamped, hands were once again shaken, and well-wishes were extended, before Tembe deplaned.

Two gleaming black Mercedes with tinted windows stood idling outside the aircraft. One, a Vito minivan, the other a Gelandewagen. Both drivers, dressed in their customary chauffeur livery, stood by the open doors. One by one, the group descended the stairs, each holding identical 'La Boutique' shopping bags.

Emily was overcome with emotion, as she hugged each man in turn and thanked them for everything. Peter lifted her off her feet and hugged her tight, whispering, "You take care of you, and keep an eye on that man. You're going to need each other in the coming days." With that, Emily's tears began to flow in earnest. Peter set her down, and with his thumb, brushed the tears away.

She gulped, and stepped back, saying, "No matter where you are, I would like to stay in touch."

Peter smiled and said, "I will never be too far, nor too busy for you, young lady."

Andrew was making his rounds of handshakes, hugs, and thanks, and he, too, had become emotional.

Patrick pulled Emily in close and told her Travis's body was scheduled to arrive later that day and would fly out the following evening on the British Airways flight to London, then connecting with them to Dallas on the American Airlines flight on Saturday and onward to San Antonio. He'll be travelling with you guys all the way. He handed her an envelope with their airline tickets, the hotel confirmation, and three thousand South African Rand. "You'll need some local currency to buy yourself a suitcase, a taxi to the airport tomorrow, and whatever else you might need to tide yourselves over till you get home." His generosity and kindness was overwhelming. He took her into his arms and said, "Anytime, anywhere, you need anything, I will be there." He released the embrace and pointed at the G-Wagon. "Your ride is waiting."

The chauffeur greeted Emily and Andrew, took their bags, and they slid onto the back seat. He climbed in behind the wheel and headed out of the airport. Forty minutes later, they exited the freeway and pulled up to the grand Intercontinental Johannesburg Hotel. A porter held their door open, and the driver handed him their bags. Emily opened the envelope and familiarised herself with the currency to tip the driver. The driver shook his head, smiled, and refused politely. "That goes for the hotel as well; all gratuities have already been paid, Mr. Kinsella's orders."

Two rooms had been booked, and they advised the receptionist that they would only require one. "In that case, let me upgrade you and put you in a suite. Check-out is usually at eleven, but you have the room until six, as per Mr. Kinsella's request. Anything you want or need from the hotel should be charged to your room." He listed off all the hotel's amenities — the pool, spa, restaurants, and bars. "Tomorrow a taxi will be waiting to take you to the airport at six pm. If you require anything, just dial nine and ask for me personally." he said, handing Andrew his card.

They were shown up to their suite, which was elegantly decorated. The ornately carved exotic wood four-poster bed stood proudly in the centre of the room. The bed, adorned with a thick white duvet cover, and curtains of mosquito netting, clung to each post. Large windows not only allowed for breathtaking views over Kempton Park and the Johannesburg skyline beyond, but also bathed the room in natural light. Oversized French doors opened onto a screened patio, where sat a bistro table and two chairs, with a commanding view of the airport. They marvelled at the marble bathroom with a shower boasting two LED-lit waterfall shower heads. There was a jetted corner bathtub with copper faucets, an elegant mixture of modern with a hint of a bygone era.

Another set of leaded glass French doors led to a cosy sitting room. Black and white photos of wildlife adorned the walls, and a forty-inch flat-screen television hung above an electric faux-flame fireplace. The black leather couch and club chairs looked inviting, and a small dining table with Queen Anne chairs sat to one side. The sideboard housed a minibar, a Keurig coffee maker, and a tea chest brimming with an assortment of black and herbal teas.

They walked hand in hand, exploring and opening cupboards, awestruck by its elegance without being ostentatious. Neither spoke for a while, and Emily finally broke the silence. "Well, this isn't too shabby at all." He grinned and drew her in close, staring down into her piercing green eyes, and brushed an errant strand of hair from her face. He tilted her head back, his lips almost touching hers, pausing, he said, "May I?"

"Well, Mr. Koch, if you must."

"I think I must." he drawled, leaning down and kissing her gently. Her full harp-shaped lips parted, and he felt the warmth and sweetness of her breath, as he closed his eyes and lingered in the moment. Their tongues probed and explored excitedly for a moment, then slowed and danced, as if to a melody only they could hear. And for a moment, the world ceased to exist.

Chapter 45

After twenty hours of flying and a combined five hours of layover time, Andrew and Emily were settling into their seats for the final leg of their journey from Dallas to San Antonio.

In the past seventy-two hours, they had drawn strength from each other, but now they were both depleted. Their reserves were sapped; they were physically and emotionally drained. Whatever needed to be said was said; whatever reassurances needed to be given were given. They sat in silence, holding hands, each alone with their own thoughts, and each feeling the gravity and sense of impending doom.

The Boeing 737 was carrying them at just over five hundred and twenty-five miles per hour towards what Andrew knew with certainty, would be the second-worst day of his life. He would come face to face with Andrea, carrying her and Travis's unborn child; Mr. and Mrs. Johnson; and his parents — all anxious, all grieving. And the closer they got to San Antonio, the heavier the weight of guilt settled on his shoulders.

His thoughts were interrupted by the pilot's announcement. He looked at his watch and couldn't believe that forty-five minutes had elapsed. He and Emily had exchanged no more than a dozen words since leaving Dallas. He looked over at Emily, who occupied the window seat and was staring at the sprawling cityscape as they descended into San Antonio. He squeezed her hand, and she turned and smiled at him. Her beautiful eyes were once again filled with sadness and trepidation.

Good afternoon, ladies and gentlemen. This is your captain speaking. We have just started our descent into San Antonio, where the weather is eighty-seven degrees and beautiful blue Texan skies await you. The local time is three fifty-five and we'll have you on the ground in fifteen minutes. Your luggage will be on carousel three. On behalf of myself and the crew aboard, we would like to thank you for choosing American Airlines and look forward to welcoming you aboard again in the near future. Cabin crew, prepare the cabin for landing.

Under normal circumstances, Andrew would have looked forward to this arrival. He and Travis would have been delirious with excitement, rushing off the plane and into the arms of their loved ones with squeals of joy, non-stop chatter and banter, during the thirty or so minutes drive home. Smoked Texas-style barbeque ribs and steaks with all the trimmings along with cold Lone Star beer, would have been served well into the night.

Andrew watched until most of the passengers deplaned before he unsnapped his seatbelt, stepped into the aisle, and lifted their bags from the overhead compartment. He shuffled back to allow Emily to slide out, and they trudged up the aisle, the last two to disembark. The flight crew cheerily thanked them and wished them a pleasant time in San Antonio. They smiled back politely, nodded, but neither could bring themselves to say anything.

Emily took her bag from Andrew once they were in the jetway and took hold of his hand as they made their way silently through the maze of corridors and escalators. Andrew slowed his pace as they approached the automatic sliding doors that led into the arrivals concourse. Passengers hurried by; every time the door opened, screams of delight and joy flooded into the quiet airside section. He knew there would be no balloons, no flowers, no welcome home banners, and no screams of excitement for him and Emily when they stepped through the doors into arrivals. He hesitated long enough that Emily tugged on his hand, stood on her tiptoes, and whispered, "Together we can do this." She kissed him lightly on his cheek. Tears were welling in both of their eyes, and it wouldn't be long before the floodgates opened again. He took a deep breath and stepped up to the doors and they slid open. He paused again briefly, but she kept a firm hold of his hand, and they tentatively walked into the cavernous arrivals terminal.

They followed the tape guidance barrier that separated the passengers from the waiting crowds. Families were reuniting with loved ones, children were being lifted high in the air and swung around, shrieking with excitement. Colourful balloons rolled abandoned on the white marble floor, dragging long lengths of shiny balloon ribbon. Wives waited for their husbands, boyfriends waited on girlfriends, parents for their offspring, all parties giddy with excitement.

Emily spotted their awaiting party first and pulled Andrew up short. She released her hand and nodded with her chin to the sombre group standing to one side. Respectfully, she slowed her pace and stopped, allowing Andrew to reach them first. Emily watched as Andrew stepped gingerly towards the huddled group. Before she knew it, Andrew had disappeared from view amid shrieks of pain and loud sobbing. He was embraced and jostled from one to another, all crying and wailing, his bag lying abandoned outside the scrum. She caught glimpses of his sandy hair from time to time, as he embraced each mourner in turn. She felt her face wet, as warm tears ran unbridled. She fished out a Kleenex, blotted her face, dabbed her eyes, and chased away the tears.

Andrew finally untangled himself and came to where Emily stood against the wall. He took her hand and brought her to meet his and Travis's family. She was brought into the throng where they all cried and hugged. Andrew hesitantly said "So, do we wait here for Travis?"

Mr. Johnson answered, "Travis is being collected by the funeral director and brought back to Bulverde. We will be able to go visit him tomorrow and pay our respects. For now, there is nothing left to do but to go home."

Chapter 46

Ingrid had kept vigil at Mac's bedside for much of the past two nights. He was recovering, slowly. She had removed the nasal cannula and was gradually weaning him off the sedatives.

He was prone to violent nightmares and would mumble incoherently in his sleep. At times, he yelled, and she could patch together phrases and sentences. He would wake, disorientated and perspiring, calling out for someone to jump. She realised he was fighting the demons of his flight that had crashed into the Irish Sea in 2006. Ingrid would mop his brow, before settling back to read; her current novel being *The Alchemist* by Paulo Coelho. She sometimes read aloud to Mac when she found something amusing or insightful.

To her, Mac was a bit of an anomaly. A seasoned airline captain, obviously not a drinker or substance abuser — she had seen his blood work — yet he, apparently by choice, had opted to fly ambulances and freight in the Congo. It was incongruous with his training. Bush pilots and airline pilots, were as different as night and day.

Following her phone call with Pierre and against everything she stood for, her curiosity had gotten the better of her. She spent a few hours researching the mystery pilot, who had arrived at her hospital with two bullet wounds and was barely clinging to life. The pilot she had spent three hours patching up.

She had only meant to read about the accident, but became engrossed in the online battle between those who knew, and those who seemed to not have a clue. She became more intrigued the more she read. Fingers pointed at the airlines, the airlines pointing to the manufacturer, the manufacturer pointing to airline maintenance, and then all of the above pointing at the pilot with over eighteen thousand hours of flight time. A man with an exemplary record. A former check ride pilot — whatever that meant. But a pilot in the middle of a messy divorce. A pilot who was distracted and quite possibly distressed. A pilot who may have tried to end it all by plunging into the sea. The rumours and accusations swirled violently, like an Oklahoma twister.

She became caught up in the various blogs, official websites, and pilot forums. There was also an inordinate amount of nonsense spewed on sites like Reddit, Twitter, and the lesser-known social media platforms Bebo and Yahoo 360, with comments and opinions that were so far from the truth. Although she knew nothing about aviation, she could tell the misinformation from the truth just by the writings. Anonymous contributors were more likely than not the ones with too much to say without evidence, facts or knowledge of aviation. She found the writing was poor, the spelling atrocious, and the use of numbers in lieu of letters frustrating. Not surprisingly, they attracted more likes and thumbs up than the coherent, knowledgeable and articulate responses. It was just the way of this world.

What she gleaned from the official reports, was that it had been an awful night — strong winds and poor visibility. She knew the plane crashed into the sea and that the rescue was hampered by the weather. Many had survived the initial impact, yet died due to hypothermia from the below-freezing conditions, before the coast guard could reach them.

She knew the plane broke into three pieces. Many of the survivors were in the tail section, a handful from the forward cabin, but none from the mid-section, which sank quickly. She knew Mac was the sole surviving crew member. She knew they found the CVR, but not the FDR. She had to look up what they were and their importance — cockpit voice recorder and flight data recorder. The former recorded voices and sounds from the cockpit, and the latter recorded many technical parameters of how the plane was behaving during the flight. The bad weather had lasted for almost a week, hindering the recovery efforts. Wreckage, luggage, and human remains were found washed up all along the Irish coastline, Wales, and the Isle of Man.

Those who knew Mac defended him vehemently. Pilots he flew with, cabin crew, maintenance personnel, and friends from all walks of life. Not a single person had anything derogatory to say about Dalton McBride... barring the trolls on social media, and they didn't count. In fact, three pilots resigned in solidarity after the final findings by the NTSB, which had irreparably damaged Mac's reputation.

The report was inconclusive but hinted strongly at pilot error. Mac had ostensibly been found guilty through both mainstream and social media, long before the official hearing concluded.

Ingrid found herself sympathising. She knew doctors — exceptional doctors — whose careers were adversely affected, and sometimes irreparably harmed, through the same channels, and her heart went out to Mac.

Chapter 47

Andrew and his father sat up front, while Emily and Andrew's mother occupied the back. Andrew's father was a big man, slightly overweight, but had the appearance of someone who worked hard, rose early, and retired early. He resembled an older version of the Marlboro Man, but with a greater focus on large food portions than cigarettes. He filled the seat of the big Suburban SUV to capacity, which was pushed back as far as possible to accommodate his large frame. He wore the clothes of a working man; loose-fitting jeans, a red plaid shirt, and scuffed, well-worn cowboy boots. He removed his cowboy hat and placed it between himself and Andrew, lest it get squashed between his head and the roof of the vehicle. Andrew had his eyes and hair, and the resemblance was unmistakable.

In contrast, his wife was petite with a heart-shaped face, slim jawline, and delicate features. Accentuated by a layered bob cut, which gave her hair a chic, messy look, and blended well with her attire. She, too, wore cowboy boots — brown and well cared for — paired with form-fitting dark blue jeans and a simple white button-front blouse, with a little ornate embroidery on the collar. They were a very wholesome family. They spoke quietly, contrary to what she had heard about Texans. She found herself having to listen carefully as she slowly grew accustomed to their deep southern accents and colloquialisms, which she found endearing.

They lumbered north on Interstate 281 and exited onto Bulverde Road, passing roads with names like Comanche Trail, Running Fawn, Arapaho Way, and Howling Wolf, a testament to those who had first lived there, some two hundred-odd years ago. About thirty minutes later, they pulled into a gravel driveway that meandered alongside lush green lawns and well-tended flowerbeds, and led up to a sprawling, white, two-story clapboard house, with a deep wrap-around porch adorned with solid wood rocking chairs and rustic, but tasteful, side tables. A mature American elm stood majestically in the centre of the manicured lawn, a well-used board swing hanging from one of its sturdy limbs, swaying gently in the soft breeze.

Andrew took Emily's bag and they made their way up the front steps onto the hardwood porch. Mr. Koch opened and held the door for everyone to enter the house. Emily noted that the door was unlocked, and suspected it was never locked. There was a bit of a traffic jam, as they all stopped in the hallway to remove their shoes. "Andrew, you show Emily her room. I've made up the bed, and there are fresh towels in the bathroom. Welcome, Emily. I hope you will be comfortable. You rest a spell, and I'll fix us some dinner." Mrs. Koch said, with a genuinely welcoming smile.

Andrew led Emily up the wide wooden staircase, down a long hallway, and into the guest room. He deposited her bag on the antique, white-painted, wrought iron bed. She gazed around the tasteful and modest room, adoring the patchwork quilt and homely touches, especially the vase full of fresh-cut flowers on her nightstand. Andrew showed her the bathroom with its clawfoot tub and shower combination. They stared at each other for a moment, both inquiring at the same time, "Are you alright?" Emily shrugged and smiled a weary smile, replying, "Ask me again after I've had a few hours' sleep."

"Well, I'll leave you to it. Get some rest. Dinner is at seven." he said, as he closed the door behind him. She knew he needed some time alone with his folks, and she was content to have a shower and a nap; she was jet-lagged and exhausted.

She showered, washed her hair, pulled on fresh underwear and slipped on Andrew's T-shirt, which she had now laid claim to. She wrapped her hair in a towel, slid under the patchwork quilt, fluffed a pillow, and fell sound asleep.

Emily woke with a start. The light filtering through the window had changed. It was no longer harsh and bright; it was soft and cast deep shadows in the room. She sat bolt upright and checked the time — it was six thirty-five. Voices drifted upward from the porch below.

She slipped out of bed and went to the window overlooking the giant elm and the front garden. Panic jolted her fully awake. In the driveway stood an ambulance and a police car. She shot across the room, raced down the hallway, bolted down the staircase — skipping the bottom three steps — and flung open the screen door, stubbing her toe with such force that she let out a shriek.

A generously proportioned man in his fifties, dressed in a dark blue uniform with a handgun in a holster and a bright gold star on his chest, leaned casually against the corner rail, holding a Smokey Bear hat in his hand. Another man, around Andrew's age, tall and gangly, also in a blue uniform with reflective stripes and plenty of pockets, sat casually on the porch rail, his legs swinging absently about a foot from the floor. Andrew reclined in a rocker, arms crossed behind his head and legs propped on the deck rail, crossed at the ankles.

All three men stopped talking and stared at the commotion as Emily came hopping onto the deck, shouting Andrew's name, the screen door slamming behind her. Andrew leapt from his chair and, in two bounds, was at her side, guiding her to the porch swing and setting her down.

"What happened? What's wrong?" he asked tenderly, kneeling down between her legs and cupping her panic-stricken face.

Emily started babbling. "What happened? Why are the police here? Why is there an ambulance? I-I-I thought it was you. I thought maybe you'd..."

"Shhh, it's okay, it's okay. Hurting myself is never an option, okay? Besides, it would kill my parents. I could never do that," he said soothingly. He glanced at her toe, which was red and would probably bruise, but the impact hadn't broken the skin. "Well, I betcha that smarts!" he said, smiling at her. "Come on, let me introduce you."

Emily glanced down, realizing she was wearing only a pair of panties and a T-shirt, and it was obvious she wasn't wearing a bra. Andrew noted her discomfort and stood, shielding her from the others. She smiled at his chivalrous manner and said, "Let me get dressed. I'll be back in a minute."

She bumped into Mrs. Koch, who was on her way out with a pitcher of homemade lemonade and a tray of glasses.

"What's all the hollerin' about?" Mrs. Koch asked, as Andrew took the tray from her. Emily heard him explaining as she went upstairs to change. She was back down in five minutes, wearing a pair of jeans and a yellow blouse, favouring her throbbing toe.

Mrs. Koch was in the kitchen, humming along to Travis Tritt crooning through the radio; *"It's a great day to be alive. I know the sun's shining when I close my eyes."* Emily paused at the door and apologised.

Mrs. Koch told Emily not to fret. "By the way, please call me Rosemary. Lemonade is on the porch, and have Andrew take a look at your toe; it took quite a licking," she said, turning back to the stove and giving the pot a stir.

Emily limped onto the deck sheepishly. Andrew was holding out a glass of lemonade and handed it to her. The two other men stood as Andrew introduced them.

"This here is Hank. He's our deputy sheriff. We just call him Bubba," Andrew said.

Bubba leaned forward and shook Emily's hand. "Ma'am, it's a right pleasure, Miss Emily."

"And this is Earl-Ray. We call him ER on account of his job and all. We work together as paramedics," Andrew continued.

ER removed his cap and took Emily's hand in a warm handshake. "Well, howdy, ma'am. Do you always make such grand entrances? You reminded me of Kramer from *Seinfeld,* only you is prettier and a lot shorter. Dang, I love that guy. Come, rest your britches a spell."

He gestured to a chair, and Emily blushed, recalling her entrance and imagining how it must have looked to the men on the deck. She sipped the sweet lemonade and smiled as she listened to the guys catching up.

She noticed Andrew had slipped deeper into his Texan accent. It seemed fitting. It suited his jeans, denim shirt over a white T-shirt, and boots. The police radio squawked, and something unintelligible to Emily was said, though the guys knew it was their cue to take their leave.

Andrew said, "Well, you best get after that." They all shook hands.

ER once again removed his hat and said, "We'll be seeing you, ma'am. You take good care now."

Bubba, always economical with words, nodded goodbye and added, "Ma'am," as he worried the porch with his heavy footfalls.

The cars left the driveway, leaving behind a cloud of dust that hung in the air. Mr. Koch appeared around the corner with Buddy, the family's well-fed and happy golden labrador.

Emily, still a bit jumpy, stepped back from the rail as Buddy trotted onto the porch, a big grin on his face and his tail wagging with such ferocity she thought he might wag himself off his feet.

Mr. Koch casually said, "Aw, Emily. Don't you pay him no never mind. He'll lick you to death if you give him the chance."

Andrew knelt down, cooing to Buddy, who, true to Mr. Koch's word, bestowed a long, sloppy kiss on Andrew's face. Andrew and Emily petted Buddy, who was clearly enjoying all the attention.

Rosemary poked her head beyond the screen door and said, "Dinner is on the table, y'all. Wash your hands now. And Andrew, wash your face if you ever expect that girl to kiss you," she added as she retreated inside.

Mr. Koch turned to Emily. "Young lady, my name is Russell, but my friends and kin call me Rusty. It's a right pleasure having you in our home. Stay as long as you like." He removed his hat, slapped it against his leg, and hung it outside the door before disappearing inside.

Emily and Andrew followed, and Buddy slumped hard onto the deck, tongue lolling as his tail thumped the wooden boards.

From somewhere deep inside the house, Garth Brooks was going on about having some *friends in low places*, and Emily realised she was in for a lot more country music. Strangely, although she hadn't liked it much in the UK or Europe, here she couldn't imagine listening to anything else.

The wide-open spaces, porch swings, cowboy boots, 'yes ma'ams', overweight dogs, sprawling clapboard houses, giant elm trees, and homemade lemonade on the porch — this was living, breathing, walking, talking country music!

Chapter 48

Gryphon Enterprises was conveniently located in the luxurious gated-housing complex known as Fourways Gardens. It was one of the safest and most affluent areas near Johannesburg, South Africa. The location afforded the team easy access to where their Gulfstream was housed at Lanseria Airport (LAN), a mere twenty-minute drive via the R552. Additionally, Johannesburg International Airport (ORT) was reachable within forty minutes via the M39 motorway. Most of their shopping needs could be found at the nearby Fourways Sandton Mall, which also boasted a number of quality restaurants.

Theirs was a sprawling, two-story, four-hundred-square-metre unit, situated amongst pristine lawns and gardens. There was a five-car garage that housed the fleet of vehicles owned by the company. The interior of the house had been completely gutted and rebuilt to suit Gryphon's needs. The lower level consisted of a welcoming reception area and waiting lounge, a boardroom that seated twelve people in ergonomic leather office chairs around a solid oak table, and a large, state-of-the-art kitchen. There was an informal sitting room with overstuffed armchairs and two comfortable settees facing a large marble fireplace.

Both Patrick and Hugh had sizeable offices, with views over the pool-deck and fifty-metre heated lap-pool beyond. Adjacent to the pool stood a twenty-foot shipping container that had been converted into a fully-equipped gym, complete with infrared sauna and showering facilities. Patrick and Hugh's respective secretaries each occupied a smaller, more modest office space. Again, no expense was spared on refurbishment, and the decor was elegant and inviting.

Simone had, by far, the largest workspace of all. Ostensibly, a glass cube filled to capacity with the latest in high-tech equipment, and the fastest, most powerful, custom-designed computer systems. In jest, she had scribbled 'WAR ROOM' on a piece of paper and taped it to her door when they first moved in. A week later, it was replaced with a permanent silver plaque bearing the same joke, courtesy of Patrick.

The upper level had been left unaltered. There were five luxurious bedrooms, all en-suite, and at the end of the hallway, a library and congregating area. This was for the crew and guests who rotated in and out between assignments. Currently, Peter and Ryan were in residence, while Patrick worked on the DRC issue of the previous week.

Ryan and Peter had already completed their morning run and were swimming laps when Patrick stepped onto the pool-deck and signalled to the men. They both paused at the lip of the pool, removed their goggles, and looked up at Patrick.

"Morning, boss. What's up?" Ryan quipped.

"Morning, guys. Sorry to interrupt. How long until you are done?" Patrick asked, his hands casually in his pockets.

They looked at each other. "We can be done now. We'll do the gym later."

"Well, take twenty minutes to shower and get dressed, and we'll meet in the sitting room for coffee." Patrick suggested.

Peter and Ryan hoisted themselves out of the pool, dried off, draped their towels over their shoulders, and headed upstairs to shower and change.

All three were seated comfortably in the sitting room. Patrick had sent out for Mugg and Bean Americanos and a selection of pastries... a favourite among the staff. Peter selected an apple strudel, and Ryan, an orange cranberry muffin, still warm. While the men ate and drank coffee, Patrick wasted no time in updating them on what was happening in Goma.

"It's a complete fucking train wreck. I'm happy you guys got out when you did. Beni, Isoro, and Bunia were overrun and are now strongholds of the M23 rebels. The blue helmets are still waffling about with no clear mandate. The National Army has been pushed back and is setting up just north of Goma. Expats are being evacuated, and Pierre has his hands full, moving his planes and equipment to Arusha, Tanzania.

To date, four hundred and seventy-eight people are confirmed dead. Forty-three villages have been razed to the ground. Nearly three hundred children have been abducted. I strongly suspect those are only the 'reported' casualties; I imagine it's far worse. Médecins Sans Frontières and all their employees were airlifted to Kinshasa and are awaiting transport out of the country. UNHRC has been ordered to leave. If the Kabila government cannot get a handle on it, it could be another Rwanda."

"This has nothing to do with us, though. We're not going back, right?" Peter questioned Patrick.

"Hell, no. Just updating you guys. However, Mike Sellars, your guardian angel pilot who talked you into Kampala, has been given clearance and a ferry ticket to collect the Caravan from Entebbe. He's flying it down to Lanseria on Wednesday morning for repairs and will be our guest for a few nights. He took the liberty to clear out your rooms at the compound and is bringing your personal effects. He will also stop in and see Mac, drop off his personal effects, and pass on our well-wishes. I thought you might want to buy him a steak and a beer."

"He deserves the whole bloody cow!" said Peter.

"And the entire Amstel brewery," Ryan added, his mouth still half full of muffin.

"So, what of our skirmish with the guerrillas? Are we being sought after?" Peter asked seriously.

"No, not a word. I believe the army has taken that credit. Apparently, Mavivi was a bit of a hot spot after you guys got away; it attracted soldiers from both sides. There was quite a bun fight – mortars, RPGs, and other heavy firepower. There was not much left when the guerrillas retreated. The army counted the dead, multiplied it by at least five, and claimed victory, so you guys are in the clear." Patrick smiled, his palms open and facing up, arms spread. He shrugged his shoulders, cocked his head, and said, "TIA, boys. TIA," the abbreviation for 'This Is Africa' – a common quip when the unexpected happens.

Chapter 49

In a private room on the second floor, Mac was recovering steadily — often napping, but no longer unconscious. In the beginning, when he was still sedated in the ICU, Ingrid had spent a number of days by Mac's side, occasionally reading to him, her voice the only sound in the sterile room. Soon, Ingrid would have the chance to meet him properly. She would get to hear his voice and have a real conversation — a prospect that filled her with anticipation.

She had been unsuccessful in her attempts to get word to either of his children. She had obtained contact details for his ex-wife via the internet. She knew little of the woman, other than she was a solicitor in a large Dublin law firm. She would have contacted her had it become necessary, but now that Mac was on the mend, she would leave it up to him.

Ingrid decided she ought to contact Pierre and Patrick to update them on Mac's progress. Pierre received the first call.

"Hello, Dr. Svenson," answered Pierre, a hint of foreboding in his voice.

She quickly put him at ease, with "Hi, Pierre. Just a brief update — Mac is out of the ICU and is recovering nicely. He's doing well, all things considered." He praised her for her work and informed her that they were evacuating Goma for the time being, due to the unrest. They would be in Tanzania until things settled down. He confirmed he would be in touch in the next few days with details of the insurance company that would take care of Mac's account. He also let her know that Mike Sellars would be in Kampala on Tuesday with Mac's personal effects, and asked if it would be possible for Mike to visit. Ingrid thought it would be good for Mac, and welcomed the idea. She proceeded to call Patrick and update him similarly. They exchanged pleasantries for a few moments and said their goodbyes.

It was just after six in the evening when Ingrid finished writing her reports. She yawned, stretched, and got up from behind her desk. She hung up her lab coat, took her keys and handbag, switched off the lights, and locked her office door. She bid goodnight to the night staff and made her way down the stairs. When she reached the second floor, she paused and decided to pop in on Mac before she went home.

His light was on, and the bed was raised, enabling him to lay at a comfortable elevated angle.

"Good evening," Ingrid greeted him cheerily. "You are looking better and better every time I see you."

He took a sip of water through a straw and said something totally unexpected. "Aye, sure. It's the moisturising cream, fabulous stuff, so it is."

She smiled broadly. "Well, Captain McBride, you certainly seem chipper for a man who was as close to death as a man could be. Mind if I chat with you for a while?" she asked, as she resettled her bag on her shoulder and pocketed her keys.

"Please, call me Mac. And absolutely, take a seat. I could do with a bit of company."

Ingrid placed her bag on the floor and sank into the chair, then shuffled it around so she could see his face.

"Are you responsible for this?" he said, gesturing to his wounds.

"If you're referring to the shooting, no! But the patching-up? Yes." she replied.

Mac took another sip of water and said, "Okay, so I realise I'm in a hospital — the lab coats, scrubs, and horrible food were a dead giveaway — but where am I? My recollection is very sketchy."

"You are in Kampala, at the International Hospital. I can fill in some of the blanks, but let's start with what you recall, and I'll tell you what I know." she replied.

He closed his eyes and seemed to be mulling things over before his eyes shot open. "Shite! I'm in Kampala?!" Mac's voice trembled, confusion etching deep lines on his forehead. "Where's everyone else? How the hell did we get here? I didn't fly... did I fly... I couldn't have! Who flew?" His stare bore into Ingrid, a mix of fear and desperation flickering across his face. Ingrid felt a pang of sympathy as Mac's eyes widened with apprehension. He'd been through so much, and the gaps in his memory seemed to disorientate him further.

She wished she could ease his frustration. "It's a bit vague, but from what I hear, one of your security men flew the plane with some guidance from a pilot in the tower. Apparently, Ryan... I think that's his name, had some basic training, but I'm not sure. He did manage to get the plane on the ground safely without any further loss of life. So, what do you remember?"

He recalled landing in Mavivi and getting the plane ready to leave; the ambush; a young man being shot and helping load the boy's body into the plane. He remembered taxiing down the runway; someone shooting at them from the front of the plane; the ripping sounds as bullets penetrated the cockpit; and then the pain and a burning sensation.

"I have snippets of someone yelling for me to engage the autopilot, but I don't recall if I did or not. I must have been carried from my seat, because I could see the cockpit ceiling, and then the cabin ceiling. I definitely remember the excruciating pain in my legs. I have a vague recollection of people talking to me, and I think I was lying prone for a while, because I remember the smell of the carpet." He paused. "That was an odd recollection," he pondered, then continued, "I don't recall anything further, until a really sharp pain in my upper leg woke me up, screaming. And again, nothing after that."

Ingrid listened intently before responding, "The boy you saw get shot didn't make it. His friend was the medic who stabilised you. And the excruciating pain you felt was probably the tourniquet that stopped you from bleeding out. We got wind of the situation and dispatched a helicopter to meet you at the plane. You were transferred here, spent five days in ICU, and now you are in a private ward. One of your guys is coming from Goma tomorrow. I'm sure he can fill you in further."

They had exchanged questions and answers, as best they could, for almost an hour. Mac was exhausted. As Ingrid closed the door softly behind her, she couldn't shake the sense that there was more to uncover — both about the events in the Congo and Mac himself.

Chapter 50

At just after eight on Monday morning, Emily and the Kochs sat down in the kitchen for breakfast. Texas-style for the men; a short stack of pancakes, swimming in butter and maple syrup, bacon, sausages, grits, and fried eggs. Emily, feeling more at ease after being welcomed warmly into the Koch household, quipped, jokingly, "Would it be safe to assume you've not heard of this global cholesterol epidemic? It's been in the papers, you know."

"Er, nope. Ain't got no time to read the papers." Rusty replied with a grin over the rim of his coffee cup. Emily and Rosemary exchanged amused looks, as Rosemary said to Andrew, "I like her."

As the women tucked into their yoghurt, homemade granola, fruit salad, and hard-boiled eggs, the mood was light, and the banter was heavy. For a moment, life felt almost normal. But Emily knew the day ahead would be challenging. As the men cleared the plates and stacked the dishwasher, Emily and Rosemary went upstairs to prepare for the visit.

An hour later, they arrived at the Johnson residence — the driveway crowded with cars. People stood talking quietly as the foursome threaded their way through the huddled groups and up the porch steps. The Kochs greeted the familiar faces of a close-knit community.

Handshakes, kisses, and introductions followed as they entered the house.

Emily stepped into the Johnsons' home and was struck by the overwhelming outpouring of support — casseroles piled high on the counter, cakes lovingly baked by neighbours, and an array of flowers and condolence cards filling every available surface. The scent of home-cooked meals hung in the air, bittersweet against the backdrop of sorrow. The Johnsons, gaunt and visibly worn, stood at the heart of it all. Emily kept a respectful distance while the Kochs and Johnsons huddled with the Baptist minister, sharing hugs, tears, and prayers.

As Emily observed the scene, memories of Travis's final moments replayed in her mind — his daring drive past the police officer, his infectious laughter, and the camaraderie he shared with Andrew. Her heart ached anew, and tears streamed down her cheeks. Andrew's gentle voice pulled her from her reverie. "Hey, you. You okay?" He handed her a Kleenex and a glass of orange juice.

She forced a smile and nodded, recalling one of Andrew and Travis's visits to her in Nia Nia. She remembered their Land Rover coming up her driveway in a cloud of dust, country music blaring out of the open windows, and Travis belting out the lyrics so completely out of tune it was comical.

The drive home was quiet, a stark contrast to their earlier journey. Emily had met so many people, learned about Travis's impact on the community, and shared in the collective grief. The funeral was to be held at the Bulverde Baptist Church, and the fire department wanted to honour Travis. The Johnsons agreed. It had been Travis's life, his commitment to the community, and his selflessness, both on and off the job. The Johnsons could not think of a more fitting way to honour their only child.

Chapter 51

Ingrid was not due back at the hospital until the weekend. She would spend the next three days volunteering at Rhino Refugee Camp, a sprawling tent city, divided into six sections, and housing nearly a hundred and fifty-five thousand refugees from South Sudan and the Democratic Republic of the Congo — each fraught with turmoil. It was, by far, the largest camp in Uganda, and arguably, the largest in the world, due to its close proximity to both war-torn countries.

The majority of the camp's population came from South Sudan, and if the conflict, and the unrest, continues on this trajectory, it is believed, by many in the field, that, by 2025, it will have produced more refugees than any other country.

Although Uganda itself is a struggling, developing nation, to date, it gives sanctuary to more refugees than any other country on the planet, and it relies heavily on foreign aid. Unfortunately, much of the funding does not make it to the camps, causing tensions within the community and their neighbouring hosts.

For the past year and a half, Ingrid had made the journey every three months or so, and she knew all four hundred and seventy-odd kilometers well. The road was old, narrow, and in poor condition — mostly tarmac, with long stretches of gravel and littered with potholes.

Road repairs and rebuilding had been stopped and started, due to previous unrest in Uganda, long before she started making her pilgrimage. Much had to do with Joseph Kony and his Lord's Resistance Army, who terrorized the region from 1987 to 2006. Although his army of upwards of three thousand strong has since been decimated, and the man himself now exiled in South Sudan, his name still evokes fear in the Ugandan people.

Kony was once the most sought-after and ruthless warlord in Africa. It is widely believed he was responsible for the deaths of over one hundred thousand civilians — mostly his own people — and the conscription of almost twenty thousand children as soldiers and child brides. In 2008, the Ugandan National Army engaged in a ferocious fight, all but wiping out Kony and his followers. They forced Kony to flee to South Sudan, and his army splintered into different factions, reducing their threat to the people of Uganda. Before Kony fled, he raided a number of subsistence farming communities and killed hundreds of peasant farmers and their families in retaliation.

Ingrid packed an overnight bag and drove to the hospital to collect the many donations she had gathered over the past three months. She pulled into the loading bay and was greeted enthusiastically by Stephen and Enoch, the two male nurses who always accompanied her to the camp. They all immediately busied themselves loading the large SUV, folding flat the last row of seats in the Nissan Patrol, and filling the space to the brim. Enoch climbed onto the roof of the vehicle, and Stephen handed him the waterproof bags and plastic lockable boxes. He secured everything to the roof rack, while Ingrid went upstairs to check in with her staff and let them know she would be back by the weekend.

Forty minutes into the journey, they pulled off the Gulu highway into a Total petrol station. They had breakfast while the mechanic checked the fluids, changed a light bulb, added air to the tyres, and fuelled the car.

Back on the road, with seven hours ahead of them, yet only four hundred kilometers to traverse, Ingrid calculated they would be safely in Arua by five in the evening — their destination for today. Tomorrow they would drive out to Rhino Refugee Camp, another hour or two's drive, depending on the road conditions. They would stay there for three nights, work for three days, and return to Kampala on Friday. The work was demanding, the time limited, but the rewards outweigh any discomfort.

For the next few hours, they serpentined and weaved along the roads, avoiding potholes and local buses that drove as though Satan himself was chasing them. On two occasions, they were forced off to the soft shoulder, as the buses sped down the middle of the road. They passed through Masindi and saw the signs for Murchison Falls — a place Ingrid planned to visit when she could steal enough time away from her hospital duties and her volunteer work.

They continued north and marveled at the changing scenery — small subsistence farms, dotted with thatched-roof mud huts. Women cooking outdoors on open fires, as children played nearby. Varying livestock, from goats to long-horned cattle and sheep, were penned close to the homes, while chickens pecked at the sun-baked, dusty earth around the huts. Men and young boys, barefooted and wearing colourful blankets, armed with long sticks, herded cattle alongside the road in search of greener pastures. They waved and smiled as they drove by.

They turned off the main Gulu highway onto the Pakwatch-Urua road, passing small fields of sweet potatoes, tomatoes, and maize — all fenced in with thorn bushes to ward off the wildlife that ventured beyond the boundaries of Karuma Game Reserve. If they were fortunate, they would glimpse some of Africa's wonderful wildlife. This was their favourite part of the journey. Ingrid slowed to sixty kilometers an hour, and everyone kept their eyes peeled for animals in the bushes beyond the road.

Coming around a corner, they happened upon two mature Rothschild's giraffes and a calf, loping across the road. Startled by the approaching vehicle, they began galloping with their tails curled upwards and necks thrusting fore and aft. The calf, frightened, scrabbled for purchase as it skidded on its ungainly, long legs on the unfamiliar asphalt surface, before bounding into the brush. The trio smiled and chatted when, not two kilometers past, Enoch spotted a herd of Ugandan Kob browsing in a clearing. Ingrid pulled the car to a stop and shut down the engine. Silence ensued, as they watched the herd with the same curiosity as the herd watched them. They were lovely antelope, with a golden-brown coat and white underside. Enoch pointed out that the males have lyre-shaped horns, while the females did not have any. He also proudly announced that, of all the animals in Uganda, the Kob was on Uganda's coat of arms. After a few photographs, Ingrid started the car and drove on slowly. They passed a troop of olive baboons, who, picking lice and fleas from each other, paid no attention whatsoever to the car. Just as they were approaching the park's borders, a bull elephant sauntered slowly across the road. He was too far away to get a decent photograph and was well into the dense foliage by the time they reached the spot where he had crossed.

The trio were elated with their sightings, and Enoch, possessing an encyclopaedic knowledge of Ugandan wildlife, regaled them with tales from his childhood. He would watch and learn about the animals of the country as a herd boy, tending his father's cattle, near the world-famous QE2 National Park. He revealed that he had wanted to be a game ranger, but fell in love with a girl who was studying to be a nurse, so he swapped his studies for phlebotomy. This started Stephen laughing uncontrollably, until tears streamed down his face, which started Ingrid laughing. "So, what happened to the girl?" Stephen pressed on, through peals of laughter. "She fell in love with a gynaecologist." That comment had Stephen slapping his thigh and rolling around on the back seat, and before long, all three were laughing so hard, Ingrid started a bout of hiccups, which set them all off again.

By just after five, they were checking into the hotel. Enoch and Stephen shared a room, while Ingrid had her own. They were all well known to the staff, and the vehicle was stored in the owner's garage. They agreed to meet at seven for dinner.

Chapter 52

The following morning, Ingrid was already in the breakfast room. Pouring herself a coffee from the cafetiere, she looked up to see a familiar face approaching her.

"Dr. Kiza. How lovely to see you!" Ingrid enthused. "Join me for coffee, will you?"

"Morning, Dr. Svenson. I will. Thank you." he said, signalling for a waiter and pulling up a vacant chair. "I heard you were in town. Good news travels fast around here. How have you been?"

"I'm well, thanks, and looking forward to catching up with the team at Rhino. So, how's the family? How's the hospital?" she smiled.

"The family's good, thanks for asking. The hospital, not so much — overworked, understaffed, not enough equipment, not enough beds, and certainly not enough money... the usual." He nodded a thanks to the waiter, refused a menu, and continued. "I had a patient come in yesterday afternoon, somebody I know — a really good guy. A self-sponsored aid worker, born in Tanzania to British parents, I believe— now living in Canada, working as a paramedic with the Toronto ambulance service. He spends a couple of months a year over here as a medic, helping refugees who present with minor ailments —

dehydration, exposure, cuts, bruises, malaria, etc. He'll give them food and water and direct them to a place where they can receive further treatment — typically the hospital or Rhino Camp. He's responsible for saving many lives on his trips. Last time, he delivered a child in the bush and brought them to us for observation.

His work is dangerous because he operates outside the usual parameters of an aid worker, with no backup. Although we've cautioned him on the dangers, he works alone and in the remotest of regions.

From what I can gather, he was last seen here at the hotel four days ago, before going out on a mission. Yesterday, he was brought into the emergency room in an awful state. It appears he was attacked. His vehicle was stolen, he was beaten, robbed, and left for dead out in the forest. He has head injuries, a broken arm, broken ribs, a ruptured spleen — that thankfully clotted — and a collapsed lung. He is in and out of consciousness. We have blood work out, and I suspect he has malaria. He's feverish and delirious.

We have two hundred and seventy beds, and over three hundred and fifty patients. Half our equipment is inoperative, and what we do have is proof that the ark existed! We have no quinine drips. We have no Fansidar. He needs to be in a hospital in Kampala with proper facilities." He finished with a big sigh, as he took a sip of his coffee.

"I'll come up and see him and make a few calls. I'll try to reach Gavin at MAF and see what we can do about airlifting him to Kanjjani and on to University Hospital." Enoch and Stephen had arrived partway through the conversation and had caught the gist. Ingrid addressed the boys. "Please, fill up on a good breakfast. I'll be as quick as I can."

The two doctors strode side by side, reporting to the hotel front desk and explaining the situation. The receptionist summoned the duty manager, who determined the medic's room as 213 and granted them access. Upon entering, they noticed cases of bottled water piled high against one wall. Cartons of military-issued MREs (meals ready to eat) were stacked halfway up the adjacent wall, and, in lesser quantities, boxes of sweets. They suspected the latter were for the children, along with a few dozen new blankets still in their wrappings, and at least twenty stuffed toys. At the far end wall stood a steel trunk, brimming with medical supplies.

They rummaged through drawers and found a Canadian passport, confirming him as Ian Cranston, thirty-seven years old. His clothes were neatly hanging in the closet, and an empty duffle bag lay at the foot of the bed. They took the passport and left everything else untouched. Ingrid charged the lads with packing up Ian's belongings and storing everything in the luggage room. She okayed this with the hotel manager before heading out through the glass doors and into Dr. Kiza's 1985 Mercedes 300TD.

Being chauffeured by Dr. Kiza, Ingrid took the opportunity to make her calls. She shared her predicament with Gavin, who confirmed that he had a Cessna 206 flying into Arua on a light freight run, so a transfer was certainly possible, but warned.

"It won't be comfortable. The seats have been removed, so he'll need to be on a litter."

Ingrid thanked him as the car pulled up to the hospital. "No problem. I'll let you know when our pilot is on the ground."

Dr. Kiza led the way through the hospital, past throngs of people, many sitting on floors or leaning on walls. Some were on trolleys in the corridors; others, less fortunate, were lying on floors on folded blankets, make-do mattresses, with intravenous drips dangling from IV poles. The entire hospital was filled with the ripe odour of infection, decay, and stale unwashed bodies. A sense of hopelessness and despair hung on a cloud of desperation.

Ian was in a room with three other patients and no dividers. He lay, supine, on a grimy cot. An IV bag hung, almost empty, from its pole, and a sheet that had probably started its life as white but now grey and threadbare was draped across him. An equally discoloured mosquito net covered man and equipment, and a tired ceiling fan whirred lazily overhead, stirring the cloying, stale air.

Ingrid had seen her share of trauma patients, yet the sight of this man's face caused her a sharp intake of breath through gritted teeth. He was totally unrecognisable from his passport photo. His eyes were swollen closed, his nose obviously broken, and, she suspected, due to the amount of swelling, there was damage to his right orbital socket. His lips were swollen and split, revealing two broken front teeth. His bald head showed contusions from the forehead to the back of the skull. She lowered the sheet and took in the bruising on his chest as Dr. Kiza handed her the chart. She read the notes, handing them back to the doctor and replacing Ian's cover.

"Do you have an operational ambulance available to transport him to the runway?"

"Yes. I can arrange that," Dr. Kiza replied enthusiastically.

He immediately set about making the call, then the pair walked back down the hallway. Ingrid noted two bodies, covered from head to toe in sheets, lying on the ground amongst the sick patients. Noting where Ingrid's eyes drifted, Dr. Kiza informed her, "We have notified their families, and they are coming to retrieve them. We have no space left in the morgue."

Silently, they walked on. Her heart went out to the good doctor. He had an impossible task.

They finally reached the exit and stepped out into the dusty car park. Ingrid was about to speak when her phone rang. She held up a finger, smiled, and answered.

"Oh, hi Gavin. Okay, that's great! Yes, I'm here now. Yes, we can. Give me a second..."

She cupped the phone and asked Dr. Kiza, "Is the ambulance ready? How far is it to the runway?"

"Ready and waiting," Dr. Kiza responded, pointing across the way towards an ageing Toyota Landcruiser that had been converted into an ambulance. "And not far. 20 minutes away."

She uncupped her palm and relayed the information to Gavin, who confirmed the pilot, Tobias, was on the ground.

She thanked Dr. Kiza, adding, "A couple of things. Could we borrow the litter? I'll make sure Gavin gets it back to you on his next flight. And could the ambulance driver possibly drop me back at the hotel?"

"Of course! Not a problem." he replied.

At the dirt runway, Tobias was waiting. Impeccably dressed in his uniform, he helped secure the litter to the floor of the aircraft. Ingrid placed the passport and medical charts into an envelope and handed it to Tobias, asking him to be sure to hand it to the paramedics at the other end.

She shielded her eyes, squinting against the harsh sunlight, and watched as the plane rose from the dusty earth, its shadow slipping silently across the landscape.

Chapter 53

Emily lay in bed, looking out of the window at the pale blue sky. She fixated on the wispy clouds drifting by, morning doves cooing, and the gentle tinkle of wind chimes floating up from the porch below. Thoughts about the day ahead were interrupted by a gentle tapping on her door.

"Come in." she said, yanking the covers up.

The antique brass handle turned slowly, and the door creaked open.

"Good mornin', Sunshine." Andrew said, stepping inside with a smile. "Brought you some coffee and orange juice." His sandy hair was still damp from the shower, and he placed the drinks on her bedside table. "Breakfast is at nine. I gotta run to Walgreens. Need anythin'?"

"Well, if you enlighten me on what a Walgreens is, I might."

"Oh, it's a pharmacy, but it sells other stuff too."

"No thanks. I think I have everything I need. Maybe just a quick kiss to motivate me to get out of bed." she grinned, tugging at his arm.

He leaned down, stared into those eyes he could never grow tired of seeing, and kissed her tenderly. When he left, the scent of sandalwood lingered. She smiled and thought, *I could get used to this man.*

Just before nine, she descended the staircase, and soulful guitar music greeted her. A gravelly voice coming from the small transistor radio was singing something about 'packing up all the dishes, and making note of all good wishes.'

"Well, good mornin', darlin'." Rosemary called out from the kitchen, where she readied a couple of eggs to poach.

"Good morning, Rosemary. I like that song. Who is it?" Emily asked, as the singer crooned, *"If I can just get off this LA freeway, without getting killed or caught."*

"Oh, you do?" Rosemary smiled. "He's a good ol' boy from Texas. From up near Abilene or Odessa, I think. Name of Guy Clark. He went to LA in the seventies, and didn't much care for it."

"It's nice." Emily said again, as the melody ended, and an obnoxious voice boomed from the radio, yelling, *"We'll beat any price, on any Ford, anywhere in Texas! We'll give you five hundred dollars in accessories, AND free air conditioning! So come on down to Trent Parker Ford, for a deal YOU don't wanna miss!"*

Emily put her glass in the dishwasher, offered to help — which Rosemary declined — then pointed at the half-full coffee pot. "Mind if I pour?"

"No, Suga. Help yourself. It's still hot. Breakfast will be another ten minutes."

Emily took her coffee and stepped onto the porch, sitting on the swing to gaze out over the lush lawn. Buddy bounded up the steps, wagging his tail. He sat at her feet and rested his head on her lap. She scratched behind his ears, laughing. "No kisses, okay?" she warned.

A few minutes later, she heard a vehicle gearing down and spotted a sage green Jeep Sahara turning into the driveway. Curious, she watched as the Jeep pulled to a halt, dust swirling. Buddy dashed off the porch to greet it.

Andrew got out, clutching a shopping bag, and smiled as he mounted the stairs, with Buddy at his heels. He kissed her, then said, "I'm ravenous."

"Where did that come from?" she asked, gesturing to the Jeep.

"It's mine." he replied, settling into the rocker and wrestling his boots off. "Had it parked in the barn when I went to Africa. I didn't wanna leave it at my place. I don't have a garage."

"Oh, I thought you lived here."

"No. I bought a patch of land a few years ago just down the road a piece. I live in a trailer on the property for now, while I build my house. Come on, let's eat." He picked up his boots, placed them next to the door, and took the shopping bag in for his mum.

As they sat down for breakfast, Rusty walked in, greeting everyone and kissing his wife. "Morning, gorgeous. You've outdone yourself again." he said, lovingly. Despite the recent strain and the upcoming funeral, Rusty's affection for Rosemary was always clear, and it warmed Emily's heart to see.

Chapter 54

Ingrid, Stephen, and Enoch pulled into Rhino Refugee Camp, three hours behind schedule, and were collectively shocked at the number of people milling about — wide-eyed, bedraggled, and weary.

"It's getting worse every time we come up here. I think there must be at least a hundred and fifty people waiting to be housed and fed." Ingrid remarked as they got out of the car. They walked into the stifling hot enrolment center, where they were greeted by an exuberant young volunteer, relief washing over his face at the arrival of the medical team.

They exchanged some general chit-chat as the refugees continued to pour in. They were processed, assigned areas, and given temporary shelter for the next few days before being moved to more permanent dwellings. A dozen or so overwhelmed foreign aid workers sat behind tatty desks, on equally tatty and uncomfortable wooden chairs, processing the constant flow of new arrivals. French, Kituba, and Lingala interpreters were on hand, all of whom spoke Swahili, the common language of East Africa.

Ingrid asked if the makeshift hospital tent had been set up and where it was situated. She also inquired about any pressing cases the volunteer might know of. He informed her that it was ready, located behind the building where they now stood, and there were no urgent cases, to his knowledge.

"How many people arrive daily?" Ingrid asked.

"It varies, but on average about three hundred and fifty. Today we've documented about two hundred, and we're not even halfway through. In the past two months, we've seen about a thirty percent increase. Last week, we registered more people from the DRC than we have in the past two years." the volunteer explained.

Ingrid reflected on the recent unrest that had brought Mac into her hospital, sent a young American volunteer home dead, and forced a flight company to relocate in a single week.

"We will go, set up, and be ready for patients in an hour. We'll be available until eight tonight. Then Wednesday and Thursday, we'll see patients from six a.m. to six p.m." Ingrid said.

Both Stephen and Enoch spoke Swahili, and Ingrid could speak French, so she asked for either a Kituba or Lingala interpreter to be available if needed. The young volunteer thanked them, handed over their room keys, and they took their leave.

The three spent the next thirty minutes unloading and setting up the equipment. By two o'clock, Stephen was taking the first shift at the triage table. Post-triage, there were five chairs set up as a makeshift waiting area, twelve beds, a minor operating and disinfecting table, and a curtained-off section for examinations that required disrobing. Four security guards were assigned to the team — two outside to control the crowd, as they surged forward to be seen, and two inside to watch over the medications and equipment.

By seven forty-five, the trio had treated forty-six refugees for a range of ailments, including malnutrition, dehydration, and two suspected cases of malaria. Those patients were assigned beds and placed on medication, rehydration, and quinine drips. A handful of children with severe diarrhea were rehydrated and given a specific diet to follow for the next few days.

By Thursday evening, the trio were exhausted, and their supplies had been depleted. They had seen nearly two hundred patients, not enough time, not enough staff and not enough supplies to see any more and there would always be more. As they tidied up and checked on their patients, Ingrid said to Enoch, "Did you know, in a first-world country, a town with a hundred thousand inhabitants — fewer people than this place — would have a fully functioning hospital with around four hundred beds, a minimum of fifteen hundred staff, and at least a hundred doctors?"

"You've gotta be kidding, right? Did you hear that?" Enoch called across to Stephen, who was adjusting the flow on an IV and chatting to a young patient.

"No way, man! I'm gonna Google it." Stephen said with a cheeky smile.

The three sat in the small staff canteen eating a bland but nourishing meal. Enoch and Stephen drank room-temperature Fanta, while Ingrid enjoyed a soothing chamomile tea. They sorted and filed the patients' notes for the next volunteer team, scheduled to arrive on Saturday.

By nine-thirty, they were struggling to stay awake. Ingrid stood up and announced, "Okay, boys, we have showers to take and bags to pack, and a long drive home tomorrow. Get some rest. See you at six."

Ingrid lay in bed that night, thinking about the poor, tortured souls forced to flee their country in search of a better life. She shuddered to think how bad life must have been, that they walked three hundred kilometers across a desert to live in a tent. She had read the stories, seen the images on the news, but even the best correspondents failed to convey what you see and feel when you look into the eyes of a person who has suffered the greatest loss of all — hope.

She thought about those eager, dedicated volunteers who travel from all over the world with a dream of saving humanity, only to leave, beaten and dejected, when they realise they cannot save humanity from itself. She wanted to tell them they did make a difference. Even if they helped just one person, it still made a difference. And that, in itself, should be good enough.

She knew some would return home stronger, wiser, and full of passion — the kind of passion that ignites the flame to challenge governments to intervene and assist. Others would go home with a sense of abject failure, scarred for life by the desperation and hopelessness they witnessed. Sadly, some would never make it home.

Dew clung to the tops of the tents, shimmering softly as the first light of dawn stretched over the horizon. The sun began to rise, casting long shadows across the camp. The trio walked in silence. The only sound was the gravel crunching beneath their feet and the distant cry of a child punctuating the stillness of the morning. They loaded the vehicle quietly and strapped the empty boxes to the roof rack.

A new wave of refugees had arrived overnight, mingling with those who were not yet billeted. They huddled under blankets, some lying on grass mats on the dry, sun-parched earth, others sat against the trees. Malnourished women were attempting to feed equally malnourished infants from empty breasts. No matter how often the trio visited the camp, they could never get used to these scenes.

The three piled into the Nissan and started the journey back to Kampala. As they turned out of the gate, they passed a new influx of refugees trudging toward the camp. Barefoot women, with babies tied to their backs by blankets. Others, with their only possessions balanced on their heads. A few men carried infants, while others pushed bicycles piled high with what meager belongings they could salvage from their homes before being forced to flee. Children, some as young as eight, walked in small groups, and the trio knew they were the unaccompanied minors, possibly orphaned by the ravages of war. An elderly couple shuffled along slowly, their clothing threadbare and hanging off their emaciated frames. Ingrid watched them all in her rearview mirror. She wondered how they had survived the roughly three hundred-kilometer walk. One thing Ingrid knew for certain; this was not in the old couple's life plan.

Chapter 55

Rusty and Andrew tidied up after breakfast, while the women went upstairs to prepare for the funeral. The service would be held at Bulverde Baptist Church, which the Johnsons and Kochs had attended since its inception in 1973. Andrew and Travis were baptized here, and were lifelong attendees. Both played in the church band — Andrew as the lead guitarist and Travis on bass, although Travis could play almost any instrument. The church was pivotal in fostering their love of aid work.

Emily and Rosemary sat on the porch speaking quietly. Even Buddy seemed to sense the solemn mood; he lay with his paws outstretched in front of him, his large head between them, and his incessant tail-wagging had ceased. Rusty and Andrew, dressed in dark suits, white shirts, and dark ties, stepped onto the porch, smiled sadly, and, without a word, the women rose, smoothed their dresses, and followed the men to Rusty's Suburban. The men held the doors open for their respective partners and closed them gently once the women were comfortably seated, before sliding into the Suburban themselves. Rusty started the engine, turned off the radio, and switched on the air conditioning before executing a U-turn and driving out onto the street.

Andrew reached into his pocket, retrieved a sheet of paper, and unfolded it. He began rehearsing his speech. Emily noticed the tears in his eyes and placed a comforting hand on his leg, squeezing his knee. He mumbled that he wasn't sure he could make it through the speech. She said nothing and just rubbed her hand along his thigh, knowing words would be inadequate. They turned onto Bulverde Road, passing the fire department, where the flag was flying at half-mast. Two fire trucks stood on the forecourt, gleaming in the sun, their emergency lights flashing in honour of a fallen comrade.

The parking area at the church was teeming with vehicles. They had a reserved parking space next to the Johnsons, who were already standing by their car with a group of people. Once alighted from the vehicle, handshakes, hugs, introductions, and gentle words followed.

The deacon poked his head around the church door, announcing they were ready, and the families assembled at the foot of the church steps. Mr. Johnson was in the center, with a heavily pregnant Andrea to his left, and Mrs. Johnson on his right. Rusty and Rosemary linked arms with Grandpa Johnson and guided him up the steps. Andrew took Emily's hand and placed his free hand on his hip, offering his elbow to Grandma Johnson. With the congregation complete, the heavy door closed behind them.

Emily was struck — first, by the sheer number of people in attendance, and then by the song choice, which was unlike anything she had heard in a church. *'I'll Fly Away'* by Alan Jackson was one of Travis's favourites. The altar was adorned with beautiful flower arrangements, and candles flickered around a silver-framed portrait of Travis in uniform. The entire assembly stood as the families passed slowly towards their assigned seats. Then, one by one, they approached the open casket to convey their private goodbyes. Travis, dressed in his firefighter 'Class A' uniform, looked at peace. Mrs. Johnson almost collapsed, trying unsuccessfully to stifle a wail. Mr. Johnson rushed to her side, drew her in tightly, and guided her back to the pew.

Memories of Travis flooded Emily's mind like a movie in fast-forward. She could almost hear his laugh on the veranda of her home in the Congo. She had known him only a few months, and there were many wonderful memories, so she shuddered to think how many Andrew had accumulated over twenty-plus years.

The same pastor she had seen at the Johnson's stood at the pulpit. "Good morning, everybody. Please, be seated." Emily glanced across the aisle at the five men dressed identically to Travis and knew they were his pallbearers. The pastor said a few words that Emily didn't quite catch — she was lost in thoughts of Travis — and only came out of her reverie when he asked everyone to bow their heads in prayer. After reading excerpts from *Ecclesiastes 3;1-8*, he asked everyone to stand and join in with *'Shine, Jesus, Shine'*, a song Travis had spent weeks teaching the kids at Sunday School. The congregation sang with such enthusiasm that it seemed they might blow the roof off the building, especially during the chorus. "Thank you, everyone. At this time, I would like to invite Travis's family and friends to say a few words."

Andrew and ER had decided, the night before, that ER would speak first. As he made his way to the stage, his nerves, emotions, and lack of confidence were on full display. He stared out over the sea of people, his vision blurred. He blinked away the tears and began. "I'd like to tell you what Travis meant to me. Trouble is, I have to be back at the fire station in two days, so…" This elicited many *amens* and tentative chuckles from the crowd. "If it's okay with y'all, would you please stand, as I pay tribute to my friend and comrade, with a lil' number we liked to do." He placed the microphone in its stand, reached behind him, picked up his guitar, and said, "Travis, I hope I do you proud, my friend." He took a deep breath, bowed his head, and after two faltering starts, sang a rendition of *'Hallelujah'* that would make Leonard Cohen proud and give Jeff Buckley a run for his money.

There was not a dry eye in the room when he'd finished. The silence was deafening, until the congregation broke protocol, unable to contain what could be perceived as the greatest of honours and moving eulogies anyone could witness. The applause drowned out the amens echoing through the cavernous church.

Emily felt Andrew's hand tighten on hers, sensing he was struggling to keep his emotions in check. Tears streamed down Emily's face as Andrew stood up and made his way to the podium. The crowd quieted and seated themselves. Andrew unfolded the note. He set it on the lectern, adjusted the microphone, and cleared his throat. He wiped the tears that continued to flow down his face and drop onto the paper, smudging his handwritten words. Emily fought the overwhelming urge to jump up, rush to the stage, and rescue him from his torturous ordeal. Andrew called the pastor over, whispered into his ear, and handed him a flash drive, before attempting to continue. His voice choked with emotion, he began, "The Johnsons have lost a son, a grandson. Andrea lost a husband, and their unborn child, a father. The fire department lost a comrade. And to all of us, we lost a true friend. A man of honour, integrity, and compassion. I cannot speak for everyone here, but I have to remember the joy, the love, and the light he gave so willingly. I will forever continue to suffer his loss, but I pray I will not sustain my connection to suffering, but sustain my connection to love." Andrew was weeping openly, and could no longer read his words. He looked up from the tear-stained page into the somber crowd and continued, "Travis brought light to this world. He brought light and hope into places where perpetual darkness and despair reside. And I believe, in his death, his light burns on in all of those he touched. I cannot do justice to Travis through words, so this is for you, my friend." he said quietly, and nodded to the pastor. Libby L. Allen's song, *'Heaven's Now My Home'* accompanied a slideshow, with images of Travis and Andrew building sandcastles on the beach as toddlers, fishing in the creek, pre-teen birthday parties, making funny faces at the camera, camping, motorcycling on the farm, Andrew's twenty-first birthday in New Orleans after Katrina, and missions in Honduras and Malawi.

The pastor closed the service and reminded everyone where Travis was to be buried. Andrew whispered to Emily, "See you at the gravesite." He stood, and took his position at the head of the casket, while the five firemen took theirs. They hoisted the casket, as Alison Krauss's rendition of *'Down to the River to Pray'*, a George Allan song from the slave songbook of 1867, filled the church with southern gospel music. They walked slowly in step and slid the casket into the awaiting hearse.

Two Comal County police motorcycles led the procession down Bulverde Road, past the fire department, where all those on duty stood to attention, with their hands on their hearts. At every intersection, Comal County police halted traffic, giving right of way to the large funeral procession, all the way down Casey Road, onto US 281 highway, and off again at New Braunfels.

At the entrance to the cemetery, two fire ladders were crossed as a tribute to a fallen hero. Graveside, Emily took a seat with the Johnsons and Kochs, as she had in the church, while the rest of the mourners stood under the warm, late morning sun. The last rites were read, before *'Old Glory'* was removed from the casket, folded, and handed to Mrs. Johnson. As Travis was lowered into the ground, the haunting sound of the bagpipes played *'Amazing Grace'*.

Emily ambled away, allowing the family some private time to say goodbye to Travis. She observed the lone piper from afar, as he stood beneath a Red Smoketree and continued to play as the gathering dispersed.

Fittingly, the wake was held at the fire station. The mourners mingled and regaled tales well into the afternoon. The reception culminated in 'the last alarm', the bell service to honour a fallen comrade.

Chapter 56

Six o'clock arrived about three hours too soon for Ingrid's liking. She dragged her tired body out of the comfortable bed and stood equidistant between an invigorating shower and her chest of drawers — home to her running gear, aka her tools of torture. She took two steps towards the shower before her conscience got the better of her.

She pulled on her running gear, and by six fifteen, she was making her way around her five-kilometre circuit. Two kilometres in, she mentally approved of her decision. The dappled sun shone through the blossoming spring trees, accentuating their vibrant colours. The deep orange African tulip trees and the various-coloured hibiscus trees, with their large trumpet-shaped flowers, ranging from deep red to peach and yellow. This, combined with the energetic, colourful morning birds, made for good running companions as they flitted from tree to tree.

The kilometres fell away quickly. Rounding the corner and beginning her descent from four thousand feet, Lake Victoria came into view. A turquoise-blue disc, the sunlight coruscating off the little white waves and hemmed in by the Rwenzori Mountains, hazy and shrouded in morning mist. She ran on — the only person on the road in her own personal painting.

Back home, invigorated from the run and a long, hot, luxurious shower, Ingrid glimpsed herself naked in front of the full-length mirror doors of the closet. She paused and took in her reflection. At forty-four years old, she was happy with the image that looked back at her. Her long legs, lithe and toned. Her belly taut, her small pear-shaped breasts still firm. Her heart-shaped face, with full, bow-shaped lips, prominent cheekbones, and striking blue eyes. She liked the small laugh lines at the edge of her eyes, which added character to an otherwise perfect complexion.

Smiling, she slid the door open, selected a pair of navy blue slacks and a pale blue blouse, pulled out items from her underwear drawer, and dressed quickly. She made her bed, closed the novel she had picked up last night but failed to get past page four, and set it on the nightstand.

Charged by a wonderful start to her day and four successful days at Rhino Camp, she drove out of her driveway with the radio on, music blaring, and singing along. She tapped her hand in time to the beat on the centre console. Her 'driving tunes' playlist contained only catchy upbeat music, while she sang and danced in her seat. By the time she pulled up to the gate, Joe Cocker was belting out 'Feelin' Alright', and she only realised it had taken her almost thirty minutes to do the usual ten-minute commute when she signed the hospital entry log.

Taking the stairs two at a time on the balls of her feet, 'Feelin' Alright' was stuck in her head. She unlocked her office door, flipped on the lights, and raised the blinds. She went through her voicemails, emails, and yellow post-it note messages. Satisfied there was nothing pressing, she spent the better part of an hour responding before slipping into her lab coat and pocketing her stethoscope. She locked the door and began her rounds.

At eleven o'clock, she was standing at the foot of Ian's bed. He was looking considerably better. The contusions were still ugly, varying in shades of purple, green, yellow, and brown, and dominating his face. His eyes were still swollen, but he was resting comfortably. She picked up his chart and scanned through the highlights; CT scans, X-rays, and blood work were performed. The findings included an indirect orbital floor fracture on the right side, a nasal fracture, pneumothorax, concussion, broken ribs five, seven, eight, and nine, malaria, and dehydration. She quickly reviewed treatments and recommendations; intravenous quinine for malaria, isotonic IV for rehydration, morphine for pain management, supplemental oxygen, needle aspiration, and percutaneous chest tube drainage.

The ophthalmologist had checked in and was waiting for the swelling to subside before performing any further tests, and the same for the neurologist. She hung up his chart, checked his vitals, closed the door quietly, and went to the nurses' station to inquire if anyone had managed to get word to his parents. They had not; they were away on safari and due back mid-week. She thanked them and went to check on Mac.

Mac's bed was raised to a forty-five-degree angle, and the iron patient-retaining bars were up and locked. He was sitting up watching Al Jazeera news when Ingrid entered the room.

"So, Mac. You're looking better! How are you feeling?"

"Aye, sure, you know yourself," he answered, with a crooked smile that broke across his ruddy features. He switched off the television and placed the remote on the table, next to his untouched lunch.

"Not hungry?" she said absently, as she studied his chart.

"Aye. Sure I'm hungry. Here's the thing though. The nurses assured me they were bringing me food. Then this arrived." he said, gesturing to the serving tray. "They told me it was food. Now then, herein lies the problem. I have tried food before, believe me when I tell you. I like food. In fact, I find food very agreeable. And this, I am almost positive, is not food."

She laughed at his response. It was the politest criticism of hospital food she'd ever encountered. She was inclined to agree. Nourishing? Possibly. Leaving the recipient begging for more? Not so much.

His notes showed there were no signs of infection, but she wanted to keep him in for a few more days — maybe a week — to get him to do some walking and monitor how much the muscle and nerve damage had affected his abilities, before sending him for physiotherapy.

She looked at her watch and said, "I've not eaten either. I was going to get something from the canteen. Can I bring you something, and we can eat together, if you like? They make an excellent chicken Caesar salad and fresh garlic bread. My treat, in exchange for a story."

"A story?" he asked, a quizzical look crossing his face.

"Yes." she beamed. "A story. Anything you want to chat about. I don't get much outside news over here, unless it's on the TV or radio, but that does not constitute a conversation."

"Like what?" he asked, smiling back at her.

"Maybe your story. How an Irish airline captain ended up flying around Africa getting shot at."

She saw the pain in his eyes, and his features quickly darkened before he regained his composure. She quickly chided herself for her impatience and said, "Or not."

He smiled back at her and said, "Maybe I will try this mush." pointing to the food on the tray.

"Well, I'm having the Caesar salad, and I think you should too. And we can just chat about anything. Sorry if I brought up a painful subject."

An awkward pause ensued, and they just looked at each other for what seemed an eternity when Mac said, "You seem like the sort of person who I may want to tell the version of the events that led me here. And I suspect some Scandinavian hospital is missing an extremely talented surgeon. And said surgeon may want to share her story with me. But I think both tales can wait a while. Agreed?"

She smiled warmly and responded, "Agreed. Two Caesar salads, with garlic bread, coming right up. Do you want anything to drink?"

"Would it be safe to assume a Jameson's is out of the question?"

"That would be a safe assumption, Mr. McBride!" she replied, nodding and smiling.

He smiled back at her. He liked the way she made him feel. "It's okay, I have some water. I'll be grand, thank you."

She excused herself and returned twenty minutes later with their food, and two chocolate brownies for dessert.

They chatted as they ate, and the conversation was easy. She asked him how his visit with Mike went, while pointing at the two suitcases, flight bag, and duffle bag that lay stacked in the corner of the room. He filled her in on the few hours they spent talking about the temporary relocation of the company and the closure of the complex where they were housed. She told him of the conversations she had with Patrick

Kinsella and about 'The Odongo Show'. She brought him up to speed with how the group was whisked out of the country and, above all, how Andrew had saved his life.

They were eating their brownies when a nurse popped her head in and told Ingrid she was required in the emergency room. A multi-casualty accident was inbound, and every available doctor was needed. She popped the last bite into her mouth and said, "Duty calls. I'll come back after my shift if you like, say around seven. If, of course, you're not too tired." She paused, one hand on the door, her head turned to face him.

"I'd like that, Doc. That'll be grand." he said, signalling with his finger and pointing to the corner of his mouth. She furrowed her brow and then realised he was pointing out an errant piece of chocolate icing on the side of her lip. "You missed a bit."

"I know. I was saving it for later." She wiped it off and asked, "Gone?"

"Gone," he responded. "See ya, Doc. Mind yourself."

Chapter 57

Ingrid returned just after seven-thirty, carrying a plain cardboard box, balancing her handbag and two cups of steaming liquid on top of it. She wrestled the door open using her elbow, awkwardly turned sideways, and bumped it open with her hip. She spun around, facing Mac, as the door swung closed, all the while precariously balancing her load.

"Well, good evening, Doc. That was a delicate and skillful balancing act, so it was." he said, smiling curiously.

Ingrid was dressed in casual jeans, a long-sleeved grey Lycra sports top, and a zip-up black lightweight fleece. She walked around the bed and placed the box on the chair. As she drew closer, Mac couldn't help but notice the delicate scent of honeysuckle enveloping him, like a memory of something long-forgotten. It tugged at him in a way he hadn't expected — a reminder of how long it had been since he'd allowed himself to enjoy the company of someone like this. The sensation was both comforting and unsettling.

"I'm going to send this down to the lab to see if it's food or not." she said, as she cleared the hospital food from the table. "Until then, we'll have to make do with take-out meals." She set the cup of tea down. "It's Earl Grey." she added. "I saw the evidence in the wastebasket earlier and assumed Mike brought it for you. The tag was still tucked under the lid. Don't say anything, I'm just observant."

She smiled, a broad smile that displayed her perfect white teeth and two endearing dimples high on her cheeks.

"Clearly." he answered.

Ingrid opened the box and withdrew a brown, foil-insulated bag. Drawing the plate out, tantalizingly slowly, Mac inhaled deeply. The smell of roasted garlic and rosemary wafted out. He sighed with pleasure and began to salivate.

Even though the contents had shifted during travel, he could tell it had been plated and garnished with pride. A large portion of rosemary garlic roasted rack of lamb sat center stage, atop a thick, biodegradable plate, surrounded by creamy mashed potatoes, a generous serving of roasted root vegetables, and a portion of honey-ginger glazed carrots.

"Bon appétit!" she said, proudly. "I assumed, being Irish, you might enjoy roast lamb."

He sat there, dumbstruck, overwhelmed by her generosity and care. The only words he could muster were, "Thank you." After a pause, he added a little humour to conceal his emotions at the touching gesture. "Now, this is the stuff I was telling you about earlier. I remember it well." he said, with a grin. Ingrid smiled back at him. For a brief moment, he felt something stir in the pit of his stomach — a quiet flutter he hadn't expected. He broke eye contact first, clearing his throat as he reached for his tea, grateful for something to occupy his hands.

Delighted he was happy with the gesture, Ingrid unpacked her meal, pulled up the comfortable bedside chair, and balanced the thin cardboard box on her thighs as a table.

The food was delicious. They ate and chatted. Ingrid told him about her day, omitting the gory details of the multi-vehicle collision that had brought eleven people into the emergency room and kept her busy for much of the afternoon. Mac shared stories of some of the flights he had enjoyed in the Congo, going into great detail about the spectacular scenery.

She mentioned her aid work at Rhino camp and her wish to visit Murchison Falls, but time was always against her. They talked about the stunningly beautiful places in Africa. Both wanted to go on a photographic safari in the Serengeti, cross over into Kenya, and visit the Maasai Mara. They both wanted to stay on the Mara River to watch the tail end of the migration. And both, they discovered, had once booked — then had to cancel — a trip to Zanzibar for work-related reasons.

Zanzibar was an enchanting island, roughly thirty kilometers off the Tanzanian mainland. Steeped in Arabic, Portuguese, Persian, and, more recently, British history. Stone Town, a UNESCO World Heritage site, was a photographer's paradise, with its narrow streets, eclectic buildings, old mosques, and the Sultan's Palace. Just beyond the town lay miles of pristine beaches, where Ingrid dreamed of soaking up the sun while watching dolphins off the coast.

Mac, on the other hand, was drawn towards the Jozani Forest to see the red colobus monkeys, the only place on the planet where they could be observed in their natural habitat. He wanted to visit the slave caves. They were equally keen on a spice tour to sample the local cuisine. They bantered playfully about the best 'things to do' in Zanzibar, almost as if they had planned the trip together.

They sipped their tea, and Mac commented that this was the best meal, and company, he'd had in a long time.

Ingrid smiled, picking up the empty plates and disposing of them. "I've really enjoyed this evening, but it's getting late, and I have an early start in the morning."

"See ya. Safe home, now, Doc."

"Sleep well, Mac."

Left alone with his thoughts, Mac wondered what he would do once discharged. One thing was certain... he wanted to know Ingrid better.

Chapter 58

By mid-June, life was moving towards a modicum of normalcy. Emily and Andrew, thrust together by tragedy and bound together by love, were smitten. Emily had moved into Andrew's trailer, and Andrew had returned to work.

Andrew was doing well, all things considered, though he had days when he would brood — but that was to be expected. Both she and space were there for Andrew, and Emily left the choice up to him.

Andrea had named the baby Travis Jr. — he was indeed the spitting image of Travis. Andrea was a beautiful soul, and she and Emily got on swimmingly. Andrea's loss was senseless, and she didn't deserve to be alone. Emily would drop in from time to time. They would take long walks, with little Travis in his pram and Buddy off-leash, padding next to them. They'd end up on Andrea's back deck, sipping iced tea — something that took Emily a while to get used to.

The Kochs had lent Emily their old Toyota Corolla, giving her the freedom to get around, and she would often stop by to have coffee with Rosemary on the porch. Buddy had grown quite attached to Emily, and vice versa. He would accompany her on long hikes through Guadalupe River State Park. Expectantly, as she stood to leave, he'd bound off the deck and plonk himself next to the car. She'd open the rear door, he'd jump onto the back seat, slobber on the window, spin around in circles before settling down, his tail thumping the seat. Emily would make a half-hearted attempt to clean the glass, nuzzle the big pooch, and mutter something along the lines of 'you're lucky you are so cute!' before rolling the window down. They'd drive off, Buddy's head outside, ears flapping and tongue lolling, in the warm summer breeze.

Andrew had shown Emily the plans for the house. As they pored over the architectural drawings, Andrew encouraged her to make suggestions or changes. She saw no need to make any structural changes but was keen to help with the interior decor and, in particular, the landscaping.

She had always loved gardens. During her travels, she made a point of visiting as many botanical gardens, parks, and green spaces as possible. She borrowed Andrew's library card and checked out the maximum number of books allowed — all on horticulture, specialising in plants that grew well in central Texas.

Rosemary, too, was an avid gardener. On their bi-weekly visits to the Koch household — Wednesdays for laundry night and tacos, Sundays for roast beef or BBQ ribs — the two women would clear the table after dinner, spread out large sheets of drafting paper, sketchbooks, and reference books, and get to work on their masterpiece.

Rusty and Andrew would either sit on the deck over coffee or hang out in the workshop, tinkering on one piece of farm equipment or another, always with Buddy not far away.

Andrew was two payments away from owning the land free and clear, making him eligible for a loan to start building their house by September. Emily had applied for, and been offered, a job as a French teacher at the local high school, starting in the fall semester. However, this meant she had to return to the UK to apply for a work permit and was scheduled to leave at the end of the month.

She hadn't seen her parents in over a year and was both excited and trepidatious about the trip.

Chapter 59

Mac's recovery had been nothing short of miraculous, though it had come at a price. He had thrown himself into physiotherapy, pushing his body to its limits, each step away from the hospital bed a victory over the weakness that once threatened to consume him. The days were long and gruelling, and on the nights when he drove himself to the edge of exhaustion, he slept soundly. The demons that usually haunted him were held at bay by the weight of his fatigue. For the first time in a long while, silence greeted him in the darkness.

Still, the cane would be his companion for a while longer. Ingrid and his physiotherapist said it could take a few months, and for Mac to be patient. They could not decide whether he was impatient or just downright stubborn when he said he would be running in a month. But even as his body healed, his thoughts remained restless, circling the same unanswerable question; Where would he go when this was all over? The truth was, he had nowhere else to go. The compound was shuttered in Goma, Clarke Aviation, now in Arusha, mothballed, and the airlines were no longer an option. He had no home to return to. No plan. The idea of facing the empty spaces of his past filled him with a quiet dread he rarely admitted, even to himself.

It was Ingrid who broke through that uncertainty, though not in the way he had expected. After his discharge, she had offered him her guest room. He had agreed, though he hadn't thought much beyond the moment.

The days in her home had blurred into weeks, both of them settling into a rhythm that felt strangely natural, as though they had been orbiting each other for longer than either realised. There were late-night conversations over tea, quiet mornings where they would steal glances at each other from across the kitchen, and moments where words weren't necessary at all.

It wasn't until one evening, after a particularly long day of appointments and rehab, that Ingrid had made the first move. She stood in the doorway to her room, a soft smile tugging at her lips, and said, "Mac, you don't have to stay in the guest room."

His heart had stuttered in his chest, his gaze meeting hers, searching for the unspoken question in her eyes. He had hesitated only for a second. Then, with a quiet nod, he had followed her.

Mac loved cooking and taking care of the house, and all the chores that came with it. Ingrid loved not having to think about meals and shopping. Mac could not recall any time in his life when he felt this good. He doted on Ingrid, surprising her with picnics in the garden, baking her favourite treats, and planning quick overnights out of the city.

Ingrid hadn't had many serious relationships. She told Mac that, when she was with him, the world seemed to blur and fade, leaving only the two of them. No one had ever made her feel so singular, so completely seen. There was a stillness in his gaze when he looked at her, as if he were mapping the contours of her soul, not just her face. When he touched her hand, it wasn't just a gesture — it was a quiet promise, a steadying warmth she hadn't known she craved. In a world full of people, Mac made her feel like the only one that mattered.

Mac wore his jovial, easy-going manner like a tailored suit — one he slipped into effortlessly when in public. But in the quiet moments, when no one was watching, shadows crept in. His thoughts often took a darker turn, leaving him adrift in a sea of melancholy. He would sit, staring at nothing, feeling as though life was moving around him — he was in it, but not part of it. His children, and now Ingrid, were the only threads that kept him tethered to the present. They were his anchor in a life he often felt was slipping away.

Mac was technically illegal in the country. His passport had not been stamped, and he wasn't ready to deal with the Ugandan home office. He reached out to Patrick for a favour. Patrick was happy to make the call and was delighted to hear that Mac was doing well. Patrick sent Mac the name and number of the taxi driver he'd used whilst in Kampala, saying he could be relied upon if Mac needed him.

Mac and Ingrid were enjoying a beautiful, sunny, midweek afternoon picnic in the backyard. A dense, six-foot-tall, multi-coloured hibiscus hedge, in full bloom, gave them privacy. He had made a Cobb salad, and they were eating it at the round garden table under a large white umbrella, sipping a palatable Chablis.

Mac, in a pair of khaki bathing shorts and bare-chested, sat opposite Ingrid, who was in a two-piece yellow bikini. He had mowed the lawn that morning and set the sprinkler going. Ingrid had put on one of her favourite pieces of music, Claude Debussy's *Bergamasque Suite* - a tranquil and sometimes sprightly four-movement piano composition. The rhythmic tic-tic-tssht of the sprinkler, and the chattering of the red-chested sunbirds frolicking in the water, created a zen-like ambience.

Their peaceful lunch was interrupted by Mac's ringtone. They had agreed on no phones at the table unless Ingrid was on call. But Mac had been waiting for this. He'd been restless all week, anxious about the visa situation hanging over his head.

"Sorry." Mac said, standing and answering the call. After a brief conversation, he hung up and sat back down, his brow furrowed in thought.

"That was Patrick, so it was. I'm to meet with an immigration officer tomorrow evening at Entebbe Airport. He'll stamp my passport, backdating it to when I arrived. That'll give me six months from then." He paused, doing the maths. "So, about three months left now before I'll need to leave and reapply from overseas."

Ingrid leaned back, crossing her legs, her face serious. "What then, Mac, are you ready to make Uganda your home?"

Mac exhaled slowly, rubbing the back of his neck. "I don't know, but what I do know is, I want to be with you. Aye, that is one thing I am certain of." He met her eyes. "I don't want to leave, not if I don't have to."

"And your Cati and Connor?"

"Aye, I need to visit the kids for sure. Connor is graduating this year, and I promised I'd be there. Also, I've got to go to Toronto to see Catriona. I can't keep putting that off. It's been almost two years, and she still hasn't spoken to me. If I don't try now..." He trailed off, his eyes darkening with the weight of it. "As you know, her mother and I had a turbulent marriage and a messy divorce. Cati took it hard, and her not talking to me is devastating. It's like watching your heart walk away from you... and not knowing what to do or say to get it back."

Ingrid had pushed her chair back, kicked an empty chair sideways, stretched out her legs, crossing them at the ankles, and had her glass poised at her lips. She looked over the rim into the tormented eyes of the man she had grown to love in such a short time, and her heart ached at the turmoil he was carrying.

"Oh, shite. Sorry. This was supposed to be a romantic and relaxing afternoon. You know, I had this all planned. Feed you, ply you with wine in the sun, convince you it was in your best interest to remove that bikini and take a cool, invigorating shower with me. Then I'd take advantage of that stunning body of yours."

Ingrid sipped her wine slowly, biting down on her bottom lip seductively. Half-closing her eyes, she raised her eyebrows, her voice now sultry and low. "So, that was your plan, Captain?"

Standing up, she walked towards the house, looking back over her shoulder. She untied and dropped her bikini top onto the ground, winked slowly at him, and said, "Well then, Dalton McBride, what are you waiting for?"

Ingrid woke the following morning to an empty bed and heard Mac in the kitchen. She slipped out from beneath the sheets, shimmied into her peach silk kimono, and padded silently downstairs and into the kitchen. She pulled up a stool and sat at the counter.

"Good morning, sir. What does a girl have to do to get a coffee in this joint?" Ingrid said, executing a terrible American accent. Mac, halving oranges to juice, turned to face her, laughing, as he crossed the room in a few big strides. He tilted her head back and kissed her deeply and passionately.

"That ought to do it," he said, smirking. Reaching behind the counter, he pulled out the carafe, poured her a cup, and returned to juicing the oranges. Ingrid smiled.

"Dalton McBride! Did I just see you walking without your cane?"

"Sure. Not my brightest moment, but you looked so damn appetising! Eggs Florentine okay for breakfast?"

The food was fabulous, filling the kitchen with warmth and the aromas of fresh spinach and creamy hollandaise. They lingered over their plates, savouring the meal and the quietness of the morning. Mac hummed and loaded the last of the dishes into the dishwasher as he waited for Ingrid.

Ingrid's footsteps echoed lightly as she trotted back down the stairs, hair still damp from her shower and smelling faintly of coconut. "I'm ready, Dalton McBride." she called, her voice carrying a hint of excitement.

Mac noticed she had four names for him; his full name, or captain, when she was playful or flirtatious; Dalton in conversation; and Mac when she was serious. He liked how it made him feel.

They finally set off for their much-anticipated outing to the equator. "It's known as the line of 0 degrees, where people like to pretend they weigh less. The gravitational pull is weaker at the equator, after all. I go there in lieu of the gym." Ingrid teased as they backed out of the driveway.

"Aye, catch yerself, Doc. You need neither." he playfully retorted.

They were making their way out of Kampala. Mac joked that the city planner must have been born in a rondavel, as they entered and exited three traffic circles in under a kilometre, and a further four in the next four kilometres, before finally merging onto the main road heading east.

"A rondavel?" Ingrid asked, quizzically, as she accelerated, pulled out, and passed another overloaded bus belching black smoke.

"It's a small roundhouse with a conical roof. You must have seen them; they are everywhere in the Congo and, I suspect, all over Africa."

The conversation flowed easily, and before Mac realised it, they had slowed down, the indicator blinking, and were turning into the crowded parking lot at the equator.

There were a dozen or so minivans and four-wheel-drive safari vehicles, all emblazoned with colourful decals advertising their companies and tours. The car park was teeming with tourists, ranging from twenty to seventy years old. The latter dressed head to toe in colour-coordinated safari gear, sporting logos from companies like LL Bean and Mountain Warehouse, and lugging bulky cameras. The younger generation wore shorts, bright t-shirts, and sandals, most armed with selfie sticks. Others had their arms outstretched, snapping selfies, and immediately checking them before uploading to Snapchat and other social media platforms.

Ingrid found a parking spot away from the crowd, a short walk to the large upright concrete circle with 'Uganda Equator' painted on the top, and the letters N on one side and S on the other, depicting the northern and southern hemispheres. People stood in the centre in all manner of poses, one foot in each hemisphere.

Ingrid shut down the SUV and they slipped out, locking the doors behind them. They wound their way through the crowd, listening to the excited chatter in accented English and a multitude of foreign tongues. They passed souvenir stands selling everything from waxed batik tablecloths and djembe drums to Uganda football jerseys and ornately carved wooden animals.

They eventually made their way into the Aidchild Cafe and Gallery — a low concrete building with a high thatched roof, which gave the interior a cool, airy feel. The rich aroma of freshly brewed coffee mingled with the scent of wooden carvings and textiles. They were still full from breakfast but decided to have coffee while browsing the 'Made in Uganda' products. Both agreed that the coffee was some of the best they had tasted. They found the coffee section and purchased half a dozen bags of medium-roast organic beans, with twenty percent of the proceeds going to the charitable organisation, Aidchild.

Mac bought a few items for Connor and Cati, while Ingrid fawned over a tablecloth and placemats. She argued with Mac when he wanted to buy them for her but finally relented. Mac placed them onto his pile and had them tally up his order. He thanked the friendly staff and paid for their purchases.

They walked outside onto the covered veranda, finding an empty table in the corner, where they watched the antics of excited tourists and their flustered guides. The guides set up large, clear water bottles on either side of the equator, pouring water through funnels to display the Coriolis effect, where the water would enter the bottle clockwise in the south and counterclockwise in the north. The guides also attempted to balance a chicken egg on a nail, but neither Ingrid nor Mac saw either experiment work to any degree of accuracy and deemed the results inconclusive.

Finally, the guides shepherded their flocks back into the vehicles. "It's like herding bloody cats!" Mac quipped. "I'm happy they are not my monkeys, and it's not my circus."

Finally, car doors slammed, engines fired up, dust billowed, and then silence ensued. In contrast to her usual cool demeanour, Ingrid found herself asking the waiter to take a touristy souvenir photo of her and Mac in the big concrete circle. The couple playfully posed and giggled like a pair of love-struck teenagers. Mac hid his cane behind him as the waiter snapped a dozen pics — the joys of digital photography.

Just after three, they piled back into the Nissan and headed to Entebbe airport to meet with the immigration officer. They were looking forward to having dinner at the Crane Cafe, where Raj's butter chicken was renowned amongst the ex-pat community. Ingrid had called ahead to make sure Raj would be making his signature dish.

Chapter 60

Andrew had been taking on extra shifts and studying for his upcoming recertification. Emily divided her time between Andrea, Rosemary, and puttering in her small vegetable garden behind the trailer. She was enjoying the southern lifestyle and had even started listening to country music... voluntarily.

"Hey, where did these come from?" Andrew pointed to a pile of CDs he knew weren't in his collection.

"I borrowed those from your mom. Oh, and a couple from Andrea." Among them were Loretta Lynn, Merle Haggard, Keith Urban, and Garth Brooks.

Although they weren't much for going out, they occasionally visited a local bar with live music. Mostly, they'd sit outside on the deck, letting the music wash over them while still being able to have a conversation without yelling.

"Don't be making no plans for Friday." Andrew said, excitement flashing in his eyes, as they sat on the near-empty deck sipping their drinks and snacking on nachos. "We're going to the Old Barn Country Bar. It's way out in the middle of a field — hay bales, old tractors, rusty cars, even a mechanical bull — the whole kit and caboodle."

Emily nodded, tilted her head, raised her eyebrows, and said, "Are we now?"

"Yes ma'am. It's the Annual Fireman's Ball fundraiser. See, the local police and fire departments have to raise extra money for work in the community that their budget doesn't allow for. By the way, darlin', we just pitched in two hundred bucks, so we gotta go! We'll drink us a couple of long necks, and gal, you best learn you some line dancing!" He stood up, stuck his thumbs in his belt loops, performed a quick two-step, and pulled out all stops on his accent.

Finger on chin, Emily replied in her crisp British schoolteacher tone, "Correct me if I'm wrong, but I think what you're trying to say is, we will consume some bottled beers and partake in some form of southern prancing. And by the way, it is 'girl,' not 'gal.'" She raised an eyebrow, a small smirk tugging at her lips, and a game of accent war was afoot.

He laughed, then took her hand, pulling her into an impromptu line dance right there on the patio. "Well, gal, reckon I'll show you how it's done... Texas style!"

She resisted at first, embarrassed, but soon found herself shuffling awkwardly to his makeshift rhythm. "I am warning you, Andrew, I shall never perfect this dancing!"

The few people on the deck clapped and cheered them on good-naturedly.

"Oh, I don't know," he teased, twirling her in place. "Might just make a country gal outta you yet."

Chapter 61

Peter and Ryan were relaxing in the office after their morning workout regime and discussing flying down to Cape Town to spend a few weeks sailing. They'd been back from Goma for six weeks and were both restless and longing for the ocean.

Simone tapped on her glass cubicle, getting their attention. Ryan, who was facing the cubicle, looked up as Simone wheeled her chair back behind her desk and signalled for them to come into the office. The two set their coffee cups on the table and strolled casually into Simone's inner sanctum.

"Morning, gentlemen." Simone said, with a smile. "Patrick has a mission for you guys. A little different than the normal protection detail. He wants to see you when he is off the phone, so don't venture too far. And before you ask... the answer is no, I cannot tell you the details."

Ryan broke into the theme tune from 'Mission; Impossible' when the intercom interrupted him. Patrick's voice, tinny through the speaker, said, "Simone, did you find the guys?"

She pressed the flashing red button and said "They're right here."

"Please send them in."

Patrick was standing in front of his desk, and as usual, impeccably dressed. Today he wore a tailored charcoal-grey three-piece suit with fine burgundy pinstripes, a pale blue button-collared shirt, and a burgundy silk tie. Ryan and Peter always felt very underdressed in his presence, yet Patrick had a way of making anyone he met feel comfortable and at ease.

The three shook hands, and Patrick gestured for them to take a seat on the sofa. He took the armchair on the opposite side of the coffee table. He detested sitting behind his desk when hosting meetings. No matter the importance, he preferred a more relaxed atmosphere.

"Coffee, gentlemen?" he asked. Both declined.

"Okay, guys. I'll get right to it. We've been asked to train a small team on close detail protection for foreign investors attending a conference in Mogadishu."

Both Peter and Ryan looked quizzically at each other but knew better than to interrupt.

"The First Somali Bank is sponsoring the Technology Entertainment Design Conference later this year in an attempt to showcase Somalia's stability, and their improvements in security to foreign investors. Coca-Cola has just opened a factory in the country, as has Hormuud Telecom. Renovations are in progress at Aden Adde International Airport. Turkey has just finished building their state-of-the-art control tower, and the United Arab Emirates have recently upgraded their hospital. In short, billions of dollars are pouring in, and they want to be the go-to place for investing in East Africa. There is talk about upgrading and renovating the port, which is ideal for goods coming out of Central Africa. Questions so far, guys?"

They looked at each other, then Peter spoke. "Are we talking about the same Mogadishu where Mohamed Farrah Aidid attacked and killed a couple of dozen Pakistani peacekeepers? The same Mogadishu where they shot down two of George Bush's Blackhawk helicopters later that year? And the same Mogadishu that houses pirates who take over ocean liners, cargo ships, and pleasure boats off its coast? If it is that Mogadishu, sure, that sounds like a jolly good time. Makes Goma look like Disney World."

Patrick smiled, nonplussed. "Yes, the very same Mogadishu, but it's been calm for the past six or so years, other than the Maersk Alabama cargo ship that was boarded and taken in 2009."

Ryan interjected, "Patrick, I trust you. You know this. I know without a doubt you will have our backs. I believe I speak for the pair of us. We are fresh out of the Congo, where nothing was supposed to happen. I think we may need some reassurances that this is not going to be another Mavavi situation."

"Fair enough." Patrick replied. "Your task is a reconnaissance mission; identify the safest ingress and egress points, threat assessment, and training of two teams. You will not be armed, you will not partake in the protection detail, and you will be out of the country before the conference starts.

We have secured a house in the Hodan neighbourhood. There are eight routes onto Jazeera Road, which leads to both the airport and docks. It is a wide, four-lane boulevard. You are ten minutes to the American Embassy compound, five minutes to the United Emirates Hospital, and fifteen minutes to Aden Adde International Airport.

We have also secured an abandoned trucking company warehouse to use for training. The interior will be set up with a gym, debrief station, weapons training and so on. The exterior is large enough for advanced driving techniques. The warehouse is only ten minutes from the safe house."

"Your Land Cruiser is, as we speak, on its way from Goma and should be waiting for you when you arrive, should you decide to take this mission. As you are aware, you're free to decline the task. I just wanted to offer it to you first."

Peter and Ryan looked at each other for a long moment, so in tune with each other, they instinctively knew what the other was thinking.

"When do we deploy?" Ryan asked.

"Thanks, gentlemen. Next Friday. SAA flight from Oliver Tambo Airport direct to Aden Adde. Simone will have all the intel and packages complete and ready for you on Monday. Go through them, and we will meet on Wednesday for a briefing."

Patrick stood up, signalling the meeting was over. Ryan and Peter stood, and the three men shook hands.

Chapter 62

Ingrid and Mac parked at Entebbe International Airport just after five-thirty. The faint smell of jet fuel hung in the cloying air, as they walked hand in hand towards the terminal. The airport concourse was quiet, almost unnaturally so, with only the hum of distant air conditioners, and the occasional announcement echoing through the vast space. According to the departures and arrivals board, there was only one inbound flight scheduled to arrive at eight. Outside, the muggy air of Uganda clung to the glass doors, while inside, the sterile chill of air conditioning cooled the terminal. Mac was feeling the strain of the day. He had been sitting far too long, and leaned heavily on his cane.

They found their way to the information booth, manned by a bored attendant scrolling through her phone. She looked up and asked if she could help, but her look and demeanour told them it was the last thing she wanted to do.

Mac, tired and in pain, was in no mood for pleasantries. He had always believed if you have a job, do it to the best of your abilities, or not at all, because there will always be someone willing to do it better. He uncharacteristically got straight to the point.

"I have an appointment with Mr. Mutesi in immigration. Please call him and let him know Captain McBride is here to see him."

He rarely used his title, and 'captain' could denote any of a multitude of positions. His tone and abrupt manner had the young woman calling him 'sir' and quickly contacting the immigration department. Ingrid wasn't used to seeing Mac so curt. Part of her wanted to chide him for it, but she also understood the fatigue that gnawed at him after long days. She wondered if her own weariness had sometimes made her less patient, especially when lives were on the line. But still, his frustration seemed... different here, more sharpened, perhaps by their surroundings.

They took a seat while they waited. A little tension hung in the air. Ingrid was about to ask if he was okay, when a portly man of about sixty years old came around the corner in an immaculate immigration uniform. He stopped in his tracks and then beamed.

"Doctor Svenson! How are you?"

Ingrid felt her cheeks flush with embarrassment as the man beamed at her. Where had she met him? His face didn't ring any bells, and she tried to keep her expression neutral, rifling through the many faces she had encountered over the past months.

"Um... hello. Sorry, I cannot recall meeting you." Ingrid said sheepishly.

"I don't expect you would. You were so busy when I saw you last. Three months ago, my wife was involved in an auto accident along with many others and was rushed to your hospital. You attended to her — seven stitches above the eye, a broken leg, concussion — and you kept her in for observation when another doctor wanted to release her. You stopped by, twice, late at night, to check on her. You were kind to her."

It all came back to Ingrid; the multi-vehicle collision that interrupted hers and Mac's first lunch.

"Oh, yes! Priscilla. How is she?"

"Very fine, doctor, very fine, thanks to you." he said, turning to face Mac, who had struggled up and was resting on his cane.

"Captain McBride. I am James Mutesi." he said, reaching out his hand.

Mac shook hands and smiled. "Pleasure to meet you, sir."

"Come with me and I will take care of your passport. It's not far."

Mac and Ingrid followed him to a small room, took the two seats offered to them, while James sat behind the small metal desk.

"May I have your passport, captain?"

Mac handed him his passport. James found a blank page, picked up his stamp, rewound the date and stamped Mac's passport.

"I can only issue you a six-month visitor visa. Usually, it is only three, but six will not be questioned. We do that for certain visitors who are engaged in aid work, research, and other important matters. As an ambulance pilot, we can use the aid work angle. If you wish to stay longer, come and see me, and I will do what I can."

Twenty minutes later, they were in the Crane Cafe, sipping fresh mango juice, and being entertained by Shadrick — the same enthusiastic waiter who had served Emily and Father O'Donnell a few months previously.

"So, what was eating you with the woman at the information stand?" Ingrid enquired.

"Ah, I'm just exacerbated by the discrepancies between the haves and have-nots. Some of those who have employment are too blind to appreciate such an opportunity, when others would view it a gift. They would be happy, if not proud, to go to work every day."

He told her of William, the crew accommodation cook, and his wife Aminata, in the Congo. How hard they worked. How much they loved being able to take care of their kids, and they were a joy to be around. Mac shifted uncomfortably in his chair, his hand gripping his cane a little tighter as he spoke of William and Aminata. His voice grew softer, more raw, and Ingrid noticed his jaw clench, as if he were holding back more than just words.

She knew he was wondering what had happened to them after the rebels had violently overrun Goma. Ingrid placed her hand on his. She was moved by his tenderness and compassion; just one of a number of reasons why she was falling so heavily for Mac.

Shadrick approached the table, excitedly, almost bouncing on the balls of his feet and rubbing his hands together, whilst apologising profusely for interrupting. A smile beaming across his face.

"You are in for a treat tonight." He leaned in, as if ready to divulge a state secret, glanced at the kitchen, as if he could get caught at any second, and whispered, "I always taste the butter chicken before I bring it out — shhhh, don't tell anyone. And tonight's is the best I have ever had!" Shadrick's smile was wide and true, but there was a brief moment — when he spoke of tasting the butter chicken — that his eyes seemed to darken, like a shadow flitting across his face. It was gone before Mac could place it, replaced by his infectious enthusiasm.

He quickly stood upright, clapped his hands, giggled, and called out over his shoulder, "You'll see. Delicious!" He brought his finger to his lips, reminding them it was a secret, as he retreated to the kitchen.

Ingrid looked at Mac, and they both chuckled.

Mac said. "Now that is a man who clearly loves his job."

True to Shadrick's words, the meal was exceptional. And Mac mentioned, more than once, it was indeed the best butter chicken he'd ever tasted and to please pass their compliments to the chef.

"I hear the coffee here is pretty good." Mac said, as he leaned back in his chair and stretched out his legs.

"No sir. The coffee is not pretty good; it is the best in the whole airport."

"There is nowhere else that sells coffee in the airport." Mac said, catching Shadrick's joke, but playing along.

"See, I told you. The best coffee in the airport and maybe all of Kampala." Shadrick said, gleefully, laughing at his joke.

"You have to be one of the most exuberant waiters I have ever met." Mac smiled. "You bring joy to dining here."

Ingrid found the exchange endearing. "Can we have two americanos, please." she asked, politely.

The espresso machine hissed and gurgled in the background. Shadrick returned a few minutes later with the coffee, two single-serving jugs of hot milk, and a white ceramic container of sugars and sweeteners.

"So tell me, Shadrick. Where are you from?" Mac enquired, with genuine curiosity.

"I am from Kitgum, in the north, sir." He answered, guardedly.

Mac did not know where it was, but Ingrid did and said, "I'll tell you about it another time. Go on Mac." She was clearly enjoying Mac's interaction with the young man and liked how Mac had the ability to make almost anyone he met feel like they were important. Mac smiled at Ingrid, a smile that tugged at her heartstrings. She laced her fingers with his, placed her elbow on the table, and cradled her jaw in her free hand, her smile never dimming, as Mac continued.

"You must know that the people who come here are either entering or leaving Uganda, and your enthusiasm is either the first impression they get upon arrival, or the last thing they will remember before leaving. You are truly an ambassador to your country. Well done, young man."

Shadrick, now appearing somewhat bashful, bowed his head, smiled, and said, "Thank you, sir."

Mac continued, "You know, Shadrick, food is not the only reason people come to a restaurant. Of course, it has to be good, but it's the service that brings them back. It matters not if it's a café in an airport, or a five-star restaurant in town, it's the customer experience that counts. And you, my friend, bring a whole new meaning to the dining experience. Shadrick, you have a gift. A true gift. Don't ever lose it, son."

Ingrid smiled and tilted her head upward, still cradled in her hand. Shadrick stood there, blinking as if Mac's words were too much to take in all at once. He opened his mouth, then closed it, his throat bobbing as he swallowed hard. The tears in his eyes glittered under the restaurant lights, one finally slipping down his cheek. "I - I don't know what to say, sir." His voice cracked with emotion, and he quickly wiped the tear away with the back of his hand.

As Shadrick turned from the table, Ingrid caught a fleeting look in his eyes. Something deep and distant that contrasted sharply with his bubbly demeanour. It was gone in an instant, but it left a faint unease hanging in the air.

"Did I say something wrong? I thought I was complimenting him."

Ingrid squeezed his hand and said, "No, you were so thoughtful and fatherly to him. Maybe he's not used to someone complimenting him. Especially from a white man. Sadly, we are on a continent where they are not looked upon as equals."

Shadrick had not returned by the time they had finished their coffee, so they paid the bill at the counter. Mac returned to the table and discreetly left a generous tip under the water pitcher so no-one else could see it. He and Ingrid loitered in the main terminal hoping to say goodnight to Shadrick.

Chapter 63

Peter and Ryan touched down at Aden Adde Airport just after four in the afternoon, and were cleared through customs and immigration by five. Both were dressed in lightweight suits and blended well with the multitude of business travellers who had travelled to Somalia in preparation for the upcoming conference in a few months. Entering the arrivals terminal, a slender man with the skintone of dark Cuban tobacco and dressed in a white Ethiopian suit — a long sleeve knee-length shirt and matching trousers — was waiting with a sign, welcoming them to Mogadishu.

They greeted the man, who introduced himself as Abshir Farah. He explained that he would be their guide, translator, and driver on call, when, and if, needed. Peter's eyes flicked to the small sign held by Abshir, noting the crispness of the paper—too new, as if it had been printed minutes before they landed. He glanced at Ryan, whose face betrayed nothing but the slight tension in his shoulders told Peter they were both thinking the same thing; trust no one.

They followed him out of the terminal and loaded their luggage into a pristine Mitsubishi Pajero. Still unsure of who was playing on whose team, and in a country he felt was a tinderbox, Ryan crouched casually by his bag, his thumb brushing the camera button on his phone. He angled it subtly, not daring to look directly at the licence plate, as he captured the shot. He wasn't taking any chances, not after what happened last time. Everyone here could be working for someone, or no one at all. But in a place like this, that's just as dangerous.

Peter sat up front, and Ryan slouched in the back seat behind Abshir, quietly taking photos through the dark-tinted windows. Ryan asked Abshir to drive them through the downtown core before taking them to their hotel.

The streets of Mogadishu unfolded like a labyrinth; children darting through alleyways, vendors huddled under tattered tarps, and heavily armed soldiers lounging at checkpoints. Peter's eyes scanned every corner, every rooftop, and every parked car that could hide an ambush. The city felt like it was holding its breath, waiting for something to ignite.

Abshir looked confused, and said, "Mrs. Simone from your office told me to take you to your house in Hodan."

"The house is not ready yet." Ryan replied. "I'll let you know when it is, and have you take us there."

Ryan wanted to do his own vetting and have Simone run the plate in case their original driver had met with an unfortunate incident. He didn't want to risk being set up. After Mavavi, both were on high alert in sketchy countries, as Ryan aptly called it before boarding the plane from Johannesburg.

"We are staying at the Sahafi Hotel. Do you know it?" Peter asked.

"Yes, sure. We are not far. You call me when you go to your house." Abshir said, handing Peter his card. "You call Abshir anytime. Okay?"

Abshir went into a running commentary of which streets they were on, where the conference was being held, and pointed out historical landmarks. He also mentioned where the Blackhawk helicopters were shot down and the American airman was dragged through the streets in a bloody battle in October 1993. Peter exchanged a quick glance with Ryan as Abshir launched into his tour-guide speech. The man seemed eager to please, but that didn't mean he wasn't a plant. Trust was a luxury neither of them could afford — not after Mavavi. Abshir might be harmless, or he might be the first piece in a puzzle they weren't meant to solve.

Just before eight o'clock, Abshir dropped them at the Sahafi Hotel, where they bid him goodnight and told him they would be in touch in the morning.

They dragged their cases behind them and sat down in the lobby bar, ordering coffee. Ryan flipped open his sat phone, and called Simone, asking her to run the licence plate and send a picture of Abshir to his computer so he could verify both. The coffee was superb, and they looked around the lobby for anything that seemed out of place.

Of course, they were not going to stay there. It was indeed a fine hotel, however. It housed diplomats, aid workers, and foreign journalists — an ideal spot for a car bomb or suicide bomber. They planned to book into the Istanbul Mogadishu Hotel, not far from their safe house in Hodan. Ryan fired up his computer, linked into a secure network, and checked Simone's email. Abshir's smiling face was on his screen, and the car checked out, too. They were relieved and would call him in the morning.

They contacted the Istanbul Hotel and reserved two rooms, while Ryan paid their bill and asked the concierge to call a taxi. Forty minutes later, they were safely in their respective hotel rooms, making plans to meet at seven for breakfast.

Settling into his new room, Peter couldn't shake the feeling that Mogadishu might be a tougher battleground than the Congo had ever been. Not because of the open conflict, but because here you didn't know who your enemy was until they were standing in front of you, gun drawn and smiling.

Chapter 64

Mac caught movement from the corner of his eye. Shadrick, head bowed, was walking slowly back towards the restaurant. His demeanour had shifted, the jovial mask from earlier replaced by something heavier. Mac gently tugged Ingrid to a stop, waiting for Shadrick to approach.

"Hey, Shadrick," Mac called softly when he was within earshot. "I'm sorry if I said something to offend you, my boy. It was meant as a compliment."

Shadrick looked up, and Mac's breath caught. The young man had been crying. His face, once full of bright energy, now looked vulnerable, almost fragile.

"What's the matter, Shadrick?" Mac asked gently.

Shadrick swallowed hard, his voice wavering as he replied, "Sir, you called me 'son' when I was serving you. And now, 'my boy.' It's been over ten years since I've heard anyone call me that. I miss my parents so much."

Mac felt a knot tighten in his chest. What had started as a simple exchange had clearly touched something deep within Shadrick—something raw and painful. He hesitated for a moment, not entirely sure what to say, then the words came instinctively.

"Shadrick, when do you finish your shift?"

"After I clean your table, I'm done," Shadrick replied, his gaze still lowered, as if meeting Mac's eyes would release another wave of tears.

"We'll wait for you, if that's alright. I'd like to talk with you, but only if you feel up to it," Mac offered, his voice full of care. He turned to Ingrid, who gave a small, understanding nod. She had an early morning, but this moment felt too important to pass up.

"We'll be right here," Mac assured him, pointing to a nearby bench.

As Shadrick disappeared back into the restaurant, Ingrid and Mac sat down to wait. The time passed slowly, each of them lost in thought.

Ingrid broke the silence. "Kitgum. That's where he's from. It's part of the Acholi land. Joseph Kony's people..."

Mac nodded, listening, as she filled him in about the horrors in the Kitgum district—how Joseph Kony, an Acholi himself, had led a campaign of terror that ravaged his own people for decades in his war against the Ugandan government. The very mention of Kony's name made Mac's stomach twist. It wasn't hard to piece together the likely fate of Shadrick's parents.

By the time Shadrick reappeared, it had been almost half an hour. He approached them with a shy smile, sitting on the edge of the bench.

"Thank you for the tip." Shadrick said, quietly.

Mac shook his head. "You earned it. You were great tonight."

They chatted casually for a while, about nothing in particular—just enough to let Shadrick relax. It wasn't long before the young man's shoulders softened, the tension starting to ebb. And then, when the moment felt right, Shadrick spoke again, his voice quiet but steady.

"Sir, I have done bad things in my life, and I am ashamed of my past."

Mac responded gently, "Shadrick, your past is just that — the past. Some can forgive. And those who can't... well, that's beyond your control. You cannot change what's gone before, but you can make a better future for yourself."

After absorbing Mac's words and hesitating a little, Shadrick began telling his story. Mac and Ingrid sat in silence as his life unfolded before them, on a worn and scored airport bench.

"It was December 14th, 2002, when the soldiers came. I remember because we had just finished school for the term. I was seven years old. It was dark, and we were asleep. I heard people running and screaming. I heard a lot of shooting. We were in our hut—my mother and father, my sister Joyce, who was nine, and my brother Joshua, who was ten. The door was kicked down, and the soldiers were screaming for us to come out.

My father was begging them to take whatever they wanted, but to leave his family alone. One of the soldiers just shot him. My mother was screaming. The soldiers grabbed her, and one kicked her in the face. They then tore her clothes off and were beating her as they dragged her by the feet out of our hut. That was the last time I saw my mother. The soldiers forced us out of the hut and set it alight.

There were more gunshots and more shouting. I saw a woman lying on the ground. She'd had her breasts cut off. There were many men and women lying dead in pools of blood. I was hit on the head and ordered to go to the group of children who were gathered at the far side of our village. I saw a soldier slap my sister and force her to join us. My brother was already with the group of screaming and crying children when I got there.

The soldiers were beating and shooting people while setting our huts on fire. The whole thing lasted about an hour. We were then tied, hand to hand, in a row and forced to march, carrying the food, water, and the heavy cooking pots they had stolen from the huts before they burnt them to the ground.

I turned to look back at the village and saw the whole place was in flames. A soldier whipped me with a stick and told me to forget about Uganda; there was nothing left for me.

We marched all night and were beaten if we cried or made any sounds. There were about fifty children in a long single line. I could not see Joyce or Joshua. When one child fell down, they were beaten, and we had to help them up. If they could not get up, we were forced to beat them while we, too, were being beaten. Sometimes a soldier would come by and shoot a fallen person, then re-tie our hands to the next person.

We marched at night and were able to rest during the day, but were warned that if we tried to escape, we would be killed, so no one tried. Sometimes a soldier would select a girl and rape her in front of us, then laugh as the girl lay crying, and say that she is now his wife.

On the third day, we crossed into Sudan. The soldiers were celebrating and taking the girls. I found Joshua, and we decided to help Joyce escape. We found her and hid her in the bushes and told her to run away when it got dark. She was found late that afternoon and brought back to the camp. They were going to make an example of her and asked who her relatives were. Joshua and I came forward.

We were ordered to kill her. I was given a rifle and was told to shoot her. I had seen what had happened to the other girls and thought she would be better off dead, so I shot her. It was then I lost all feeling for anything. I think that is what the soldiers want—people who have no feeling or fear of death.

I was a child soldier for six years. Maybe I killed more than a hundred people. We fought against the Ugandan government army and raided lots of villages. My brother was killed in one raid, and a year later, I was injured and pretended I was dead. When the LRA left, I threw my gun away and went back to Kitgum. I was so ashamed of what I had done—killing so many people, and especially for killing my sister. I didn't want to talk to anyone. I was so afraid all the time. I was afraid of the national army. I was afraid of the police. And I was afraid of the LRA. I was afraid that if anyone found out about my crimes, they would kill me. I went to Lubujie camp, and they took me in. I said I was an orphan and that my family had been killed by the LRA."

Shadrick took a deep breath, staring at the ground. Then continued, "I lived in Lubujie for five years. I met a lot of people who came to help. They put in wells so we could have water. Others came with the Red Cross and the UNHCR. There was an American actress who set up a drama school and taught us acting. Some of us acted out what had happened in our lives, and I think that helped a lot of us... but then they stopped coming."

He faltered. Ingrid and Mac sat in stunned silence. Their hearts heavy, tears filling their eyes.

"People were getting sick from malaria, and there were no more doctors visiting. Many people died. I decided to come to Kampala to find work. I try to make people happy now... because I made so many people so sad."

Mac folded Shadrick into his arms, holding him tightly as the young man sobbed into his shirt.

Mac and Ingrid's drive home was one of quiet contemplation. Shadrick's story had left them both emotionally drained. It was just after ten when the garage door closed behind them.

Mac knew for certain that his life would never be the same after spending just an hour with this exceptional young man. He had not only witnessed the very worst of humanity; he'd been forced to be a part of it and survived. He thought about Cati and Connor, unable to imagine them enduring what he had heard tonight. He desperately wanted to talk to them, to tell them he loved them, to tell them to be safe, and to be thankful for every day. He did not think he could share tonight's story with them, especially not with Connor, who was a sensitive soul.

Ingrid, too, was deep in thought. She'd seen a lot in the camps where she volunteered, but she was never alone with a patient long enough to hear their heartbreaking stories. She suspected that many of the patients she had helped might have equally traumatic stories to tell.

They flipped on a few lights as they entered the house. Mac poured himself a scotch and cursed the fact that he had given up smoking — he could really use one now. Ingrid kissed him goodnight.

"I won't be long for bed myself." Mac reassured her.

Mac left the scotch untouched and went for a long, hot shower. But no matter how hot the water, or how much soap and scrubbing, he couldn't wash away any of the sadness he had heard tonight. He dried off and slipped into bed next to a sleepy Ingrid, kissing her gently before snuggling close. Ingrid fell asleep with Mac's arms wrapped around her. Mac quietly untangled himself and went back downstairs.

Mac sat at the kitchen table, the dim light casting long shadows across the room, as he stared at the blank page before him. His hands trembled slightly, the weight of Shadrick's trauma pressing heavily on his chest. He wasn't sure what to write or how to begin. How do you put into words the gratitude and fear that come from realizing your children live in a world that, on the surface, seems so distant from Shadrick's? Yet, beneath that surface, the same darkness lurks, waiting for an opportunity to strike.

He thought of Cati — her fierce independence and how she always seemed one step ahead of the world, ready to conquer whatever came her way. And Connor. Sensitive, thoughtful Connor, whose heart was always on his sleeve. Mac feared for him most. The weight of the world could crush his gentle spirit.

He took a deep breath and started to write, his hand steadying as he focused on them.

Dear Cati and Connor,

It is late here in Uganda, and you are so far away, but there are moments when a father's heart feels so full that he has to put down the things he wants to say before they fade away. Tonight was one of those nights. I won't go into detail, but I met someone. Someone who has been through hell and came out the other side. It's made me realise how much I love you both, how much I want to protect you, and how lucky we are to live in a world where the horrors others face aren't our own...

He stopped, realizing that his words felt hollow. How could he describe what Shadrick had been through without terrifying his children or diminishing its gravity? He scratched out the last few lines, frustrated.

His mind wandered back to Shadrick. Mac's heart ached for him — a boy forced to grow up too fast, who had seen too much. And yet, here he was, brave enough to tell his story. Brave enough to keep going.

Suddenly, Mac realised the letter wasn't just about telling his kids how much he loved them. It was about giving them a sense of the world outside their bubble. It wasn't just love he needed to impart; it was perspective. They needed to understand the importance of kindness, resilience, and gratitude.

He grabbed a fresh sheet of paper.

Dear Cati and Connor,

Tonight, I met a young man named Shadrick. He's not much older than you, Connor—maybe 21 or 22. He's been through things that I can't fully understand, things I would never want either of you to experience. But what struck me most about Shadrick wasn't just what he survived, it was the strength he has — the way he keeps moving forward despite everything. It reminded me of how important it is to be kind, to be grateful for what you have, and to help others when you can. You two have big hearts. Never forget how powerful that can be. I miss you both so much and cannot wait to see you.

Love, Dad x

He read it, re-read it, then folded the letter carefully, placed it in an envelope, and addressed it. He would mail it to them in the morning.

As he slipped back upstairs, he felt a strange mixture of heaviness and relief. Shadrick's story was now a part of him, woven into the fabric of his own life. And while he couldn't change the past or undo the suffering the boy had endured, maybe, in small ways, he could change the future by raising Cati and Connor to be the kind of people who would make a difference in this unkind world.

Chapter 65

Ten days before Emily was due to go back to the UK to secure her visa, the stillness of the morning was broken by the growl of a big truck idling outside the trailer, followed by the sound of air brakes being set. Voices and other diesel engines, belonging to other trucks, pulling to a halt and setting their brakes on the outskirts of their home, followed. She rubbed the sleep out of her eyes, stretched, and realised Andrew's side of the bed was cool. He must have been up for a while, she surmised. She swung her legs onto the floor, scrabbled for her jeans, and hoisted them on. She went to the closet, slipped on a t-shirt, glanced in the mirror, slipped it off again, found a bra, fastened it, and pulled the t-shirt back on before walking out onto the little deck, still shaking off the sleep.

Andrew, shirtless and dressed only in his boots and jeans, was standing at the rail, blowing on a mug of steaming coffee poised at his lips. The sun, cresting the trees, highlighted his unruly sandy hair and cast a long silhouette of him along the deck. Without turning to face her, he stretched out his left hand and handed her a mug of tea. She stepped up to join him at the railing.

"Mornin' Darlin'. Say good morning to our future." he said as he draped his arm over her shoulder, pulled her in close, and kissed the top of her head.

Her usual idyllic view of open prairies, tall grasses, and wildflowers stretching for miles was today replaced by a fleet of construction vehicles lining the road. A bright white Peterbilt truck stood nearest the driveway, its engine grumbling under its long hood. Two tall CB antennas, one on each mirror, stood shaking in time with the vibration of the engine. A low-stepped trailer, attached and loaded with three large, bright yellow pieces of construction equipment — only one of which she could identify as a bulldozer—was first in line. Two dump trucks were parked behind. One, tagged with a trailer, carried another piece of unidentifiable equipment, and the other, trailerless, had its door and window open. A pair of cowboy boots, crossed at the ankles, rested on the window ledge, their owner slouched in the seat, a cup of coffee in one hand and a cell phone pressed to his ear.

Two four-door pickup trucks brought up the rear of the convoy, their doors all open. Men were spilling out, toting coolers and sipping coffee, their hard hats tucked under their arms, chatting and laughing as they made their way up the driveway. Their conversation only halted long enough for a 'howdy, folks' greeting before resuming their conversation and destination.

A flurry of activity soon began. Equipment was fired up, the banging of ramps being dropped onto the hard earth, heavy chains clattering against the metal beds of the trailers as the equipment was freed from its bindings. The machinery was carefully driven off the trailers and up the driveway. Andrew and Emily walked off the deck and followed the dust trail beyond their trailer towards the site of their new home.

The foreman arrived a few minutes later, driving up to the site with a mobile office in tow. He parked, got out of the truck, and walked casually up to Andrew and Emily. He greeted Andrew by name, and Andrew introduced him to Emily. He shook her hand and simultaneously tipped the front of his hat with his index finger.

"Howdy, ma'am."

They walked the site together, laying out the plan of action and time frame before returning to the truck. He pulled out the plans that

Andrew and Emily had poured over for so long and unrolled them on the hood of the truck. They went over them one more time, ensuring this was the final draft and that everyone was on the same page.

Andrew and Emily were housesitting for his parents. Emily would miss them on their return, as she would be heading for England before they were due home, leaving Andrew to rattle around the house with Buddy.

They packed what they thought they might need but were not overly concerned. They'd pop back every few days to see the progress on the dig. Andrew threw on a clean t-shirt and tossed the two duffle bags into the Jeep, its top now removed for the summer. They waved goodbye to the builders as they drove out, spurred on by the promise of a hearty breakfast, as a truck arrived with two green porta-potties on a trailer. Andrew stopped, leaned out the door, and exchanged a few words with the two men before pointing out the foreman and wishing them a good day.

Rusty and Rosemary were leaving that night to help with a school-building project after the devastating monsoon hit Assam and Arunachal districts in the northeast region of India. The storm had claimed nearly two hundred lives and displaced almost two million people, making it the worst monsoon to hit India since 1998.

This was a massive group effort, with close to three hundred members volunteering for three weeks, from twenty-three participating Baptist churches from all corners of the United States. A forty-foot container full of clothing, blankets, toys, medical supplies, and bottled water — all privately donated — had set sail ahead of the party. It had landed, cleared customs, and was currently on route to the site.

Pulling into Rusty and Rosemary's driveway, Buddy, hearing the vehicle, came barreling around the corner and escorted them the last fifty meters. Buddy's tail was thrashing wildly, his head up, looking at Andrew as he greeted the affectionate pooch. They climbed out of the Jeep, and Buddy did his rounds, greeting them both before leading the charge up the porch and flopping down in front of the door, barring their entrance.

"Okay you, just lie in front of the door and thump the porch with your tail. Interesting tactic for stopping would-be burglars." Andrew said to Buddy as he patted his head and stepped over him, Emily following. "We've gotta work on your guard dog routine!"

Andrew kissed his mom, yelled 'hi' to his dad, who was in the kitchen preparing breakfast, and then went upstairs to deposit the bags in the guest room. Rosemary fussed over Emily. "Well, look at you, all tanned and all! Good Lord, gal, every time I see you, you look more country — and I'm here to tell ya, you wear it well! Come sit." She patted a stool at the kitchen counter. "Rusty is making his famous huevos rancheros for breakfast. Rusty, Honey, hand me that there coffee pot, will you? And two cups."

Later that afternoon, they packed Rusty and Rosemary's luggage into their car and drove them to the airport. Heartfelt goodbyes were exchanged, and Andrew and Emily watched as his parents met up, excitedly, with the other church members at the check-in desk. They were to stopover in Boston for the night and meet other volunteers before connecting to India the following evening. Andrew and Emily watched them through security, as Rosemary paused and blew kisses in their direction, picked up her hand luggage, and disappeared into the throng of travellers. Emily believed at that moment that Rosemary was one of those women who just had to show up, and things would already be better.

Andrew was proud of his parents. He had long since known that they could not sit by and watch the devastation unfold on television. They were among the few who actually got up, pressed the pause button on life, and pressed resume when they returned. They might have to press rewind to catch up, but they always managed. Times were often lean when they returned, but as Rosemary would say, "We were comfortable when we left, and we'll be comfortable again, and that is a luxury not everybody has."

Emily pressed into Andrew, stood on her toes, kissed his neck, and said, "This may sound corny, but I believe I have found out what belonging feels like."

"Yep, they kinda have that effect on a person." Andrew took her by the hand, and they began walking out of the terminal. "Ready for dinner? I've been waiting for a special occasion to take you to this great little restaurant, but, heck... you *are* the special occasion, Miss Esposito!"

Emily smiled and retorted, "Well, who could resist an invitation like that? And from such a slick, silver-tongued devil, with an irresistibly charming accent."

Soon, they were walking into one of the most visually appealing, quirky restaurants she had ever visited. She marvelled at the rustic charm of its reclaimed hardwood and rusty corrugated iron-clad walls. The exposed rafters, mismatched furniture, comfortable couches, and built-in wine racks spanned a warren of brightly painted rooms.

After meandering and enjoying the local artwork, they asked for a table on the patio. They perused the menu, and it all sounded excellent! They settled on bruschetta, a meat and cheese tray, a barbecue brisket pizza, and a bottle of house red. They listened to the chorus of cicadas as Andrew pointed out some of the stars and constellations.

Back at home, with Buddy fed and snoring on the tiled kitchen floor, Andrew resumed his tutorial of the northern skies, upon a red-checked blanket under the giant elm. He pointed out Cassiopeia, Cepheus, both Ursa Major and Minor, among other annually visible constellations. Emily gazed into the carpet of stars, her head on his chest, as he traced Scorpius and Sagittarius lightly on her arm.

Her eyes locked onto them in the sky. "And what about Libra?" she interrupted.

"I'm not sure I can find it. It's not the brightest of constellations."

"Careful, Mister! You are entering treacherous waters that could land you on the couch." Emily teased.

"Honey, it's a well-known fact. Libra is just... dim."

"That's it!" Emily exclaimed in mock indignation. With a playful glint in her eye, she straddled him, launching into an impromptu assault of tickling and laughter. But within moments, the laughter melted into something deeper. She traced her fingers down his chest, her touch light, deliberate. As she slowly unfastened his buttons, he followed suit, unbuttoning hers. Their lips met... soft at first, then urgent. He slid her blouse from her shoulders. His hands moved down her back, his fingers nimbly undoing her bra. As the fabric slipped away, she gasped softly, her breasts free, her erect nipples grazing his chest.

Her breath warm against his neck, she kissed the hollow of his throat, moving downward across his chest, her lips brushing his skin with aching slowness. Her tongue flicked over his nipple as she worked his belt loose, her fingers deftly unfastening his jeans. He groaned against her skin, his hands mapping the curve of her waist, the swell of her breasts, the arch of her back. Their movements were unhurried, savouring each discovery.

Emily shimmied down his legs, tugging off his boots before peeling away his jeans and underwear. Moonlight spilled over them, silvering her bare skin as she stood before him. His breath caught at the sight of her, luminous and unguarded, the night air wrapping around her like silk. He reached for her, but she lowered herself to him first, pressing her body against his, her warmth, her softness.

He drew her down onto the blanket, his lips tracing a slow path over her stomach. She gasped as he parted her thighs, his breath hot against her, his touch reverent. She ached for him, her body arching instinctively, welcoming. When he hovered above her, she guided him closer, pressing against him, the sensation making her tremble. Their bodies met in a slow, exquisite rhythm, a dance as old as time. She moaned into his ear, her fingers tangled in his hair.

They moved together, lost in each other, exploring, discovering, deepening. Every kiss, every touch, carried a silent promise, something unspoken but understood. They were no longer just lovers in the night; this was something more, something lasting.

When release finally claimed them, they held on, limbs entwined, their breaths mingling in the warm summer air. The stars above winked like silent witnesses. The night was alive with rustling leaves, the distant cry of a coyote, and the steady chorus of cicadas. Wrapped in the afterglow, Emily traced slow circles on Andrew's chest, pressing a lingering kiss to his shoulder. Neither spoke. They didn't need to.

Chapter 66

Peter and Ryan were having a working buffet breakfast. Peter was busy re-reading the bios of the two four-man teams that were scheduled to arrive in the morning. Ryan was checking on the whereabouts of their Land Cruiser, which was a day late in arriving. Peter had already called Abshir. He was on his way and would be joining them for breakfast shortly. The hotel buffet was an eclectic mix of local Somali dishes and Western breakfast staples. The scent of cardamom-spiced coffee mingled with the humid sea air that filtered through the open windows. Outside, the distant hum of traffic was punctuated by the occasional call to prayer, a reminder of where they were.

Abshir had no sooner sat down and started eating when Ryan's phone rang. Ryan answered, listened for a moment, then looked frustrated.

"What do you mean, you can't find it?" Ryan rolled his eyes. "Well, it's a big enough hotel... ask someone."

Abshir nodded at Ryan and signalled for him to hand over the phone. Ryan shrugged and handed Abshir the phone. A few hesitant words were exchanged until a common language was established, then a rapid-fire exchange of words, and Abshir disconnected the call.

"Okay, I'll go find him. He's at the Madina Hospital, it's not far."

As Abshir started to get up, Peter motioned him to sit and finish his breakfast, saying the driver was already a day late, and another half hour wouldn't matter. Abshir smiled gratefully, sat, finished his breakfast, and asked for a few rolls, assorted meats, dates, and a coffee to go, indicating it was for the driver. He took the bag of food and coffee and said he would be back soon.

Peter looked at Ryan and said, "I like him."

"Me too. The driver was irritating the fuck out of me. He was standing outside a huge hospital and didn't have the sense to ask where the Istanbul Hotel was?" Ryan grumbled, as he finished his coffee.

Peter could always tell when Ryan was workout-deprived; he became sullen, judgmental, and fractious, and the smallest of things irked him.

An hour and a half later, they checked out, paid the driver who had delivered their Land Cruiser, and tipped him handsomely. Peter and Ryan were both pleasantly surprised by the driver's neatness, his methodically organised paperwork, and receipts. Equally impressive was how clean the vehicle was, considering it had just completed a two-thousand-four-hundred-kilometre journey over some punishing terrain in Uganda and Northern Kenya. The man himself was dressed with fastidious care. He looked nothing like a man who had driven for over fifty hours and slept in a car for a week. Quite the contrary. His two-piece suit did not have a wrinkle in it, his white shirt crisp, and his pale blue tie knotted perfectly. He was clean-shaven and could have accomplished that feat using his shoes as a mirror.

"If we abort the road trip down to South Africa after this job, I wanna use this guy to deliver the vehicle to Joburg." Ryan muttered aloud, after realising he had made a bad call about the driver, who had exercised due diligence by not wanting to leave the vehicle unattended while he went inside a hospital to seek directions. "I need to go for a run and find a gym, before I kill something."

"Yes, you do, my friend!" Peter responded, smiling and punching Ryan on the arm.

They started their vehicle and followed Abshir. As they weaved through the narrow streets of Mogadishu, the city felt like it was holding its breath. Sturdy concrete houses stood shoulder to shoulder with crumbling, bullet-pocked walls. The streets were alive with a cacophony of vendors hawking their wares and children darting between donkey carts and tuk-tuks. Peter kept his eyes moving, alert to the unusual stillness in certain areas — places where the locals seemed to know better than to linger. Finally out of the city, they both let out a deep breath and sighed. The yards became bigger, and there were far fewer buildings per block.

Abshir stopped, put his hazards on, and signalled them to pull in behind him. He darted across the road and banged on a heavy steel gate with a man-door in the centre of it. They listened as he spoke with someone on the other side. Then, the man-door opened and a female's face looked at Peter and Ryan before smiling. The door closed, and the big steel gate slid open. Abshir signalled them to follow, and the two vehicles drove in, with the gate sliding closed behind them.

As Peter and Ryan alighted the vehicle, Abshir was kissing the woman on both cheeks. He then turned and introduced her.

"This is my sister Amara. She is a doctor at the UAE hospital. This is her house, and you are most welcome." Abshir said, his voice filled with pride.

"Hello and welcome. Which one of you is Peter and which is Ryan? You know, you white people all look the same to me." Amara said before her lips parted, revealing a brilliant smile and laughing. "You should have seen your faces. There is nothing similar between the two of you, barring, of course, your keen alert eyes. Come on in, let's get you guys settled. You have the entire place to yourselves. I'll be using the guest house for your duration. The team you are training will be staying with Abshir. We are both an equal distance from your training grounds at the old Swift trucking depot."

Amara stood out, her long dark hair falling loosely over her shoulders, a colourful scarf casually draped around her neck, more accessory than tradition. There was a playful sharpness in her gaze, a boldness that matched the lilt of her slightly Canadian-accented English. In a place where most women moved cautiously, Amara strode with the ease of someone who made her own rules. She wore neither a hijab, niqab, nor khimar. She was exotically beautiful and seemed not to be aware of it.

She showed them where everything was, offered them coffee or tea, and something to eat — it was the Arabic way — the only tradition she still honoured, as far as they could tell. She handed them the keys, the remote for the gate, and her business card, which had the hospital address and phone number. She flipped it over, where she had handwritten her personal cell phone number, and said, "This is the best number to reach me if you need anything. I've gotta run. Nice meeting you both. Abshir, are you still coming for dinner tomorrow? Call me if anything changes."

"I'll be there. See you at seven, habibi." Abshir called back, as she walked into the courtyard.

Peter and Ryan unpacked and changed into their running gear. Ryan tapped on Peter's door.

"I'll be waiting downstairs whenever you're ready."

Peter was right behind him and joined him in the hallway as they descended the steps together.

Abshir was sitting at the kitchen counter drinking a Turkish coffee when the men entered the kitchen.

"So, the house is not ready yet?" he said, referring to Peter's comment from yesterday. "Oh, and Ryan... do I have any outstanding driving or parking violations, seeing as you ran my licence plate?"

Smiling, his halting English was replaced with impeccable diction. "Don't worry, gentlemen. I would have done the same. A country brimming with corrupt leaders, locals who do not trust each other, and kids with more guns than the military. Yes, indeed, I would check everyone out."

Peter and Ryan looked at each other and then back at Abshir, before Ryan spoke.

"So tell me, Abshir. What's your story? Both you and your sister have impeccable English, obvious wealth. If this is your sister's house, and you are the male, yours must be bigger. What is your connection to our company?"

"The first two I can answer." Abshir said. "The third? You will have to ask Simone. It was she who reached out to me. The abandoned yard that you will be using was our father's trucking company. He was a successful businessman. My mother was his accountant and, before that, a brilliant lawyer, who could not practise in her field due to her gender. She had a natural-born talent and was often sought out to fact-check and coach. It worked well when the male lawyers won, and not so much when they lost. So instead, she worked with my father. And they did well — well enough to send us to school in Canada.

My parents were killed during the unrest. Their trucks were either stolen or burned, their property seized, and their bank accounts looted. A lawyer friend of my mother's brought a suit against the government, which at first would not budge, until they started receiving calls from foreign investors threatening to abandon deals as word spread about the illegal property seizures. They finally acquiesced. They did not give back everything, but we did get a house each, the trucking depot, and the insurance money from vehicles that were stolen, but not ones that were burned. As for their other assets, no one seems to know what they were, where they were, or their worth as all the papers were destroyed. New deeds, ownerships, and corporations were formed — all forgeries done from the highest levels, of course, but once the originals were destroyed, the new ones became the only ones.

After receiving a bachelor's degree in forensic sciences with criminology from the University of Toronto, I returned here and became an investigator for the military police. I recently resigned and am consulting with a team of experts, advising the government on launching our own national intelligence and security agency. It could be ready to go as early as next year. As you know, we are trying to re-establish ourselves as a sovereign stable country, hence all the investment and this upcoming dog-and-pony show.

"As for Amara, she studied medicine at McGill University in Montreal.. She still lives there, has her own practice, and married a doctor. She seems happy. She volunteers here six weeks a year, and the pair of them help out in some place or another. Almost every year, Mother Nature unleashes her fury, most often in some already desperately poor country, so they follow the devastation and do what they can. And, that, my friends, is the abbreviated life's resume." Abshir concluded. Peter scrutinised the man's face, searching for any cracks in his carefully presented story. Was this just the truth, or a version of it, shaped to put them at ease? Abshir had charm, sure, but charm could be a mask.

Abshir discarded his traditional dress, revealing his hidden running gear. "Mind if I join you for your run? I can show you the least congested areas."

Peter couldn't help but feel that the man had many more layers yet to peel back. For now, they would run. But soon, they would need to figure out exactly who they were running with.

"Sneaky little bugger." Ryan mused.

Chapter 67

The American Airlines Boeing 787 Dreamliner touched down just after seven in the morning at London's Heathrow Airport, with a chirp of the tires as they made contact with the wet runway. Emily was sitting over the wing and watched with fascination as the spoilers deployed, the engine thrust reversers engaged, and the plane protested, shuddered, and shook as the speed fell off rapidly. It was evident that this big, beautiful aircraft was more at home in the clouds than on the ground. The plane finally slowed and began its turn onto a taxiway through the grey, dawn mist and rain that, seemingly, nine out of ten times, was there to welcome passengers to London. They stopped momentarily as a Lufthansa A320 barrelled down the runway, took off, and disappeared into the blanket of fog. Its flashing strobe light was the only evidence remaining that an aircraft was cocooned in the greyness.

It struck Emily that everything was lacking in colour. The dullness was only broken by the bright yellow reflective vests worn by the ramp workers and the flashing lights of the vehicles charging about the ramps. The aircraft came to a halt at the jetway, and she could see its reflection in the terminal windows. She thought the plane looked sulky, not unlike a child who had been summoned too soon from the playground. She watched through the raindrops beading on her window and the rivulets streaming down the slick wing to the flurry of activity as the train of baggage carts arrived. She heard the sound of the cargo doors being opened.

The ding of the seat belt indicator brought her out of her trance, and she turned to see people standing in the aisles, wrestling baggage from the overhead bins. She remained seated and people-watched until the doors were opened and they started filing out. Finally, Emily stood, stretched, pulled her bag down, and followed the crowds into the sprawling, bustling terminal building.

It was still early. Emily had completed immigration procedures and went in search of coffee. She settled onto a stool at a high-top table at Caffe Nero, ordered a tall cappuccino with an extra shot, and a pain au raisin. While she waited for her order, she rifled through her bag and pulled out her Oyster card. She still had roughly fourteen pounds of credit available — more than enough for the trip to Vauxhall station. She checked her watch; she still had three hours before her appointment at the embassy, although the train journey would chew up just over an hour of that.

She asked the barista where she could pick up a SIM card. Emily was directed to the next level, where she discovered an impressive array of vending machines housing all manner of mobile phones and accessories. Simply insert your payment card, select your preferred service provider, data requirements, minutes, and text allowances, and 'hey presto' - you have a SIM card! Emily was back at her table in under five minutes, ordering her second coffee and setting up her phone.

Just after nine, Emily was settled on the train. She stared out into the drab morning. Rows of attached houses with dark, inky, solid-fuel smoke billowing from their chimneys, clawing its way like oily fingers reaching for the low, oppressive blanket of cloud, as the train hurried past. A cheery, albeit recorded, voice was announcing upcoming stations. "The next stop is Hounslow East. This is the Piccadilly line." She had not been back on home soil in over a year, and the familiarity of the canned announcements made her smile. Emily listened to "Mind the gap. Stand clear of the doors, please." for three more stops, and by South Ealing, she had plugged in her headphones.

Her parents had originally wanted to meet her flight, but Emily had persuaded them not to. The traffic in London was a nightmare. Furthermore, her father was a stereotypical Italian driver. His hand signals would not be found in any driver's manual anywhere on earth. Emily joked that road trips and diazepam went hand in hand in the Espisito family!

By the time she had changed at Green Park, onto the Victoria Line, and alighted at Vauxhall station, the sun was struggling through the clouds. She was feeling upbeat. Familiar territory, walking along the Thames, George Harrison in her ears, keeping her company with 'Here Comes the Sun.'

Her visit to the American embassy was relatively quick and surprisingly uncomplicated. She was relieved when they told her that her visa would be ready next Thursday, and by lunchtime, Emily was sitting at a corner table at the Ebury Wine Bar. She tucked into a Croque Monsieur and was sipping a pleasant Chardonnay as she waited for her room to be readied upstairs. The lunch crowd was relatively quiet, so she took the opportunity to send a handful of text messages with details of her temporary phone number. No sooner had Mrs. Esposito received her daughter's message, she was on the phone.

"...and don't go wasting your money on that awful train food — you'll need a hearty appetite when you arrive. I've organised a little 'welcome home' lunch for you. I've invited Mrs. Briggs from next door... ooh, and I bumped into Sue and Trevor in Waitrose yesterday... they cannot wait to see you. What about Layla from school... do you still speak to her... I..."

Emily looked up at the approaching waitress, her eyes almost willing her to ask her something... anything... so she could cut the phone call short. As if reading her plea, 'Chloe' said, "Your room's ready. Can I get you anyfink else?"

"Oops. Gotta go, Mum."

Emily declined 'anyfink else' and asked that the bill be charged to her room. She followed the waitress up the narrow carpeted staircase to the first-floor landing, down a long narrow hallway to her room. After she was let into the small room with its quaint antique furnishings, she was handed an old-fashioned four-inch skeleton key on a large wooden fob with the number six burnt in the centre. She was reminded about dinner, breakfast, and checkout times. Emily thought about ordering a pot of tea but decided that what she most wanted right now was a good long nap. She thanked and tipped Chloe, locked the door, drew the heavy curtains, sent Andrew a text asking him to call her in three hours. She slipped off her outerwear and crawled under the duvet.

Chapter 68

It was a bright, sunny Texas day. Andrew was early to work and, by eight o'clock, had already finished his inventory on the ambulance and was restocking for the day ahead, when his phone alerted him to Emily's incoming text. He closed the rear doors, sat down on the big step bumper, and read her message. He smiled and thought, *'Short and sweet, just like her'*. He spent a few seconds looking at her face on the screen, ran his thumb down her image, and thought, *'Dang girl, I love you'*. As he slipped his phone into his pocket, it began to ring. Assuming it was Emily, unable to sleep, he picked up immediately.

"Hey, Andrew. It's Andrea."

"Oh, Andrea. Hi... um... how you been? Sorry, I'm at work. Hey, can I call you later? Is everything okay?" Andrew responded, stumbling over his words, not sure why she was calling and obviously uncomfortable.

"I know you're at work. You're always at work. Or working on your house. Or taking care of one thing or another. You are always unavailable, and no, later won't work." Andrea replied in frustration, her words filled with hurt and anger. She continued, her tone softening. "Andrew, I know how difficult losing Travis has been for you. You were best friends. You were like brothers. But he was my husband, my best friend, and the father of little Travis. I've seen you three times since the funeral… three fucking times in six months. And each time, something has been more important than me. And you know what's killing me? You've barely looked at little Travis. You and Travis used to sit, rub my belly, and talk to little Travis, competing with each other on who was cooler, his daddy or his uncle Andrew. Well, his daddy is no longer here, and he sure as damn it needs his uncle Andrew. We all lost someone special and irreplaceable that day. I don't want to lose my friend, too." She paused, her breath hitching, gathering herself.

Andrew's chest tightened as he braced for the rest. Andrea was sobbing now, her words punctuated with hiccups and short, rapid breathing, making her last words barely audible. But he did hear. And his heart felt like it was breaking all over again. Tears of pain and guilt fell down his cheeks as he recalled promising Travis that he would take care of Andrea and little Travis, as he was wheeled off on the gurney at Entebbe airport.

Andrew felt like a heel. He knew he had been avoiding Andrea. He felt guilty that he made it, and Travis didn't. Felt guilty that he was happy, or as happy as one could be under the circumstances. Guilty that he was in love with Emily. While Andrea was alone, with a little boy who looked more and more like his father every minute. She'd lost her soulmate and best friend, who had died in a place that barely made it onto a map, in someone else's war, before he could even meet his child.

He was silent for a minute, and then, hoping that he didn't screw up by throwing some levity into the tense conversation, he said, "I'm mighty apologetic, Andrea. I ain't been a real good friend, for sure. What say you I come by after work and visit a spell? I could have me some of your famous sun-sweet tea. You need anything from town, Suga? I'm fixin' to be done by three."

Andrew had purposefully drawled on his words, as he and Travis would do when flirting and teasing with Andrea. Andrea started laughing through her tears.

"God, Andrew, I've missed you! And no, I don't need anything from town." She paused. "I'm just glad you are coming over."

Andrew rubbed the tears from his face and said, "Yeah, me too. I'll see you this afternoon. Promise."

Andrew picked up Buddy after work, went back into town, and headed to the florist. Most everyone who had lived in Bulverde for the better part of their lives knew Andrew and Travis, and were well aware of what had happened. The florist was no exception; she had been classmates with the two, and she'd struggled through making the funeral floral arrangements. She was also close to Andrea — both were self-appointed anthophiles. She had to explain this to Andrew as she busied herself selecting the appropriate flowers for his 'sins' as she called them.

"White Lilies, symbolizing commitment and rebirth. Yellow roses, for your friendship — not that you deserve to be her friend," she said playfully, and smiled, letting him know she was joking, "and... hmm, let's see... oh, yes, Campanula — perfect. That, my friend, represents gratitude."

"Dang, girl! Well, I'd sure be grateful if you let me keep some money in my billfold!" he said, looking at the huge bouquet that she'd added some baby's breath to before wrapping. She knew Andrea would want to arrange them herself. Andrew thanked and paid her. He had just pushed the door open, the old-fashioned bell still clanging, when she called after him.

"Hey, you. We all miss him. Whenever I see you, I still expect to see him a few steps behind. I'm glad you are reaching out to Andrea... she needs you now more than ever. Now git, before I cry. Oh, and say hey to her from me."

Andrew nodded, tipped his hat, and headed for his jeep.

Andrew arrived just after three-thirty, Buddy padding next to him. He had not been to their house since he had returned to Texas, and it pained him how neglectful he had been. Prior to leaving for Africa, he had all but lived with Travis and Andrea. Although the small wooden bungalow was looking a little tired and in need of a few new boards on the porch, the flower garden was stunning. Andrea had planted almost a quarter of an acre of flowers, plants, and wild grasses, to attract hummingbirds and butterflies. The patch of Duelberg Salvia was almost three feet tall, and its purple trumpet-shaped flowers were being enjoyed by a kaleidoscope of monarch butterflies, as was the scarlet-coloured Hibiscus, now almost five feet in height. There was not a window without a colourful window box, all in full bloom, and potted flowers led up the wooden steps and dotted the porch.

He opened the old wooden screen door and rapped on the bright yellow door he had painted two summers ago. Andrea called him in. He entered the house, and it was like stepping back in time. He half expected Travis to pop his head around the corner and offer him a beer. Andrea was sitting in her oak and wicker rocking chair beside the bay window, gently rocking back and forth. Sunlight was filtering in through the ivory lace curtains, highlighting her flaxen hair. She was nursing young Travis, and he thought she had never looked more radiant. For fear of being overcome by emotion, he dared not speak. He simply placed the flowers on the coffee table along with his cowboy hat, walked over, and kissed her on the cheek. He noticed a tear slide down her tanned face and knew he was the cause of it. She cleared her throat and looked down at Travis, who had stopped feeding. She withdrew him from her breast, closed her nursing bra, and buttoned up her shirt, before handing Travis to Andrew.

"This is your uncle Andrew. In time, you will come to know he is a bit of a donkey, but you will also come to love him." she said, her eyes never leaving him. Andrew cradled Travis, who was sound asleep, and rocked him gently as Andrea got up and hugged him. She went into the kitchen to put the flowers in a vase and poured the iced tea. Andrew felt sheer joy as he held little Travis — the resemblance to his daddy was overwhelming.

"The flowers are beautiful. I bet Terry picked them... and I'm sure she told you what each meant. She has a heart of gold, that girl." Andrea called out from the kitchen.

"Yes, she does! I like her. She says hey, by the way." he called back at her, his eyes never leaving the sleeping baby.

They sat on the porch and talked late into the night. Andrea fed little Travis a few more times. Andrew burped him and fussed over him when he was awake, and when he was in his bassinet, Buddy lay close by in protective mode. They ordered burgers and fries from Max's Roadhouse. Andrew had a beer, and Andrea another iced tea. Before Andrew left, he promised to stop by on Saturday morning to replace a few of the porch boards, and Andrea knew better than to argue with him. She just asked, "Still like your eggs sunny side up?"

As Andrew descended the steps, the soft creak of the wood beneath his boots echoed in the quiet night, a reminder of the life that once filled this home. He could almost hear Travis call out, "See you at work tomorrow, bud." But the familiar voice dissolved into the cool evening air, leaving a hollow ache in its place.

He paused at the bottom of the steps, taking in the faint glow of the porch light and the soft murmur of Andrea's voice from inside, soothing little Travis to sleep. The world had shifted, but in this small pocket of time, in this house that carried so many memories, it felt like something of Travis still lingered.

Andrew took a deep breath, the scent of fresh-cut grass mingling with the cool breeze. *"See you on Saturday."* he murmured to himself, more a vow than a plan, before heading towards his jeep.

The road ahead was dark and quiet, but for the first time in a long while, it didn't feel quite so lonely.

Chapter 69

The Cessna 172 droned steadily, its shadow skimming over a patchwork of green and gold that stretched to the horizon. Mac adjusted the trim, glancing at Ingrid, who sat quietly beside him, her gaze fixed on the ever-changing scenery four thousand feet below. Dense forests gave way to sprawling savannahs, the terrain wild and untamed — a striking contrast to the sterile confines of her daily life in the hospital.

For Mac, this flight was more than just a scenic tour — it was a triumph. After months of tests and endless paperwork, he had finally regained his flight certificate. Passing the medical had been a personal victory, one he hadn't dared to celebrate too loudly. Now, as the Cessna hummed beneath a cloudless sky, he felt more like himself again, back in control of the one place that had always made sense — the air.

Over the following eight months, their free time was filled with flights and discoveries. Mac flew her to Murchison Falls for a mid-week escape, and to Kibale Forest, where they hiked to see chimpanzees, who unceremoniously flung shit at them from high up in the treetops!

One of the most memorable flights was when Mac flew Ingrid, Stephen, and Enoch to Rhino Refugee Camp on one of their missions. It was the boys' first time on a plane, and their emotions ran wild — nervous laughter, forced bravado, and finally, pure awe. By the time Mac descended to five hundred feet above Karuma Wildlife Reserve, all nerves had vanished. They were snapping pictures, mesmerized by the view below — elephants wading through waterholes, giraffes browsing on flat-top acacia trees, and herds of antelope grazing the sprawling scrubland. Watching the wonder on their faces, Mac couldn't help but smile. He wasn't sure who was more exhilarated — Stephen and Enoch, seeing their world from a new perspective, or himself, seeing it through their eyes.

The most important trip of all, was the one Mac had planned with the utmost care and attention.

"We'll be in camp in time for lunch. We should start seeing wildlife as we descend over Lake George." Mac said, over the drone of the engine, breaking the silence as they cruised above the endless landscape.

Ingrid smiled faintly but didn't look away from the view. At one hundred and forty miles per hour and five thousand feet above the earth, the land below seemed vast and untouched — a living, breathing canvas. "I can see why you love this. I never grow tired of these views." she murmured, her voice tinged with awe as she traced the winding ribbon of a river below with her eyes.

"It's only the beginning." Mac's grin widened, as he adjusted the throttle and began their descent.

They had booked the luxurious Mweya Safari Lodge, renowned for its breathtaking views and meticulous attention to detail. Their first day consisted of a relaxing spa session followed by a sunset cruise along the Kazinga Channel, surrounded by the largest concentration of hippos in Africa. But the highlight came at dawn.

As the first light of morning stretched across the horizon, a private hot air balloon lifted them above the savannah. Below them, elephants stirred in the golden mist, their silhouettes merging with the land as the sun spilled warm light over the world.

At eight hundred feet, with the earth hushed beneath them, Mac turned to Ingrid. He took a breath, his pulse steady despite the weight of the moment. Then, he dropped to one knee.

Ingrid's breath hitched, her hands flying to her mouth as her eyes filled with tears. "Mac..." she whispered, a tremor in her voice.

He reached for her hand, his fingers warm against hers. Ingrid, loving you has been my greatest joy. You're the best thing that ever happened to me and I want to spend the rest of my life proving it to you. Ingrid Svenson, will you marry me?"

A laugh bubbled from her lips, part joy, part disbelief, as she nodded through her tears. "Yes." she managed, her voice breaking as she laughed again, wiping her eyes. "Yes!"

The ring sparkled in the early light as Mac slipped it onto her finger — a perfect fit.

Chapter 70

"Good afternoon, ladies and gentlemen. This is your captain speaking. On behalf of myself and the entire crew, I'd like to thank you for flying with us today. It has been our pleasure serving you, and we look forward to welcoming you aboard Ugandan Airlines again soon. Whether you're here for business or pleasure, we wish you a pleasant stay in Dar es Salaam."

Mac and Ingrid touched down ahead of the East African Physicians Conference in Dar es Salaam where Ingrid was one of the keynote speakers. Mac tagged along, and together they planned a week-long getaway in Zanzibar after the event. It was a place both of them had longed to visit, and they mused at the serendipity of neither having been able to make the trip before, both revealing how, each time either of them had contemplated the possibility, work or one thing or another had got in the way. They romanticised that it was fate. That the island had been waiting for the right moment. Waiting for them.

At the luxurious Hyatt Regency Kilimanjaro, Mac and Ingrid were led up to their lavishly decorated suite. Its floor-to-ceiling windows offered commanding views of the silver sandy beaches and the Indian Ocean beyond, turquoise and glimmering in the mid-afternoon sun. The ocean became white and foamy as it lapped at the shore, erasing traces of recent human traffic and leaving behind shimmering sand, like millions of tiny diamonds reflecting in the sunlight. Pleasure crafts and Arab dhows rocked gently in the shallows, their sails catching the soft breeze.

Ingrid stood facing the pale blue skies, her heart lightened by the beauty around her. The only blemish in the infinite blue was a dual contrail, already dissipating and forming wispy cirrus clouds from a long-out-of-sight jetliner. Mac slipped his arms around her, drawing her back against his torso. He swept her hair over her shoulder, gently kissing the nape of her neck and whispering, "I love you, Doctor Ingrid Svenson."

She leaned into him, a soft smile spreading across her face. "And I love you, Captain Dalton McBride."

Over the next three days, while Ingrid immersed herself in the conference, Mac dedicated his time to working out in the gym, relishing access to equipment he had missed in Kampala. He swam laps in the pool overlooking the ocean, the salt on his skin mixing with the sweet scent of tropical flowers wafting through the air. Long runs on the beach were accompanied by the rhythmic crashing of waves, a soothing backdrop to his thoughts.

Ingrid always managed to sneak out to meet Mac during her breaks, the vibrant energy of their love pulsating in the brief moments they shared. They dined alone each night at the open-air rooftop restaurant, admiring the breathtaking views of the harbour as the sun dipped below the horizon, casting hues of orange and pink across the sky.

Midway through the after-conference party, Ingrid felt she had fulfilled her social obligations. After kissing cheeks and exchanging cards, she slipped away, eager to reunite with Mac.

She hurriedly boarded the elevator to their suite. Mac stood at the window, his gaze fixed on the ever-changing sky, when he heard the key turn in the lock. The door swung open to reveal Ingrid, barefoot, high heels in hand, radiating warmth and joy.

"Hi, Honey. I'm home," she quipped playfully, tossing her shoes aside. She dropped her bag and closed the door behind her, skipping across the room into Mac's waiting embrace. He kissed her deeply, lifting her off the ground and swinging her around before she broke away and dove onto the king-sized poster bed. Rolling over onto her back, she purred seductively, "I hope you didn't make dinner reservations."

Later, freshly showered and savouring their room-service dinner overlooking the harbour, moonlight danced on the ocean's surface, while lights from nearby boats twinkled like stars fallen to earth.

As they discussed their future plans, Mac and Ingrid found themselves aligning on a vision that felt almost dreamlike. The idea of a fresh start, shedding past lives, and rediscovering themselves was exhilarating. Each knew from experience how quickly things could change, how life could be ripped away without warning. They'd both seen it happen, though in different ways; Ingrid with the death of her parents, and Mac in the nightmare he was still living in after his accident. They were well-acquainted with fragility and impermanence, and albeit a cliché, they wanted to 'live well, laugh often, and love much'.

As they looked out over the harbour, the city lights casting reflections across the water, it felt like a new beginning shimmering on the horizon.

Chapter 71

Emily's afternoon nap had appeared to completely scupper any chance of her being able to get back to sleep that evening. She tossed and turned, no longer used to the sounds of city life — the constant flow of traffic, horns blaring, and the sound of steel on steel as the trains rattled by. Emily pounded her pillow and wrapped it around her head in an effort to drown out the din. Outside, patrons spilled out of the pubs, debating ferociously whether they should go to the chippy for fish and chips, to the Indian takeaway for a curry, or grab a kebab.

This inane debate, in which she learned that the chippy was closer than the Indian and that the kebab was cheaper than cod and chips, went on for the better part of twenty minutes. Finally, someone mentioned spring rolls, and they all happily trotted off — she assumed in the direction of the Chinese.

She had spent the better part of the last year falling asleep to either the nocturnal creatures of Africa or the chorus of cicadas in Texas. The latter was also accompanied by the soft, deep breathing of the man she adored — and the man she was missing every minute they were apart.

Eventually, in the small hours of the morning, jet lag and exhaustion took their toll. The streets below finally became still, and she fell into a deep slumber.

She awoke a few hours later, wrestled herself free from the bedspread, and staggered sleepily into the bathroom. She turned on the light, quickly turning it off again as the harsh glare assaulted her eyes. She found the toilet by memory and sat down, cursing the cold seat. Finished, she turned on the shower, undressed, and waited in the dark, shivering and muttering as it remained cold — before it dawned on her.

"Duh! Electric shower, stupid," she mumbled out loud. Swatting her hand around in the dark, she felt the pull cord and tugged. A red light illuminated, and a few minutes later, she stepped under the hot water.

She towelled off, dressed, and made her way down to the breakfast room. She looked at the 'included continental breakfast' on offer... unimpressed. Though she'd been on a number of continents, she couldn't recall any of them ever serving orange cordial, bran flakes, and pre-packed muffins.

The waitress, who was no more in the mood to be there than Emily was, approached the table. Emily smiled. "Hi. Can I get poached eggs on...?"

The waitress slowly shook her head. "Scrambled or fried."

"Okay... scrambled, please, on sourdough."

She shook her head again. "Sorry. White or brown."

"Ahh. Brown then, please. Latte?" Emily enquired, hopefully.

"That'll be an extra four pounds," she said, in a can't-be-arsed tone, "or you can 'elp yourself to tea and coffee over there, included in the price." She lifted her head and pointed with her chin towards a sorry-looking beverage station.

"I'll have a latte." Emily forced a smile.

"One l-a-t-t-e." The waitress echoed, whilst feeling the need to write it on a notepad, lest she forget the order. "Jus' to let ya know, it's a twenty minute wait on food." The inflection at the end of the sentence left Emily not knowing whether it was a question or a statement, and they were left staring at each other awkwardly.

Lack of sleep, the tone, and the pettiness of a four-pound cup of coffee on top of an already extortionate room rate, irritated Emily. She wanted to say, *Look, I'll give you ten pounds if you'd just shut the fuck up and bring me my latte.* Instead, she smiled and said, "No problem."

Two hours later, Emily's train was pulling into the station at Milton Keynes, greeted enthusiastically by her parents and a dozen friends. A banner was strung up on the railings, boldly spelling out *WELCOME HOME EMILY*.

B-l-o-o-d-y h-e-l-l! Emily thought.

As she alighted, bouquets of balloons and flowers were thrust into her hands. There were hugs and kisses galore, as streamers and confetti rained down to shrieks and whistles. Everything was present, shy of a marching band and a parade. Emily adored her parents and friends. They always went all out for her, and this welcome-home gathering filled a hole in her heart left by Andrew's absence.

Emily's parents' VW Passat led a convoy of cars, filled with friends and neighbours, to Towcester, some twenty minutes away. They had reserved a table at the Navigation Restaurant, set on the Grand Union Canal, for her welcome-home lunch. The entourage crowded around four wooden picnic tables under umbrellas. Emily's friend, Janine, had arrived early and decorated the tables with balloons, and the banner was now tied to the picket fence next to them.

Though embarrassed by all the fuss, she knew it was just how her mum and dad were. Her mind went fleetingly back to how different Andrew's arrival home was. She suspected, under different circumstances, it would have felt much like this, knowing Rusty and Rosemary. Funny, she thought, how similar, yet different, they were from her own parents.

Lunch was a rowdy affair. Everyone was eagerly talking, catching up on Emily's adventures and asking what she'd been doing for the past eighteen months. No one brought up her near-miss in the Congo, though she suspected it was on everybody's mind. She was grateful not to have to relive that horrific day — at least, not today. She knew she'd have to go through it at some point during her stay.

As the afternoon gave way to evening, much of the group had either left or were preparing to leave. The tables had been separated, and now it was just Emily and her parents, sitting quietly and watching the narrowboats navigate the canal, waiting their turn at the locks. Emily's dad popped the balloons and placed them in the bin, as her mum draped an arm around her shoulder, telling her for the umpteenth time how happy she was to have her home.

Emily grew increasingly concerned that her mum might think she was home to stay. She realised they'd need to have that conversation in the morning, lest she ruin the afternoon. Her dad bent down and kissed her on the top of the head. "Do you want anything else, Pumpkin? Or should we head home?"

"No, I think I'm done, Dad. Thanks for a lovely day." she said, standing up and hugging him. Emily and her mum walked hand in hand towards the car, as her dad went in to pay the bill.

Although it was only eight o'clock when they arrived home, Emily was knackered. All she wanted was a long, hot soak in the bath, to climb into bed, and call Andrew. She followed her dad into her room, as he set her bag down and turned on the light.

The room hadn't changed, still white with soft pink accents. Half-used bottles of nail polish and old perfumes sat atop the dressing table. The familiar, worn crochet blanket stretched across the bed, as if waiting for her return. The walls, adorned with framed academic achievements and faded posters, seemed frozen in time, echoing the hopeful ambitions of her younger self. Everything about the room — the faint floral smell, the soft colours, the quiet orderliness — brought her back to her high school and university years, to a time when life had felt simpler, her dreams closer and clearer. It still held that teenage-girl charm, like a snapshot of the past, preserved.

She flopped onto the bed, stifling a giggle, as it squeaked loudly. Images of her making out with a boyfriend, whose name she'd long since forgotten, bounced to the forefront of her memory.

Her dad smiled and asked, "You okay?"

She nodded. "I'm fine. Just happy to be home."

"It's so nice having you home, Pumpkin. Sweet dreams. See you in the morning."

Chapter 72

Peter and Ryan stood at the front of the makeshift training centre, their eyes scanning the eight men before them — hardened soldiers chosen for a new mission. There would be two teams of four, each team protecting one VIP. These men were not just soldiers; they were veterans of countless missions across hostile territories. Of the eight, only two had ever held escort duty — former American special forces, now turned contractors. All eight, however, were battle-hardened veterans, and it was Peter and Ryan's task to chisel off a little of the GI Joe look, hone their urban awareness skills, and train them in this new environment.

Peter had the men stand at ease, their legs slightly spread, their hands folded behind their backs. He introduced himself and Ryan, and their objective. Ryan moved out of the direct line of sight of the group and observed. He noted two of them whispering and smiling every few minutes. Ryan, soundlessly and with the speed of a cheetah, advanced on the two. In a single fluid motion, Ryan locked one man's arm, yanked him off balance, and swept his legs out from under him, sending him crashing to the floor. The second trainee barely had time to react before Ryan tackled him, putting him down.

It was a blur of motion, and from where Peter stood, the reaction time of the two downed trainees was sloppy. He had seen them speaking through still lips and smiling; he knew Ryan would move but did not imagine that it would be so swift and final. Peter joined Ryan, who was glaring at the two soldiers, almost goading them to do something stupid. Peter waded in, extended his arm to the one man, who finally grasped it and was hoisted to his feet. Ryan did the same, but his assistance was dismissed, and the man got up on his own.

"Now, gentlemen. That is what happens when you don't pay attention." Peter said.

Abshir was standing in the back of the gym. Peter called him over and whispered a few words. Abshir nodded his head in agreement.

"You're all dismissed. Take a break. You two, stay." Peter said, pointing at the two who had disrupted the class. "Abshir is our local eyes and ears on the ground. He is also a highly trained soldier and intelligence agent. He's going to lead you on your runs for now, but his primary role is intel and local knowledge. It will behoove us to pay attention to him. It could save your lives."

The group filed out, got into their running gear, and Abshir led them outside. Peter and Ryan knew that they'd be gone for at least forty-five minutes. Peter gestured to a couple of chairs and told the guys to take a seat. The two begrudgingly sat, still smarting from the humiliation, but saying nothing.

"Okay, guys. I know you are exceptional soldiers, well-trained and combat-hardened; however, this is not the forum to be cavalier. This may not be as dangerous as Iraq, but lest you forget, these people downed two of your choppers a few years ago. They dragged the airmen through their streets, humiliated the American military might, and had you guys off their soil in less than a month. So, do not underestimate them and your mission. Check your ego and attitude at the door, or use the door to exit. Your choice."

Ryan jumped into the conversation. "This is not only about how good you are, but also about how good we are as trainers. So far, we have an exemplary record, and we want to keep it that way. We were both career soldiers," he said, pointing at Peter, who was leaning against the wall, 'just like you. But we had to learn a whole new skill set to do what we are teaching you. It is lucrative, it's demanding, and it's rewarding every time we thwart an attack, either pre-mission or during a mission. Pre-mission is preferable, but sometimes we, too, are blindsided, so there is no margin for error. Survival means you are never, never, never caught being distracted as you were earlier. I'm not going to scold you like children; you are men, and men I respect, so I'm going to leave you alone for five minutes. If you want to stay, great, and if you want to leave, we'll arrange your transport to the airport. If you decide to stay, be in your running gear and join us. As far as we are concerned, this matter is closed."

Peter and Ryan left the room, changed, and were limbering up in the parking lot when the two men came jogging up in their running togs.

"Five k's in thirty okay for you guys?" Ryan said, smiling as they jogged out of the compound, passing Abshir and his group coming in.

The remainder of the day was all classroom — learning the ingress and egress routes, option A's, B's, and C's of how to get out to a safe house in the event things went bad, either en route, during, or leaving the seminars. The street names were hard on a Caucasian tongue and therefore difficult to remember, but it had to be done. There were no do-overs in this game. You either won or were dead, and winning was, of course, preferable.

Tomorrow would be a series of dry runs through the city in their disposable cars, while they awaited the arrival of their armoured land cruisers. Tomorrow would also decide who was best equipped as the driver of each team. It was not based solely on their driving capabilities, but their ability to recall all the routes, think on the move, communicate clearly whilst under duress, and act and react appropriately in highly stressful situations.

Chapter 73

Mac and Ingrid, having completed their check-in and immigration procedures at Julius Nyerere International Airport in Dar es Salaam, went to the duty-free shop to purchase wine, coffee, and a couple of bottles of decent champagne.

An hour later, they were walking across the apron, following another thirty or so holidaymakers towards the awaiting Precision Air de Havilland Dash 8 turboprop for their quick twenty-minute flight to Zanzibar. Ingrid was resting her head on Mac's arm and was snuggled in close as they handed their boarding passes to the flight attendant. Both were excited. The attendant looked at them, pointed her finger, smiled broadly, and said, "Honeymoon, right?" Ingrid blushed, and Mac kissed the top of her head but did not correct the kindly flight attendant. "Follow me." she smiled, and led them to the front of the aircraft. Although there was no business or first class, she gave them two seats just behind the cockpit, which had ample legroom, and asked if they would like a mimosa or champagne. Ingrid smiled at her and said, "Oh, a mimosa would be wonderful."

After a pleasurable flight, a cheery welcome from immigration, and a short shuttle, they arrived at the Zanzibar Beach Resort, a few kilometres from Stone Town... and their home for the first three nights.

The beach resort was a sprawling, single-story, whitewashed hotel under a beautiful thatched roof. The room, although not the Hyatt Kilimanjaro, was spacious, comfortable, and had a lovely holiday vibe. It opened up onto a stone patio, also under thatch, that looked over pristine gardens and lush lawns that trailed down to the sparkling white sands of the wide beach and the warm waters of the Indian Ocean.

After settling in, Ingrid slipped into a white bikini, and Mac into his blue rafting shorts. They spent the early afternoon frolicking in the warm ocean and walking along the beach, stopping for cocktails under the swaying palm trees. Later, Ingrid took her beach towel and spread it on the sand, asking Mac to slather her in sunscreen as she settled in to read her novel.

Mac opted to sit at a table in the shade of a palm tree to read his book. He found he was unable to concentrate; he was often distracted, his thoughts drifting regularly to him and Ingrid. He could not believe how blessed he was to be with her. She made him feel alive — a feeling he had not had in many years, if ever. He looked at her lying on her front, her wide-brimmed straw hat shading her face. Her book lay on the sand, her hands were clenched into two fists, resting atop each other, with her chin resting on top of them. Ingrid was not only beautiful to the eye; she exuded everything that was pure and good in this world. To Mac, Ingrid represented perfection — the depth of her eyes, like the brilliant blue of the ocean on a cloudless day, and her hair, the colour of summer wheat. He had never known anyone who could capture and hold him still with their sheer presence. Mac was smitten. A warmth enveloped him as he watched Ingrid basking in the sun, her laughter ringing like music over the soft sound of waves. He couldn't imagine a life without her joy, her laughter, or the way she made every moment feel like a dream.

After a restful night, a twenty-minute run on the beach, an invigorating swim in the ocean, and a hearty breakfast, Mac and Ingrid stood outside in the bright morning sun, awaiting their guide. Hand in hand in the tropical garden, drinking in the briny air and listening to the rolling waves as they tumbled gently onto the shore, Ingrid squeezed Mac's hand to get his attention.

"Dalton." she said, removing her sunglasses so he could meet her gaze. "I just wanted to say thank you. Since we met, I've felt different — like I've woken up to something I didn't know I was missing. I've never put much stock in the idea of soulmates, but maybe I was too quick to dismiss it. I don't know how to express it, but I do know I'm grateful for it."

Words eluded him; he simply removed her sunhat and kissed her tenderly. He felt her lips part, a silent invitation. "I feel the same." he murmured.

The tender moment passed when a Toyota Hi-Ace minivan pulled up beside them. The driver jumped out and asked, "Are you Mr. Mac and Mrs. Ingrid?"

"To be continued." Mac whispered, as he handed her hat back. They greeted the driver and both slid into the bench seat in the rear of the van. The driver closed the door, got in behind the wheel, turned and smiled at the couple. "My name is Sammy. Karibu Zanzibar!"

Mac responded with, "Jambo bwana. Asante Sana." Surprised, Sammy asked, "Do you speak Swahili?"

"Only enough to get me into trouble!" Mac chortled.

Sammy turned out to be an excellent guide and a great raconteur. He had grown up in Zanzibar, was a history teacher, and worked as a guide at weekends and during school vacations. He revelled in retelling the colourful history of the island. There wasn't a single place in Stone Town — or as the locals call it, Mji Mkongwe — that he did not know about. He knew the area intimately, and seemingly every shopkeeper, museum curator, restaurant owner, and a number of touts that plied the streets, looking to introduce tourists to other guides for a small fee.

By the end of their three-hour tour, they had visited some wonderful historic landmarks. The Old Fort, dating back to 1699, the oldest building on the island. Tembo House Hotel with its ornate Arabic-style doors. A private tour of the House of Wonders, a former Omani palace, and Mercury House, museum and former home of Queen's legendary singer, Freddie Mercury. The three lunched on the rooftop at Six Degrees South, a restaurant affording spectacular views over the old town with its tight winding streets and busy harbour. The afternoon was spent in the vibrant Darajani market, where they purchased a few trinkets and colourful sarongs for Ingrid. The busy day culminated in a tranquil boat trip — the wizened, old Arabic dhow operator sailed them back to the hotel just as the sun was setting.

Mac woke early and lay watching the ceiling fan whirl slowly above the canopy of mosquito netting. Breathing in the mixture of salt air that drifted through the open window and the earthy notes of the thatched ceiling, he gently propped himself up on the pillow and watched Ingrid's deep, peaceful, rhythmic breathing. Her chest gently rising and falling. He took in her entire form. Lying on her side, her hair a tangled mess sprawled out across her pillow, her one long naked tanned leg atop and contrasting with the white bedding, her arms curled upward, clutching the comforter to her bosom. He watched her until the sun began to light the room. The lacy drapes ebbed and flowed as the breeze filled the room, beckoning him to come and sit on the patio and watch the morning come alive.

He slipped out of bed, pulled on his shorts, quietly took the coffee machine out onto the patio, plugged it in and made a pot. He ambled across the lawn and sat at the table under the thatched umbrella. He was lost in the morning's awakenings and the birdsong when he heard the door click closed. He turned as Ingrid stepped onto the lawn, barefoot in a white hotel robe.

"Ahh, there she is... Sleeping Beauty." he said as he pulled out her chair. He fetched her a coffee and placed it on the table. She looked up at him and pursed her lips. He bent down and kissed her before he sat down.

Ingrid tilted her head, her eyes twinkling over the rim of her coffee cup. "I roll out of bed looking like I've been dragged through a hedge backwards, and you always have something lovely to say. You do wonders for a girl's delicate ego, Mr McBride."

Mac grinned, reaching over to gently brush the hair from her face, the intimacy of the moment hanging in the air like a charge. "Well then I'll do my very best to keep it intact." he said, voice low and teasing.

She laughed, the sound like warm honey, and leaned in to kiss him softly. "Well then I think I might just have to keep you."

Mac felt his chest tighten at her words, a rush of affection sweeping through him. And for a heartbeat, the world outside seemed to disappear.

They sat in quiet contemplation and appreciation for a while and bade a reluctant farewell to their beautiful surroundings, before moving inside to shower and pack. Sammy would be arriving at nine-thirty, ready to take them to Pingwe Beach for the remainder of their stay.

Chapter 74

Emily had been home for two weeks and had spent most of her time catching up with old acquaintances, lunches with girlfriends, meandering the streets of Towcester, and an entire afternoon at her favourite book store. It had been in the Dunning family for over fifty years and had barely changed. It was the kind of bookstore that had a maze of towering old wooden shelves. Narrow aisles between the shelving displayed handwritten signs, letting patrons know which section they were in. The kind of bookstore that still smelled of aged paper and hardbacks. The old wooden floor was scuffed from years of use and little maintenance. It creaked and groaned as one navigated the narrow spaces. She wondered how on earth a place like this managed to survive in a world of Waterstones, W.H. Smith, and Amazon.

Emily had frequented the shop her entire life, from kindergarten through university, and had come to know the Dunning family well. It was unclear whether Mr. Dunning was pushing eighty or dragging seventy. He was, as always, impeccably dressed. Dapper some might say. Today, wearing two pieces of his three-piece suit, the jacket was removed and hung on an antique valet behind the counter. He wore charcoal pinstripe trousers, matching waistcoat, starched white shirt, its sleeves rolled up and secured with silver retaining bands, and a colourful bow tie. His customary silver chain retaining his pocket watch was tucked into his waistcoat pocket.

The old door bell jangled and he came out from behind the counter with the aid of a silver-handled ebony cane, a beaming smile crossing his wrinkled face when he saw Emily step inside. His body had aged but his mind remained sharp and he greeted her warmly through thin lips hidden in his heavy grey beard. "Emily Esposito! My, my. What a wonderful surprise! It's been far too long. I trust you are keeping well? I hear you have had an exciting few years, enlightening the minds of our youth on a global scale. Please, regale me with a few yarns. You could grant an old man half an hour, could you not? And besides, it's dreadfully quiet in here and rather blustery out there."

She looked at him quizzically wondering how he had known. He smiled, his slate grey eyes twinkling mischievously behind his bifocals. He picked up on her curiosity. "Your mother comes in on occasion, sometimes just to chat, but often to buy a book. She still supports this tired old establishment." he said, sweeping his arm, gesturing to his life's work, before pointing to two well-worn antique, green Queen Anne chairs by the window. Emily took a seat and waited for him to shuffle over and sit next to her. The half-hour chat extended to two happy hours, only interrupted by a handful of customers. The last customer had left and twilight was setting in.

"Well, I'd best be on my way. I have a bus to catch." she said.

"Yes, I must be getting along too. Sandra will be wondering where I am." Referring to his wife of fifty years. He shuffled out of his chair and walked her to the door. "Well, it's been lovely catching up, my dear. Delighted you're back." Emily popped up her umbrella and made a dash for it. "Oh... and good luck with the UCLAN interview!" he called after her, as he flipped the closed sign and locked the door.

As she stepped off the bus, Emily's mind was still racing. UCLAN interview? What had her mum said to him? Emily's discussion with her mother was long overdue! She crossed the street, threw open the little iron gate and strode purposefully up to the front door. She barged in. She was fuming. Trying desperately to keep her tone neutral, she called out into the house, "Mum? Are you home?" The answer came from the back patio. Emily put her bags on the kitchen counter and slowed her pace, breathing deeply.

She found her mum sitting at the small bistro table, drinking a cup of tea. Her gardening gloves neatly folded on the table and an array of gardening tools in a small wheelbarrow, all cleaned and ready to be packed back in the shed. Emily glanced around the small walled garden, which was beautifully landscaped, and she thought of her own garden. The one she had designed with Rosemary. The one she was so looking forward to creating when she got home.

She pecked her mum on the cheek and pulled up a chair opposite. She looked up and saw what she might look like in twenty or so years. Emily considered her mum pretty. They had the same inquisitive blue eyes and curly, strawberry blonde hair. Her mother had aged well and although sporting a floppy white hat, her hair pouring out on all sides, no makeup and a smattering of freckles along with a few mud smears, she looked good.

She reached across the small table and took her mum's hand. "Mum, I spoke to Mr. Dunning at the bookshop. He thought I'd come home to stay... shhhh, don't say anything yet. I am not staying mum. I love you and dad to bits, but I have a home now, or at least a place I want to be. I love Andrew with all my heart. And I know you will love him too. Where he is, is where I belong."

"Em... Sweetie... just hear me out... I bumped into Mrs. Hearn at UCLAN..."

"Oh, for God's sake, mother!" She knew her mum meant well, but this was getting old. "I know all of that!" Emily snapped, frustration bubbling over. Her mum had always wanted her to work at the university's language department and it had been a long-standing bone of contention between the two of them.

"Simmer down, Emily! I was just saying that I ran into her at Tescos a few weeks ago and told her you were coming home. She said they could use a teacher like you with your language skills and that she would put in a good word for you. That's all." Emily knew that was not all. She was almost positive that sometime in the next week Mrs. Hearn would be invited for dinner, or they would be invited for lunch... and Emily knew she would need to end this now.

"Mum. You are not listening to me."

"Em. Sweetheart. I worry about you... we both do. Your father was beside himself when you were almost killed in the Congo. We both were. Now you are home, we want you to settle down and stay. You're not a teenager anymore, Emily, traipsing around the planet to God knows where! And for what? To help in places that don't want or need your help! For God's sake, Emily, it's time to stop! It's time to come home!"

"Look, Mum... I'm sorry about giving you a scare when I was in the Congo, and I'm not going there again. But as sad as it makes me, something good came out of that horrific ordeal. I met a man. A kind, wonderful man. A man who loves me, and I am going to try to make this work. Andrew and I are going to try. We're building a home together in Texas and..."

"Texas! Listen to yourself! Where school shootings and mass killings are normal?! People running around like it's the... fucking wild west! And the gun laws? What a joke! Ha! You'd be safer in the bloody Congo!" she snapped, standing up abruptly and shoving her chair back. "I am not having this conversation with you. You need to look to your future... and it is not in the wild bloody west." She grabbed her gloves, tossing them into the wheelbarrow and marched off to the garden shed, the wheelbarrow bumping along ahead of her on the uneven crazy paving.

Emily took her head out of her hands. She glanced at her mum hanging up the garden implements in the shed, sighed and walked inside. Her heart ached at her mother's anguish, but there was no use trying to talk to her now. She would broach the topic again when they had dinner — with her dad at the table things may go smoother — but for now, all she wanted to do was have a long, hot soak in the tub and call Andrew. She picked up her bag, and went upstairs to draw a bath.

An hour later, Emily was in her comfortable old grey sweatpants and Andrew's baggy Dallas Cowboys t-shirt, hair wrapped in a towel, lying on her bed fidgeting, waiting, willing Andrew to answer, as the phone purred in her ear. He picked up the phone with a cheerful, "Well, hello Darlin'!" She beamed at the sound of his voice. She could tell he was at work — announcements were coming over the tannoy, the sounds of big engines running and doors opening and closing. "Gimme a minute, Suga. I need to go outside where I won't miss a word." he yelled over the din, gesturing to ER he would be at the picnic table. "Dang, Gal, when y'all coming home? I miss the bejesus outta ya!"

They talked nonstop for half an hour and shared what was going on. He told her he had seen Andrea. She told him she had a fight with her mum. She told him she felt claustrophobic in England. He told her he was rattling around in an empty house. She told him how much she missed him. He relayed the same sentiment and added that even Buddy was missing her. She asked after his folks and he told her he had heard from them and they were well and happy. They were due home next week. They were never at a loss for words and felt like they could continue talking for hours. Their conversation was cut short, however, when Andrew had to attend a call-out. They exchanged 'love yous' and kissing sounds before ending the call.

Emily slipped on her house shoes, and plodded downstairs.

She could hear her parents talking in hushed tones before she entered the kitchen. Her dad was still in his shirt and tie, his jacket draped over the high back counter stool. A glass of wine sat untouched next to him and her mum was making dinner. Her eyes were red and she had obviously been crying. Emily's mood softened and her heart went out to her mum. She rarely cried, and she knew it had everything to do with the feud they'd had earlier.

"Hi!" she said, kissing her dad on the cheek before going around the counter and embracing her mum. "Can I give you a hand?" Emily proceeded to strain the peas, as her mum finished plating up the gammon steak and mashed potatoes. She removed her apron and they all settled around the dinner table. She watched as her mum took a couple of bites of her food and then slowly moved the remainder absentmindedly around her plate. She definitely was not finished with their afternoon's discussion, and Emily braced herself for what was coming.

Emily decided to nip this in the bud. The tension was palpable and she did not want their last few days to be ruined. She loved her parents and they had rarely argued. They'd supported and encouraged her every decision and she desperately wanted them to support her on this. This, the best and most important decision of her life to date. The silence stretched between them like an invisible wall. Her mother's tear-streaked face was a silent plea for Emily to stay. Her father's steady presence felt like a gentle anchor. Emily's heart ached, but she knew what she had to say. The words spilled out before she could stop them. "Mum. Dad. I love you both so much, but I need to move on with my life. I know you want me to be happy, and I really am. I love Andrew, and my life in Texas. Other than here, I have never felt more at home."

"Em... Love..." her mother interrupted.

"No, mum. I haven't finished."

"Let her finish, — We raised her to speak her mind, so let her. When she's finished, then we'll have our say." her dad said, over the pair. "As you were saying, Pumpkin."

"Thanks dad. Mum, this is not the first time you're hearing this — I've been telling you for months. I've found someone special, Mum. I want to be with him. To have his children even. Andrew and I are building a house. We are building a life together in Bulverde. I've made some amazing friends there, and they are good to me. They love and care about me, they look out for me. I've got a job in a small school teaching French — I'm excited about that. You know all of this. I feel, and have been made to feel, so welcome. It's a wonderful, small close-knit community, the kind that takes care of each other... and I love that. I really feel I belong. You two have always wanted the best for me and I have finally found what is best for me. All I ask of you is that you support my decision, as you always have... that's it."

Emily's dad patted her hand, squeezed it and said. "Pumpkin, as always, we will support your decisions. We raised you to be independent. We trust you. You are twenty-four. Everything we could have taught you has been taught. We'll always be your parents, but the days of parenting you have passed. We just want you to be safe and happy... and if you are, I, for one, will sleep well at night."

Emily's mum blotted her tears with a napkin. She took a deep breath, cleared her throat, and said. "Alright, Sweetie. Your dad's right as usual. I'm sorry I got carried away today. As long as you are safe, that's all that matters. You have our blessings and support... and don't forget, you will always have a home here."

"So... when do we get to meet this Michael character?" her dad said, teasingly.

Emily slapped his arm. "It's Andrew, dad!" She replied, feeling the tension dissipate. "We were hoping to come for Christmas. I know he really wants to meet you. Family is very important to him." Emily couldn't shake the feeling that the distance between her and her mum was still there. It had lessened, however the worry in her mother's eyes remained. But for now, it was enough.

Chapter 75

Sammy was waiting in the reception area chatting with the desk clerk, when Mac and Ingrid entered the lobby. He greeted them enthusiastically, took their bags despite Mac's protests, and carried them to the awaiting van. Once aboard, he began his running commentary on the landscape and the history of the island.

As was typical in Africa, the road surfaces were a mixture of partially paved, partially gravelled, and partially potholed — the latter having the majority. The first hour and a half was a bumpy ride. The last forty minutes was beautiful, cruising the coastal road to the tip of the peninsula that led to Pingwe Beach. Sammy slowed as he navigated the narrow streets, passing vendors and their colourful shacks, hawking everything from diving tours and dolphin excursions to beachwear, Maasai blankets and wood carvings.

After a series of turns, he stopped outside the bungalow that Mac had rented, and they all clambered out of the vehicle. Open-mouthed, taking in her surroundings, Ingrid placed her hand on her chest and sighed audibly. "Oh, wow, Dalton. This is beautiful."

Sammy insisted on carrying the bags, including the groceries Mac had asked him to collect the day before. He placed everything in the simple but well-equipped kitchen and asked if they needed anything else. He handed them a list with restaurant recommendations, names, and places to get the freshest seafood. Sammy cautioned them about locking up the place, dealing with beach touts, and what to say to ward off any further harassment. Before leaving, he reminded them about their dinner reservation. It was a unique experience; a restaurant set on a rock, situated less than a hundred metres off the coast, aptly named '*The Rock*', where one had to either wade, swim or hire a boat to get there, depending on the tide.

Sammy wished them an enjoyable stay and said he'd be back in three days to collect them. They accompanied him outside and watched as he drove off with a cheery toot. They stood in the sand-garden, waving, behind the small ornate wrought-iron gate, before turning to explore the little bungalow.

Set directly on the sugary sands, it was an idyllic, whitewashed, A-framed building with a traditional makuti roof — rough-hewn wooden poles, exposed from the inside, and covered with overlapping palm fronds.

Inside, it boasted an oversized bed, supported on four sturdy wood posts, with the ever-present mosquito netting draped elegantly over it. The kitchen, although compact, would do for all their needs. The interior walls were lime-washed, giving the little cabin a bright, airy feel. The living room was dressed in calming coastal palettes of whites and blues, with distressed wooden accents, giving a fresh but weathered look. The salty ocean air was carried inside on a gentle breeze, bringing with it the white muslin floor-to-ceiling drapes that hung at the large wooden-framed doors leading out onto the deck, with its wicker seating. The small, but perfect-for-two, bistro table had a commanding view across the pristine beach to the turquoise blue ocean.

"Look, if I am missing, that is where you will find me." she said, pointing to a double bed-swing beneath a linen sunshade at the edge of the garden, surrounded by palm trees and no more than ten steps from the wide white beach.

"Well, I'm sure I won't have to search too hard... because I'll be on it, right next to you!" he grinned. "Right. Go on with you... the ocean's waiting." he said, playfully slapping her on the bottom before racing her inside.

They quickly unpacked, stocked the fridge and pantry, and threw a bottle of wine in the ice bucket. They changed into their swimwear and headed out to the beach, fingers interlaced. Ingrid's bright red sarong blew in the breeze, her free hand held down her wide-brimmed straw hat, and Mac felt he'd never seen anything more beautiful. He snapped a picture of it in his mind's camera and stored it for later review.

Ingrid picked up her pace as she shed the sarong and hat, unlaced her fingers from Mac's, and crashed through the shallows. When she was knee-deep in the surf, she dived in, with Mac in pursuit. Ingrid came up first, running her hands down her face, sweeping her hair back, and letting it fall down her back as Mac surfaced. She shrieked with the excitement of a child. "God, this water is perfect! Everything is perfect. Turn around, look at our cottage. Isn't it just adorable?"

Mac wiped the warm salty water from his face. "Aye... it'll do."

She splashed water at him. "You didn't even look. You, Captain, are incorrigible!"

They cavorted and splashed about in the water for a while longer, before Mac said, "I'm turning into a frickin' lobster here. This Irish skin doesn't fare well in the midday sun. Besides, I'm getting hungry."

"I am, too. So, what's for lunch?" They jogged through the surf and headed back up the beach, hand in hand.

"I'll rustle up something light to tide us over. I don't want to ruin our dinner tonight." he said, scooping up Ingrid's discarded sarong and hat.

They took turns rinsing off in the outside shower and went inside. Mac made grilled cheese sandwiches and a basic salad, while Ingrid set the table and opened the chilled chardonnay. She poured two glasses as they sat, inhaling the salty air, feasting on the stunning view, and the simple food.

Ingrid washed up after lunch and found her novel, a Tana French 'whodunnit' based in Dublin. Mac was engaged in the amazing life of Nelson Mandela through his book *The Long Walk to Freedom*, recommended by Ryan. They lay head to toe on the covered swing-bed, with its unobstructed views of the beach and ocean beyond. Ingrid was the first to be lulled to sleep by the waves and sea breeze, her book slipping out of her fingers and falling onto the sand below. Mac soon followed, placing his book on his chest, removing his sunglasses, and closing his eyes.

Ingrid woke Mac just after five and excitedly pointed to a stunning sunset. High cumulus clouds the colour of pewter, outlined in red, with bright flashes of yellow, peeking through where the clouds met. Their eyes were drawn to deep shades of red, fading to tangerine, saffron, golden, and ending in a blinding wash of yellow, as it met the ocean. So intense, it appeared that the entire horizon was set on fire and the ocean itself seemed as if someone had painted it amber while they dozed in the sun. So brilliant were the colours, the palm trees were mere silhouettes, swaying in time with the sound of the surf.

They finally tore themselves from the stunning vista and went inside, showered together, and dressed for dinner. Ingrid chose a simple sleeveless v-neck white cheesecloth dress that fell just below her knees, and Mac wore camel-coloured loose-fit shorts with a short-sleeve white linen shirt.

They closed and locked the door, leaving a few lamps on for their return, and walked out over the beach and into the calm, warm ocean. Mac carried their sandals as they waded out to the restaurant at low tide, Ingrid gathering her dress and holding it high on her thighs. They ascended the short flight of stairs as the water lapped at their feet. Reaching the open-air patio, they were immediately transported to a page right out of a Hemingway book. Hand-carved wooden tables adorned with twinkling candles and low-back canvas directors' chairs sat atop a beige flagstone floor. Large potted plants were scattered about, and tiki torches flickered in the fading light, as thin tendrils of greyish-blue smoke rose and dissipated in the light breeze.

Ingrid let her dress drop and slipped into her sandals before they went inside to check on their reservation. They stepped through the glass concertina doors onto the beautifully polished hardwood floor and were greeted by the manager, who gushed and welcomed them enthusiastically before showing them to their table by the window. A waiter arrived with menus and took their drinks order. Both Mac and Ingrid agreed, in all their travels, this had to be one of the most romantic and fitting places for two people in love to spend an evening.

Their drinks arrived, and they ordered the fish carpaccio with coconut, lime and chilli as an appetizer. They could not decide on what fish dish they wanted, so opted for the seafood platter to share. Once the waiter left, and they had feasted on the elegance and romance of the setting, Mac raised his glass, fingers steady but his voice slightly hoarse. He held her gaze. "To the most amazing woman I have ever met, the woman who has given me purpose." Ingrid's hand instinctively covered his, a soft touch grounding them both in the moment. "I proposed to you not because I wanted to live with you, but because I simply cannot live without you. Ingrid, I want you to be the last thing I see at night and the first thing I touch in the morning."

Ingrid's eyes shimmered with tears of love that threatened to spill out if Mac said another word. "I love you so much, Dalton McBride. I will always be eternally grateful that we met, but please know you did not have to go to such extreme measures to do so; flowers would have sufficed!"

"What... so I didn't need the bullet wound? And now she tells me." he said, as they touched glasses and sipped their wine. Mac continued in the same vein with a halfway decent Humphrey Bogart impersonation from *Casablanca*, one of their favourite movies.

"Of all the gin joints, in all the towns, in all the world, she walks into mine."

They both giggled as he physically impersonated a drunk Rick Blaine. Ingrid reached over, took his hand, and followed suit. Putting on a forlorn gaze, she replied, "At least we'll always have Zanzibar." It was not difficult for her to impersonate Ingrid Bergman's accent. She smiled and looked into his eyes and said, "Seriously, Dalton. Thank you for everything. I mean it."

After the most romantic evening — an unforgettable meal in a setting like no other — they strolled back to their bungalow. The warm breeze carried the scent of salt and frangipani, wrapping around them like an embrace. Laughter filled the quiet night, soft and unguarded, their fingertips brushing as if the touch alone could hold the magic of the night in place.

They never made it to the door. The bed-swing beneath the palms beckoned, its canopy shifting with the wind. Mac pulled Ingrid into his arms, their bodies swaying with the rhythm of the ocean. His lips found hers, slow and searching, tasting the remnants of wine and something sweeter — something uniquely her. She melted against him, her breath catching as he pressed her closer.

The world blurred into starlight and whispered gasps. They moved in harmony, the gentle breeze caressing them as they became one, the creak and groans of the swing mingling with their sighs. Beneath them, the sand held the warmth of the sun's memory, and above, the cosmos stretched endless and infinite — just as this moment felt.

Later, breathless and slick, their clothing strewn haphazardly on the back patio, they stumbled naked inside. The bed welcomed them in a spill of soft linen, and they found each other again — this time unhurried. Their lovemaking was tender and deep, revisiting the places they had already memorised, yet discovering something new with every touch. Ingrid straddled Mac rocking back and forth, savouring his every contour, her body glistening in the candlelight that flickered, painting golden strokes, illuminating the rise and fall of her breasts.

Wrapped in the afterglow, Ingrid rested her head on Mac's chest, her arm stretched out, watching the light dance on her ring. She smiled against his skin, pressing a kiss over his heart, where his love pulsed steady and sure. Outside, the waves whispered against the shore, but all Ingrid heard was the quiet symphony of their love, echoing long into the night.

Chapter 76

Ryan sat in the front passenger seat of the lead vehicle, his stopwatch counting down the minutes. The driver was speeding down one of the many egress routes they had mapped out and practiced over the past few days. The rest of the A-team were in their positions; one at each rear window and the last one in the floor of the baggage compartment, sitting upright in a custom-made four-point seatbelt, much like those found in aircraft cockpits, facing aft. Peter and Team B followed closely behind, with Peter watching the seconds tick away on his stopwatch. This was the least desirable route, with narrow streets often teeming with traffic, high-rise apartments, and even lower ones with rooftops that would make excellent ambush vantage points.

It was late at night, and traffic was light, but Ryan and his team had to remain vigilant for cyclists and pedestrians who often ignored crosswalks and traffic lights. The big V8 engines roared, and the extra light-bar blazed brightly, lighting up the road as if it were daytime. Abshir trailed the group in his personal car as a precaution, in case they encountered local police. He could assure them that all was okay and that they were on a training mission. It had happened a few nights ago on Airport Road, just beyond the airport perimeter, and it took a number of phone calls to resolve the situation, causing the team to lose momentum for an hour.

The vehicles screeched to a stop. Doors flew open in unison, and the men swiftly took cover at the front of Aden Adde International Airport, eyes scanning the dark horizon for any hint of movement. They were unarmed for the practice procedures. Ryan clambered out of the vehicle, checking his stopwatch. "Nine minutes and twenty-six seconds. We need to shave off another minute and a half. Again!" he said as they all piled back into the vehicle. He talked into his wrist mic and told Peter they were running it again.

It was four in the morning when they finished their last dry run — twelve in total — and everyone was exhausted. "Good job, gentlemen. Let's hope we don't have to use the Corosso Somalia route. The Solidarieta traffic circle is always a disaster, and there's no way around it. I don't like the only other option of Via Gibuti to Via Asciaa, unless we can get the locals to clear the flats, but I don't trust that either." He looked at Abshir apologetically.

Abshir grinned. "You are a wise man, Ryan. I would not trust us either. Present company excluded, of course." His smile never dimmed.

"Okay, gentlemen. Lock up the vehicles, hit the hay, and let's meet at ten to go over what we've covered." Ryan announced, as he and Peter went into the house. They chatted for a while and agreed to meet at eight for a run and be in the briefing room by nine-thirty to wait for the group. "You happy so far?" Ryan asked.

Peter responded, "They are a good group. They work well together. So, yes. And you?"

"Yeah, I'd trust them to protect me. I just wish we could've done some live ammunition training, but I think they know their way around weapons. They've all seen combat and, after reading their jackets, they've all performed well under fire. So, in short, I think they're ready."

Peter and Ryan were in the warehouse when the group filed in, just before ten in the morning. "Morning, gentlemen. Grab a beverage, and take a seat." Peter said, as he drained the last of his coffee and joined them at the urn to get a refill. Ryan was at the whiteboard, checking off tasks completed and what still needed to be done. The group had not only met every requirement but had excelled in a number of them, especially the blindfold test through the maze of streets. Peter, Ryan, and Abshir would stop the vehicle, have the team get out on the busy streets, remove their blindfolds, and let them ascertain their location and make the best decisions for an escape route, on foot if necessary. Their spatial awareness techniques were almost perfect, and their decision-making as a team was excellent.

With just ten days to go before the conference began, and booths arriving daily, Peter and Ryan decided to take the group to the conference hall for a reconnaissance mission. They had covered every possible angle outside the venue and only needed now to find the best escape routes from within the hall.

Once everyone was seated, Ryan began. "Okay, guys. We've done all we can to date, and you are as prepared as you can be. The conference begins in ten days, and your VIPs are arriving in eight. We are going to concentrate on the hotel where they are staying, and the conference hall, from now until their arrival, covering every possibility. A snatch and grab is our biggest concern and should be yours too. Questions, anybody?"

Only a handful of hands were raised, and Ryan fielded the questions, finishing with, "Yes, the assigned drivers will stay in their vehicles outside the conference hall. Yes, you will all be staying at the same hotels as the men you are protecting. And yes, Abshir will stay on as your liaison. He will also be the man who clears your weapons upon their arrival, and is in charge of getting them back out legally. So, no loss of equipment, or you'll end up in a not-so-pleasant place for a very long time. And no, Peter and I will be leaving when your charges arrive. Our task was to make sure we assisted you in every way possible and keep our employer apprised of your progress, who, in turn, would relay it to yours. And yes, you all got gold stars!" Ryan said, eliciting laughter from the group.

"Gentlemen. Your mission is simple; keep them safe, get them home, keep yourselves safe, go home, and get paid." Peter said from across the room. An hour later, the two groups picked up their security passes and badges and wandered the cavernous hall, amid the hustle and bustle of booths being erected. Where booths and workers had not yet arrived, a taped outline showed where they would be staged so they could see the layout and obstacles in the event a premature, hasty departure was required. Peter picked up brochures, detailing the visiting companies and their respective booth numbers, and cross-referenced them with the layout plans, looking for any inconsistencies. At a quick glance, there weren't any, but he would study them closer tonight.

By two o'clock, the echo of hammering and chatter filled the hall, as things took shape. The team studied the space, snapping photos and mapping the best escape routes. Workers looked on, amused, as they ran drills through the half-constructed maze. They would return every day and run scenarios, right up until the opening day. At three-thirty, the group descended on the elegant Sahafi Hotel, a hub of activity, with local businessmen and expats mingling, many huddled in tight groups, all vying for business in this new, burgeoning market.

"If this mission turns to custard here, it'll be a shit-show." said one of the guys, as he surveyed the numerous unsecured places where a snatch and grab could occur.

Abshir responded, "We will have a team of handpicked men, whom I can vouch for, in plain clothes, naturally. They will be scattered around the area 'twenty-four-seven', as you Americans like to say. You will be introduced to them on Wednesday, and they to you, so that no-one becomes a casualty of friendly fire if things turn to pudding... or however you say it."

"Custard. But pudding works, too." Peter said, as he slapped Abshir on the back.

Back at base, they grouped around the large conference table. The photographs were uploaded and enlarged on the sixty-inch screen. Peter stood at the head of the table, operating the remote control with one hand and using a pointer with the other, as they discussed the most viable exit routes. A large architectural rendering of the hotel floor plan and grounds was affixed to one wall, and the group flipped between both. After two hours, four possibilities were decided upon, and code names were attached to each.

"Tonight, and for the next three nights, we'll do dry runs, and I think that will cover every eventuality. If not, fall back on your skills and get your charges out safely; that is your only goal." Peter said, concluding the meeting.

Ryan added, "Relax. Enjoy the days. Get some rest. Our nights are going to be busy. You guys are as ready as you will ever be. Good job, gentlemen. See you all in the vehicles at twenty-one hundred hours."

A week later, two days before the businessmen were due to arrive, the training centre was packed up. The vehicles were inspected and repairs made where needed. Firearms had arrived. They were cleaned, loaded, and locked in the gun cabinets. The team gathered around the pool deck, enjoying a barbecue. The mood was festive, with smoke rising into the warm afternoon sky from wood fires set in forty-four-gallon drums converted to barbecues. The smell of steaks, sausages, and lamb chops filled the air as rock and roll music played.

Peter and Ryan opted not to drive their Land Cruiser back to South Africa; instead they booked the SAA flight to Johannesburg for seven that evening. They were anxious to get home. Their training mission was complete, and they were happy with the results, as was Patrick Kinsella.

Peter decided that after the debrief in Joburg, he would head back to Cape Town, reunite with The Wanderer, and sail into the Indian Ocean, taking him to Reunion, Mauritius, and Seychelles. Beyond that, he had no plans; he would take it as it came.

At four-thirty that afternoon, they wished the team good luck and piled into the car. Abshir was at the wheel, and fifteen minutes later, they were standing outside Aden Adde Airport. Peter gripped Abshir's hand and pulled him into a quick embrace. "We couldn't have done it without you, Abshir. You're a good man."

"Yes, Abshir. You are a hive of information! You're as cunning as a fox, and if everything turns to pudding, as you say, with your plans, we could always use someone with your skills at Gryphon, now that Peter is leaving us." Ryan said.

"Thanks, Ryan. I will keep that in mind, but for now, I have to do all I can to get my country back on track. But I thank you for the offer, all the same." Abshir replied. The men shook hands, exchanged warm embraces, and parted ways.

"Oh, Abshir. Please tell Amara thanks from us and wish her every success in her work and a safe trip home." Peter called over his shoulder as they entered the terminal.

Abshir responded with a final wave over the roof of the car. "Will do, and a safe journey to you as well."

Chapter 77

Emily felt a flurry of excitement as her flight touched down in San Antonio. Andrew paced the terminal, craning his neck and struggling to get a glimpse through the crowd every time the arrival doors opened. Finally, he found a place behind the barrier, directly in front of the glass doors. He held a custom-made old-fashioned wanted poster that he'd toiled over all morning using his limited Photoshop knowledge. 'WANTED' blazoned across the top in heavy font, a super-size image of Emily's smiling face beamed out from underneath, and below that 'Saucy Minx - Recently Arrived From Heathrow' - a nod to 'Love Actually', Emily's all-time favourite movie. People chuckled as they passed by, and Emily could not contain her laughter when she saw it. She picked up her pace, weaving through people to reach him.

"Well, aren't you a strapping Marshal?! Guilty as charged. Arrest me, cuff me, take me in!" she said seductively, as she sidled up to him, wrists pressed together.

Andrew laughed as he dropped the poster and wrapped his arms around her, pulling her close enough that she could feel his heartbeat under the rush of voices and announcements filling the terminal.

They held onto each other a moment longer, letting the world around them fade into the background. Passersby hurried past, but neither of them seemed to notice or care.

Finally, he pulled back, but kept her hand in his, as he grabbed her bag and led her towards the exit. "Come on, let's get you outta here." he said, flashing her that smile she'd missed for so long.

They stepped out into the thick Texas warmth, and Emily immediately felt the dry, sun-baked air settle over her like a welcome blanket. Andrew's Jeep was parked close by, its top down and seats already hot from the summer sun. He tossed her bag in the back and opened the passenger door with an exaggerated bow. "Your chariot, you Saucy Minx, you."

She slid into the seat laughing, as she felt the leather warm against her skin. Andrew hopped in beside her, and soon they were speeding down the highway, the wind whipping through her hair and the familiar Texas landscape stretching out before them. Eyes closed, head back, she breathed deeply, immersed in the sounds and scents. She glanced over at Andrew, his hand resting casually on the gear shift, and knew in an instant she was home.

"I can't believe you're finally back. It felt like forever." Andrew shouted over the wind, a twinkle in his eye. "Ready for the best ribs in Texas?"

Cars lined the driveway. No sooner had they parked, than Buddy came barrelling towards them, his big head nuzzling Emily as if he'd been waiting for her all year. He dashed in joyous circles, skidding on the gravel driveway and kicking up dust in a frenzy. He bolted around the giant elm tree and crashed through the rose bushes; four legs and seventy-five pounds of pure, excited destruction.

Rosemary trotted down the porch steps. "Andrew, would ya settle that dang dog down, before he tears up my roses again! Mercy, it looks like the circus came to town!" She turned to Emily with a wide, warm smile and flung her arms around her with genuine affection. "Welcome home, Suga. Ain't been the same here without you."

"Easy, Buddy-Boy!" Andrew said, wrangling the over-excited dog, who licked him enthusiastically. He turned to Emily. "Dang, girl! You sure get everyone excited 'round these parts. Let's get these here bags upstairs and get us some grub."

As they made their way onto the porch, the sound of country music and lively chatter carried on the smell of mesquite wood fire wafting from the backyard. Emily abruptly halted on the second-to-top step, with Andrew a step below. She turned and was face-to-face with him. She flung her arms around him and kissed him deeply. He set her bag down and drew her in, embracing her tightly.

"Y'all need to git yourselves a room!" Their passionate kiss was interrupted by ER, who stood grinning with Andrea beside him and Travis asleep in his pram. ER removed his cowboy hat and loped towards Emily. "Dang, it's good to see you, girl! Your man here's been moping around worse'n a lost pup." He glanced at Andrew. "Told him you'd be back, but I'm reckonin' he needed to hear it twice."

"That so?" Emily said, winking at Andrew.

ER swept her off her feet onto the porch and swung her around in circles, kissed her, and said, "Now don't you be leavin' no more." He set her down gently, put on his hat, and continued, "You best git on 'round back. We got us a sure-fired barbecue fixin' to be et." Emily watched him escort Andrea around the side of the house before they went inside.

"Did I miss something? Andrea and ER?" Emily said, as they climbed the stairway.

"I'll tell you all about it later." he replied, setting her bag down. "See you downstairs."

She emerged onto the back deck in fresh clothing and was immediately met with laughter, music, and the smoky aroma of mesquite-grilled ribs. Colourful Mexican lanterns were strung from the trees. ER and Rusty were at the grill, flipping ribs and drinking beer.

"Welcome home, Em!" someone hollered, and before Emily could react, a cold beer was pressed into her hand. She turned to see Andrea, all smiles. "Figured you might just be parched."

Andrew appeared at her side, his arm slipping effortlessly around her waist. "Didn't I tell you we throw the best welcome-home parties?" he drawled, before stealing a quick kiss.

Old Crow Medicine Show's rendition of Wagon Wheel blared from the large speakers and she was pulled towards the makeshift dance floor. The familiar rhythm of a two-step filled the air. Soon she was twirling and giggling, and for the first time in a long time, she didn't have to wonder where she belonged. She knew.

Chapter 78

Time had flown by. Lost in work and social engagements, Mac and Ingrid could not believe it had been almost half a year since their trip to Zanzibar. Mac had returned to Ireland to attend Connor's high school graduation and to reunite with Cati, and on his return, unbeknown to Ingrid, he had secretly made a detour to Zanzibar to close the sale on the Pingwe Beach cottage he and Ingrid had stayed in during their visit.

He had contacted Sammy, who made some discreet inquiries and introduced Mac to the owners via telephone. The proprietors were an older couple returning to their native Italy later that year and selling their beach bar and rental cottage business. They'd discussed the matter over the phone and haggled for a few days. The owners wanted to sell the five units, bar, and restaurant as a package. But Mac wanted that one cottage at any price — within reason — and finally persuaded them, with an extra ten percent, to sell him the one he and Ingrid had made so many wonderful memories in during their short stay. It helped that the couple were returning to Europe, allowing Mac to deposit half the funds into their Italian bank account, thereby reducing taxes, red tape, and fees on the foreign currency being taken out of Tanzania.

Ingrid had settled back into her daily routine. She missed Mac while he was away. And his love of cooking and doting on her was sorely missed! Ingrid always looked forward to mealtimes. Not only was the food scrumptious, but it was also a display of his love and affection. Prior to his departure, Mac had made a selection of her favourite dishes, divided them into single-serving portions, and frozen them. Each meal came with a personal Post-it note, reminding her of his love; some were witty, some heartfelt, and a few simply said "Eat me!"

Mac arrived home just before the holiday season; delighted to be back with Ingrid, elated that he and his daughter had repaired their rift, and overjoyed that his son had been accepted to Dublin's Trinity College.

The two weeks surrounding Christmas and New Year were filled with endless celebrations. The hospital staff party; Christmas dinner with a few select friends; the flying club ball; and several neighbourhood gatherings.

By mid-January, Mac and Ingrid had worked off the extra pounds from the holiday season, and were snuggled on the couch. Mac had his feet propped up on the ottoman and Ingrid had her head in his lap. They were reading, drinking wine, and listening to Cole Porter in the background, as Mac absently ran his fingers lightly through Ingrid's hair. She placed her bookmark in her book, closed it, looked up at him, and said, "Dalton, Sweetheart?"

"Hmmmmm." he replied.

"Dalton." she said again, sitting up and crossing her legs under her to face him.

Mac closed his book, noting the perturbed look on her face and gave her his full attention. "Aye. What's troubling you?"

"You had another one of your nightmares last night. Don't you think it might be time to see someone about it, talk it out? To see you in so much distress really breaks my heart. It pains me to watch you wrestling with your demons like that — the way you thrash about, sweating, and shouting. Dalton, if you think telling me will help, I'm here for you. You know I'll walk through hell with you if it eases the pain."

Mac saw the anguish on the face of the woman he loved and admired. He'd put this off for too long, it was time to tell her. She had earned the right to know. He had planned to do it in Dar es Salaam, but the timing never felt quite right, and so he brushed it off, hoping it had passed. It had not.

Mac stood up, a tormented and conflicted look crossing his ruddy features. "Aye, it's about time." That was all he said. He went upstairs and returned with his laptop and a memory stick.

Mac and Ingrid sat on the edge of the couch, knees touching, her hand gently on his back as he fired up the computer on the coffee table. He inserted the memory stick and paused — inwardly trembling — dreading listening to the recording again. The last time he'd heard it was at the final inquest. Images of him sitting alone in front of the panel with a simulated version of the flight playing on the huge screen flashed through his mind.

He pressed the play button and held his breath. He increased the volume when he heard faint cockpit audio coming through the computer's speaker. He listened to some communications, then forwarded it to the part where everything started to go horribly wrong. He made a few more adjustments, paused it again, and looked at Ingrid. "I'm not sure how much of this you will understand, but I'll narrate where I can." He proceeded to play.

Paul Davidson, Mac's co-pilot, was the first to break the silence. *'Mac, that coffee is running through me. I need to take a leak. Want anything while I'm out?'*

'No thanks, you work away.'

He explained to Ingrid that they had been waiting for clearance for smooth airspace as they were about to fly into some inclement weather. The controllers were busy delaying flights and rerouting others. It was a busy night, and the weather was worsening. Mac let the recording continue. There was a distinct click. Mac explained it was Paul unfastening his seatbelt.

Static filled the air when the controller authorized their descent. *'Shamrock Air one-nine-seven, clear to descend to flight level one-seven thousand and maintain current heading'.*

Mac had responded, *'Shamrock one-nine-seven, clear to one-seven thousand and maintain'.*

Paul's voice said, *'You okay, or should I stay?'*

'I've got this. You go on, and get yourself back and strapped in. We're in for a busy one' Mac replied.

He paused the recording and explained, "You'll hear another click as Paul opens the cockpit door. All hell broke loose and he never made it out. I believe he was thrown back into the cockpit and knocked unconscious when the plane went into an unauthorized nose-down attitude, or nose dive. Are you sure you really want to hear this?"

Ingrid squeezed his hand tightly and just nodded. He pressed play.

A loud bang filled the silence. Mac explained, "That was the yoke crashing into the instrument panel".

Then on the audio you could hear Mac's voice, surprisingly calm. *'Mayday Mayday Mayday Flight control, Shamrock one-nine-seven. We are in an uncontrolled dive. Repeat. We are diving. We have lost pitch control, hydraulics, or horizontal stabilizer malfunction.'*

'Say again Shamrock one-nine-seven' came the response from the flight controller.

'Shamrock one-nine-seven. We are diving. Coming through one-eight thousand feet' Mac responded, a cacophony of audible warnings; the overspeed clacker, sirens and chimes blared.

'Sink rate. Sink rate. Whoop-whoop. Whoop-whoop. Pull up. Pull up. Overspeed. Whoop-whoop. Whoop-whoop. Pull up. Pull up. Overspeed. Whoop-whoop'.

Ingrid put her fingers to her temples, her face scrunched in anguish. She was well aware it was a recording, but it was Mac's voice, which made it all the more real. The sounds were chaotic, shocking and urgent. She felt like she was in that cockpit... and it was terrifying!

Mac paused the recording, putting his hand in Ingrid's lap. "I needed to arrest the dive, so I did everything possible to slow the plane and regain control. I disengaged the autopilot, reduced the power settings, deployed the flaps, slats, speed brakes, and even attempted to lower the landing gear — tasks I would ordinarily have had my first officer perform. I didn't know what had happened to him. I was pulling back on the control column, my arm wrapped around it, using every bit of strength I had and my free hand to adjust all the settings. It finally levelled out at eleven thousand feet."

'Centre control, Shamrock one-nine-seven. We are at one-one thousand

feet and sort of stabilised. Not sure how long for. We need vectors to the nearest airport and a block of clean air to troubleshoot' came Mac's calm voice.

'Stand by Shamrock one-nine-seven' was the response from the controller. That was the last communication Mac answered before the nose pitched down again.

'Centre control, Shamrock one-nine-seven. We have a jammed stabilizer or something. We are diving again. We are in an uncontrolled nose-down attitude coming through six thousand feet' Mac said as the audible warnings once again filled the cockpit.

'Sink rate. Sink rate. Whoop-whoop. Whoop-whoop. Pull up. Pull up. Overspeed. Whoop-whoop. Whoop-whoop. Pull up. Pull up. Overspeed. Whoop-whoop'.

The recording continued as Mac explained that he slammed the throttles forward and kept yanking hard on the yoke and, moments before impact, the nose began to rise. He said "I knew it was too fast, too low and too late... but I kept flying." The alarms continued to shriek as a new chilling warning sounded. And the computerized Ground Proximity Warning System started repeating, *'Too low, terrain. Too low, terrain. Too low, terrain. Pull up. Pull up'* and started a countdown of feet above the sea. *'Four hundred. Three hundred. Two hundred...'.*

Mac told Ingrid through halted, pained words, "I knew we were going in, and I knew we were too fast... but still I tried to get it straight and level. My left wing impacted the water first. I was thrown violently forward. The next thing I knew, I was standing knee-deep in water in the cockpit, staring back into what was left of the aircraft. The plane had broken apart, as you know from what you found out online. I was looking into where the cabin should have been, and most of it was gone.

A young girl, maybe fifteen or so, was standing on a seat, staring out into the sea. She did not have a life vest, but I told her to jump anyway. I promised she would be okay, and so she jumped. I followed... but she was swallowed up by the blackness of the sea and I never saw her again.

People were bobbing in the frigid water. I yelled to them to get to the wing that was still floating. The rest you know. Paul's body, among others, was never recovered."

Mac sat for a few seconds, his face buried in his big hands, muting his sobs. "Paul's wife wouldn't even take my calls. She told the media I was responsible for his death. She was, and probably still is, adamant that I was trying to mask my suicide in an aircraft accident. She told the press it cost her a husband, and their seven-year-old daughter, a father."

Ingrid couldn't speak. She had heard the man she loved fight that plane all the way down. Okay, so she maybe didn't understand all the technical jargon, but she certainly knew her Dalton, and his dogged determination was evident right up to the point of impact.

For months, she had witnessed him wrestle that plane in the small hours of the morning, seen his anguished face, and listened to him plead with that young girl to jump. In her opinion, he deserved a medal, not the life sentence he was enduring. Ingrid's heart ached. She wanted to scream at the injustice of it all, to cry out for the lives lost. But Mac needed her to be strong. She swallowed the lump in her throat and gently pulled him towards her, wrapping him in her arms. Ingrid held him tight, grounding him.

Mac stood slowly as if in a trance. He ejected the drive and held it in his palm for a moment, the weight of it so much heavier than its size suggested. Six years of torment lived inside that tiny object. With one last deep breath, Mac snapped it in half and tossed it into the bin, where it belonged.

Chapter 79

Emily and Andrew had moved into his parents' home due to the ongoing construction of their own house. The incessant noise from the building site had made it difficult for them to sleep, study, or unwind, and with Andrew working shifts and Emily teaching at school, this arrangement made the most sense. They returned to their trailer on weekends, however, savouring the quiet when the heavy equipment lay dormant, with only the chorus of morning birds to wake them and distant coyotes howling them to sleep.

When Andrew wasn't working, Rusty and ER would drop by, lending a hand with the house or running equipment, while the women laboured in the garden. Rosemary and Andrea were regulars almost every weekend, and together, the three women poured their energy into transforming the yard into a vibrant oasis.

Sunday evenings were sacred, reserved for fresh lemonade on Rusty and Rosemary's porch. The sight of the three women, grubby and tired but bubbling with laughter, was a testament to their hard work. Their chatter filled the air as they discussed progress, plans, and the little joys of life. The tantalising aroma of Rosemary's Sunday roast wafted through the house, a family meal that was non-negotiable - there were three things you don't miss... church, your funeral and Rosemary's lunch!

After lunch, Andrew and Emily would swing on the porch glider, coffee cups in hand, marvelling at the changing colours of the trees as daylight faded into twilight. Conversation always flowed freely, sharing equally and enthusiastically about their life plans. They would talk late into the night, often losing track of time. Emily would recount work-life stories of a challenging child, or a student facing difficulties at home. Andrew, likewise, shared his grief over a lost patient, or his joy at witnessing a miraculous recovery.

At times, they talked about Travis — a bitter sweet reminder of what they had lost, and what had brought them together. Andrew still struggled with it. During those moments, Emily would grip his hand tightly, allowing him the space to mourn silently.

As their own bond deepened, they mused about ER and Andrea's blossoming relationship. Andrew enthused how good he was with little Travis, the way he fussed over Andrea's well-being, and how they seemed to balance each other perfectly.

In a quiet moment, Andrew said, "Y'know, ER and Andrea were a thing for a few months before she got together with Travis."

Emily nodded, remembering what Andrea had told her. "Yeah, she mentioned that! Apparently it came to an abrupt end when Travis showed up at school on his motorbike. And that was it! They rode all over the county — no helmet — just shorts, T-shirt and sneakers. He didn't even have a licence!"

"Yeah, that was Travis... carefree and devil-may-care." Andrew replied, a wistful smile on his face. "Teachers said he'd either end up a convicted criminal or save the world. He tried hard at the latter, and failed miserably at the former. I don't think I'll ever stop missing him."

Chapter 80

It was December 21st and, as planned, Emily had whisked Andrew away to England to spend Christmas with her parents. As she had anticipated, they immediately fell in love with him, drawn to his warmth and charm.

Emily and her mum had gone into town for a spot of last-minute shopping, and Andrew seized the opportunity to take her father for a pint at the local pub. With anxious anticipation, he broached the subject that had been weighing on his mind.

Christmas Eve arrived with the kind of peaceful, snowy evening that only England could offer. The cosy living room was aglow with twinkling lights, festive decorations and the crackling warmth of the coal fire. Bing Crosby's *'Little Drummer Boy'* played softly in the background, filling the room with a nostalgic, magical atmosphere.

Andrew had been up and down the stairs and in and out of the bathroom more times than you could count. His heart raced and his mouth was dry. He gathered all the composure he could muster, gently taking Emily's mulled wine from her hands and placing it on the table. He took her hand in his, the warmth of their connection unmistakable.

"Em," he began, his brow clammy and his voice wobbly, "I know we've only known each other for just over a year, but from the moment I saw you sitting on that there concrete porch in Nia-Nia, the wind blowing your hair and the sun highlighting your freckles... well, I knew right then you were someone special. Hell, I told Travis you had to be the most beautiful creature I'd ever seen. From that moment on, I wanted to know everything about you."

Emily had never seen him this nervous. It was endearing. Then Andrew dropped onto one knee. She felt her throat tighten as her eyes welled with tears, a blend of joy and disbelief. Andrew continued, his voice steadier and impassioned "I love you. I have since the moment you took my hand and said 'Hi', and I'll never stop loving you. Emily Esposito, will you marry me?"

Tears flowed freely, Emily's heart swelling with happiness, as she looked to her father, who nodded his approval. Her mother's hands flew to her mouth in shock, her face a portrait of astonished joy. Andrew opened the box. The sight of the elegant platinum band, its brilliant round-cut diamond flanked by two pear-shaped emeralds, stole Emily's breath.

With giddy excitement, she stretched out her left hand as Andrew slowly guided the ring onto her finger, his smile wide with love, before he stood to shake her father's hand. "I'll cherish your daughter, sir." he promised, his voice sincere. Emily's mother burst into tears, overwhelmed by the moment.

They returned to Texas on New Year's Eve, jet-lagged but exhilarated. Met by a gushing Rusty and Rosemary, and their jubilant reaction to the engagement, they stayed awake, ringing in the new year together before finally collapsing into bed... exhausted, but happy.

Spring arrived, and brought with it Emily's parents, who visited for the completion of the house. The two sets of parents bonded effortlessly, enjoying numerous day trips together, experiencing all that central Texas had to offer.

On days when her parents weren't out exploring the countryside, Emily, her mum, Andrea, and Rosemary worked together in the garden, tending to the flowers. Little Travis revelled in the mud, his innocence and carefree joy always uplifting.

Andrew and Emily had set their wedding date for mid-September, eager for an outdoor ceremony in their garden. The time between their engagement and the wedding passed in a flurry of flowers, planning, and preparations, but as the warmth of the impending marriage loomed, the school budget cuts were announced, and Emily's world tilted. Her beloved French programme was being cut from the curriculum, therefore losing her job and hence, a part of her own identity.

Andrew took a few days off, and together they visited the Immigration Department to update her status. After submitting new paperwork, letters from the school and Andrew's parents, Emily began to feel a glimmer of hope. The process took time, but in the end, their efforts were rewarded with an open work visa, allowing her to seek employment in any field.

By summer, Emily was working as a hostess at *The Vine in the Village*, the eclectic wine bar she and Andrew loved. Her enchanting accent and captivating stories quickly won over both staff and customers, and the camaraderie she found there completed her happiness. Despite the ups and downs, life had a way of surprising her. She missed teaching, but she could always tutor on the side, and for now, this job was fun.

Chapter 81

Mac kept his purchase of the island cottage a secret from Ingrid. He had enlisted Sammy to oversee the painting and redecorating — and also asked his thoughts on the possibility of opening a scenic flight business to add to the list of activities available to the bustling tourist trade. Sammy agreed it was a great idea, and Mac started contacting the relevant agencies and applying for permits. The process proved daunting, fraught with bureaucratic hurdles and endless red tape. But Mac's tenacity paid off, and by late summer, all the required documentation was in place.

Now, he was on the lookout for a suitable single-engine aircraft. It had to be a high-wing plane so passengers could enjoy unobstructed views. He was considering the Cessna 172 or 182 when he stumbled across an advert for a 1955 de Havilland Tiger Moth — a magnificent two-seat open-cockpit biplane, restored to its former glory by an aviation enthusiast. Unfortunately, the man's ill-health prevented him from future flying, and so this beauty was available for a very reasonable forty thousand dollars.

Mac flew to Nairobi and made his way to Wilson Field, where the plane was hangared. He took her up for a quick flight, and after fifteen minutes, he was hooked. He authorised the transfer of the money the very same day. He decided to keep the plane at Wilson Field until he was ready to move it to Zanzibar. This, too, would be a secret he had to keep until the right moment. He loathed keeping secrets from Ingrid, yet the thought of surprising her with his plans thrilled him.

Ingrid had been working a double shift that day. This gave Mac the opportunity to return from Nairobi and be home forty-five minutes ahead of her. The steaks were already out of the fridge, warming up to room temperature. He tuned in to BBC World Service Africa while he blended a batch of Montreal steak seasoning. Ingrid came in, exhausted. He poured her a much-needed glass of wine and sent her upstairs to soak in the tub while he continued preparing the meal. He was buzzing with excitement about his purchase but had to stop himself from spilling the beans too soon.

After dinner, in the cool of the evening, the lake stretching out below them, they strolled and chatted. Above them, the stars twinkled, their reflection shimmering on the calm waters of Lake Victoria. During the moments when their conversation lapsed into silence, and they both took in the beauty surrounding them, Mac realised how much he had never really noticed before. Life with Ingrid made everything feel vivid and full of purpose. Before her, it had been pretty much black and white, with varying shades of grey. Now, it was in full colour, bright and brimming with hope.

Back home, 'La Vie En Rose' playing softly in the background, they settled into a game of Rummikub. The coffee table was cluttered with numbered tiles as Mac frowned at his rack, debating his next move.

"You're stalling." Ingrid said, stretching out her legs and nudging his shin with her foot.

"I'm strategizing." Mac corrected, squinting at the pieces. "Big difference."

She smirked and took a sip of wine. "You can strategize all you want, I'm still going to win."

Mac exhaled dramatically, rearranging tiles for the third time before finally placing a cautious set on the table. Ingrid's eyes flicked over his move, then, with an infuriating lack of hesitation, she laid down a perfect sequence, dismantling one of his groups in the process.

"You're ruthless!" he groaned.

"You knew this when you invited me to play." She leaned back, satisfied. "You're the one who keeps believing you can beat me."

Mac shook his head, grinning as he refilled their glasses. "One of these days."

She clinked her glass lightly against his. "Keep dreaming, Dalton."

Chapter 82

As 2013 approached its conclusion, Andrew and Emily sat in their kitchen over bowls of fettuccine carbonara. CNN was showing footage of the devastating super-typhoon bearing down on the Philippines. "Shit!" Andrew reached for the remote and turned up the volume. They watched a harried reporter standing knee-deep in water, the winds battering a little-known city some eight hundred and fifty kilometres south of Manila. By morning, Tacloban would be known worldwide as the city that endured the strongest typhoon ever to make landfall — three hundred and fifty-kilometre-per-hour winds, a seven-metre storm surge, and three hundred millimetres of rain in just twelve hours.

"Oh my God! Those poor people." Emily murmured, eyes wide as the footage played. Roofs were already peeling off, flung through the air like scraps of paper.

"What the hell are they all still doin' there? The government should've started the evacuation hours ago. This is gonna be a disaster of biblical proportions." Andrew said in frustration. The image changed to a well-dressed weatherman discussing the satellite images that filled the screen in swirling red. He predicted that Typhoon Haiyan, or Yolanda as it was called in the Philippines, would make landfall in Eastern Samar and spread to the Visayas and Leyte districts between three and four in the morning local time. Andrew switched the television off when more mundane local news began to air.

Andrew pushed his pasta aside, picked up a piece of garlic bread, and clenched it between his teeth, as he opened his laptop and pulled up a map of the Philippines. "H-o-l-y shit!" he said, chewing on the bread. "They had an earthquake last month, and now this. Can these people not catch a break?!"

Shortly after the holiday season ended, Emily was working a quiet shift at the restaurant when a group of young Filipino nurses came in for a late meal after a long shift at the hospital. Emily overheard snippets of their conversation about how Typhoon Haiyan had killed over ten thousand people in just six hours. However, the official reports kept the death toll under ten thousand, enabling the Filipino government to control the disaster's narrative. Emily did not fully understand the implications, but grew more interested when she heard one of them saying they had raised four thousand dollars and much-needed medical supplies to send over. Unable to contain her curiosity, she said, "Sorry to interrupt, but I couldn't help overhearing your conversation. Are you talking about that typhoon that hit in November?"

"Yes, it was bad. So many people died. Tacloban is still a complete mess and aid isn't getting through to those who need it. I used to work there and my mother still lives there, so it hits close to home for me." said one of the nurses. Another chimed in, "I'm from Cebu, the neighbouring island. I did my training at Divine Word Hospital in Tacloban, and right now, it's the only operating hospital in the region. We used to have four big hospitals — now there's just the one. My friends still work there; they tell me things are getting worse by the day. A surge in dengue fever, chikungunya, cholera, and typhoid is on the rise due to stagnant and poor drinking water." A third nurse put down her fork and looked up at Emily, with an anguished look. "We all knew someone who died. My cousin died, her husband too, but the kids survived. Who is going to look after them? They're eight and nine years old."

Emily wasn't sure how she could help, but she took their phone numbers anyway.

During the following family Sunday lunch, Emily mentioned her encounter with the four nurses. It wasn't long before the disaster dominated the conversation, everybody at the table pitching in their concerns about what was happening in Tacloban.

Andrew sat quietly for a while as suggestions on how to raise money and supplies were thrown back and forth. "Y'all know it won't get there." His voice was low but firm. "These people are needin' help. And I've got plenty leave stacked up... I don't know that I can just sit here doin' nothin'." Emily looked at him, her heart racing. She knew what he was about to suggest before he even said it out loud.

After much finagling, cashing in of favours — and a modicum of grovelling — they were all set. By mid-January, they were on a flight to Manila with two duffle bags full of medical supplies donated by the four Filipino nurses, combined with Andrew's donations from firehouse suppliers. They had six bags in total to hand-deliver.

Twenty-two hours and two stops later, they finally touched down at Manila's Clark Air Force Base. They'd chosen that option instead of Ninoy Aquino International Airport because they'd heard they might be able to hitch a ride on one of the aid flights into Tacloban. Failing that, they could still purchase a ticket on one of the regional budget airlines operating from Clark.

They collected their bags and were held up in customs, as an officer went through their donations. Andrew's medical supplies were spread out on the long metal table, as were Emily's notebooks, pens, pencils, crayons, and English study materials, when a man in uniform wandered by and asked in an Australian accent, "G'day. You volunteers for Tacloban? Mick O'Rourke, Australian Air Force. We take off in two hours. There's a group assembled in the cafeteria. Go grab yourselves a coffee and see the liaison officer. She'll put you on the manifest."

Andrew thanked him profusely, as the customs officer instructed them to pack their bags, thanked them for volunteering, and welcomed them to the Philippines.

As the plane circled the city, the devastation below was staggering. What had once been a thriving urban centre, now resembled a war zone — half-collapsed buildings, the remnants of homes scattered like toys tossed in a child's game. Andrew's stomach knotted. How the hell had anybody made it through this? Most everyone had similar varying comments as they craned their necks to see through the few available windows of the massive Hercules C-130J.

After disembarking and thanking the crew, they walked across the tarmac. Dense, humid air settled on their skin. The smell of salt and decay filled their lungs. Debris was piled high in a field adjacent to the runway — broken glass, splintered wood, evidence of lives torn apart.

It had been two months since the typhoon made landfall, and still, not a single window was intact at the airport, including the control tower. There was no respite from the cloying, oppressive balmy weather, and Emily and Andrew were drenched in sweat by the time they made it to the taxi rank out front. Tuk-tuks, colourful jeepneys and battered sedans all vied for their business.

It was eight in the evening when they finally reached Divine Word Hospital. They were enthusiastically received by Tala, who had been asked to meet them and get them settled in. She apologised that the accommodation was sparse — it was originally designed to accommodate the on-call emergency room doctors. She warned them it could get quite loud, as it was adjacent to the ambulance drop-off point. She asked if she could get them anything, and when they declined, she told them that Dr. Mariano would meet them at eleven in the morning to arrange some shifts for Andrew and give him his identification badge. She bid them goodnight and left them to unpack.

True to Tala's words, the sounds of gurneys clattering and orders being barked, interspersed with sobbing and wailing, filtered down the tiny corridor and into their room. Red, white and blue strobe lights from the ambulances constantly filled the room via the small jalousie window. Andrew took in the accommodation, which consisted of two single beds, a wooden desk, and little else. There were nails in the wall and a few wire coat hangers hanging from them. The bathroom had a cold-water-only shower and toilet. "Well, ain't this quaint." He smirked.

"What?" Emily called above the noise, cupping her hand behind her ear for comic effect. They chuckled tiredly from their respective beds. It certainly wasn't The Ritz.

Chapter 83

After Mac shared with Ingrid the final moments of the doomed flight that altered his life, Ingrid had told of her own trauma at losing both parents on the same evening to a drunk driver, and how from that moment on, she'd struggled to find purpose in life. She had thrown herself completely into her work and despite being a good doctor and compassionate aid worker, she felt like an empty vessel adrift at sea with no anchor, until Dalton came along. A brighter future now beckoned.

Ingrid was working her final notice period at the hospital, and the couple were already deep into the process of planning their future, constantly reimagining their next steps, often settling on one idea, only to alter it again the following week. They felt they had so much catching up to do — eager to explore, taste, and embrace the freedom they'd only truly known since their worlds collided almost two years ago.

Their dining room table was strewn with maps, hastily made itineraries, discarded plans, dog-eared travel books, and pages torn from magazines. After weeks of mulling over their options, Ingrid finally said, "There's too much choice. Dalton, I'm leaving the first trip up to you. Surprise me!" With Mac's clandestine 'Operation Zanzibar' already in progress... this was music to his ears!

Before embarking on their new life, Ingrid had made one final commitment. She had pledged to assist a group of non-profit doctors she'd met at the conference in Dar es Salaam. They had asked her to consult on setting up a small trauma center in the Cuando Cubango province of Angola, focusing on treating landmine victims and providing rehabilitation for amputees. Ingrid reassured Mac she wouldn't be anywhere near the minefields. She was there only to advise and help link the hospital with potential donors.

This little stretch of hell, almost a hundred square kilometers, had approximately one thousand two hundred minefields. Angola had the highest density of landmines per square kilometer in the world, second only to Egypt. These mines were a tragic legacy of the Angolan Civil War (1975–2002), which erupted following the country's independence from Portugal. This bloody and violent conflict was a Cold War proxy, with the Soviet Union and the United States supporting opposing factions. The very same three liberation forces that ousted the Portuguese government and declared independence in 1975.

In 1997, the same year as her death, the late Diana, Princess of Wales had walked through a partially-cleared minefield in the area. That brave and selfless gesture shone a spotlight on the use of landmines in war. In Angola, feuding guerrillas would lay mines in a haphazard manner with no mapping or record of the locations of these deadly ordinates. Thus, not only did the enemy suffer, but local civilians also bore the very same fate. To date, the landmines, now some eighteen years beyond the end of the war, still kill or maim nearly five thousand people per annum. They stifle village growth, and although two agencies have worked tirelessly in the area for over fifteen years, it's expected that it will take another thirty-plus years to locate and destroy the last of these mines that decimate its citizens and hinder the economy.

With four days left at the hospital and a week before her departure for Angola, Ingrid had made the most of her remaining time with Mac. It proved more difficult than one might imagine — Ingrid had been invited to farewell dinners, hospital events, and a surprise party. At the hospital's formal farewell gathering, colleagues praised her for the profound impact she'd had on their lives. It wasn't surprising to Mac that Ingrid had touched so many hearts.

On a bright Sunday morning, Mac drove Ingrid to the airport. They held hands and chatted all the way to the check-in desk. At the terminal, they shared a passionate kiss, and Mac hugged her tightly. "Safe home." he said, his voice barely rising above the noise of the crowd. Ingrid turned, blowing him a kiss, as she melted into the sea of passengers.

Mac spent a busy Monday cleaning the house and doing laundry. By Tuesday afternoon, he'd packed his luggage, set it in the hallway by the front door, and received a call from Ingrid, albeit brief, who was waiting to board the one-hour helicopter hop from Menongue to the rural clinic. In anticipation of her return in a little under two weeks, Mac had purchased Ingrid a one way ticket to Zanzibar and placed it on her pillow. Despite numerous attempts to find the right words to reveal the long-held secret, he finally wrote a simple note with just four words... *'Meet me in Zanzibar.'*

Chapter 84

Andrew woke at daybreak. He had slept fitfully, a little apprehensive about what would be required of him — he had never worked on this side of the ambulance before. Dressed in his scrubs, he kissed Emily, and told her he was off in search of coffee. "Back in a flash."

He rounded the corner and stepped into the emergency room, which was bustling with activity for six in the morning. He stood in the little alcove and took in the scene. There were about sixteen beds lining the two walls; beyond that was the nurses' station, then the paediatric area with three beds, and the pharmacy at the far end of the room. To his left sat a desk at the entrance, which served as the triage and pre-admittance area, and as he walked towards the exit, he passed a small room, marked 'Minor Surgery'.

Andrew greeted the young male nurse at the table. "Good morning. Do you know where I can get some coffee?"

The young man stood up and said, "Ah, good morning, doctor. We heard there was a new volunteer doctor arriving. Welcome!"

Andrew corrected him, jovially. "I'm not a doctor — I just get to play one in the ambulance. I'm a paramedic."

Adon laughed. "I've almost finished my shift. If you give me ten minutes, I can walk with you to the coffee shop. There's a nice little

Australian-owned restaurant across the street; good coffee, great breakfasts and very popular with the ex-pat community. Perfect place to meet fellow aid workers and volunteers."

As Adon completed his paperwork, Andrew decided to pop back to the room to get Emily out of bed and see if she fancied breakfast. Emily was already up and dressed, perched on the edge of her bed, going through one of her bags. She seemed deep in thought.

"Hi, Hon. Oh good, you're up. Let's go git us some breakfast." Andrew said.

"Hey babe, how is it out there?" Emily enquired.

"A little daunting. Everything okay?"

"Oh, yeah... just feeling a bit lost is all, trying to come up with something to justify my existence. What if I'm not able to teach here — who knows what schools are left?"

"I'm sorry, hon, I just don't know at this point. Let's ask around. One thing's for sure, you certainly won't be short of something to do — just look at this place! Hey, maybe you could initiate a food programme or somethin'?" Andrew said, as he hugged her and then caught her up on his meeting with Adon. As they approached the emergency room, he signalled to Adon and pointed at the exit. Adon nodded, and Andrew and Emily waited outside for him to finish up. There were at least a dozen people sitting on chairs under the corrugated awning waiting to be tended to, and Andrew surmised that this was what represented a waiting room.

Adon stepped out a few minutes later, introduced himself to Emily, and led the way down the side of the hospital. They crossed the busy thoroughfare, alive with the hum of activity, but emanating an undercurrent of strain. The air smelled faintly of saltwater and diesel, a constant reminder of the recent devastation. The heat was oppressive, and the distant chatter of vendors and the clang of construction reverberated around them.

They passed a few more demolition sites, Adon commenting all the way. "Here it is on the left," he said. They crossed the road, teeming with pedestrians, most under colourful umbrellas, chatting amicably as they sidestepped debris and dodged a graffiti emblazoned jeepney.

They took an outside table on the road-side patio and ordered full

English breakfasts and cappuccinos all round. Adon gave them a rundown of what had happened that fateful November morning and promised to give them a tour of the most devastated neighbourhoods, or 'barangays'.

Adon talked nonstop, pausing only when he ate or to take a sip of coffee. "...you couldn't have imagined it in your wildest dreams." He went on. "The storm surge was so high, it carried ten ocean freighters right into the downtown core. The statistics are heartbreaking — thirty thousand fishing boats destroyed, thirty-three million coconut trees uprooted, over a million homes lost and four million people displaced."

"Oh my fucking God, I can't even get my head around that!" Emily said, stunned. "How far are we from the sea?"

He took a sip of coffee and answered, "Well, to give you an idea, our hospital is two kilometres from the sea and we were swimming in the emergency room, actually swimming... gathering what equipment and medical supplies we could, before the water almost reached the ceiling. We were fortunate enough to only close for a week before being able to reopen. We used to have four major hospitals in Tacloban. Now, it's only us and the Eastern Visayas Regional Medical Centre that are operational. Tacloban Doctors is scheduled to open in a few weeks... but Bethany, where Médecins Sans Frontières has a tent-hospital, will probably never reopen."

Emily glanced at her watch, aware they had been in the restaurant for over an hour and a half. Andrew, the severity of the situation sinking in, was completely captivated as Adon spoke and had lost all track of time — he could have easily listened for hours. He had seen devastation before, but nothing like this — this wasn't just destruction; it was the entire obliteration of lives, homes, and history.

"I'm sorry. Andrew, you have a meeting with Dr. Mariano in thirty minutes. We'd better get back." Emily eventually interrupted.

Andrew hurried to pay the check, and asked Adon when he was next on duty. Adon said he would be on at nine that night.

"Okay, buddy, I guess I'll see you later then. And thanks for the chat, man. I've really enjoyed your company." Andrew said, sincerely, taking Emily's hand and embarking on the lively jaunt back to the ER.

Dr. Mariano not only managed the emergency room, but was also the chief orthopaedic surgeon — and, Andrew later came to discover, the most renowned in the Philippines. He would also come to realise that this was true of many of the doctors working at the hospital during his stay — most were leaders in their field.

After a brief introduction, Dr. Mariano turned to Emily, his smile soft but perceptive. "Are you in the medical field, too?"

Emily shifted on her feet, tucking a strand of hair behind her ear. "No, actually, I'm a teacher... or I was. I'm just trying to figure out how I can help."

His expression brightened. "A teacher, really? My wife is a teacher. She's been helping out at one of the barangays. The schools are gone, but she's trying to make do, teaching wherever she can."

Emily's face lit up, and she leaned forward. "Do you think I could meet her? I'd be happy to help in any way possible."

"I'll introduce you at lunchtime, if you're available. I think you two will get along well." Dr. Mariano's voice softened, as if recognising the uncertainty in her eyes. "There's always something to be done, Emily, trust me. You'll find your place here. You must be exhausted from your flight. Why don't you two relax today, wander around, get a feel for the place, then start tomorrow? We're always short-staffed at night, so for the next few days, if you could work the graveyard shift from nine until seven that would be most helpful. We can swap that around by the end of the week. Does that sound okay?"

"Sure, no problem. What would you have me do?" Andrew asked.

"How about you man the triage desk and jump in where you're comfortable? I will have one of the nurses who speaks Tagalog help with the translations, but a good many people speak English, so I think you'll be fine. And Emily, don't worry about having nothing to do. There is more work to be done than there are hours in the day, believe me." Dr. Mariano glanced up at the time on the wall clock and said he had to prepare for surgery, but not to hesitate to contact him if they needed anything.

"I have bags full of medical supplies that were donated. What should I do with those?" Andrew asked, just as Dr. Mariano was turning to leave.

"Dr. Ignacio will be in shortly. She will happily take them from you.

Go to the nurses' station and see Gabriel; have him call you when she gets in. Thanks for everything, Andrew. We really appreciate you and Emily being here." As he was turning the corner, he stopped. "You and Emily eat pizza? I was thinking there's a restaurant that just reopened last week across the street... does great Italian food."

"Yes, sir, indeed! We eat pizza."

"Great! How about two o'clock for lunch? See you there." Dr. Mariano said, his smile reassuring. Emily's shoulders relaxed slightly, her eyes regaining their sparkle, as she envisaged a path forward beginning to take shape.

Chapter 85

Mac sat on runway seven in his open-cockpit aircraft, wearing jeans, a heavy, distressed leather jacket, leather gloves, a replica WW1 sheepskin flying helmet, and a pair of flying goggles. He could not help feeling like Biggles, the main character from the W.E. Johns novels he had loved to read as a boy. *The White Fokker* and *The Camels Are Coming* were two of his favourites.

The Tiger Moth had to be hand-started using the propeller. The plane possessed no electrics, and thus had no radio, so Mac had purchased a small but powerful handheld radio and contacted the tower for clearance. He had filed a 'visual flight rules' flight plan, with several stops, due to the plane's limited fuel capacity.

His first stop would be to refuel in Moshi, Tanzania. He was excited, as this took him over Amboseli National Park in southern Kenya, which bordered Kilimanjaro National Park. Both were teeming with an abundance of wildlife, including large herds of elephants. Standing sentinel over these breathtaking parks, Mount Kilimanjaro towered nineteen thousand three hundred feet, its peak snow-capped year-round. From there, he would fly east, with fuel stops at Korogwe, Tanga, and then the final leg over the Indian Ocean to Zanzibar.

Mac received his clearance to depart, and the old bird trundled down the runway. Looking out the side of the cockpit, he kept her straight until the tail lifted off the ground, and he could see through the small windshield. The tail wagged slightly in a mild crosswind, as if bidding farewell to its old home, before lifting off. Mac had not flown taildraggers in a long time and was loving the feeling of the simplicity of the old girl. This was flying in its purest form — stick and rudder, no electrics, and a simple instrument panel. Mac levelled off at four thousand feet and maintained a comfortable speed of one hundred and ten kilometres per hour. It was going to be a long, slow day... and he was looking forward to every minute of it. At this altitude and speed, he wouldn't miss a thing!

Mac flew to the west of Mt. Kilimanjaro, granting him a view like no other. With Mt. Meru further to the west, and Kilimanjaro National Park below, flying in an open cockpit at eight thousand feet, he marvelled at the mountain towering a further twelve thousand feet above him. The little plane did not have the altitude to fly above the mountain, so he simply circled it in awe, at times spotting small groups of climbers making their way up from different sides of the massif. Climbing a mountain was not something he had ever considered, but if he were to do it, this would be the one — the vista would be spectacular!

Mac landed at Moshi Airport and arranged for a bowser to fuel the plane. He calculated his fuel burn and was pleased with the six and a half gallons per hour consumption. The attention that his canary-yellow plane garnered, took him by surprise. The ramp crew, maintenance personnel and pilots alike all wanted photos of his plane. Some even posed in front of the aircraft, asking Mac to borrow his flight helmet and jacket for the shot. He knew then he had made the right choice with the purchase — everyone loved the old girl.

"So, what's her name?" asked a KLM pilot, as they chatted about the plane. Mac had not thought of naming her, but the first thing that came to mind was Ingrid.

"Ingrid. Her name is Ingrid." Mac said, feeling the familiar warmth that came with saying her name. It was a perfect choice — a representation of resilience and grace — qualities both she and the plane shared in their own ways.

After paying the landing fees and fuel bill, and calling ahead to

Korogwe to ensure they had fuel for his next stop, Mac bid farewell to a waving crowd, all wishing him well. He turned the plane around and taxied, waiting for clearance for take-off. Korogwe was just two hundred and sixty kilometres away, barely fifteen minutes in a jetliner, but a two-and-a-half-hour flight for Mac. He was travelling no faster than a car, but with much better views and... oh, so much more fun, he thought to himself. The hours slipped by as he soared over patchworks of green and gold, the soft hum of the engine blending with his thoughts.

Mac touched down — the first grass runway he had landed on in almost thirty years. Memories of his earlier flying career came flooding back, towing gliders to build hours every weekend at Gowran Grange Glider Club, just outside Dublin. His arrival at Korogwe solidified his feelings that the Tiger Moth was indeed the right choice, as a crowd gathered, once again asking for photographs of him and his plane. He wished he had time to entertain the children who begged him for a ride and who pawed his plane lovingly. He spent an hour hoisting the kids into the plane for photographs, their parents and friends capturing the moment while they giggled and posed in the cockpit. Their excitement was contagious, and their beaming smiles contrasted with their dark faces, melting Mac's heart. The little joy it brought to those much less fortunate than most, lifted his heart and carried him through the day. He found himself recalling their laughter and smiling all the way to his next refuelling at Tanga, the last stop before flying over the Indian Ocean to his final destination.

Sammy was waiting for him when he arrived in Zanzibar and guided him through the maze of offices he needed to visit to ensure the plane was registered correctly, customs was satisfied, and a hangar was secured. It was well after nine that night when Sammy dropped him at the cottage.

Mac looked at the beautiful hand-carved wooden oval sign hanging on two chains, gently blowing in the wind. It read *Nyumba Ingrid*. Mac looked quizzically at Sammy, who was beaming. "It means 'House of Ingrid' in Swahili. I carved it myself."

Mac was touched, genuinely speechless at Sammy's wonderful gesture. He ran his fingers over the wood, acknowledging the thoughtfulness and dedication that had gone into that level of workmanship. Thanks to Sammy, it was as though Ingrid had already begun putting her stamp on their future home. Mac put his arm around Sammy's shoulder. "It's perfect." he murmured, his throat tightening. Mac knew they were going to be so welcomed, and so happy. It already felt like home.

Sammy gave Mac a quick tour of the refurbishments he had been tasked with overseeing. The results were incredible, and he knew Ingrid would absolutely love the old clawfoot bathtub that stood atop the newly-installed terracotta tiles in the bathroom. In his usual organised manner, Sammy pointed out all the receipts neatly laid out on the table, before he took Mac through to the bedroom and showed him the safe he had installed in the cupboard.

Sammy opened the safe and withdrew an envelope containing just over three hundred dollars, handing it to Mac. Realising it was his change from the renovations, Mac handed it back to Sammy. "A bonus, my friend, for everything you've done. Use it well, for you and your family."

Sammy protested. However, Mac insisted, and Sammy was overjoyed. "I'd better get home. It's almost eleven and Justina will be waiting up — she'll want to know everything!" he laughed. "That woman would not be able to wait until morning to hear how you are... and especially how you like the home improvements."

"Thanks again, my friend! You're a legend. I can't wait till Ingrid gets here. She's going to be blown away. Goodnight, Sammy. Send my love to Justina... and tell her I love the place! Safe home, now!"

Chapter 86

Andrew and Emily had settled into life in the demolished city of Tacloban. Andrew was working five nights a week, from nine until seven, while Emily had established a drop-in school in barangay sixty-eight, also known as Anibong. Her classroom was set up under the bow of the 'Eva Jocelyn', one of the huge freighters washed inland during the super-typhoon. Classes were held from eight in the morning until one in the afternoon, and typically, there were anywhere from fifteen to thirty children in attendance at any one time.

After his nightshift, Andrew would accompany Emily to the school, then volunteer his medical services to those in the barangay who either could not afford to visit the hospital, or were afraid their few remaining belongings would be robbed in their absence.

Then, early afternoon, their duties carried out, they would stroll back towards the hospital. If time permitted, they would sit in Sunzibar Café, known for its unusually unique, but delicious, nacho salad. But more often than not, they would grab a burger and fries at Jollibee's, the Filipino fast food chain that had opened up a mobile concession on Avenida Rizal, just three blocks shy of the hospital. This was not only convenient, but half the price of the McDonald's they passed along the way... and far less crowded. They would often bump into other aid workers there, stopping to chat and catch up on each other's progress, and the latest plans for rebuilding the city. There was a strong camaraderie among the volunteers.

Continuing their walk home, Emily gazed around her environs, always noting something new to comment on, no matter how many times they passed the same area. She marvelled at the tenacity of the Filipino people. "It's awe-inspiring," Emily remarked. "Most have no running water, no electricity, live in half collapsed buildings, and yet they always appear happy."

"Yip. It's been just over three months since the disaster, the streets are still one almighty mess... hell, there are ships where houses s'posed to be, and y'know what... I have not heard a single complaint, not one." Andrew said. "You shoulda been in New Orleans after the shock wore off the townsfolk when Katrina hit. It was hotter than a billy goat in a pepper patch with folks fussin' 'bout every little thing! Y'all could not fix anything quick enough!"

"We really do take so much for granted back home. Not only do we want everything done right now, this minute... we expect it. Demand it. This experience really is a wake-up call."

They waited for a Tuk-Tuk to pass before darting across the street towards the hospital entrance, dodging traffic. They both smiled at a little motorcycle racing past, piloted by a young man wearing shorts and sandals, his open shirt blowing in the wind, his wife or significant other, sat side-saddle in her crisp, white nurse's uniform, holding a novel in one hand and a multi-coloured umbrella in the other.

"Dang! You sure see some weird shit 'round these parts." Andrew said, kissing Emily and heading back to the room to get some sleep.

Andrew in his bed, and Emily in the cafeteria grading her pupil's schoolwork, both pondered how humbled they were by the graciousness and resilience of these people... and how grateful they were for this rewarding opportunity, despite the circumstances.

Chapter 87

Ingrid was deeply ensconced in her work in Angola. She and Mac would endeavour to speak every two or three days, but the communications were hit and miss. Often the call would be disconnected midway through a conversation, which frustrated them no end, but it was part and parcel of living in remote areas and they were used to it. Ingrid told Mac during one call that she was not exactly in the middle of nowhere... but she could see it from the hospital window. Mac had laughed at her quirky sense of humour and longed to have her back.

In their latest conversation, she had pleaded for him to tell her where they were going when she got back, but he sidestepped the question and feigned a bad connection. He was desperate to tell her there was a ticket waiting on her pillow, and a taxi arranged to the airport. She didn't know about the beach house; she didn't know about 'Ingrid' the Tiger Moth; she didn't even know Mac had been speaking to her from Zanzibar! It was killing Mac. With each passing day, the burden of secrecy grew heavier, but he knew the surprise would be worth the wait.

Mac and Sammy had become firm friends. He and Justina had stopped by the bungalow a few times for a meal or a drink, and Justina couldn't wait to meet Ingrid. One night, while chatting, Mac asked, "Sammy, would you come up for a wee ride with me, show me some of the landmarks from the air, so I'll be able to point them out to paying guests?"

"Oh, I would love that! I get to be your first passenger." He said, excitedly, his enthusiasm contagious. "How about tomorrow after school? I can pick you up at two o'clock if you like."

"Ah, don't trouble yourself. I'll cadge a ride with Ernesto; he's going into town for supplies tomorrow. But if I could get a ride home, that'd be grand!" Mac responded, before turning to Justina. "Please, Justina, would you tell your man, business is business, and friends are friends. He argues every time I try to pay him for his taxi services." Mac shook his head, grinning. "I'm telling you, Sammy, you keep refusing my money, and I'll start handing it directly over to Justina." He winked at her.

Justina chimed in. "Please do! Dar es Salaam has some lovely dresses." she teased.

"Okay, okay, you win!" Sammy laughed, throwing his hands in the air. The couple stood to leave, the men reiterating that they'll meet at the airport tomorrow at two. Mac shook his hand and kissed Justina. "If you ever want to come up for a ride, Justina, you let me know."

Mac was at the airport early the following day and had wheeled the plane out of the hangar. He was talking to the young signwriter who had brought along script samples. Mac chose his preferred font and a vibrant red for the artwork, and the young man set to work, ready to paint *Ingrid* on the cowling. Mac, meanwhile, sat in a canvas folding chair in the bright, morning sunshine and plotted the best scenic flight route with which to take in as much of the island as possible in an hour. Mac looked up from his notes periodically to watch the young man's progress and smiled as *Ingrid*'s name began to take shape on the aircraft.

Zanzibar was eighty-five kilometers in length and thirty-five across at its widest point, and Mac had calculated that he could not circumnavigate the entire island in an hour. He would need Sammy's expertise in getting the best results, but for now, he surmised that he would take off and fly south, turning east over Jozani Forest, then north up the coast over Chwaka Bay to Ras Nungwi, then south along the west coast over Tumbatu Island, then finally Stone Town and back to the airport. He calculated that this route could be flown in fifty minutes, which gave him ample time in his allotted hour for photographs, should they happen upon a pod of dolphins during the trip, or maybe an extra circle over Stone Town.

The artist had finished his preparatory sketch of the name and asked Mac if he liked it before he proceeded to paint. Mac loved it, and stepped back, imagining it in red.

"It's looking great! I'm grabbing a Coke. Would you like one?" Mac asked, as the young man began mixing his paints to get the exact colour match.

"I'd love a Fanta Grape if they have one? If not, Fanta Orange, please." he replied gratefully. "I think it is going to look magnificent when it's finished, Mr Mac. A good colour choice."

Mac walked into the terminal and was immediately surrounded by a group of curious people enquiring about his plane, excitedly firing questions at him about what he was doing. Mac filled them in on his plans and spent the next thirty minutes fielding inquiries and scribbling his name and contact number on bits of paper, while others entered his contact details directly into their phones. He apologised that his website was not yet functional, and business cards were not yet ready, but confirmed he would be fully operational within the month. Instead, he handed out Sammy's cards, stating they could contact him for all their touring needs, transportation, and scenic flights. Finally, he was able to break away and order the drinks.

Mac had every confidence that this business was actually going to work. He wandered back to the plane and felt his heart lift at the sight of *Ingrid* now coming to fruition in bright red. It would be a 'wow' moment when Ingrid finally got to see this, Mac thought. She could never have guessed that their someday-dreams were already here, taking shape, just waiting for her to arrive.

Sammy arrived just after two o'clock and spotted *Ingrid*'s name emblazoned on the aircraft. "Oh, now she's ready for business! She looks great!"

"Thanks, she sure does! Right, are you ready for our maiden voyage?" Mac said, setting up the handheld radio. He handed Sammy a pair of headphones, leaving him to study the route on his map, while Mac walked around the plane performing a pre-flight inspection. "Okay, let's take her up. I hear the scenery is better from up there." Mac quipped, as he put on his jacket.

Sammy slipped into his windbreaker and started to clamber into the back seat. "No, no! You sit up front; I sit in the back." Mac instructed. Sammy looked confused and startled, his eyes bulging in fear.

"I fly it from the back, and the passenger sits up front." Sammy remained bewildered and still a bit hesitant. "Relax, I saw this in a cartoon once. I think I can do it," Mac said, holding a poker face for as long as possible, before bursting into laughter at Sammy's expression. "God, I wish I had a camera. Your face was priceless!"

He helped Sammy with his seatbelt and plugged in the headset before settling into the rear seat. Twenty minutes later, they were passing over Jozani Forest at three thousand feet, turning north, towards the coast. Sammy finally became more at ease and began pointing out places of interest, giving Mac snippets of information and historical facts.

Just after they had reached Ras Nungwi and were beginning their southbound leg down the west coast, Mac asked Sammy if he wanted to take the controls and feel what it was like to fly. Under Mac's careful instruction, Sammy put his feet on the rudders and his hand tentatively on the stick. He could feel Mac's input on the controls, following them gingerly. Mac released the controls and allowed Sammy to fly for five minutes before telling him. "Hey, Sammy. You know you've been flying the plane by yourself for the past five minutes?" He leaned forwards, showing Sammy his hands to prove the point. Mac took back the controls and landed at the airport. Sammy was in post-flight ecstasy, talking non-stop about how amazing it was, how fantastic the addition of these scenic flights would be to the tourism industry, and how he could not wait to add it to his website and brochures.

Mac called Ingrid just after six that evening. He was still giddy with excitement from the day's events and struggled to keep it to himself. This proved easier, however, when Ingrid had plenty to talk about. She revealed that, although the work was rewarding, she was definitely looking forward to returning home next week. She relayed how glad she was that it was not her responsibility to deal with all the red tape surrounding the importation of goods needed to make the project a success. She told of the group's dismay at having to return to Luanda twice already to meet with officials trying to charge import duty on donations, treating the project as a profiteering scheme, as opposed to a not-for-profit endeavour. She informed Mac that the oil industry had made Luanda the most expensive city to live in in the world, surpassing Hong Kong, and how this had led to greed in every sector, including hospitals, with the poor and sick suffering the most.

The connection was not great, as per usual, and they found themselves having to repeat sentences, over and over. They both agreed that they would rather catch up in person when she got home. They professed their love to one another and managed a couple of half-heard 'miss yous' before the call spontaneously disconnected, unable to reconnect.

Mac grinned, holding the phone tight even after the line went dead. The house was ready. The plane was ready. And for Mac, the greatest gift of all was yet to come — the moment Ingrid finally stepped through the door. Until then, the waiting was all he had. Like a kid on a countdown to Christmas, six more sleeps, he thought. Just six more.

Chapter 88

Two weeks before Emily and Andrew were due to return home, Andrew's shifts in the emergency room had become gruelling. Dengue fever was on the rise, cases of cholera and typhoid were increasing daily, and the queue of patients waiting outside the ER was relentless. In addition, trauma victims would arrive by ambulance almost hourly, most from motor vehicle accidents. The strain was evident.

It was approaching two in the morning, and there was finally a lull. Andrew and the nursing staff folded and wrapped bandages while sipping coffee, at last able to hear the quiet background music. The moment of calm didn't last for long. Two ambulances screeched to a stop outside, sirens blaring and lights flashing.

Andrew, Adon, and Gabriel rushed to meet them. Due to overcrowding, triage had become standard practice in the ambulances themselves. They found eight patients inside, seven suffering various non-life-threatening injuries, while one showed no vital signs. All were young, between sixteen and twenty. At first, Andrew assumed it was a car accident, but it turned out to be two motorcycles and a pedestrian. All were dressed in shorts and sandals. None had worn helmets. Andrew shook his head.

They admitted, treated, and released most of them. One girl, no older than sixteen, had suffered a broken arm and severe abrasions to her body. She sobbed in pain as Andrew spent over an hour cleaning and dressing her wounds, before admitting her with pain medication.

The ER finally settled again. Just before five in the morning, the peace was shattered, when the doors burst open and a woman stormed in, followed by three men. They shouted in Tagalog. Andrew didn't understand the words, but the look on the nurses' faces was a tell-tale sign that this was not good. Then he saw it.

A machete in the woman's grip. A gun in the man's hand.

Shouts exploded through the ER. A nurse screamed. Andrew's pulse pounded as his mind locked onto the immediate threat — the gun. The man was only a few feet away. He was scanning the room, clearly looking for someone.

Andrew had no time to think. Instinct took over. In one swift motion, he lunged, swinging a powerful punch into the man's jaw. Bone met bone with a sickening crack. The man collapsed instantly, the gun clattering to the floor. Adon scooped it up before anyone else could react.

The woman turned towards Andrew, grasping the machete tighter. He read the intention in her eyes — she was about to swing. Before she could, he lashed out, kicking her legs from under her. She hit the floor hard. Security burst in, wrestling the woman and the unconscious man into handcuffs. The other two men bolted, disappearing into the night.

It was only after the chaos had died down that Andrew caught his breath, and the story unfolded. The girl from the motorcycle crash was the girlfriend of the rider who had died. His parents were blaming her for his death and had come to kill her.

Andrew exhaled sharply. "Man, they was wound up real good, ready to get 'er done. They was gonna shoot 'er right here in the ER! Dang, I thought they was gangbangers lookin' for drugs." he muttered, his accent thickening in his exhaustion.

The tension in the room cracked as Adon tried to mimic Andrew's drawl, sending everybody into fits of laughter. It was a much-needed moment of levity, the staff collectively breathing a sigh of relief.

By the time Andrew's shift came to an end, he was running on empty. He trudged back to the room and collapsed onto the bed. He was recounting his night to Emily, as he drifted off, mid-sentence. Emily slipped off his shoes, kissed his forehead, and tiptoed out, leaving him to sleep.

Emily poured herself a cup of tea and settled herself down in the quiet cafeteria, for a stint of marking paperwork. The cleaner, mopping the floor, smiled at her. "Magandang umaga, Emily."

"And good morning to you, too." she replied with a warm smile.

She loved learning Tagalog and took every opportunity to practice. "Kumusta?" She enquired, asking the cleaner how she was.

"I am fine." the cleaner replied, delighted with her English pronunciation.

Tomorrow, we'll change it up, Emily thought, already planning her next phrase.

Though she tried to focus on marking, her mind wandered. The violence in the ER was disturbing. No matter how many times she told herself that these things happened everywhere, she couldn't shake the lingering unease. Was it just bad luck, or had Tacloban become more dangerous in the aftermath of the storm? She shook off the thoughts and returned to her papers.

Andrew woke late that morning... with no inkling of the extraordinary events that would soon pull him into a whirlwind of chaos he was not expecting.

He hurriedly dressed and found Emily still buried in exam papers. "G'mornin', Darlin'. Ready for breakfast?"

"Well, hello! You were out like a light and sawing logs before I could kiss you. Interesting night? And yes, I'd love some breakfast. I'm famished!" she said, stuffing her books, papers, and laptop into her bag.

"And you can still find stuff in that bag?" he enquired, teasingly, stepping back just in time to dodge a playful swat.

As they cut through the emergency room, the place was in full swing — overwhelmed and understaffed. Andrew paused.

"Gimme a minute, Hon. I just wanna check if they need help." he said, kissing Emily.

"Okay, I'll meet you at the café. I need a cappuccino."

Andrew approached the nurses' station, and they assured him that reinforcements were on the way. As he headed for the door, a voice called out his name. He turned to see a short man, mid-forties, in light blue scrubs, wearing a welcoming smile.

"I've heard a lot of good things about you, Andrew. Thanks for all your help."

Andrew shook his hand. "I'm sorry, I don't think we've met."

"Dr. Cruz. Hospital director and neurosurgeon."

Andrew blinked in surprise. A neurosurgeon, here?

"I didn't realise we had a neurosurgeon!" he muttered to a nurse, as Cruz gave orders to his team.

"Uhuh, we're fortunate. There are only two in the country as esteemed as him — the other's in Manila."

Andrew watched as Dr. Cruz explained a case to the nurses, his quiet authority evident in every word. There was something about him — an air of gentle confidence, a calming influence amid chaos.

Andrew stepped out of the hospital, dodging an incoming ambulance. He welcomed the midday heat — the sunlight and warmth replenishing. The hospital's urgency faded behind him, replaced by lively chatter from the café.

Emily was chatting animatedly, surrounded by a large group of aid workers from a variety of organisations. Their laughter and easy conversation made it feel like an entirely different world. Andrew squeezed by, exchanging greetings, and sat down next to her, asking if she had ordered breakfast. "Not yet." she replied. "I was waiting for you. This is Tomas, Sven, Jo-Jo, and Pete." she said, waving at the harried waiter, holding her index and middle finger aloft, indicating two of their 'usual'. He nodded and smiled, calling out over the din, "Five minutes, Miss Emily."

Andrew leaned back in his chair. Thoughts of the night before still looming heavy, at odds with the airiness of the laughter-infused chit-chat around the table. One thing was certain, every day held surprises. Some light, some dark. Out of sight, but just around the corner.

Chapter 89

Ingrid stood next to the helipad, awaiting the chopper. She and Mac talked on the phone, excitement brewing that she'd be home the following day. Mac had arranged for a taxi to pick her up and take her home, where she would discover the note on her pillow, and the ticket to Zanzibar. Ingrid, of course, knew nothing of this — she assumed Mac would be there to greet her. And so she went on.

"Can you tell me where we're going when you pick me up? As soon as I see you... before we even leave the airport. Pleeease."

She was like a persistent toddler. Mac found it amusing.

"Aye, aye! Sure, you know yourself, of course I will..." Mac assured her, then added, teasingly, "...maybe!"

Ingrid moaned with feigned indignation.

As the sound of the approaching helicopter grew louder, its rotors thrashing the air, Mac concluded, "Go on now, be off with you, and get yourself back. I'll see you tomorrow. Safe home. I love you."

Ingrid had to shout over the wash, her finger in one ear and the phone pressed hard against the other, she yelled, "My ride's here, my love." Turning away from the approaching Jet Bell Longranger, she bent over to hear him better and finish the conversation. "I can barely hear you, but I love you and I'll see you tomorrow."

Mac responded, "Love you too, my sweet. See you tomorrow."

The following morning, Mac and Sammy stopped off at the florist, and Mac purchased a large bouquet of flowers before they headed to the airport. He was delirious with excitement and nervously checked his watch as the traffic crept forward.

"We have plenty of time, Mac, don't worry. We'll be there an hour before it lands." Sammy said as he shifted gears. Sure enough, the traffic picked up the pace once they turned onto airport road.

"Aye, Sammy, I know. I'm just eager to see her again, and nervous at the same time. I'm just hoping I've done the right thing. I made all these decisions without her knowledge. What if she doesn't like it?" Mac responded.

"She won't like it. She'll love it! You told me it was her favourite place, and she loves you. I know about love, and that woman adores you, but for the life of me, I can't figure out why." Sammy smiled.

"Oh, you're a craic, so you are!" Mac said with raised eyebrows, playfully punching Sammy on the arm and chuckling, as they pulled into the airport.

They found an empty table, and Mac set the flowers on it. He pulled out his phone and checked for messages. Then Sammy said, "The flight is delayed, now due at twelve ten."

"Ah, shite. If you need to go, go on. We'll get a taxi home."

"Hakuna Matata, bwana. I'm free all day. And I'm not going to miss the look on her face when you show her Nyumba Ingrid." Sammy retorted.

"Fair enough. Right, two large coffees coming up then — we're here for the long haul." Mac left his satchel on the floor, his phone on the table and went to stand in line. He guessed everyone else in the queue was resigned to the same fate, waiting for the delayed Precision Air flight. Sammy had abated Mac's worries about Ingrid not liking the house, but as he stood in line, his mind drifted again. *Why had she not called when she got home? Maybe she's toying with me. Yeh, that sounds like her - making me now wait for her reaction, because I made her wait with this secret. Ha. Or maybe there just wasn't time to call. A delayed flight from Luanda to Johannesburg, then another flight delay from Joburg to Kampala, she wouldn't have arrived home until two in the morning. Yes, that makes sense. Or has she read the note and is disappointed it's Zanzibar again? Oh God, I hope it's not that. But she doesn't realise I've bought OUR cottage. Ah, she'll love it. Sammy's right, she'll be blown away.*

He settled on that thought and smiled, as the barista brought him out of his daydream. "Will that be everything, sir?"

Mac's phone was buzzing on the table, incoming call. Sammy looked up and saw Mac busy paying, then glanced down at the phone. Ingrid's face lit the screen.

Mac, balancing two coffees and two apple turnovers, glanced over at Sammy. Sammy, answering Ingrid's call, gave Mac the thumbs-up signal. "Hello, Miss Ingrid, it's Sammy. Mac is just getting coffee. Hold on, he's on his way back."

Mac assumed Sammy would have answered his phone for one reason only; Ingrid was calling. He headed for the table, treading carefully as he walked, negotiating people and suitcases, trying not to fill the saucers before he made it back.

Sammy stopped talking, shocked at the voice on the other end. A man, a stranger with a heavy accent he couldn't place, was talking to him from Ingrid's phone.

"Hello. Is this Dalton McBride?"

Sammy stammered, "Er...no, I'm a friend. Who is this?" A concerned look spread over his dark, cherub-like face.

"I am Dr. Monterio from Josina Machel Hospital in Luanda, Angola. I need to speak to Mr. McBride."

"Just a second." Sammy said, dread creeping in and taking over his whole being. Mac was smiling as he set the cups and pastries down. Sammy froze and struggled to get his words out, when Mac grabbed the phone. "Hi, Sweetheart. About bloody time." he beamed, winking at Sammy.

There was a pause. Mac's face drained of all colour. He stumbled, caught the edge of the table to steady himself, upsetting the coffees, the cups and saucers crashing to the ground, coffee spilling off the table and onto the floor. Sammy was up in an instant, coming to Mac's aid as he tried to sit, slipping off the edge of the chair, before slumping into his seat. "No... no... no." he repeated, in between breaths.

Sammy could only hear one side of the conversation, but he knew it was bad, and clasped his hand to his mouth. People stopped and gawked, others came close. Sammy ran interference and halted their approaches.

"No, it's not possible. Are you certain it's her? How can you be so fucking sure! You never saw her before! Aaaagggghhhh... FUCK!" he screamed into the phone. He tossed it onto the table. "This can't be happening. This cannot be happening!" He staggered out of the terminal, crashing into people and trolleys, tears rolling down his cheeks, before collapsing to the ground. Mac felt his knees hit the asphalt. Sobbing loudly, his chest tightening with each breath, he choked on air and bile, his hands scraping against the rough ground as his world splintered.

Sammy retrieved Mac's discarded phone. Dr. Monterio was still talking. "Mr. McBride? Mr McBride, are you still there?"

Sammy answered and introduced himself as Mac's friend. "Please... what's happened?"

"Dr. Svenson and four colleagues were killed yesterday in a helicopter accident in the east of the country. I apologise that we were unable to make contact with you sooner, but her cellphone has only just been retrieved. I'm truly sorry for your loss."

Sammy was hurrying out of the terminal, Mac's satchel banging into his hip, while talking to the doctor and trying to process what he was hearing. "Please, doctor, take my number, and text me yours. I will call you later. I have to find Mr. McBride." He gave the doctor his number, thanked him, and disconnected.

Sammy found Mac curled in the fetal position next to his van. He slowed his pace as he approached, uncertain what to do next. He sat down on the warm tarmac and leaned against the car, helpless, as he watched his friend sobbing like a child on the ground next to him. "Why her?" he wailed, "Why my Ingrid? Why a woman who gave so much and asked so little in return? Could he not find anyone else that deserved to die? Well fuck him!" Looking to the heavens, he added, "Fuck you! FUCK YOU! Aaaagh... fuck you." Spittle and drool dripped down his face, mixing with his tears.

Sammy's phone rang, and he muted it. It rang again, and he

switched it off, before helping Mac into the passenger seat and closing the door. Mac slumped against the door, his eyes tinged with pain and suffering, as they drove back.

"What am I gonna do? She's my world, Sammy. I can't do it. Oh, God! I can't..." Mac had begun hyperventilating between sobs, and Sammy wondered if he should take Mac to the hospital. He posed that question to him.

"For what, Sammy? For fucking what?! So they can save me, so I can go through life without her? No! I am not going to the fucking hospital. Just take me the fuck home!" he barked, spittle landing on the dashboard and windshield.

As they neared Pingwe Beach, Mac said, "Stop here, Sammy. I need some cigarettes."

Sammy had never seen Mac smoke and was confused, but did as he asked. Mac searched for his wallet to give Sammy the money. "Later, Mac. Just wait here. I'll be right back." Sammy said, getting out. "What brand?"

"Camels. Two packs."

Sammy made the purchase and got back in the van. Mac's head was in his hands, and the wailing had not abated. Sammy assumed it would not for a long time.

Sammy drew up outside the cottage and watched Mac stare at it for a while before he got out without saying a word. Sammy rolled down his window. "What can I do, Mac? I can stay. I can do whatever you want me to do. You just tell me, Mac." Tears now fell from Sammy's eyes, as he watched the man who had become a close friend falling apart... and did not know what to do.

Mac looked around, bewildered, hoping Ingrid might suddenly step onto the patio, her laughter breaking this nightmare. After a moment of staring between the ocean and patio, he said, "You can fuck off now, Sammy. I'm no good to anyone. I'm just one big fucking dark cloud, who kills anything that gets too close, so... go on, just fuck off! GO!" He said it with such venom, as he wrestled the 'Nyumba Ingrid' sign off its chain, taking with it the post it was attached to, and flung it over the small fence. "And take your fucking sign with you!" he spat out, as he stepped into the house and slammed the door.

MEET ME IN ZANZIBAR

Sammy got out of the van, picked up the sign he had made for Mac and Ingrid and put it on the back seat. He clambered in, and drove around the corner, finding a place to park. He switched his phone on and saw he had seven missed calls from Justina and a dozen or so from numbers he did not recognise, but assumed they were business calls. He rang Justina, who immediately went into a tirade. He let her finish her rant; she had every right to, she was worried. It was not like him to have his phone switched off.

She finally finished, with "Well, where are you?" followed by silence.

He replied through tears and heartache, "Ingrid is gone. She was killed in a helicopter crash yesterday in Angola."

Sammy could hear Justina's gasps, before she finally shrieked, bombarding him with a flurry of questions.

"I can't answer anything right now." he interrupted, his voice faltering. "I just need to focus on Mac — he's a complete wreck. I'm staying in the van tonight — I need to be close by. I'm scared he might do something reckless." he said, trying to sound more confident than he felt.

"I'll make sure he's okay and keep you posted. I love you Justina." Sammy hung up, wiped his face and stared out at the ocean. Thunder heads were gathering, the wind shifted, the sun dipped lower. And the weight of night crept closer.

Chapter 90

"So, are you guys coming to the party tonight at Radio Abante? It should be a lot of fun! Music. Beer. Dancing." Tomas asked, again. Andrew and Emily, who were on the periphery of the group as they worked independently from the aid organizations, had originally declined the offer graciously. After much cajoling from the group — especially Jo-Jo, also from the UK and one of the few women in the group, who had begged and pleaded with Emily to come and keep her company — the two finally acquiesced and asked where they should meet. Sven said they had arranged transport and would pick them up outside the hospital at eight.

Loud music spilled out of the jeepney as it pulled up to the hospital. Andrew and Emily climbed aboard, and quickly realised they were at least half a dozen drinks behind the already raucous crowd. They each accepted a Red Horse beer and joined in the merriment, all singing and making a botch of the Pharrell Williams song 'Happy'.

They disembarked at the Radio Abante complex; a large, sprawling L-shaped house with wide corridors, large meeting rooms, all opening up onto a huge garden with tropical plants, trees, and a koi pond — a focal point that seemed to take up much of the spacious yard. Loud reggae music boomed from the bar and dance floor area which had been set up against the ocean-facing wall. While some people were swaying to the music, others were standing at the bar, chatting.

The group that Andrew and Emily travelled with soon dispersed, and were lost in the crowd. Tomas, Jo-Jo, Andrew and Emily found a vacant table and chairs on the veranda. They sat, conversation flowing for a while, until they noticed a number of people on their phones, talking urgently and pacing the corridors. Andrew heard snippets of the conversations and knew something was afoot.

"No, I don't know. Yes, I'm sure. I think we can... okay, get back to me." came one of the pacing men's voices.

"Yeh, it happened this morning. She's eight or ten... I really don't have all the details." came another one-sided conversation.

Different variations on the same discussion came and went, piquing Andrew and Emily's curiosity. Andrew stopped one of the volunteers — a strapping lad from the Midwest of the United States — to ask what was going on. He brushed Andrew off with a dismissive wave, and continued talking animatedly into his phone.

The small group shrugged it off and continued their conversation until the young American returned and apologised to Andrew for his brash behavior. Andrew had cooled on his need to know what was happening and said, "Ain't no problem, man. None of my concern." turning his attention back to Emily and Jo-Jo. Tomas had left to get a round of beers.

When Tomas returned, he filled the group in on the flurry of urgent calls. "So, two men got into an argument today at a shoe shop. One shot the other in the chest — big fucking .45 caliber gun — he's dead. But apparently, the bullet exited his back and struck a little girl in the head! The different aid agency worker bees are calling their head offices in Manila, Hong Kong, New York, London, or wherever they are based, trying to get permission to help."

"Well... do we have any more information? Where is she now? What time was this? Where was she shot?" Andrew was yelling over the din of the music, just as a song ended. His words carried around the back garden, and echoed through the doors into one conference room.

"Ah, fuck. Bad timing." Andrew said as all faces turned to look at him and the other three. The young strapping American volunteer ambled over again and said, somewhat condescendingly, "She was shot in the head."

Andrew, now exasperated, replied, "I know that, man! What town?"

"What does that matter? She needs to be airlifted to Manila — she needs a neurosurgeon." the American volunteer replied.

Andrew just shook his head and said, "Hell, man! That dog won't hunt! Ain't no way you're airlifting her with a bullet still stuck in her melon. Y'all best have plan B! But hey, do what you gotta do." He turned back and placed his hand in Emily's lap, rolling his eyes.

Andrew could not let it go. A kid could be dying and would certainly do so if it was left to this disorganised, albeit-well-meaning, group. He stood up and started asking around, searching for anyone who could give him more details.

He was introduced to Paddy, who was running the radio station and responsible for airing the news earlier in the day. Andrew followed him into a meeting room, with the handful of volunteers who had been making the calls earlier.

After a few introductions, Andrew — who was a firm believer in 'Fail to plan; plan to fail' — said, "Alright, y'all, what time did it happen? What town was it in? 'Cause that's gonna tell us which hospital she's in. Do we know if she's still breathin'?"

They all started talking over each other, giving their opinions and speculations, much of them based on rumours and hearsay, with few actualities. Andrew found himself becoming frustrated, thinking, other than the quiet Irishman, Paddy, the rest were 'all hat and no cattle'.

Finally, Paddy ushered the well-meaning group out and brought Andrew up to speed with as many facts as he had in his possession. "It was at ten o'clock this morning in a town called Palo, this much I know. I believe she is eight years old. She was not the intended target — just wrong place, wrong time. I know her family has no money; no one does after the typhoon, of course. And honestly, I don't know where she is, or if she is even alive." He concluded with a tired smile.

"Okay, well that's a start. She'll probably be in EVRMC." Andrew looked at his watch. It was just after ten. "Shoot, man. That was twelve hours ago. It'd be a miracle if she made it this long." Before Andrew could think through his words, or even consult with Emily, he said, "I need me a motorcycle to get to the hospital. If she's still kickin', then we can figure out what to do from there. Sound good?"

"Aye, sure. That's logical," Paddy responded, tossing Andrew the keys for his little motorcycle. "It's the red Honda 250 in the hallway. Don't crash it! The helmet is behind you. Mind yourself and call when you have news. Here's my card."

Andrew stopped by the table, helmet in hand. "I'm gonna check on the kid. Can you get a ride home with Andre and Jo-Jo if I'm not back? If she's alive, it's fixin' to be a long night!" he said, kissing Emily and making his way down the corridor.

Forty minutes later, he was standing in a dimly lit hospital room, flanked by Dr. Fuentes on one side, and a frail, frantic woman on the other, who cried, wailed, hugged, and thanked Andrew, telling him she had been praying that he would come.

Andrew looked down at the tiny girl and asked what her name was. Dr. Fuentes said it was Nanette Lucello and that was her mother, which Andrew had already surmised. At present, the doctor was keeping Nanette's blood pressure elevated with the aid of dopamine and keeping her comfortable. Both she and Andrew knew that was doctor-speak for 'she would certainly die if nothing was done' — and done soon.

Dr. Fuentes said she knew Dr. Cruz well, but sadly this family could not afford to have him perform the required surgery. Before he could think, Andrew was asking for the charts and x-rays... and planning a call to Dr. Cruz.

Just after midnight, Andrew got word that Dr. Cruz had been woken up, would take a look at Nanette, and was on his way to Divine Word Hospital. Now all Andrew had to do was organise getting Nanette there. He jumped back on the bike, and headed to Divine Word, where Adon had already commandeered the ambulance. The pair drove to EVRMC, loaded Nanette and her mother, and raced back again to Divine Word Hospital — Adon behind the wheel and Andrew in the back, monitoring her vitals.

By two in the morning, the little girl was on the operating table and Dr. Cruz was battling to save her life. Andrew stood outside, watching, and praying she would make it, when Emily rounded the corner and ran into Andrew's arms.

"Is she going to be okay?" she asked.

"Not sure. Dr. Cruz has just begun surgery." he responded, kissing her forehead and telling her to get some sleep.

"No, we are going to see this through together. God, I love you, Mr. Koch. You never cease to amaze me." she said.

Andrew squeezed her. "Love you too, Mrs. Koch. Y'know, I don't believe in coincidences, but it seems like fate put me right in that little girl's path."

Emily furrowed her brow and asked, "How so?"

"Well first off, I wasn't 'sposed to be in that emergency room yesterday mornin' when we were headin' out to breakfast. Hell, if I hadn't stopped by the desk, I wouldn't've even known we had a neurosurgeon! Wouldn't've met Dr. Cruz, neither. And I damn sure didn't wanna go to that party last night, but I went anyway. And here we are. That little girl had a .45 caliber round stuck in her head for over twelve hours, like she was just waitin' for somethin'. Against all odds, she made it. This ain't her time to die. She was kept here for a reason, I reckon."

Just after five-thirty in the morning, Dr. Cruz was speaking in hushed tones to Nanette's mother, and hugged her. He then came to Andrew and Emily, looking drained, and said, "I think she'll make a full recovery. We removed twenty-seven bone fragments but could not remove the bullet. We almost lost her, but she fought on. She will have to go through life with the bullet in her brain. Other than the possibility of mild seizures, which we can treat with medication, she should be fine. We've set up a room for her and her mother, and she will stay with us for a week to ten days before she is released."

Andrew shook his hand and thanked him profusely, asking if he could see her. Dr. Cruz praised Andrew for his desire to save Nanette and said, "She's in recovery, but sure, go in. Her mother wants to see you too."

Andrew and Emily went into the recovery room and stood at the foot of the bed. Her mother, still wailing, was sending praises to the Lord, and Andrew. The only word Andrew understood was 'Salamat' — thank you in Tagalog. The attending nurse translated the rest for him and Emily, who just nodded and hugged the tired woman before they took their leave.

Andrew only made it part way back to their room before he stopped short and leaned against the wall.

"Y'know, I don't believe in coincidences, but it seems like fate put me right in that little girl's path."

Emily furrowed her brow and asked, "How so?"

"Well first off, I wasn't 'sposed to be in that emergency room yesterday mornin' when we were headin' out to breakfast. Hell, if I hadn't stopped by the desk, I wouldn't've even known we had a neurosurgeon! Wouldn't've met Dr. Cruz, neither. And I damn sure didn't wanna go to that party last night, but I went anyway. And here we are. That little girl had a .45 caliber round stuck in her head for over twelve hours, like she was just waitin' for somethin'. Against all odds, she made it. This ain't her time to die. She was kept here for a reason, I reckon."

Andrew slid down on his haunches, sobbing. Emily stroked his head and waited until he had said what he wanted to say and his sobbing abated, before giving him a hand up and guiding him to their room. He collapsed into bed, dead to the world, after only two hours of sleep in the past thirty.

Emily wandered down to Hotel Alejandro and wrote notes that Nanette was alive and well, posting them on all the various conference room doors that housed the aid agencies, with a sense of pride that her husband was responsible. She knew he would take no credit — for him, it was all in the line of duty.

She paused outside the Save A Child Foundation office, remembering comments from the gathering last night, when the larger agencies were approached for their help with the little girl who got shot in the head, their responses were unanimous 'Sorry, but it's not in our mandate'. "Well, what the fuck is in your mandate?" She hissed at the closed door. She loved partaking in aid work, but was so glad to be self-sponsored. She would never be bound by the red tape and have to listen to words like this from anyone, especially when a child's life was at stake.

Chapter 91

Mac swept all the framed pictures of him and Ingrid off the mantle with a back-handed swipe and went directly for the liquor cabinet. He took out a bottle of Jameson's, removed and crushed the cap, and gulped. His trembling fingers unwrapped the cigarette packet, and he lit his first smoke since Goma, almost eighteen months ago. He inhaled deeply, coughed, swore, kicked the dining room chair over, and threw the vase of flowers he had purchased the previous day against the wall.

"Oh God! Why Ingrid? Why not me? Why now, when we had everything ahead of us? Tell me, God. Go on!" he screamed at the ceiling. "Why did you need her more than I did? I'll fucking tell you. You are a fucking jealous God, that's why! It says so in your fucking book of fables, fantasy, and folklore. It says it right there, in Exodus, 'I am a jealous God.' Well, you fucking well are! Jealous of my happiness. Jealous of Ingrid's happiness. Well, fuck you! And damn you to hell!" His voice broke. "Why couldn't you just leave us to be happy?"

Mac stormed through the house, looking for more things to destroy in his anguish. He went outside, but all he saw was Ingrid. Ingrid lying on the lounger; Ingrid lying in the sun, her head in her hands, reading and smiling at him. He walked beyond those haunting images and onto the beach, but there she was again; Ingrid, running beside him in the morning; Ingrid, holding tight to her sun hat, her flaming red sarong blowing in the breeze and then, in slow motion, the sarong fluttering onto the beach as she discarded it before diving into the surf.

Mac couldn't bear it. He stumbled back inside, each new memory driving him deeper into the bottle, but still, the pain wouldn't subside. He slumped onto the wicker settee and buried his head in his hands, staring at the floor. Tears pooled on the broken frame that once held the first picture they had taken together — him and Ingrid at the equator, their first date. Every encounter thereafter better than the last, and their love grew stronger every day... until some stupid fucking helicopter pilot killed her.

"Fuck him!" Mac muttered. "I hope the bastard suffered. And if he didn't die, I'll find the motherfucker and kill him myself."

Sammy remained nearby until nightfall. He drove closer to Mac's house, watching and listening for signs of trouble. He knew Mac was awake; he could hear doors banging and objects being broken inside the house. He listened to Mac curse and wail for hours until the house became eerily still around ten o'clock. Although it pained him to hear Mac destroying the house, the sudden silence scared him more.

He called Justina almost hourly. When he told her things had gone quiet, Justina urged him to check on him. Sammy found the front door unlocked and cautiously entered. The living room looked completely different from that morning. Broken glass littered the floor, a dining room chair lay on its back, and paperwork and photos were strewn everywhere. The only sound in the room was the noise of the old record player, its needle spinning at thirty-three revolutions per minute, endlessly scratching at the end of the album.

"Mac?" Sammy called out.

No response. He ventured deeper into the cottage. Mac's clothes were scattered around the bedroom, but he wasn't there. As Sammy walked down the hallway, he kicked an empty liquor bottle, which spun and clattered against the wall. He cursed under his breath. The bathroom door was closed. He knocked gently, but there was no answer. Gingerly, he opened the door.

Mac was lying in the clawfoot bathtub, one arm dangling over the side, still clutching an almost-empty bottle of Jameson's whiskey.

Sammy quickly stepped inside, pulling the plug to let the cold water drain. Mac's lips were tinged blue, and his body was cold. "Oh shit, he's dead!" Sammy said aloud, panic rising in his voice. Sammy pressed his fingers to Mac's neck, and his own heart froze until he felt it — a pulse. Faint, but steady. Mac was alive. Sammy breathed a sigh of relief.

It took all of his strength to lift Mac, dropping him once, before finally getting him into bed. He found a hot water bottle, boiled the kettle, filled it, and placed it under the covers. Then he located outdoor blankets in a wooden chest and layered them on top of the comforter. Satisfied that Mac was warm, Sammy called Justina.

"Mac passed out drunk." he told her. "The house is a mess, but he's okay."

Sammy hung up and surveyed the destruction. He began cleaning up, placing the broken frames and scattered photos of Mac and Ingrid back on the mantle. He picked up the broken glass and turned off the turntable, setting the stylus back in its place. Finally, he lay down on the couch and nodded off.

Sammy woke shortly after sunrise. He stepped outside and called Justina. "How much money do we have on our credit cards?" he asked. "I have to buy a ticket for Mac to go identify Ingrid's remains in Luanda, and I think I need to go with him. He can't do this by himself. If there's enough, can you find a way to get us there today? And is it okay with you?"

"Of course it is." Justina replied. "Why would you even ask? He's our friend. If we don't have enough, I'll find a way. I'll get back to you as soon as I can."

"Thank you, my angel. I love you." Sammy said as he hung up and walked to his car. Both he and Mac would need coffee, lots of it... and Mac would certainly need paracetamol.

Chapter 92

Sammy located Dr. Monterio's details on his cell phone and called Josina Machel Hospital. It was just after eight in the morning. He told them that he and Mac would be arriving at four that afternoon and would come directly to the hospital.

Justina had not only booked their flights, but the hotel and car rental too, in the most expensive city in the world. The cost almost depleted their cards and what little savings they had. She knew Mac would make certain they got it back.

Mac had protested about going. He was still belligerent and filled with anger, until Sammy lost his patience. "You know, she was my friend too! And I am not going to let her lie in a steel box until they put her in a pauper's grave in some shit-hole country she does not belong in." Tears leaked from his eyes and raced down his face as he continued. "If you don't want to go, fine. I'll go myself and bring her back. This is her home and she needs to be here. Besides, Justina pulled out all the stops... and depleted our bank accounts, so now I am committed, and I'm going with or without you. Now, pull yourself together. I have to go home and pick up my passport and some clothes. Take a shower; we leave in an hour."

He stomped out of the house and closed the door behind him, the full weight of what happened yesterday taking its toll, as he climbed behind the wheel and wept... for Ingrid and for Mac's unnecessary loss.

Few words were exchanged as they made their descent into Quatro de Fevereiro International Airport over the beautiful Bay of Luanda. The scenery was stunning, yet Mac saw nothing. From the beginning of their journey by car, through two subsequent flights, Mac merely dawdled, trancelike, behind Sammy.

Sammy picked up the rental car and they made their way to the mortuary with the aid of the GPS. The roads were more congested than he would have imagined, and they were soon in a traffic jam. This worried Sammy, as Mac was becoming more and more fidgety the closer they got to the hospital. He was afraid Mac would bolt if the car stopped. He double-checked that the doors were locked as they approached Zamba 2 Bridge and could see the hospital looming just across the water. The GPS instructed, in its mechanical, cheerful voice to *'take the next left onto Rua Samba Road, proceed for eight hundred metres and your destination will be on your right'*.

They parked and made their way into the hospital, following signs for Charon's waiting room. They passed grief-stricken people supporting each other. Some snivelled quietly into handkerchiefs, while others were inconsolable. Sammy knew they would soon be one of those two-person clusters who people passed en-route to visit their worst nightmare. They were directed to the waiting area and were asked to take a seat while the kindly nurse called for the doctor.

Dr. Monterio arrived a few minutes later, grim-faced and solemn. He greeted the two men with a variation of the usual 'I am sorry we had to meet under these circumstances, and I am so sorry for your loss.' And asked them to please follow him.

Sammy wondered how many times he had said that in his lifetime and how often one could say it before it sounded insincere. They followed the doctor into the mortuary which was sterile and cold, the faint hum of refrigeration units punctuating the silence. A sharp, clinical scent of disinfectant lingered heavily in the air, only barely masking an underlying hint of decay. A metallic, earthy tang clung to the walls and seeped into the senses, unsettling and unforgettable; death seemed to surround them. Sammy knew this was going to be the worst moment of Mac's life, the moment when reality would hit him the hardest; the woman he loved on a steel tray in a morgue.

The doctor located Ingrid's door and slid the tray out. "Whenever you're ready, Mr. McBride. Take your time."

Mac said nothing for a while, staring at the form lying beneath the clean white sheet. Eventually, he sucked in a deep breath, nodded his head, and mumbled, "I'm ready." The doctor drew back the sheet. Shock and devastation contorted Mac's features. He had to steady himself on the tray next to Ingrid's badly broken and bruised face, and the sobbing started again. Sammy had to avert his eyes and, he too, began to cry.

Mac breathed deeply and, through the sobs, asked if he could have a moment alone with her. The doctor nodded, and he and Sammy left the room. Mac found a chair and pulled it up next to Ingrid's face. He spoke in a soft tone, barely above a whisper, "Oh God. My love, my beautiful love. What did they do to you?" He gently stroked her hair. "What am I going to do without you? You were my everything; I am so lost without you. I'm begging you, please don't leave me." His body juddered with silent sobs.

"I'm so sorry now I didn't tell you my surprise. You know that cottage we stayed in in Zanzibar; the one you loved so much? Well, I bought it for us. We named it Nyumba Ingrid — it means House of Ingrid. Actually, Sammy named it; he even carved a sign for you — it's beautiful, you'd love it. He's been my partner in crime, helping me get the place and making it all beautiful. Ah, Ingrid, it's lovely. I know we'd have been so happy there. Every day with you was filled with promise, with joy and happiness. You took that glimmer of hope that smouldered deep within me, and made it burn so brightly. You reintroduced colour to my life. And now I am back in the dark.

Please, God, let this be an awful nightmare. I will do anything to have you back, back at Nyumba Ingrid, back where you belong, where I can keep you safe. We still have so much to do, Ingrid. And I've not yet finished telling you how much I love you and what you mean to me. I'm so alone, Ingrid. I'm so scared and empty. Sweetheart, how do I go forward without you by my side? Tell me, my love."

Mac stared at the woman he loved so deeply. The room was still, and the silence was deafening. He stood, apathetic to the tears streaming down his face, and bent over, kissing her gently on her cold lips "Rest now, my love. Rest now."

Mac staggered on legs that could barely carry him, finally collapsing into Sammy as he left the room, Mac's silent grief turning to gut-wrenching sobs.

While Sammy drove, Mac sniffled and grieved quietly, blowing his nose periodically and blotting his eyes with a handkerchief. Sammy carried their bags into the large lobby of the Hotel Presidente, where they were greeted warmly and given the key to their room. Mac fidgeted, mumbled, and shuffled behind Sammy — not unlike Dustin Hoffman in the movie *Rain Man* — into the elevator, along the carpeted hallway, and into the room.

Sammy dropped his bag on his bed, choosing the one closest to the balcony in case Mac had the mind to try something stupid. He apologised to Mac that he could only afford the one room and hoped Mac didn't mind sharing. Mac merely nodded, opened the minibar, and in the absence of any Irish whiskey, took out two mini bottles of Scotch. He poured them into a tumbler, looked at it, and added a third before stepping out onto the balcony and lighting a cigarette. Sammy followed him out, and both men leaned on the balcony's railing, staring out over the curving boulevard and beyond to the Atlantic Ocean. Neither man spoke, as Mac smoked and sipped on his drink until twilight approached and the street lights began to twinkle below them.

Mac finally broke the silence with a voice husky and gravelly from the constant crying and incessant cigarettes. "Sammy, if it were not for Connor and Cati, I'd have walked out here and jumped. But I couldn't put them through what I'm enduring, so I won't do it. You're good friends, both you and Justina, but for now, my friend, I just need to be alone. Leave me out here to grieve by myself for a wee bit longer. Would you do that for me?"

"Okay, sure. I'll be inside when and if you need me." Sammy responded hesitantly, as he stepped back inside and sat facing Mac from the edge of his bed. He was not going to let him out of his sight. He called Justina relaying that although Mac was a mess, he thought he would be okay, and that they'd be home tomorrow afternoon as planned. Sammy then called room service and ordered two hamburgers and chips, the cheapest thing on the menu. They needed something to eat. He suspected Mac had eaten nothing in the past thirty-six hours.

The food arrived, and Sammy gently tapped on the glass balcony door, summoning Mac inside. Sammy told him sternly that he had to eat, when Mac began to protest and headed straight to the minibar for a refill. Mac relented and sat at the little table and ate the burger. Sammy handed him a bottle of water and said, "Here, Mac, maybe some water before you have another drink, please."

Mac looked up, and it seemed to Sammy that this was the first time Mac had actually registered he was sitting with his friend. He uncapped the bottle of water, downed it quickly, then asked Sammy for another, which he slowly sipped. "Sammy, you're a great friend. But I need some time and space. I'm not going back to Zanzibar with you tomorrow. I don't know that I can ever go back. I'm not sure where I'm going, to be honest. My life was mapped out — my life with Ingrid — but now I really don't know. All I know for sure is, I want to be alone."

There was nothing to be said. Sammy just nodded his understanding, and squeezed Mac's hand in a way that said, 'You know I'm here'.

Chapter 93

Mac left Luanda for Dublin a week later and booked into the Jury's Inn on Parnell Street. He called Connor, asking him to come over and see him. Connor was surprised that his dad was in town, but noted something felt off and hurried over. His dad looked awful. It was clear he was drinking and smoking again. Mac shared what had happened, and Connor could see how deeply it had affected him. He proceeded with questions that Mac could not answer.

"Dad, what are you gonna do? You gotta have some kind of plan. Are you going back? Are you coming back here? Where do you wanna live?"

Mac just shrugged, shook his head, and muttered, "I really have no idea, Son."

In the months that followed, his life became a blur of peripatetic indulgence; a fugue state of trains and planes, dimly lit bars, and the bottomless clink of glasses. From the cobblestone alleys of Prague to the shadowed corners of Parisian bistros, he wandered with no destination in mind, chasing oblivion like a spectre just out of reach.

Each city seemed to absorb a piece of him, its streets marked by his staggering gait and the sting of alcohol on his breath. Yet the pain still greeted him every morning. Steadfast. Taunting him. *'Where to today,*

Mac? Where are we going? I don't mind. I'll always be there. I won't abandon you'. He'd been woken up by police in a London bus shelter at four in the morning and told to move on. He'd woken up on a beach in Costa Brava, Spain, as the sun came up. He'd been inside a few drunk tanks in various cities on the continent. And thrown out of several bars. Now he found himself in Gothenburg, Sweden, at the headstones of Ingrid's parents.

He sank down onto the frozen earth, leaning against the rough headstone as if seeking some small comfort. The icy drizzle carried on a stiff breeze, stinging his face like a thousand needles, chilling him to the core. His voice was barely a whisper as he spoke, fragmented words tumbling out — words that even he knew made little sense.

"I'm... I'm sorry. But I couldn't... I couldn't keep her safe. I tried to protect her... but I couldn't." He pressed his hand into the earth, as if reaching for something beyond his grasp. "If you're really... up there somewhere... with her..." A bitter laugh escaped him, laced with doubt, incredulity and the ache of countless unanswered questions. He stared up at the cold, grey sky as if searching for a sign — any sign — that there was a God, but his scepticism ran deep. "I just hope I'm wrong." he murmured. "I want to be wrong. Not for me, but for Ingrid and her parents. I want them to be together again. I don't want Ingrid to be alone... ever."

Both Connor and Cati were often on the receiving end of garbled messages, either from or regarding, their father. More often than not, they were from the local constabulary or concerned citizens. They were troubled by his darkness, and worried that their dad was drinking himself into an early grave.

One day, when Cati and Connor were both in Dublin, they got a call from a police station in Amsterdam. Mac was being detained for disorderly and drunken conduct. They needed to nip this in the bud. Cati asked that they hold him until morning, and they would be there to pick him up.

It would be that call that would ultimately save Mac from his downward spiral into oblivion.

Cati, Connor, and Mac sat in Mac's hotel room later that day. The kids were both shocked at their father's appearance. He was gaunt, dishevelled, smelled like a distillery, had not bathed for days, and was sporting at least a week's worth of stubble.

They took turns attempting to talk sense into their father and guilting him back to reality.

"Dad, you can't just tear everything down now." Cati said, her voice trembling as she sat beside him. She squeezed his hand, trying to make him look at her. "Ingrid gave you a second chance at life — she saved you. You owe it to her to make the best of life."

Her eyes brimmed with tears as she continued, her voice quiet but intense. "I saw how much she meant to you, how much you meant to each other. Don't let that love go to waste. Don't let the pain of losing her consume you. You're still here. That means you've got something left to give. And we're still here, Dad. We need you. I need you."

Connor, across from Mac, wiped at his eyes, tears rolling down his young face. He wasn't sure how to handle this, how to reach his father. His voice was choked with emotion as he spoke.

"You and Ingrid, from what you told me, both went through hell. You found something in each other, something worth fighting for. Don't just give up now. Don't let this destroy you." He looked at Mac, his voice cracking. "I'm still your son, Dad. I'm still here. And I want my dad back. Every time I get an unknown caller, I don't wanna have to think 'Oh, God. What's happened?' I love you, Dad. But more importantly, I need you. Please."

Mac didn't answer immediately. He closed his eyes, his chest tightening as he tried to process their words. He had never been good at this — at talking, at letting anyone in. But there was something in their voices, something that reached into the fog of his mind.

And their eyes — Cati's pleading; and Connor's, full of unspoken fear — told him they still saw something in him worth saving.

"I..." His voice broke. He tried again, but his throat was tight. "I'm sorry... I don't know where to begin."

Cati leaned forward, her hand still clutched around his. "Dad, you don't have to figure it all out right now. You just... need to start. Please. Take that first step. For us. For Ingrid. She wouldn't want this for you. She wouldn't want you to waste away. She'd want you to live again. You can do it, Dad. You can still fight. For us."

Mac sat there, his hands trembling. For the first time in a long time he'd felt his heart move. He felt something other than the suffocating weight of grief. He didn't know how to fix himself. He didn't even know where to start. But at that moment he felt at least there was a flicker of possibility

"I'll try," he said, barely above a whisper. "I'll try... for you, for Ingrid. Aye, I'll give it a go."

Cati and Connor exchanged a smile of cautious hope, their expressions softening.

Mac wasn't sure what would come next. He didn't know how to undo what had been done, how to fix the broken parts of him. But something had shifted slightly. He was here. And maybe, just maybe, that was enough to begin with.

Chapter 94

Andrew's final shift on Friday brought with it the usual suspects; the little gang from the emergency department — Adon, Gabriel, Alicia, Jamal, and Lena. These were the key players in what had come to be known as 'The Nanette Heist'. Unbeknownst to Andrew at the time, protocol had been broken when Nanette was transported from EVRMC to Divine Word, without proper authorisation. Lena said Adon had, in fact, stolen the ambulance.

"I prefer to think of it as 'commandeered' the ambulance, in a life-and-death situation." Adon said with a smirk. "What was it you told me, Andrew? Oh yes — 'It's better to beg for forgiveness, than ask for permission'."

Alicia, usually the quiet one, snorted. "Ha. Listen to you, Adon, with your fancy new words — 'commandeered'! You fucking stole it; say it like a Filipino!" She tossed a bag of gauze at him and darted behind Andrew for cover. Peeking out from under his arm, she teased, "Have you been sneaking into Emily's English classes, Adon?"

Andrew laughed, pulling her in for a quick hug. "I'm gonna miss you guys. It's been an honour working with every single one of you, let me tell ya. In my job, I never get to see the inside of the emergency department — but now that I have, boy, I have a whole new found respect for what you guys do. Especially under these conditions, with this equipment — or rather, the lack of it. Y'all should be proud."

Gabriel and Lena had slipped away unnoticed, and soon the off-key strains of 'For He's a Jolly Good Fellow' rang through the paediatric ward. Gabriel led the charge, arms outstretched, balancing a cake adorned with flickering candles — the touching gesture having been baked by Alicia and decorated by Lena the night before in the hospital kitchen. At the back of the group, Emily was singing along. Andrew turned to her, shaking his head with mock indignation.

"Dadgummit! Y'all are killin' me! And you — you knew about this?" He wagged a finger at Emily, feigning outrage.

Slices of cake were passed around before the team went swiftly back to work, preparing for what they called the 'baliw shift' — the crazy shift. Fridays brought with it car crashes, stabbings, domestic abuse incidents, and patients having one too many 'wobbly pops' — a phrase Andrew had imported from home that caught on with great enthusiasm.

As the night wore on, the already overburdened team ran on empty. It was not only a Friday, it was the end of the month and payday, which always exacerbated the chaos. Four patients had died, either in the ambulance or shortly after arrival. At least two dozen others had been 'patched and dispatched'. By the time Andrew's shift ended, exhaustion weighed on them all.

In the scrub room, they said their goodbyes, promising to stay in touch — though Andrew knew the reality. He had seen it before. You meet wonderful people, you promise to write, and for a while, you do. But time and distance creep in, and before you know it, years have passed. It wasn't sad or contrite. It was just the way of things.

Chapter 95

It had been almost six months since Sammy and Justina had last heard from Mac. They knew he was somewhere in Europe and, apparently, alive — his hangar fees and taxes on *Nyumba Ingrid* were still getting paid. But they couldn't help but worry.

It was the peak of the busy season and Sammy was getting ready to pick up clients for a half-day tour of Jozani Forest, when his phone rang.

"Sammy's Tours. Sammy speaking." he answered, swallowing the last of his coffee.

"Jumbo, Bwana! Do you do scenic flights over Zanzibar by any chance?"

"Mac! Oh, man, it's good to hear from you. We've really missed you. So, what have you been up to? Are you okay?" Sammy's words tripped over each other, racing to get out first.

"Aye, sure, you know yourself. I'm okay. Coping." He could sense Sammy's relief at hearing from him after so long. Mac led him along for a bit, bringing him up to speed on some of the places he'd been floating around since they last met.

"So where are you at the moment?" Sammy finally enquired.

"Zanzibar." Mac said, smiling his first honest smile in almost six months.

Sammy gasped in disbelief, shocked and thrilled at the same time.

"Fancy meeting me at the airport this afternoon? I have something to show you." Mac continued.

Sammy explained that he had a tour but could be at the airport by three.

"That's perfect, Sammy. I can't wait to see you." Mac replied.

"Likewise, my friend. Welcome home. I hope you are here to stay."

"Aye, that I am, Sammy. This is where I belong." They disconnected the call and Sammy called out to Justina in the garden.

"You'll never believe it! Mac is home!" he said excitedly.

Mac had spent the morning clearing cobwebs from the plane and washing her until she gleamed. He had just finished drying her with a chamois and was running his finger lovingly over Ingrid's name on the cowling when the young signwriter walked over and greeted Mac warmly. Mac explained what he wanted, and the signwriter got busy with his task. The mechanic had come by the evening prior, drained the fuel, refuelled her, performed a thorough inspection, and had given the old plane a clean bill of health.

Just after three, Sammy showed up and greeted Mac enthusiastically. He drew him in for a tight embrace before holding him at arm's length, saying, "Mac, you look like shit!"

"Aye, go on with yourself!" They both embraced again, laughing.

Mac indeed looked like shit. He was pale, had lost weight, and his once-trim physique had softened. His hair was shaggy and unkempt, the toll of months on the road clearly visible. He hadn't had a drink in three weeks, but his battle with cigarettes was ongoing.

"Let's grab a coffee. I have something to show you." Mac said excitedly as he ushered Sammy towards the terminal and ordered them coffees and pastries. Sammy was elated at the turnaround he saw in Mac, compared to when he had last seen him.

"First things first, Mac. You reimbursed us way too much money when you left; like a thousand dollars too much! Justina has been fretting about how to get it back to you. So here it is." Sammy said, handing Mac an envelope, as he stirred sugar into his coffee.

"Sammy, my friend, you saved my life. I could not have managed without you and Justina. Besides, you lost a lot of work over the days you were minding me. Keep it. It really doesn't come close to what I owe you and I don't want to hear any more about it! Come on, bring your coffee with you. You have to see this." Mac could no longer contain his excitement as they walked towards the hangar. Sammy saw the bright yellow plane sitting on the apron and, as he drew closer, noticed the name.

"Oh, Mac, that's perfect!" Sammy said, a lump in his throat. Mac lovingly caressed the new wording and smiled. "Aye. I think it's a fitting tribute." He stepped back and admired it for the umpteenth time. Still in fire engine red, it now read, *'Spirit of Ingrid'*.

"Come on, finish your coffee. We have a plane to fly. Let's go already!"

As the plane soared over Pingwe Beach, the wind rushed through the open cockpit, and the ocean shimmered below, a brilliant blue canvas stretching into infinity. Mac spoke through the headset; "Sammy, take the controls will you. Your plane. Keep her straight and level, like I taught you."

"Er... okay, boss... my plane. Hey, you're not gonna jump are you?" Sammy joked.

"No, Sammy. I'm bringing Ingrid home." Mac carefully placed the urn on his lap and closed his eyes in quiet prayer;

Ingrid, my love. I was blessed in finding and falling in love with you; I know this, and I know how fortunate I was to have you love me. I will remain eternally grateful for the time and love you gave me. I know you are gone from this world, but I will always carry you in my heart. And that is where your home is, now and forever, with me, in Zanzibar. Thank you for everything, my darling. Rest now; your work here is done.

He opened the urn and watched the ashes scatter over the beach, a sense of finality settling over him. "Stay close. Be free, but never far."

Mac took the controls. "Thanks, Sammy. My plane." He said, banking hard and heading back to the airport.

Later, Sammy dropped Mac at *Nyumba Ingrid*, and Mac slowly got out of the van, filled with mixed emotions. He passed the sign that had been repaired and ran his hands lovingly over the carved wood. He entered the spotless house, where the pictures had been reframed and were in their rightful place, and the refrigerator was stocked with the essentials. Sammy hung back at the door as Mac inspected the house before turning to Sammy and saying, "You?"

"Justina. All Justina." Sammy replied.

After Sammy left, Mac grabbed a bottle of water from the fridge and made his way out to the patio. The wicker settee creaked its familiar creak beneath him as he sat. The swing seat still swung gently in the ocean breeze. And the moon rose.

He had battles ahead, but at least he was home. He tapped a cigarette from the pack and lit it with a steady hand. "One day at a time." he whispered to himself, a silent promise he was finally ready to keep. "One day at a time."

The End

Afterword

The Aid Worker Security Database (AWSD) meticulously records significant incidents of violence against aid workers, with data spanning from 1997 to the present. Established in 2005, the AWSD stands as the only comprehensive global source for this critical information, providing an essential evidence base for analysing the evolving security landscape of civilian aid operations. (AWSD is a project of Humanitarian Outcomes (humanitarianoutcomes.org)

I extend my heartfelt gratitude to the Aid Workers Security Database for their invaluable work in documenting these incidents. Their efforts are crucial in raising awareness of the risks faced by those who dedicate their lives to humanitarian service. To learn more about their work please visit their website at https://www.aidworkersecurity.org

The chart below depicts the amount of Aid-Workers killed, kidnapped or seriously injured whilst on assignment. They are listed by country alphabetically and the numbers are totals from 1997-2024.

Country	Total Affected
Afghanistan	1351
Algeria	12
Angola	53
Argentina	1
Armenia	1
Azerbaijan	5
Bangladesh	35
Benin	1
Bolivia	2
Botswana	1
Burkina Faso	51
Burundi	45
Cambodia	4
Cameroon	86
Central African Republic	241
Chad	54
Chechnya	44
Chile	1
Colombia	21
Congo	7
Cote D'Ivoire	11
Dominican Republic	1
DR Congo	433
Ecuador	1
Egypt	1
El Salvador	9
Eritrea	5
Ethiopia	149
Fiji	5
Georgia	3
Guatemala	8
Guinea	9
Guinea-Bissau	2
Guyana	1
Haiti	89
Honduras	5
India	6
Indonesia	30
Iran, Islamic Republic of	2
Iraq	163
Israel	8
Jordan	16
Kashmir	1
Kenya	84
Kosovo	10
Kyrgyzstan	3
Lebanon	13
Lesotho	3

Afterword

Country	Total Affected
Liberia	17
Libyan Arab Jamahiriya	39
Madagascar	8
Malawi	14
Mali	256
Mauritania	5
Mauritius	1
Mexico	14
Mozambique	21
Myanmar	93
Namibia	1
Nepal	4
Nicaragua	4
Niger	46
Nigeria	206
Occupied Palestinian Territories	478
Pakistan	258
Papua New Guinea	9
Peru	1
Philippines	23
Poland	1
Rwanda	15
Saudi Arabia	1
Senegal	9
Sierra Leone	16
Somalia	575
South Africa	5
South Sudan	878
Sri Lanka	91
Sudan	615
Swaziland	1
Syrian Arab Republic	586
Tajikistan	24
Tanzania	13
Thailand	5
Tunisia	5
Turkey	7
Uganda	67
Ukraine	124
Uruguay	1
Venezuela	1
Vietnam	1
Western Sahara	4
Yemen	195
Zambia	3
Zimbabwe	2
Grand Total	**7830**